P9-CDP-692

The Fox

Arlene Radasky

Copyright © 2008 Arlene Radasky
All rights reserved.

ISBN: 1-4392-1175-2
ISBN-13: 9781439211755

Visit www.booksurge.com to order additional copies.

DEDICATION

This book would not have been written without all the support and love from my family; my husband Bill; my biggest fan, my mother Lori; Rhonda and my other writer buddies who helped me stay on track.

Thank you.

CHAPTER 1

82 AD NOVEMBER

I will die when I choose to die.
And as I die, my thoughts will be of Lovern, the
Fox, a man who taught me to live, to talk to the
gods, and to love. We failed to change the future,
and now I beg the goddess Morrigna to allow my
daughter a safe journey. I have only time for one
more passage dream to tell our story.
Then, I shall die.

72 AD OCTOBER

Peat smoke darkened the room and firelight struggled to glint off the weapons behind Uncle Beathan, our clan chieftain. I kept my eyes on the weapons so I did not have to look at him. A bronze shield, two spears and two swords – one short, and one long – were balanced against the wall. The sword hilts showed our smith's interpretations of animals, trees and the spirals of life. If I squinted just right, the bear, Uncle Beathan's name sign, shrugged its shoulders as if alive. When he was in a better mood than today, he let me touch them. I wished I had worked with my cousin to create this art.

We stood in front of my uncle's table like thieves as he ate goat cheese and bread, crumbs falling into his beard. My hands were sweating. I held them behind me. I jumped when he spoke. "Jahna, you will marry Harailt."

He had sent Braden to summon my mother and Harailt, as well as me. Harailt's father, Cerdic, was there, too. No good ever came from being summoned. Beathan would usually send the girl who did his cooking, Drista, to ask us to join him for family discussions. Drista, a farmer's daughter honored to be chosen by Beathan to serve at his table, was almost at the marrying age and would leave Beathan's home soon. He would pick another and another to come to him, until he married.

When our chieftain sent his warrior, Braden, we knew he wanted to discuss important clan matters.

I did not want to be in his lodge that afternoon. Uncle Beathan's dogs chewed on old pork bones under his table. The smell made my stomach churn.

Mother did not look upset when she glanced down at me. I wondered how we could be mother and daughter. As a small girl, I held up our polished bronze and compared our faces. She told me I was vain. I told her she was beautiful. I felt like a young goat next to her. Mother's hair was long and straight, the colors of autumn, amber laced with gold and red. Her brother Beathan's hair was similar. Hers smelled of herbs when she washed it. She wore it loose. Mine was black as a raven's-wing and never where I wanted it. I wore mine tied back. Her eyes were blue as clear snow water, mine the color of mistletoe leaves with oak splinters. She reached Beathan's chin, and my head came to his lower chest. Smiles were rare on her solemn face, and I seemed not to know how to be serious. She blended into our family, the village, the clan. I was like none of them. She told me I was like my father, a trader from the south. I wished I had known my father.

Beathan sliced another large piece of cheese and stuffed it into his mouth. My stomach groaned. Chewing, he continued. "However, Cerdic. You do have a rich farm. You will be able to provide your son with sheep and pigs to start his own family. And he will inherit your land one day, goddess willing." He drank long from his cup of mead.

Cerdic was a small man with arms strong enough to lift one of his sheep out of a ravine and shoulders broad enough to carry lambs. Harailt, like his mother, grew tall, thin and quiet. His shorter father looked up to him but Harailt heeded his father's wishes.

Blankets and pieces of clothing were strewn all over my uncle's home. Bridles and parts of his chariot lay on the table in the midst of repair. His hunting dogs laid asleep on his bed, or at his feet, gnawing on the remnants of last night's dinner. In the gloom of the room, we had to be careful not to trip over whatever was on the floor. My aunt used to straighten after him, but she died two planting seasons ago.

"And Jahna."

I looked straight at him. Shards of light reflected in his sky blue eyes. I shivered.

"You have seen sixteen harvests," he said.

I knew I was past the age of marrying. Most girls younger than me were married and had several children hanging onto their skirts. I had foolishly thought Uncle and Mother would let me choose my mate.

"It is time for you to start having babies of your own. You will marry. I will hand-fast you to Harailt at Samhainn, to be blessed by the gods. Now go! I am still hungry. Girl! Mead!" He belched. Drista dashed in, balancing an overflowing mug and more cheese.

Stunned, I hung on to my mother's arm. As we left his lodge, Uncle Beathan's words rang in my ears.

"But Mother," I said. "I have watched Braden for a long time. It was him I hoped to marry. I was waiting for him to ask Uncle for our hand-fasting. Now, I have to marry that—that—farmer."

"Shush, girl," my mother said.

I did not care if Harailt heard me. I had known him all my life; we played as children, but I had never thought of marrying him.

I did not know if the tears in my eyes were caused by the sun or disappointment.

I overheard Cerdic as Harailt and his father walked away.

"It is too bad you could not have married Sileas. Her hands are callused from hard work. Her father taught her well. Jahna does not know how to work the land. She has lived with her mother, weaving, and her hands are soft. She will not like to work outside in the fields."

Yes, I thought, I weave cloth. My hands did not have the grime of the fields on them, but they were still strong hands. Would Harailt only want to marry someone with dirty hands?

"We must do what Beathan decrees," my mother said. "He is the ceann-cinnidh."

I glanced over and saw Harailt's shoulders slump.

The moon, full then, was now a sliver. I stayed angry and sullen most days. I spilled water and half swept the floor. My mother finally lost her patience with me one day and grasped me by my shoulders.

Turning me to face her, she said, "You will be married to Harailt. And you will be happy. Beathan has said you will marry so you—will—marry. Stop behaving as if you were a lost puppy."

My dream of Braden faded and I accepted my fate. I supposed I liked Harailt. His ear-length, rust colored hair, swept back with lime-wash, looked comely. His face though not as handsome as the warrior's face I had admired for so long, was not ugly. He kept his red beard trim, and his hands were large enough to catch a baby lamb being born. He was a good farmer who smelled of harvest grain. I could marry worse.

The day before Samhainn, the day our hand-fasting would be officially announced, Mother asked me to go to the drying rack in our yard and bring in the last of our blue yarn. I stood in the sun, thinking of the upcoming ceremony. Would Harailt kiss me after the announcement? Only my uncle and cousins had ever kissed me, and then only on my cheek. I touched my lips and wondered if I would know what to do.

"Jahna!"

I sighed, not wanting to go back to the loom. The sun was high and white clouds floated in the bright sky. I had been cold in these days of rain, and felt the golden warmth as a gift from the goddess. I hoped for the same weather tomorrow. It would be nice to be warm and dry on the day of my hand-fasting.

I waved my hand to show I heard. "One moment, Mother." I saw Harailt coming from our smithy. He walked toward our house from Finlay's work-hut, carrying a repaired plow on one shoulder. "Harailt is coming. I wish to speak to him about the giving fires."

He passed me and did not stop, though I thought I had seen him look my way.

"Harailt," I called.

He stopped walking but did not look at me.

"Come with us to the ceremony," I said. "Come early so we may talk. I would like to arrive at the fires with you."

He sighed and looked at me as if speaking to his little sister.

"I will ask my father," he said. "He may need help with the animals. Maybe my sisters will be enough help. If he says I may come, I will be here in time to walk with you and your mother." He started down the hill.

"May the gods protect you from evil tonight," I called.

He answered, "And you," without looking back.

I hoped he would come to take me to the festival. He had been busy with the harvest, and I, making cloth for winter cloaks, so our visits had been few and hurried. We would need to learn to live together quickly, and I was ready to try. We would not have the usual full season to live together before marriage. My uncle had shortened our hand-fasting time. Maybe he worried one of us would protest the marriage.

I wrenched the bitter-smelling blue wool off the rack and ran to my mother, my hair flying free from its tie again.

"Jahna, do not run," she scolded. "You are old enough to be respectable. We still have good sunlight so we can weave more before we go to Beathan's."

I added the wool to the overflowing baskets next to our loom, which stood on the other side of the room. A window cut into the stone and mud wall just above it let in the afternoon light. It would be hard to leave Mother and this home I had known all my life.

Taking a deep breath, I inhaled the scent of the wool and dyes, a mixture of herbs and trees, bitter and sweet. A smell I grew up with. I learned to weave and spin with these smells as I learned to walk. My fingers were soft from the wool grease and stained from the dye. We had finished dyeing until next spring and my hands would soon lose their blue tint. I did not mind.

I loved the color and patterns we designed with the dyed yarn. I had created the clan plaid we wove by using woad blue to represent our sky and red from the alder tree to portray the blood of our clan. Uncle Beathan had declared it the colors of his warriors.

I had other pictures in my head filled with color and wished I could bring them to life, but mother did not approve of spending my sunlight hours doing anything other than weaving after the shearing of the sheep. We traded cloth for food, and pictures had never fed anyone in her family. So I wove, both cloth and dreams.

"Mother. Will you miss me when I am married?"

"That is a silly question. You have lived here longer than I had hoped. Beathan was good to me and let you stay longer than I expected. Now it is your time to become an adult. I am proud that you are going. You will give up your childish ways and act as a young woman. Now hand me that yarn and ask no more questions."

The shuttle flew in my mother's fingers like a bird through the leaves of an oak tree as she lifted the yarn and created the pattern. As I watched, my life memories played through my mind, especially my travels into other bodies – my passage dreams. I had visited two other people in my mind and prayed to the goddesses daily to allow me to continue to have those dreams after my marriage. I hoped they were not one of the childish things my mother told me I would have to give up.

I was much younger, about ten harvests, when I had my first passage dream. At dusk, the peat smoke lay harsh in our lodge and I longed for fresh air. I sat on a stool, watching the spindle and whorl twist my wool. In no more than a blink and a small dizzy spell, my heart told me that I looked out of another person's eyes. My mind said it was impossible.

I glanced around, afraid and breathless. I was in a small enclosure with strange things around me. Something looked like our polished bronze, but much more reflective. I did not understand what was happening, but I heard the goddess whispering, telling me not to be afraid.

A hand that belonged to the body lifted the bronze-like thing, and the face of a girl my age was reflected back at me. Us. Her large eyes, color same as my own, looked frightened. She wore her black hair like mine, but her face was not mine. The Goddess Morrigna whispered into her ear, too, that all was well. I felt her shoulders lose their tension. Questioning brows raised over our eyes.

I heard wind blowing and we turned to a hole in a wall to watch trees bend and sway. A skin did not cover the opening, yet the cold wind did not blow in.

The Goddess Morrigna said, "You are together, yet separate. You are connected through the wisps of time. This is a gift of life. Accept and learn."

I whispered my name, "Jahna."

She said, "Aine."

The picture was gone. I was still balanced on the stool, watching the spindle, and surprised that I was not on the floor asleep. Morrigna whispered the name in my ear again. "Aine."

When I asked if others had passage dreams, Uncle Beathan shook his head. "No. But if I could travel unseen, I would spy on other clans to make sure they had peaceful thoughts about us. Imagine, being able to listen to war plans, unknown to others!" He laughed. "Let me know if you hear about horses faster than ours. We need to look for new stock, and I want to know where it is best to go." He pushed me out of his way and continued on to his lodge.

Mother did not laugh but looked at me with suspicion, so I kept my dreams secret from everyone except Ogilhinn, our druid priest. Just before he died, he had assured me my dreams were god given.

The noise of mother's shuttle brought me out of my reverie. "Girl, the work will not get done on its own. There is much wool to spin and you stand with your mouth open like a chick waiting to be fed. Now we must go to Beathan's. Get our cloaks. I will take my light one but you should wear your hooded one. You may need to go outside and bring in firewood." She stood and stretched her hands. "I wish Beathan would marry again," she said as her fingers popped. "He has mourned enough since Gavina died. I hope he finds a woman that pleases him soon. I tire of serving his evening meals."

Our empty yard was quiet, and the sky clear, as mother and I stepped outside. The moon began showing its full body over the mountains.

"We will hear many stories about the spirits of last year," said Mother. "This evening meal is always one filled with tales. Remember, many of the stories are not real. Men try to impress each other with stories bigger than the man's sitting next to him."

Beathan's yard noisily filled with the warriors and others who followed him like puppies. My mother and I worked our way through them and went inside where a spitted hog dripped fat that popped in the fire. Root vegetables and onions boiled in a pot and heat filled the room like a blanket. We set out the mead buckets and mugs, eating as we worked.

A commotion outside told us Beathan had arrived. We placed the pork in front of his trencher. He was the honored man tonight and all nights in his lodge. He would carve the joint.

"Let me through! I smell meat, and my hunger is enough to eat a full stag!" With a laugh like a wild boar's roar, Beathan pushed his way into the room. The noise grew as hungry men followed, all expecting to sing and eat with the chieftain. He clumsily dropped something from his shoulders to the floor.

Startled, my eyes traced the shape of a man. A captured prisoner? Was he alive? One of Beathan's pony-like, black hunting dogs lay down next to the stranger's body and licked his face. The man flinched. He was not dead.

The fire burned high, and with the torches there was enough light to study him.

"I warn all of you," said my uncle. "Let him sleep. He will be busy tomorrow. If he wakes, we will feed him."

The man laid still, even though the noise grew behind us. The tables filled with men. Mother and Drista passed overflowing buckets for them to dip their mugs into.

I crept closer and crouched next to his chest. His odor slipped through the smell of the other men and the fire smoke. He was not unwashed, but had spent many nights outdoors. His red hair splashed loose over the brushed dirt floor. His worn shoes were stuffed with straw. He wore a sorrel brown weave I had seen on traders from the south: a shirt with long pants, his body wrapped in a short cloak of the same color and tied with a thin cord. An empty dirk sheath was tied to his belt. He looked thin, hungry thin, but had strong shoulders. A leather pouch lay on the floor near his feet, painted with a design I had never seen before. I picked it up, stared at it for a moment, and dropped it when the stranger groaned.

Beathan laughed, walked over to the stranger, and took the man by the arms, easily lifting him onto a stool next to him. "Come, priest. Come up to my table and have some meat and bread. Drink my mead. We have much to discuss about the giving fires tomorrow."

I picked up a tray of bread and stood next to Beathan, studying the man's face as it became visible through the smoke-filled room. I guessed him to be about twenty seasons. He had an intelligent, broad forehead. His gently sloped nose was not large. A beard, the color of an iron pot left outdoors, covered his cheeks and chin. His sharp eyes were a curious blue, not of the daytime sky, nor of flowers, but midnight blue. He seemed tired, yet wary.

The stranger stole a look around the lodge, then reached down and picked up his pouch. The crowd fell instantly quiet.

Beathan reached behind him and clapped him on his back, almost pushing the stranger off the stool.

"I have his dirk," my uncle said. "He is no threat."

The talking and shouting began again. The man laid his arms and head on the table and did not move except to breathe.

"Women!" Beathan said. "Bring us more to drink and eat! This day has been difficult and long. I have a story to tell. Where are my sons?"

Finlay, tall like his father, with arms and shoulders strong from working as our smith, and the oldest, Kenric, a hand shorter but also well muscled, came into the lodge together, sat by the fire, and ate with the men as we listened to their father's story.

"Yesterday, Cerdic told me of raiders by the river. He had watched them for two days. I decided there was not time to go for my warriors when I came across them by our river, so I charged into the group and fought like a demon."

The stranger lifted his head, looked at Beathan, and smiled. I lost my breath. He was more handsome than the warrior Braden.

"They ran as fast as they could. All except this one. He did not run. I asked why, and he said the gods and goddesses were protecting him. Only a druid would stand like that in a battle with me. I found a priest on Samhainn eve! It is a sign that we will be blessed for the giving fires on the morrow. More mead!" He pounded on the table.

Beathan's sons and other warriors gathered around Beathan, slapped him on the back, and poured out praises. I knew he would not go into battle alone when so many warriors were at his call. I glanced at my mother who shook her head but wore a smile. We knew his tale was bigger than the truth, but we enjoyed listening. My uncle's stories were often more exciting than the storyteller's.

The druid's quick hands began stuffing bread into his mouth. He reached for his dirk but when his hand touched the empty sheath, he looked at Beathan.

"Here is your dirk, priest." Beathan stabbed it into the table in front of the druid. The druid pulled the short weapon out of the table and sliced some meat from the joint, eating as if it had been a long time since his last food.

As the meal ebbed, Kenric brought out his alder whistle and played notes that trilled like birds in the trees at dusk and the rapids of the river. I loved his fast music. He often played it to please his father. Fingers and hands began to drum the tables in time with the tune. I started to hum.

The druid untied the strings of his pouch and took out a longer whistle. His playing brought in the sounds of the ponies and the wind in the trees. I began to sway, spin and fling my hair. My eyes were open but not seeing the smoke-filled room. I was in the forest, riding the ponies. Then I noticed the music had stopped.

"Druid," Kenric asked. "Why did you stop playing?"

Breathless, I ceased dancing and looked to see him staring at me. I dropped to my knees, my legs unable to hold me. What did he see? He tore his wise, night blue eyes from mine, and turned to Finlay.

"It is late and I must prepare for the early ceremony. Has the sacred wood been laid for the fires?"

I could not move. My body seemed to made of stone. I knew his voice.

"Yes, in two stacks beneath the hill," said Finlay.

The druid nodded.

I began to breathe again, and watched him. Suddenly, his eyes caught mine and he tipped his head to me as if in recognition, but his face was unreadable.

"The stables are secure and you are welcome to sleep there if you do not wish to stay and drink more," Beathan called over the noise. "Although, if the spirits come to visit, you may come back. We will be singing and drinking through the night. On the morrow, my sons and I will escort you to the fires."

"My daughter and I will bring water early," my mother offered, "so you may ready yourself for the ceremony."

"The stable will be good," said the druid. "I will sleep well there. The animals will keep me safe and warm."

My mother said, "We are going home. My daughter and I will take you."

He turned to my mother and me. "I am ready, if you will show me the way."

The men's songs and the smells of mead and meat slipped into the night as we stepped through the door. There were few others outside. All were wary of Samhainn's eve.

"I forgot, I must talk to Drista about tomorrow's meal. She must start some dishes before she leaves for the fires," said Mother. "You take the druid to the stable and wait for me."

The druid and I were alone.

I pointed to the stable door, and walked behind him. Filled with questions, I asked, "Where are you from? Why did you stop playing and look at me so?" He stopped and shivered as we arrived at the stable door.

"Take my cloak. It is hooded," I offered, slipping the heavy plaid off my shoulders. I held it out for him. "Here, it is lined with soft wool and will be warm for the night." When he reached for it, our fingers touched. My body felt as if it were pierced by sharp knives. My heart raced like a herd of running deer in my chest. We both pulled back, my cloak in his hands, his eyes surprised.

He said nothing, but looked at me as if he could see my soul.

I had to learn who he was. "What is your name? Where are you from? Why did you stop here?"

"Too many questions for a late night. Call me Lovern. My clan name is Fox. I wear the fur of the red fox on my arm." His shirt covered his arms and I could not see the band of fox fur, but my heart again stampeded.

"What is your name?"

"I—I am Jahna," I struggled, my voice almost gone, my body weak. In a passage dream, I had visited a boy who hunted a fox. This voice was the same.

"Jahna?" he whispered. Moonlight reflected off his piercing eyes, revealing confusion. "Jahna?" He stumbled as mother took my arm.

"Sleep well, druid," she said as she rushed me home. I stole a look over my shoulder to see him watching us. My mind roiled with thoughts. Was he the boy I had met in a dream?

My second passage dream was the first time I had visited the boy. I was eleven seasons old. Like the time before, I was sleepy in a room filled with peat smoke when dizziness crept over me. I blinked and saw through his eyes. His mind told me he was alone and hunting, hiding himself from his prey in a small shelter. Close to sunset, the clouds were turning hunter's pink, and he knew his prey would show soon. Startled by my coming into his mind, he lost sight of the path he had been watching. I felt his impatience. This hunt determined his adult name. The goddess touched his mind and his fear was gone.

His body tensed as a shadow crossed the path. A stunning red fox stepped out of the brush with a rabbit squirming in its mouth. The fox stood, watchful, for two breaths, and carried the rabbit into its burrow. The young man cursed. He wanted to capture the fox before it escaped underground. He crossed the path holding a small knife, reached into the hole, and grasped the snarling, biting fox. He pulled it from its burrow, sliced its neck and held its body above his head, warm blood running down his arm. I could not tell whose blood it was, his or the fox's. The bite wounds would leave scars but the feeling of triumph in the boy's heart overshadowed the pain. He was sixteen seasons old. I whispered my name and awoke. I tasted blood that morning.

I was thirteen, and he eighteen, the second time I visited. He sat on a rough log. The smell of sweet smoke and blood wafted around me, and I began to feel ill. An older man knelt beside a fire. He added leaves and small plants to its flames. A small goat, just sacrificed, lay on a rock. The young man's hand held his small bronze blade, covered with goat's blood. His mind told me he sacrificed the goat to ward off a threat to those he loved. I sent him calming thoughts of safety. I whispered my name as the goddess bade me and left.

Home, I listened to rain and the god's wrath, thunder, outside. Unease filled my heart for the rest of that day. I feared for the young man in my dream.

After leaving the stable with Mother, I did not sleep, thinking of the druid in the stable, the boy he had been in my passage dreams. I tried to determine why the gods had given me my dreams and why they brought the boy, now a man, here.

I arose before sunrise. Wrapped in a blanket, I ran to our fire and blew on its coals. It came to life and spread light and warmth throughout our home.

"Thank you, Goddess Morrigna, for protecting our fire and home," I said, uttering our daily prayer. I dressed quickly. On tiptoes, to get as far from the cold floor as possible, I dipped a jar deep into our water urn. I shivered as I poured icy water into our boiling pot and fed a small block of peat to the glowing embers.

"Do not waste the fuel," mother protested. "We must quench the fire soon to relight it from the giving fire."

"Yes, Mother. I wished to start the grain cooking before I carried wash water to the druid."

"Oh, yes. The druid. There was a feeling in my bones last night that he might harbor trouble. I do not know whether we should ask him to stay in our village. I must discuss this with Beathan."

Mother's feelings were often right and even Beathan listened and took counsel from her. "Do not be long with him. I will need you to carry the offering to the goddess today. Are you not meeting Harailt to walk to the ceremony?"

Oh, Harailt! Beathan would announce our hand-fasting today. How could I have forgotten? I poured warm water into a jug to take to the priest and measured barley and Mother's favorite herbs into the now boiling pot.

"That smells good. Thank you for starting it." I heard her groan as she got out of bed and started dressing. "Today you will be looked upon by the whole clan when hand-fasted to Harailt. You should wear your yellow dress."

"Yes, Mother." I smiled. She still thought of me as a child at times. I would be married next week! I wondered if she would then think of me as a woman.

My light cloak belted, shoe laces loose in my hurry, I pulled open our door to leave. Not quite dawn, fog hid sun as it started its long climb from behind our mountain. An iron gray sky harbored small touches of moss-flower pink reflected in the haze. The animals were still snug in stables or homes, protected from wolves, and the cooking fires were small. Bumps on my arms from the coolness of the air made me glad I carried the jug of warm water.

At the first rays of light, birds started their possessive chirps. Listening carefully, I heard no owls; they must be in from their hunts. Mother said a day started with an owl song was a favorable day. I prayed the gods looked in on me today even though no owls sang.

I hesitated at the stable door, unable to go in. What should *I say? Would I ask, Priest, have you ever had anyone visit you in your mind?* He would think me a fool.

I jumped when he cleared his throat. He stood in the darker shadows of the already dark stable. My eyes grew accustomed to the lack of light and his hands rested on the pony. Its ears reached forward as if listening. Lovern straightened to his full height, almost touching the roof of the structure, and slowly nodded to me.

"Come in." He hesitated, then said my name as if forgotten then remembered. "Jahna."

His straw-filled, tousled hair looked as if he had wrestled a demon all night. My cloak lay in a crumpled ball on the stacked hay in the corner. Caution edged his familiar voice. "I am thanking this animal for bringing me here and protecting me last night. I have come a long way. I feel I may have found the end of my journey. I trust the gods to tell me today."

"I have warmed water for your washing. Are you finished with my cloak or will you use it today?" I asked.

"I did not use it last night and will not need it today. You may take it." He nodded to it, his hands still on the pony.

"If you would like some milk to break your fast, I can milk a goat. Beathan would not mind."

"No, I will not break my fast until after the ceremony."

I hesitated, not ready to leave. *I needed to know more about this man. What journey?* What will the gods tell him today? "You may use my light cape today if you wish. I can give it to you now. If you wear it, the members of our clan will recognize you as a friend and welcome you more easily. You should wear our colors – if you think you will stay in our village for a time."

"I will not need your cape today," he said gruffly.

Was the fog affecting his voice or was he uncomfortable with me here, alone?

He stepped closer, his face a mystery, his sinewy, muscled arms bare. It was then his scars and armband became visible. I had been in his mind when he received the wounds that caused his scars! He was from my passage dream! I could not move or breathe. He reached down, picked up my heavy cloak, and stepped next to me. Currents of energy ran through my body. I watched him intently, thinking myself ready to run if I needed, but deep in my mind knowing I could not. He leaned in, and the heat of his body and mine combined.

"We will have a journey together. The Gods Dagda and Morrigna protect me," he whispered into my ear. Opening my cloak, he laid it across my shoulders. His hand rested on me for an instant. I trembled, and felt his breath on my face. His eyes never left mine. Was this a frith, a sign from the goddess? What kind of journey was he speaking of? Questions overcame my thoughts, but I could not form them into words.

I remembered the women teasing unmarried girls around the well, laughing, "The first male you meet on Samhainn is the man you will marry." He was the first male I had seen on this sacred day!

"No. No! I will marry Harailt," I said. "I am promised. Our hand-fasting will be announced at the ceremony today. You and I cannot make a journey." I twisted out of his reach. My legs finally worked and ran me back to the safety of the known, the safety of my home.

He was there. Dependable Harailt. Waiting at my door, ready to go, dressed for a ceremony in a new tunic, and hair brushed back from his face with limewater. His dirk sheathed and tied at his waist. I ran up to him, breathless, trying not to look as flustered and confused as I felt.

"I've just come from the druid and I have to get water from the well. Please go help Mother." I took the wooden bucket to the well, filled it, and was tripping back when Harailt came out of the house with Mother.

"We will start gathering the goats," Mother said. "Get dressed. Bring the blanket and the oak log for the fire."

I went in, emptied the bucket into the water jar and found my leather bag with our gift to the goddess, the blanket we wove, folded inside. The oak brand that would bring the giving fire home lay next to the pit. Mother had smothered the fire with earth and emptied it of its ashes. Laid with small kindling, it stood ready for the new fire. I found my yellow dress lying on our bed and pulled it over my head. I combed my hair, hoping to gain some control, and wore it unfettered. I retied my shoes, pinned my cloak and stepped outside.

The noise and smells of the day rose to a level seen only on days of ceremonies. The people of the farms and homes around us were gathering for the event.

I heard a loud rumble of sound behind us as I followed Harailt and Mother. A war chariot passed, pulled by two ponies, driven by Beathan. Riding on either side, each on his own pony, were Finlay and Kenric. Kenric carried an oak log filled with the embers of fire that would light the giving fire. The druid, Lovern, stood next to Beathan in the chariot. I gasped. How handsome he was, red hair flying free. He was almost as tall as Beathan and had Beathan's plaid cape pinned around him and his own pouch hanging over his shoulder. My thoughts and feelings were confused. Would he look at me? Did I want him to?

Lovern's eyes did not stray as the chariot rushed by.

I stepped between Harailt and my mother and we began the walk to the ceremony.

Looking back at my life, I understand I was unborn until the night Beathan carried Lovern, the Fox, into his lodge. I started living when he played the music of the wind and I danced.

CHAPTER 2

APRIL, 2005

"Little Mouse, are you ready to be a life partner with this man?"

"Yes, Uncle."

I knew I was to be with this man for the rest of time. Happiness filled me as a red thread tied our clasped hands together. My heart sang.

I woke up humming the melody of the music that floated in my ears, the sound of men's voices singing, and the music of a pipe. "Wow, that was vivid," I told the dust bunnies under my bed as I reached for my slippers. I never did like to clean house. I looked at my wrist to see if the red thread was still there. No. Just my watch telling me it was time to get up. A dream. I remembered similar dreams, and the peacefulness they brought me. I wished I could feel like this all day. "I wonder if the dream had anything to do with Jahna? If only-" My phone rang.

"Hello?"

"Hi, Aine. This is Kelly. Are you at work?"

Kelly supervised one of my crews during the week. She and I were friends and often met for lunch or went out on

Saturday nights if I wasn't working. I hadn't spent much time with her lately as I'd worked almost every weekend for the last five weeks.

"Hi, Kelly. No, I took this weekend off. I just woke up. What are you doing up so early?"

"There is a blasted work gang right outside my window. They started their jackhammer at seven this morning! Can you believe it? I was calling you to find out who these jokers are and put in a complaint."

"Ummm. You know, Kelly, we don't handle every job that goes on in London. How do you know they aren't digging for a new sewer line?"

"Oh, Aine. I knew you'd find out and get a call in. I just wanted one more hour's sleep. Oh well. Since we're both up, do you want to meet for lunch?"

"No, I've some things I need to get done today. Thanks. Say, are you going out tonight?"

"Is it Saturday? Darned right! It's been too many Saturday nights without you. I thought you'd a new bloke and were afraid to introduce him to me, afraid I'd steal his heart with my new short skirt!"

"Oh, now I've got to come to see how short this one is. I'll join you tonight. Cheers."

I sighed as I pushed end.

A new boyfriend. That would be nice. Does this mean I'm lonely? No, I don't think so. I've dated several times since my divorce, but I didn't have a steady. I couldn't connect or feel comfortable with anyone. I might have been scared because of my experience with my ex, Brad, but I hoped not. Late at night, when I couldn't sleep, I rationalized that I was waiting for the perfect man, a life partner. I thought I had him once, but blew it. Then we met again last summer. I didn't know if I would ever get another chance at fulfillment, but if I was going to get one, this was it. However, I had some work to do if I was to have any chance at all.

I crossed the room to wash my face. I loved my flat: small, efficient, and –most important – within walking distance to my office on Upper Brook Street. It was located over a bookstore, and if I took a deep breath I smelled the dust, glue, ink, and paper from the new and well-read used books from downstairs rise between the cracks of the centuries-old floorboards.

I was happy. At least I kept telling myself I was.

I toasted a bagel and ruminated about my job. After lots of soul searching, I'd taken a job with Michael Goldsmith Corporation, MGC, as a field archaeology supervisor. It was hard to admit I was working for a big company.

While in college, obtaining my degree in archaeology, we debated about the big corporations that were going to take over our work someday. I promised myself that I'd never work for one. I guess some promises couldn't be kept. Something had to pay for food and rent.

I worked hard to gain the position I had with MGC, and headed the Cultural Resource Management division for London. This archaeological field was new and I was inventing a lot of it as I went along. MGC was a consulting company that worked with construction companies and conducted pre-construction discovery research for all local permits.

If an ancient site was found during construction, our job was to survey and research the site before the continuing construction or rebuilding. We made sure history was preserved in a timely manner so the construction companies involved didn't go bankrupt.

I used the newest toys, the Geographical Information System, and ground-penetrating radar. I cataloged finds, marked them for preservation, dug them up and sent them off to a museum. I wrote the reports. It paid my bills and I was working as an archaeologist. What more could I want?

Well, a productive dig on my Scottish Highland hill would be perfect and I'd been planning this adventure for several months.

A cup of tea, a bagel slathered in butter and marmalade, and day planner in hand, I slumped into my oversized chair and stared at the poster I'd taped over my desk, an enlarged picture of the hill I wanted to work on. Family photos were boxed up to free a wall for this picture. Its presence kept me focused on my future goal and filled my little home with hope.

I opened my planner to my to-do list. The GIS didn't have the hill listed as a pre-known site. I received the farm owner's permission to conduct research on the hill and applied for the necessary permits. I even had a small amount of money, just enough to start. I'd begged a loan from my aunt. She always believed in me, even when I made senseless decisions – like marrying Brad.

Now, after months of preparing, I was ready to get a team together; a cheap team, preferably a free team. I planned to call Marc Hunt, a Professor of Archaeology specializing in Pre- and First-Century Celts at the University of Birmingham. His grad students needed fieldwork. I prayed he would say yes. This could be my second chance.

We had a history. In college, we'd fallen in love with the Celts and each other. The way we planned it, archaeology would never be the same after we graduated. We were going earn our doctorates and astonish everyone with our research. I thought I would be working next to him for the rest of my life.

It ended when Brad Teller stepped into my life.

Marc and I'd been dating for several years. One summer, the university offered him a chance to work a site in Cambodia.

I was a year behind him and was scheduled to take classes that summer. I couldn't believe he said yes. I was hurt he wouldn't stay with me and find a job here in London. After a fight the night he left, I avoided his calls the rest of that week. I was thick-headed and I paid for it.

Brad showed up at a party one night. He was attractive and I decided Marc wasn't going to have all the fun. Who knows what he was doing in Cambodia? Brad and I danced one dance and then he never let me out of his sight. I thought he was romantic. It was what I thought I wanted from Marc. Looking back, I couldn't understand how I let myself be fooled by him. It was as if the dark Welshman cast a spell on me. I didn't feel towards him the way I felt towards Marc. I loved Marc. I never loved Brad.

Six weeks later, we were married in a civil ceremony. His lovemaking was clumsy and unfulfilling and he started abusing me soon after our honeymoon. I never called or spoke with Marc again while Brad and I were married. I gave Marc no explanation. I didn't have one for myself. We left England and worked all over the world, never thinking about coming back to Great Britain. It seemed that Brad was running from something.

My friends sent me rebuking letters, telling me not to stay with Brad. My best friend Susie wrote long missives begging me to come home. She told me how hurt Marc was and that if I came soon he and I might be able to repair our relationship. Thinking about going home made my heart ache, but for some God-forsaken reason, I was trapped. Trapped as if I were Brad's slave.

I stopped answering Susie. Her letters stopped coming, and I was glad. They made me think about my life. I didn't want to think about it then.

I did menial work for Brad, transcribed notes, and ran errands. Every time I tried to make a suggestion toward his research or create a place for myself, he told me I was stupid and told me to stop interrupting his work process. I cried myself to sleep night after night. At the end, when he touched me my skin crawled. I couldn't stand the way he smelled.

Brad tore my self-confidence to pieces. I believed I would never be able to work on my own.

We were in Africa when a letter came from George Wyemouth, my mentor. He wrote that his wife had died. Shocked, I realized I would never get to see Sophie again. His beautiful Sophie, the love of his life. To her chagrin, he often told the story of stealing her from another man's arms. He had to assuage her family with proof of his love for her before they could marry in peace. He often said he would have fought a bear for her if necessary.

Now, George needed me. His letter was disjointed and difficult to read. Here was a man whose socks were folded in order of their color in his drawer, and he couldn't write a simple letter. I had no choice – my heart pulled me to go to him.

When Brad found out, we argued for hours. Our shouting match emptied out into the hall of the apartment building. When the neighbors' doors started to open and people stared, he grabbed my arm and pulled me back inside. I resisted and he hit me. His closed fist crashed against my chest and his open palm connected with my cheek. Up until then, for a long, awful fifteen years, he verbally abused me, but this was the first time I was afraid for my life. I left the apartment and stayed in a hotel. The bruise on my face wasn't bad, I could cover it with makeup, but the bruise over my heart grew and was painful for days.

One thought fastened itself into my brain: I'd paid my penance. I didn't need to stay with him anymore. I wouldn't have a physical rescuer, but George's letter opened my soul, and the light poured back in. I phoned home, my aunt wired money for a plane ticket and I left Africa. I left Brad.

I came back to London, filed for a divorce, and helped George through his grief. We walked, talked, and mended our hearts together. In my heart, I felt certain that I repaid George, my mentor, my adopted uncle, a long-owed debt.

I went to a party at a friend's home. The hostess invited a hypno-therapist, Rhonnie Craig. Her explanation of the process was fascinating and I couldn't resist, so I made an appointment to see her.

"We'll work together on this," Rhonnie said. "I'm going to take you to a place and find the power inside yourself that'll allow you to have good relationships. You may have a history with strong men in this or past lives, but we don't have to travel through each one to help you now. I want to draw on the good relationships you have with men in this life, your father, brother and any others you may have or have had, to make you aware of your strengths."

We drew on my family and the love I had for Marc. I cried and then remembered what had attracted me to Marc so long ago. I learned I could love again. I would love someone who would love me and let me be me, not hold me down.

After my sessions with Rhonnie, I felt like I had been freed. She helped me vanquish my guilt over my decision of marrying and then leaving Brad. The sessions gave me a new perspective on my life. I could see a productive future of my own now. Rhonnie became a very good friend.

When I went to work for MGC, Marc and I would run into each other at conferences. We said hello, but nothing more. Every time I saw him, my heart fluttered but I told myself it was because I was jealous of his position as a Ph.D., teaching and doing research, not anything personal.

Last summer I decided to try some fieldwork again. Marc just happened to have a project that I was interested in. The University of Birmingham funded Marc and through a friend I heard he was working a Bronze Age tomb near Fort William.

I had time accrued so I took three weeks. I must've had a brain freeze when I made the decision to just show up one day.

There I was, perched in front of him, his team working up the hill. His deep blue eyes filled with questions as he contemplated me. Concentration lines further furrowed his brow. His lips, framed by his full, burnt umber beard, formed a tight line. His hand ran through his collar length rust hair, pulling it back. I was shocked when I saw gray at his temples. In my mind, he was timeless. We weren't supposed to age. But here was proof of the flight of our lives.

"Aine MacRae. What are you doing here?"

"I heard you were working here and had a few days off. I would love to work. A volunteer job, anything, just so I can get my hands back into the Celt world I love. I see Romans all day long in London and need a change."

He became even more wary. "I don't know, Aine." His mouth screwed up, and his jaws clenched. He hesitated and said, "I could use another pair of hands, but I don't want trouble. Where's Brad?"

I shrugged. "I haven't spoken with him for years. We didn't separate on the best of terms, as I'm sure you heard. I'd love to help here for a couple of days. I'll do anything you need, even go for tea."

"Well, I guess we could use some help categorizing and labeling. At least you're familiar with the era."

"Great! Exactly what I wanted, a working vacation."

It was strange standing there in front of Marc. I couldn't describe the feelings that were racing through me. I had a hard time catching my breath. Marc had gone on without me. He'd married Darlene, a tall, blonde American biologist who said she loved him for his Scottish accent. I remember my stomach lurched and filled with finality when I heard about his marriage. I silently wished him luck. I was miserable.

They both taught at the University of Birmingham until she died, three years ago. You would think, with all the money spent on research, that there would be a cure for breast cancer by now. Maybe that was where I should have been spending my time – with the living, the people who needed help now, not in the dirt with the long dead. But there I was.

I looked up at the entrance to the tomb dug into the side of the hill. Behind us stood a tent that covered the workstations where we sifted, sorted, and cataloged the cave contents. I loved being here at this time of year; the blue harebells bloomed among the sparkling granite boulders. There was a path worn in the grass from the tent to the slippery shale trail leading up to the tomb's entrance.

"May I go in and look?"

"Yeah, come on. It's one of the best-preserved tombs in this area. I think it'll date to about the beginning of the first century from the looks of some of the artifacts. We've found several burial offerings. Wait 'til you see! An artisan made the bronze swords. It's the swords and the shield that makes me think it's a chieftain's tomb. Most of the burials in this area were cremations. It's a real find to get a full skeleton."

We slid and slipped up to the entrance. Marc leaned in and asked everyone to take a tea break. Two young men and a young woman crawled out in single file and stood up.

"Thanks, Dr. Hunt. Gosh, it's cold in there. I need to get my sweater," said the young woman.

Marc introduced me to his students Tim, Matt, and Lauri.

"This is such an exciting project," Lauri said.

She was so young! "So you like to be stuck back in an unstable cave? Well, I can say that if you can work there, you can work anywhere. You'll do well in this business," I told this, smiling, brown-eyed wrinkle free, straight-toothed, and innocent face.

She donned a huge smile and bounced into the tent after her friends.

"God, Marc. She – they're just kids," I said, shaking my head.

"Yeah, the older we get, the younger they are," he replied. He turned to me after following them into the tent with his eyes, shook his head and said, "All so idealistic. They have a few more years with me and then off to find jobs on their own. Good luck to them."

"My company is always looking for good people. If you are referring them, I might be able to pull a few strings," I said.

"I'll remember that when the time comes."

Marc and I got to our knees and crawled in, avoiding the electric cable. The darkness spilled away from a large lamp set up at the end of the cave, lighting the walls and their scooped out cavities. The clay was cool beneath my hands. The air was dry and carried a familiar odor. It reminded me of the Parisian catacombs I toured as a child, where bones were piled to the ceilings. The catacombs smelled like the butcher shop I used to follow my mother into on Skye.

Someone had carved the tomb out of a small cave. It ran back about four meters and was about two meters high. With Marc leading and carrying a large flashlight in one hand, we came to the first carved out ledge. There were the bronze shield and swords that a chieftain would carry into battle while riding his chariot. I could see the outline of his bow, but it had deteriorated. Marc was right; the work that I could see on the hilts of the swords was wonderful, intricate yet strong. This was further proof of the artistic bent of the earliest Scots.

Further on there were a few small ledges with some unrecognizable items I assumed to be clothing and other burial offerings. We continued to the last and largest ledge, the resting place of the skeleton. Marc stopped at its feet. I sat and looked at the skull and upper body.

"Oh, Marc. This is remarkable." I leaned closer to look at his neck vertebra, as his head seemed to be positioned at an odd angle. A shiver ran down my back. "Oh, wow! He was decapitated!"

"Nice, Aine. You haven't lost your touch. I noticed it right away, but my students didn't see it until I pointed it out. It will be good to have you around, even for a short time."

Everything was going well; I enjoyed every day. In my heart, I knew this was where I should be. It all seemed familiar, the valley and the boulders on the hill. My arm hair prickled every morning when I looked up at the tomb.

One morning, the fog was deep and heavy. I should've known there would be trouble on a day like this. It was too Emily Brontë-like. Perfect for drama. I think Brad knew I was there and wanted to cause trouble. He'd lost his funding for all his foreign work and had to come back to England. I heard he was doing follow-up conservation reports for different historical societies, none of his own research. I had also heard his next assignment was on the Isle of Lewis.

Brad never respected Marc and had been jealous of him. When their paths crossed, as they did in this business, there was always a careful dance around each other to avoid talking. This time, however, Brad interrupted their dance. I was unaware he was there until he crossed the path and grabbed hold of my arm.

"What makes you think you can do this kind of work?" Brad said, his face in mine. "Working for a huge corporation doesn't teach you how to do exacting research like this. Who let you in here?"

His breath made me nauseous and I started trembling. I thought I was over him but he could still make my vision start to go white.

Marc walked up, pried Brad's fingers off my arm and slipped between us, acting as a shield.

"You two are sleeping together, aren't you! I knew you would start rutting again. Had to go for old fruit though, huh, Marc? Wouldn't any of the young things you work with do you?"

Marc's shoulders braced at those comments. "No. We aren't sleeping together. But if we were, it wouldn't be any of your business. Leave! Now! I don't want you here on my site."

Brad's eyes lost focus just as they did the night he hit me. He lunged, trying to get around Marc to me, and Marc decked him with a single punch. It didn't take much; Brad, 5'6" and overweight, didn't match up to Marc's 5'10" and lean strength.

Brad's nose looked broken. "I'm not done with you, Aine," he said through his blood-filled hand as he left. "Or you, Marc. You think you're so high and mighty."

I stepped in front of Marc so he couldn't see Brad walking away. It was all I could do at the time. "Marc. I am so sorry. I didn't think he would find me. Are you OK?"

"Yeah," he said and rubbed his knuckles.

"Do you want me to go back to London?"

Marc grabbed my shoulder, looked me in the eye and said, "Don't ever let him treat you like that again. You're better than that. Don't let him chase you away from anywhere or stop your dreams again. Walk your own path!" He stomped to the tent. Tim, Matt, and Lauri looked on with open mouths.

Marc seemed to be very careful never to let us be alone together again, and I hoped I had not irreversibly damaged a future friendship. I tiptoed around him, trying not to get into his way.

I think I redeemed myself at the end of the project, though, when I found a bronze bowl that'd been overlooked by everyone else. It was under a rock, outside the tomb, and I knew exactly where to go to find it. No one ever asked me how I knew it was there, which was a good thing. They never would've believed me. How could I tell them that I'd dreamt about it, that Jahna showed me where it was?

We all celebrated on our last night together. Marc shook my hand and thanked me for coming. I left, feeling as if I were leaving something important behind but I didn't know what.

When his report on the tomb came out, he listed me as an associate.

Last October, my mood echoed the gray rain-filled skies of London. Trapped indoors more than I liked by reports and other paperwork, the walls of my cubicle seemed too close in on my desk. Trying to keep work permits updated and the actual work flowing was almost impossible. Working conditions in some of the locations was unsafe, so several sites close to being ready for construction to start or continue were delayed. I was getting daily calls from the construction bosses, and was ready to do a rain dance in reverse—anything to stop this horrid weather. It was on a lunch hour when, daydreaming about the work being done in other sites, I started browsing the local archaeological web sites. One from the Isle of Lewis jumped out at me.

Brad Teller, known for his overseas work, was working on the site alone when he allegedly raped a local woman and was killed by her irate husband.

It was dated three weeks after he accosted me and left Marc's site last summer. As I read the article, I became nauseous. I'd lived with that man for fifteen years. How could I've been so stupid? I didn't mourn him; I mourned the lost years I had spent with him and the loss of my personal goals. For several weeks after I read the article, I dreamed about walking the Highlands. Snippets of a hill overlooked by a mountain and three smaller hills floated in my mind when I woke up after these dreams. After all the construction had finally started, I decided to take a few days off and hike. I needed the time outdoors.

I trod along the rocky paths of the Scottish Highland and camped in the rain, heading *somewhere*, but nowhere in particular. Then, rounding a small rolling hill, I saw it. The clouds lay heavy just above its summit but one ray of sunlight was peeking through, creating a halo effect. I knew, I just *knew* I was supposed to be there. The feeling of recognition, similar to the one I had on Marc's site, was strong.

I got to its summit and the ever-present rain stopped for just a few moments. I criss-crossed the even ground and saw the hill-fort in my mind's eye. It was in a perfect position. Visibility was good in three directions. The oak trees in the distance were far enough away to allow a warning if anyone tried to come up to the fort. The meandering stream that ran through the oak grove proved water was available. The strong, squat mountain behind was close enough to provide a protective wall for the back of the fortress. The meadows were clear, and there were the farmer's long-haired cattle foraging in a bog-like depression. I turned around several times to take in the whole view. Something was missing. Several things seemed out of place. Suddenly a flock of sheep pictured itself in my mind.

"There should be sheep on this land," I said to myself. "They should be right over there." But they weren't there. I was confused. The sheep should have been there. But why would I wonder where the sheep were? I'd never been here before. I didn't even know if the farmer who owned this land had sheep.

Well, most farmers raised sheep in this part of Scotland. I made a mental note to ask him when I came back. I knew at that moment I would.

As I wandered over the grounds, I stopped on a slight depression that would've been close to the fort's walls. I stopped to eat my lunch there. As I sat, a warm, hand-like weight rested welcomingly on my shoulder.

I planned my return while I worked the rest of the winter in London.

I longed to work on that hill, the hill in my picture. I'd completed all the necessary steps. I'd found money, just enough to support a few others and myself for about two weeks. With a few people and rudimentary equipment, we could begin a dig. After we found what I knew was there, money and other resources would come pouring in.

Now I just had to convince Marc to come with me. I needed his team. My instincts told me he was the one to call. I said a small prayer to the gods and asked for his understanding.

Oh gosh, why was this so hard? After hesitating and stalling until the morning was almost gone, I dialed.

"Hello, Marc? This is Aine. I've a proposition for your students and a favor to ask of you."

CHAPTER 3

LOVERN

72 AD November

The fascinating young woman, Jahna, who danced in front of me last night, left me reeling in confusion. It was my first night in the company of men in the many nights of my journey, and I was exhausted. While I lay on the floor, she came close enough to allow me to smell lavender from her hair.

They sang to praise the stories of their *ceann-cinnidh*. I played to entice a glance from her. Beathan expected me to stay for the Samhainn ceremony. Now I had to stay not only for the ceremony, but to find out why the gods led me here. For I am Druid. The gods and goddesses talk to me.

They spoke to me last night.

After my meal of bread and mead, I required quiet hours to purify myself, to allow my songs to rise to the gods. The young dancer guided me to the stable. I asked and when she told me her name, my legs weakened. I shuddered. My thoughts had been invaded by her twice before. In the dreams, she looked through my eyes. She was there at the hunt for my namesake, the fox. And again after the sacred sacrifice to stop the Roman invaders. Could I be in danger here with her? Her name, Jahna, haunted me for years.

I undertook this journey to survive. The gods guided my steps. It was a search for her.

I circled the goats and ponies, secure in the warmth of their bodies. I had walked for many nights wary of the unknown; tonight was not an exception. I wished to speak with my teacher Conyn, but could not. He had been captured by the Romans, was now a slave. I mourned my loss of contact with him.

Jahna left me her cloak. I wrapped myself in it to know her. Her scent – lavender, some herbs for cooking and some unknown to me – lay heavy on the wool. I reached into my bag and took my stones into my hand. Three times, I traced the path of the labyrinth. My mind calmed, ready to hear the gods. I covered my face with her cloak and opened my mind to those who wished to speak.

The goats bleated. The ponies neighed, and one came close enough to warm my neck with his breath.

The gods and goddess came, surrounded in light. I spoke to them. "You have guided my hands to be able to heal. You have calmed my spirit when I have been in question about the needs of others. I have a need. Why was I led here?"

I interpreted the music of their answers in my vision.

Lugh spoke first. "Lovern," he whispered, "you are tired. Your mind is heavy with indecision. Here you may sleep and renew your body for the morrow. Then you must decide whether to go or stay in this village. Your journey may be complete if you chose to stay. But understand, danger is never out of sight. There is death hanging over these people."

Arwan, the god of my underworld, the one I called on every Samhainn, spoke next, in a coarse, deep voice. "Your journey may end here. Or it may continue if you choose to go. If you go, you will meet and learn from many more people, but your heart will remain unfulfilled. If you stay, you will learn why your paths crossed here. It is for you to choose."

Then three voices, woven into one, Queen Morrigna, sternly said, "Hear me, mortal. Fear me if you stray. You are commanded to teach the one who carries the blood of her people. You are commanded to guide the one who will soften the paths of the dying. You will mark the day of her marriage. It will not be to the chosen one. She holds the dreams of your future in her hands. It is to Jahna I commit you. Jahna is your burden. You may choose to leave and wander alone for eternity. You may choose to stay and learn to love and cry. It is your choice."

I listened. The gods gave me directions. I gave my life to the gods. I am Druid.

The night was long. My blood boiled. The gods had spoken, and the task of finding Jahna's connection to the gods had fallen on me, if I stayed. I knew not whether the dangers that Lugh described were caused by her or directed to her. I must act carefully until I made my decision. My body overheated. I threw her cloak off and removed my shirt.

As night ended, I stood by the pony that carried me yesterday. Then she came. Jahna. She brought warm, cleansing water and we talked. To start our journey, I told her the gods have crossed our paths, one over the other. I watched as she ran away. I wondered what was in her heart, why she ran. But I did not have time to wonder long.

Beathan lunged noisily into the stable, his hair brushed back, his chest bare. His plaid cape was fastened around his shoulders and hung over his yellow *braecci*, covering tree-trunk like legs. His boots were long and laced with a length of red hide. He hawked and spit at his rooster. It ran as if familiar with this morning routine.

"Did you pass the night well, druid?" Beathan growled. An extra plaid cloak hung off the crook of his elbow.

"Blessings this morning to you. May the goddess ride on your shoulders today," I said.

"She can ride if she can hold on. I expect a fine ceremony and a full harvest for the next year. Ask her for a gentle ending to this gods-forsaken dark season. The storms have been hard this year."

"I will ask. I cannot promise."

"Ach. You priests never promise anything. I have found the gods listen to those who please them the most. I pray you please them."

He turned away from me, laid the cloak on a rail, and threw a handful of grain to his goats. They stumbled over themselves trying to get to it. He laughed. "Hand-fasts will be announced today after you speak. The couples will marry soon. A good way to start a new season of growth. The young woman who danced in my home last night, Jahna, is one of them."

He turned to his ponies and gathered the harness for the chariot into his massive arms. The rattle of the metal buckles blended with the morning call of the roosters and prattle of waking people outside the stable.

"Plentiful harvests and ample butchering is what I ask. We must give a bull to Arwan and Morrigna today," he said as he lifted the harness over the pony's withers.

"Is Jahna going to be hand-fasted to one you choose?"

"Yes. She is my kin, I chose a good match for her. I did well."

Even though he did not face me, I imagined his smile. He was proud to be the chieftain and make these decisions. He had chosen for her. This was what the goddess meant. She was not to marry the chosen one. Now I must convince this mountain of a man that the marriage was not to happen.

"*Ceann-cinnidh*, Beathan," I said. "I beg you to listen well. The goddess spoke with me about Jahna last night."

Beathan stopped buckling the harness, stood to his full height and turned to me, questions in his hooded eyes as he measured me from head to toe.

I stood tall, still covered by his shadow. "The Goddess Morrigna ordered Jahna not to be betrothed today." I stepped in front of the pony so Beathan could not leave the dark stable until he absorbed the goddess' words. I was ready to fight for the goddess' demand. "I do not know what goddess Morrigna's plan is for Jahna's future, but I know I must be involved," I said.

His body tensed. A low growl came from his throat. "What do you mean, you must be involved? You have just arrived. What do you know of Jahna?"

"Jahna is the reason I am here. My journey was a long one. Many dangers were involved. I left to avoid death but arrived here by the calling of the gods. Last night they told me that Jahna is the reason I am here. I do not know more than that."

The grey, early morning light hid his eyes. I could not assure him with mine that I spoke the truth.

I silently prayed. *Morrigna, whisper in his ear. Tell him I speak with your words.*

I said, "The goddess led me here but I do not know what she plans. I must study Jahna, know her, and then the goddess will guide me."

Beathan did not move, even his breathing seemed to stop. I strained not to speak until he answered. His jaw clenched, and his eyes closed. Then his eyes opened slowly and trapped mine.

"Sometimes, this goddess asks the impossible," he said. "Why you? Why not one of my warriors?"

"That is the answer I will give you after I have spent time with Jahna. She is the one who holds the truths to these questions. She is the one the goddess will speak through. I must learn if she has the clan's good will at heart."

"The clan's good will? *The clan's good will?* What do you know of my clan's good will? We have fought hard to have a little bit of peace. Jahna was born of my sister and during her lifetime no ill has come to the clan. Why would this change?"

"Good Chieftain, I do not say there is harm coming to the clan. I only know I must find out why I am here. The gods have given me a choice and I choose to stay."

After a long moment of silence, Beathan's face hardened into an iron mask. "I will do as the gods ask. You are a priest. You must speak the truth on Samhainn. But know this, druid. She is of my family and if you harm her without talking to me first, I will have your head on my wall." The pony's ears stood up as it felt Beathan's hands stiffen on its back. "She is your millstone while you are here."

"I will not harm her without your permission. Betroth the man Jahna was to marry to another woman. Jahna will not marry him," I said.

"Harailt," Beathan said as if just remembering the name. "Hmm. He did want to marry the farm girl, Sileas. I will announce it today."

He pointed his large hand at me and said, "I warn you. Do not anger me. You do not scare me, Priest. I will hunt you like a dog if I decide to kill you."

"I do only what the goddess wishes me to," I said, bowing my head. *I must find out why the girl Jahna invaded my mind.* Now, I had Beathan's permission to talk to her, to question her, to know her.

"We will ready my chariot. You ride with me. My sons will come on their ponies. Wear this." He threw the plaid to me as he led the pony outside. "We will go soon."

I swung the cloak over my shoulders and fastened it with the acorn-topped pin attached to it. I slung my bag over my neck and, when Beathan called, climbed into the chariot, his sons on either side.

We passed Jahna, her mother and a young man I guessed to be Harailt. I did not look at Jahna. To be prepared for the ceremony, my mind must be free from outside thoughts. I was to perform the sacrifice of the Samhainn giving fire. My mind was clear; I meditated on my songs. I did not think of Jahna again until later.

At the ceremony field, there were two stacks of oak logs far enough apart to allow the passage of people and animals. The clan gathered and talked among themselves excitedly. Most were wearing the plaid Jahna had woven. It was the first time I had seen a clan dressed in the same colors. I felt the strength of the bond it created as I looked over the clan. Beathan was right to ask all to wear it as a sign of brotherhood and fealty. I walked to the sacred circle drawn around the piles of wood and waited. The crowd began to call for the ceremony to begin. The men led the bull to me.

"Here is the earthen vessel to be used in the ceremony," said Finlay, handing me the small pottery cup that would hold the blood of the sacrifice.

I crossed to the bellowing sacrificial bull. Two grown men hung onto ropes fastened to its neck, its front legs hobbled. Frightened eyes rolled and froth flung from its mouth as it tried to escape. I laid my hands on its forehead and looked deep into its eyes. It calmed as I spoke.

"I call the god Arwan and the goddess Morrigna to attend our ceremony and ask the blessings of both to fall on the clan, the harvests and the animals. I thank you, sacred bull, for giving your life today. You will call the gods to us and have them hear our prayers."

I raised my dirk to the sky and plunged it into the bull's neck. Its blood spurted into the cup I held against its straining neck. He flew into a rage and blood sprayed, covering my arms. Two more men leaped forward to further restrain the enraged bull.

I drank and passed the cup to Beathan. He drank. The blood was warm and tasted of metal. I heard the call of the birds over the bull's screams, and looked up. The sky over us was black with ravens.

"This is the sign of Morrigna. The Queen is here and blesses the clan," I shouted and I raised my bloody arms to the ravens. The crowd cheered, then quieted as they began to feel the tension of the next few moments. If the sacrifice did not go well, the clan would feel the wrath of the gods.

I nodded to Finlay to carry up the sacred sword. He stood, the bull's shoulders at his chest, raised it, and plunged it into its back. The sword pierced its heart. The bull raised its head as if surprised, fell to its knees and then, as we raced out of the way, rolled to its side with a huff, dead. A good sacrifice.

I told the gathered clan, "The peaceful death of the bull is the sign the god Arwan is here. He will bring good hunting and a good harvest for next year." There were cheers and shouts of happiness among the people.

Beathan walked forward and commanded attention with raised arms.

"To celebrate the coming planting season of the Clan," Beathan shouted to the muttering crowd. "We will have marriages."

"I betroth Maira and Clyde." He raised his hands for the couple to come forward.

I heard shouts of congratulations.

"Gara and Lyel."

Again, I heard wishes of good luck and a healthy family.

"Harailt and…."

My eyes searched and found Jahna, next to Harailt on her tiptoes, steadying herself on his arm. He seemed to be pulling away from her.

"Harailt and Sileas."

The crowd grew quiet. Jahna jumped when Beathan finished the announcement and then stood still. She stared as Harailt walked to a young woman, I assumed was Sileas, and kissed her. I watched Jahna turn and run towards the lake. After a moment of stunned silence, the crowd cheered again. Harailt, a grin on his face, did not notice as Sileas's eyes followed Jahna with concern.

I could not follow Jahna. This was the goddess' moment. I stayed to light the Samhainn fire.

I sang,

"These we shall burn today:
the rowan in the shade,
the willow near the water,
the alder of the marshes,
the birch under the waterfalls,
the yew for resilience,
the elm of the brae,
the oak, shining of the sun,
the hazel of the rocks, and
the pine for immortality,
to call all the gods and goddesses.
To bring the clan health and food and peace.
To bring honor and prizes and strength to the warriors.
To bring music and mead to all in the coming spring."

Kenric passed me a burning oak brand. I let it fall on one stack and then the second, creating two purifying fires. The heat burned the hairs on my arms as I threw in the cup used to drink the blood.

"Let the fire receive the bull." I directed the body of the bull to be thrown on the first fire. "You may now pass between the fires, bring your animals, and be purified for the new-year. Be protected and comforted by the gods. Give your sacrifices and light your brands to rekindle your home fires as you pass."

The farmers and warriors lead families, ponies, cattle, sheep, and goats between the fires. All threw in a gift – harvested grain, wool, or other items – and reached out for a piece of the fire to take home. I watched as Wynda, Jahna's mother, threw in a piece of plaid cloth. The air filled with smoke that carried the smell of burning meat and wool to the sky.

JAHNA

Why was I passed over and not hand-fasted to Harailt? I was worthless and abandoned. I ran to the lake and fell to its muddy bank, confused. My life had ended. The ravens were gone. I sat next to a lake that was deathly still. The smell of burning animals drifted in the air and choked me. I was alone; the clan was passing through the fires to be purified and I was not there. My arms crossed my breasts, and I shook as I cursed.

"How could you refuse me? How could you leave me alone?" I screamed at the iron sky.

I folded into myself, knowing I would never be the same. I would not be able to face the clan again. I sat as the sun traveled through the day, and the sky darkened with the coming intolerable night, shivering in my aloneness.

"Jahna."

I had not heard him approach. I jumped when he spoke.

"It will be dark soon. You must come back to your home," Lovern said.

"How can I? I can never go home. I have been cursed," I whispered.

"No. You have not been cursed," he said.

I lifted my tear-stained face, brushing my stringy hair away to look at him.

"I told you this morning in the stable. We shall find out what our path is together. You could not be betrothed," he said. "I spoke with Beathan and he acknowledged what the goddess has asked of you."

He kneeled beside me as I sat up, wrapping my cloak tightly around myself to shield him from touching me.

"I was supposed to be with Harailt after the fires, celebrating. We were going to go back to his farm and eat a meal. Where is he now?" I asked.

"He is with his betrothed," he said.

"You come here, not invited, and destroy my life. You invade my dreams and do not let me sleep. You convince Beathan that I should not be married to Harailt, yet you do not tell me why! I am cursed for knowing you. I wish I had never seen you! What is it you want from me?" Bewildered and angry, I slapped him. I hit him and struck him until I yielded to the ground again, sobbing. He knelt, defiant, through my tirade.

"I envisioned our future together. The goddess gave me your dreams. Now, we must determine why. I must be sure in my mind what our destiny is, Jahna," he said.

He was quiet as the moments passed and my sobbing eased.

As he gave me time to calm myself, I remembered what I experienced in my passage dreams. I was content to be with him, and I wanted to help him at those times. I knew he was spiritual and determined. But for me, confusion still reigned.

He changed my future. He destroyed it. I do not know what was to be ahead of me. He said we have a destiny together. At least I would not be alone.

"My future. Our future," I said, wiping my face with the back of my hand. "We have a journey to take." I looked at him, remembering my passage dream. "There was blood on your arms."

"Yes, your mother gave me some water to wash after the purifying."

He thought I meant the blood from the bull. I meant the blood of the fox.

"She also gave me food. I brought you bread and boiled pork," he said.

I salivated. I had not eaten for many hours.

I stretched to take the bread and pork. He held it just out of my reach. I looked up at him and scowled with hunger and annoyance. He had caused me to be here, and now he played with me. I hated him again. I wanted to be anywhere but here right now.

"I must ask you to swear to something before you eat," he said.

"I do not see why I need to swear anything to you. You have taken away my life. Why should I talk to you at all?"

Lovern stood. He was not as tall as Beathan, yet he towered over me with a sharp, appraising look. I saw the muscles of his jaw working under his beard. His eyes were intensely blue-black. I was not as brave as I wished, and I trembled.

"Beathan, your chieftain, has given me leave to talk to you. I am a druid. You must obey me. You must obey my demands, or I will take you to be tried before the clan council," he said with authority.

If he spoke with the council about my dreams, they could accuse me of being evil. I could be a sacrifice at the next quarter ceremony. I could not explain my passage dreams. I grew frightened.

I stared at him and asked, "What do you want me to swear?"

"I have two questions. You must look in my eyes and swear the truth of your answers. I will know whether you are telling falsehoods."

Standing as tall as I could, I only came to his chest. My dress and cape were dripping mud and wet grass, and I shivered. I looked into his deep eyes in the darkening daylight, and I noticed his full brows pull together, creasing his forehead.

"I must know whether you have been influenced by a man in any way," he said.

"Influenced by a man? Pff. What a stupid question. I am a loyal clanswoman; of course a man had influenced me. Beathan, my chieftain–"

"Have you ever lain with a man?" he interrupted.

"No! I have lived with my mother and never have let any man touch me. Ever!" Now, I was beginning to wonder if that would ever happen.

He nodded and continued, "Have you ever harmed or wanted to harm anyone through your dreams?"

I stood there, looking at him and remembering my passage dreams. I felt his emotions when we were together in the dreams. I felt his excitement of the hunt, his fear at the sacrifice. I felt the confusion of the girl I visited, Aine. I wanted to convey peace and comfort to both, never anything harmful. A moment passed, his eyes narrowed and jaws clenched, and he began to move away from me, taking the food.

"Wait!" I reached out and grabbed his arm. "I swear I have never wanted to harm anyone in my life, awake or in my dreams, except you just a few moments ago. I am hungry, cold, and tired and you have destroyed my life. You withhold food from me and threaten me with the council. You tell me my mother and chieftain approve of this treatment. I want to strike you!" Anger writhed in my stomach. Then, my shoulders sank. I knew could not hit him. Beaten, I turned from him and cried, "I do not want to be here."

I put my face in my hands, and sat back down on the cold ground. The sky was grey, filled with cruel clouds. The glaring sun was leaving, setting behind the three hills. I told the truth and could do no more. Let him take me to the council. I did not care. I folded in upon myself.

He laid his cape across my shoulders. It was still warm from his body. I relaxed, enveloped in his odor of earth and acorns. He gave me bread and meat; I ate. Then, he lifted me into his arms. His body warmed me and I stopped shivering. My head rested on his shoulder. I fell asleep with the rocking of his body as he carried me home.

The following morning, I woke up in my own bed.

At breakfast, my mother told me the gods and druids often changed the plans of men.

"So it is," she said. "So it is."

She told me I was to meet the druid by the lake where we were last night. I did what I was told. I put on my dress, combed the grass from my hair, and went to the lake.

A storm was coming. The sky darkened, and rain scented the air. As I walked past others on the path, a few people wished me good morning and I was surprised. I did not expect anyone to acknowledge me after yesterday.

When I arrived, he was waiting. He wore the cloak and acorn pin Beathan had given him. His unbound red hair blew around his face in the wind. His clean-shaven face was unusual as the men of my clan wore beards. He was more handsome than the warrior Braden, and my breath caught in my throat. I was disappointed in myself. I did not want to like him. I hardened my thoughts about him.

"I am glad to see you are well today. Did you get some rest and food?" he asked.

"Yes," I said, curtly.

"I told Beathan we have no need for the council. I did not tell him about your dreams and our meeting in them."

The wind began to blow harder; my skirt stung my ankles as it whipped around. What did he want of me?

"I still have some questions in my mind. I do not understand why we have this connection. We must find out together. In a dream, the goddess showed me both you and I standing on a mountain, looking over this valley. We were protecting it and each other. I must understand our bond to know what is expected of us." He looked at me with concern on his face.

Maybe he is right. Druids often had dreams of the future. But I feared his words in my heart. Why would my clan need protection?

"The wind is bringing in a storm with a bitter edge to it," I said as I wrapped my arms around my shoulders. I wished I had worn my oiled cloak.

He looked up at the dark, cloudy sky. "It will not rain for a few hours more. I want to walk around the lake with you."

He opened his arms and invited me to walk next to him, warmed under his cloak, his arm around my shoulders.

"What is the name of this lake?" he asked, pointing his chin at the wind blown waves.

"Loch Dubh. Black Lake. It is black during all the seasons. I am told other lakes are blue."

"You have never seen other lakes?"

"No. I have never been away from here. Except in my passage dreams."

We walked further. He was quiet until we reached the high point of the shore. The wind was stronger, and I leaned into it to stand upright. We stood on the bank and looked out over the lake. The hills were behind him now, and he looked like a warrior, standing against the wind with his hair blowing away from his clean, strong face.

"It is here our chieftains made sacrifices before and after battle," I observed, pointing to the lake. "Kenric told me there are iron and bronze swords down there."

"Has there been a human sacrifice here? I feel lingering souls," he asked.

"There were several when I was very young. Warriors taken in clan battles. I remember feasts, and after, the heads on our gate. Mother told me it was common during her childhood. She said some of the heads of our clansmen hung on other fences. It was the way of life. Since Beathan has been chieftain, though, battles are rare. He brought peace to this valley. His wife was from the clan we often fought. They talked a truce, and she came to live with us as his wife. We have no reason for a human sacrifice. The animal sacrifices seem to placate the gods. There have been no battles or threats in recent times."

I was still unsure how I felt about him. I did not trust him. The gods had guided him here, so he said. I asked the gods to guide me through his actions. My uncle and my mother gave my life to him, but I would not do so as easily. I would not give in to him unless he proved his worth to me. He would not have my spirit unless I gave it.

Lovern looked into the distance as if he saw riders on ponies fleeing across our farm fields. His brow filled with furrowed rows. His arm slightly pulled me closer to him, while I wanted to pull away. I stayed near him only for his warmth.

"No threats. No threats yet," he quietly murmured as we turned to walk home in silence.

CHAPTER 4

JAHNA

73 AD January

Time was not my friend.

The moon passed through her cycle before Lovern and I spoke again. A slow fire burned in my belly, fueled by discontent and confusion. Bothersome questions repeated and grew to command my thoughts during sleepless nights.

My mother and I still helped serve the evening meal to my uncle, his warriors, invited clansmen, and the druid. While the warriors and my uncle boasted the bravado stories of hunts and mischief, I stared at the lodge's packed dirt floor. To avoid Lovern, I walked to the end of the benches and placed the bread out of his reach. My mother or Drista refilled his mead. I watched. Lovern ate sparingly and drank little. He rarely smiled. He did not start conversations but viewed the evening gathering until someone tossed him a question or comment. He petted my uncle's dogs and fed them bones and scraps from the table.

When Lovern's dark, assessing eyes caught mine, I stumbled, balance lost at his glance. As I passed one night, he grabbed my wrist and pulled me to him. The laughter and chatter around me was gone from my ears. The air grew silent. My hand shook as I steadied myself against the worn table and tried to push away, unbidden tears tracing my cheeks. I stared into his indiscernible face until his eyes softened, almost imperceptibly, as if he had come to a decision. His mouth formed a smile as he slowly released my arm. The noise of the room came back, and I fell away from him.

My mother found me huddled against the stone wall, hidden by the smoke of the peat fire, my quiet tears falling to the dirt floor. Mother frowned, turned to leave and beckoned for me to follow.

A war raged inside me. I had passage dreams of him as a boy. I knew him before he came to my clan. Why was the boy, now a man, here? The gods were testing me. There was no one to counsel me. Mother's ear was not sympathetic for my dreams and worries and Ogilhinn, my druid friend, was dead. So I observed, alone, unobserved. Or so I thought.

Lovern left the hilltop to visit farmers' abodes daily. I followed, out of sight, and watched as he kneeled to talk to children, touching their cheeks with kindness. He spoke with the mothers and wives and gave them potions. His hands moved in conversations with the farmers while they surveyed the pigs. He seemed benevolent from a distance. Sometimes my doubts eased while I watched him. Lovern said the gods had spoken, that we had a journey to make together. If the gods speak, then we must listen. We built our lives around that rule. But, I was still wary.

One afternoon, when the sky darkened with the clouds that lay threatening overhead, Lovern stood tall in the center of the hill fort. His feet were spread wide, and his arms were crossed. His eyes followed me like a hawk flying over a field mouse. I went to the well, fed the animals, and swept my home. Defiant, I kept my face turned; he learned naught from me. Or so I thought.

It was the season the gods sent the dark times, the beginning of our year. Now, the sun rested longer and our daylight was short.

Mother breathed with more difficulty on the days the lamps were lit. The smoky air in our abode clotted her lungs. She sometimes rose at night and rushed outside. She stood on her tiptoes, braced against our wall, her neck stretched and her mouth reaching for air. I followed and covered her hot body with a blanket against a chill that seeped into my heart, as she panted like a dog that had lost to a rabbit in a chase. Cords in her thin neck strained as she coughed up the bad air that invaded her body. I had seen others with the same breathing pattern while accompanying Ogilhinn.

I knew a few of the healing arts. Ogilhinn taught me about some herbs and medicines. What I learned was not sufficient to feel skilled enough to help the ill often, but my soul pulled me to help when I could.

I tried to calm her, gave her heather tea and soured cow's milk. I said prayers to Airmid, for healing. Mother hated the drinks, but they seemed to ease her distress. It was all I knew to do. The sun's victory over the storm meant no oil lamps were needed to weave. We both celebrated the reprieve.

The sun was out the morning he and I spoke again. My mother's loom glowed in its filtered, golden light. It had rained steadily for three days and we celebrated the sun's muted, temporary warmth.

Anxious to be outside on such a rare day, I stood and appraised the center of the hill fort. The offal was gone, washed down the hillside by the cleansing downpour. Dogs, free from boundaries, ran and chased fowl and each other until they could run no more. They returned to their masters, tongues hanging and spittle strung behind.

All who lived on the hilltop took advantage of the lull in the storms to sweep the floors of dwellings and stables. Homes gave up their animals to be tied outside, while women spread clean straw on the floors and refreshed beds. The scent of fresh-cut juniper wafted through the air.

Activity buzzed like bees finding the first spring flowers. The colors of the multi-layered green mountains were vivid. But warning lay in the light blue sky in the form of a grey cloudbank on the horizon. The next storm would be here today or tomorrow, and the north wind carried a dampness that caused me to shiver.

On my way to refresh the water for our home and animals before the next storm, I met other women from the hill homes. There was water stored in barrels by our doors for this chore, but we still came to the well when the rain stopped. Even in the mud and cold, gossip overruled convenience.

"Jahna! Jahna!" The firm voice was familiar, its owner hidden by an oiled, hooded cloak cut from wool my mother and I had woven. Slim, work-worn hands drew back the hood, bronze hair fell to her back in waves, and I was eye to eye with Sileas.

I stepped forward and grasped the hand she held out to me. Perplexed, I tried to sort out the feelings that were running through me in the seconds I had before I spoke again. She had married Harailt, but I was not disconsolate.

The path I was to follow was with Lovern, although it was difficult to find. Sileas and Harailt had been in love for many years, since childhood. The gods made the right match; the right promise was kept. The goddess was watching over both Sileas and me. I hugged her to my heart, felt her body relax in my embrace, and my voice returned.

"Sileas. I have not spoken with you about how pleased I am for you and Harailt. There were so many around you on your marriage day, and I did not want to bring you distress. I always knew you and Harailt should be together. You and I are friends, and I need your friendship around me. I do not wish to lose that attachment, ever."

"Oh, Jahna. I worried that you would never forgive me. I also want to keep our friendship strong." Her light blue eyes clouded. Was it the cold or something else that affected them?

"I have been concerned about you since Samhainn and I saw you fly away when our betrothal was announced. I would have come to your home, but the weather has made some of our sheep ill, and I have been busy making the marriage bed for Harailt and me."

I knew of the things that needed to be done to create a new household. She had moved into the dwelling Harailt shared with his father, Cerdic, but she was making it her own now. She crafted a warm and comfortable bed in her new home. A bed where her children would be born.

Her round face broke into a small grin, but fell solemn again. "Harailt's father is ill. His breathing is difficult, and he coughs all night. Yesterday, I saw him spit blood when he did not know I was watching." Her shadowed eyes showed the concern of one who knows the result of a cough with blood.

I touched her warm cheek with my cold, dry hand and said, "I will speak with the druid and I will come myself to see Cerdic."

"I must go now. It is time to start the day's chores."

I said, "Good bye, friend. Go with the gods. I will come to your home soon." She walked to the gates, and I turned back to the well.

I dropped the iron-ringed wooden bucket into the dark hole. The wet rope burned my fingers. The bucket filled with frigid water. I heard Lovern whisper my name behind me. I hesitated, decided to ignore him, and then, groaning with the effort, I began to pull up the full bucket. As I tugged at the heavy load held by the scratchy rope, he laid his warm, soft, long fingers over mine. I relaxed my aching, raw fingers and released the rope into his hands.

Hand-over-hand, he pulled it up easily. He stepped in front of me, leaned against the stone wall and lifted the bucket of freezing water out of the well. I held out my water jug, and he filled it, pouring without a drop lost. He turned to the other women in line and, refilling the bucket with ease, filled three more jugs. He assured them with prayers for safety from the coming storms. The women bowed their heads in respect, and to thank him, and hurried back to their homes, families, and warm fires.

I waited. He had not spoken with me for two weeks. I did not want to be the one to start a conversation, but I had promised Sileas to speak with him. He watched the others leave and leaned over me.

"Jahna."

His voice burned away my promise to Sileas.

"You and I are going to the forest today. Take the water home to your mother and meet me in the stable. Be quick, the storm is coming."

Surprised at his tone, anger filled my belly and caused my hands to tremble. Water spilled from my overfilled jug and soaked the doeskin slippers I had worn on this errand. It was the voice of a master to his slave. How dare he give me orders after not talking to me for so long?

"I will go nowhere with you," I said. "Why do you think you have the right to order me to come? You have not spoken with me in two weeks, and now I am supposed to follow you like a goose? No, I have work to do with my mother. I will not meet you anywhere."

His sinewy body pressed me closer to the well. I stared up into his face, framed in the morning sun, and saw iron in his eyes. He took one step back and placed himself between my home and me, between my past and my future.

"Jahna. It is time to start working together. I have much to teach you, and we have much to do together. Many need us here. I had a dream last night about you. We must start today." His deep blue eyes locked onto mine, and I could not move. What was in our future that caused me to be so cautious?

His hand touched my forehead and the village vanished. As if drawn on the sky, I saw Lovern and myself with our hands raised, praying to the gods. We asked for their forgiveness. I was in a sacred place—all was calm. My heart was sad—a dreadful time was ahead, and we asked for help for our people.

Just as quickly, the vision's grip released me. Dizzy, I tripped forward and almost dropped my heavy water jug. The bright sun blinded me.

Even with my passage dreams, I had never had a vision like this. One that I knew to be the truth of my future. I shook my head to move aside the wool that wrapped my brain. While imprisoned in this confusion, I realized my anger was gone. As if someone whispered in my ear, my heart knew the anger would not return. Lovern and I had a path to follow, and Morrigna was leading us. I knew I would not argue anymore. I straightened and caught the start of a grin, the recognition of my acceptance, on his face. He also knew I was starting another way of life, with him.

"I will meet you soon," I said. My muffled mind was full of questions as I walked quickly to my home.

Later, in the stable, the breath of the animals lent a sweet grassy smell that helped soften the odor of waste. Lovern stroked Beathan's favorite war pony, careful of its impatient movements.

"I wish to find oak-grown mistletoe. We must gather some to protect us from the coming winter storms. I noticed as I walked around the farms and hilltop homes that there is little of the old mistletoe left inside them. Beathan said you would know of the mistletoe oak tree."

"Yes, I do know of such a tree. It is not close. How will we get there before the storm?"

"I have spoken with Beathan. I told him today was the beginning of our search for the truth in the words of the gods. That you and I both agreed to work together. Pleased, he said we could use those ponies." He pointed across the stable.

"These are his oldest and slowest. Still, Uncle Beathan is very generous to allow us their use."

We tied the leather to the ponies' backs, slipped on the bridles, and led them outside into cold gusts of wind. I mounted, wrapped my cloak around and under my legs for protection from the cold weather, and tugged up my hood, its braided cords tied. Lovern wore his light brown cape over the same clothes in which he had come to us. I shrugged and shook my head at his choice. The ponies broke into a comfortable gait down the hill and toward Bel's Copse with me in the lead.

Bel's sacred oak grove was an hour away by pony. Druids had designated it sacred many years ago. Only our chieftains, druids, and a selected few were allowed entrance. It was there the mistletoe grew and where we gathered the dry oak for the quarter fires. When I was a child, I went there to learn from Ogilhinn.

Ogilhinn and my mother were the only people of our clan who knew of my passage dreams.

He invited me to the sacred copse after mother told him of my unquiet nights. She feared I was ill after I told her of my first passage dream, and asked if he knew of a healing spell or drink that would give me restful sleep. I think Ogilhinn invited me so he could watch over me as a mother watches a growing child. He began to teach me the healing arts. He would allow me to nurse the injured, sick, and dying of our clan.

It was then I told him of my passage dreams. He told me the dreams were a gift from the gods, and I would, one day, find the reason for them.

"The sight came to me," he said, "when I blessed you as a newborn. You were working, helping your clan in ways not yet known. A man will come into your life to guide you. You will find your path to the gods. There will be a great trial for you and your faith will be tested. Do not lose your way and you will find peace after death."

I knew him to be a visionary. He often foretold the future of members of our clan. I remembered when he told Trannis not to go near the river without his friends. Trannis fell into the river while hunting. He did not know how to get out and was saved by his friends. I secretly prayed my test would not come to me for many years.

Both Ogilhinn and I had prayed and stood vigil while Gavina, Beathan's wife, was ill. A mist lifted from her and floated over her body. I looked around and saw no one else noticed it. A thought came to me. In a whisper, I told to it to cross the river. In an instant, the mist was gone. She was dead, her spirit shuttled to the land of the dead by the ferryman.

Then Ogilhinn became ill and died. He left me incomplete in my knowledge of helping the sick and injured and I had been afraid to do too much of this work alone. I could not harm any by weaving so I stayed with my mother. I thought the way I would help my clan was to weave my cloth, and the test Ogilhinn spoke of was marrying Harailt – so I believed.

Now, my understanding of my life's plan had unraveled and twisted like the path leading to the sacred woods. I wondered what lay ahead.

At the far edge of the copse grew a stunted oak. Lightning had damaged one of its largest branches near the trunk. As we sat on our steaming ponies under the tree, we could see bunches of mistletoe. Its golden-green leaves, burdened with white berries, grew out of the tree's injury.

"I have a dress of that green, and see?" I opened my cloak to show him the inside. "I lined my cloak with felt woven from the color. I love it."

"I noticed. The color is good fortune. It brings Morrigna's protection to you. Your eyes look more gold than green when you wear the dress."

I was surprised. He knew when I wore my green dress. He had kept his silence and secrets.

He reached across the width of the pony's distance and touched a loose tendril of my hair.

"You have been touched by the goddess. Your hair is one of her signs, the color of her ravens. Your dreams are another."

Shyly, I looked back into the leafless oak tree. "Here is where we find Bel's sacred mistletoe. Here is where you asked to be."

We dismounted, and he shimmied up the oak tree and unsheathed his dirk to harvest the mistletoe. Being careful of possible weakness of the branch, he harvested all the stems with berries leaving the green leaved stems with no berries to continue growing. There was enough to give one branch to each household of our clan for this new year's protection and fertility. As he cut them loose, he dropped the stems to me. I wrapped them in a cloth and slipped it into a pocket inside my cloak. He slid down out of the tree, sheathed his dirk, and readjusted his small bag.

"What is that design? I saw it the night you came to us," I asked as we remounted our ponies.

Lovern reached behind and pulled the soft leather pouch to the front. He covered the drawing with his right hand and closed his eyes.

He opened his eyes and said, "My druid teacher, Conyn, first drew it to help me learn to meditate. It is a seven-ringed labyrinth. I copied it and use it when I talk to the gods. I will teach the meditation to you someday. This bag never leaves me. It carries my past and future life."

At that, the sky, which had lowered and darkened to the color of bruised lavender, began to rain in torrents.

"Follow me! I know where we can get out of this," I shouted through the thunder, trying not to get a mouthful of water while talking.

Our ponies wove their way through the trees and jumped the small stream that formed rapids with the rain. I stopped at the foot of a hill and tied my pony to a holly bush. He did the same. Wildly searching through the undergrowth, with rain beating on my head and back, I found the start of the trail.

"Up here," I yelled. I shaded my eyes with my hand, peering through the wall of rain, to make sure he was following. The wind whipped his light cape. His long, rain-darkened hair clung to his face, yet his eyes were sharp as an owl's.

We fought our way up, slipping on muddy rocks, reaching out for each other at almost every step. Finally, the mouth of the cave appeared before me. It was smaller than I remembered. I hoped no other animal had found it and decided to use it for refuge from this storm. He edged in front of me, lowered to his knees, and disappeared inside. Tucking my cloak and dress up around my thighs, I crawled through the entrance. Stones punched into my bare knees and water sluiced down my back from the hillside. Grunting, I crawled and dragged myself until I ran into his huddled form and fell into a heap myself, gasping. The cave opened into an area large enough for us to sit upright. I wrinkled my nose at its close and fetid air. We caught our breath.

"I did not expect the rain to come so soon or so hard," I said as I untied my hood. "I am glad we harvested the mistletoe. The storms this season seem to be stronger than any I remember."

After I unfastened the oak pin, I shrugged my cloak off. It had kept me dry. I had woven the cloth and cut it myself. After Mother sewed it, I rubbed it with the oils boiled from the wool after gathering. It had repelled most of the rain, even the small waterfall at the mouth of the cave. Only the hem of my dress and my shoes were wet. Sitting next to me, Lovern shivered in the cold, grey light that lit the cave. Our breath steamed in front of us.

"Take off your wet cape and come here, under my cloak," I said. He had warmed me the same way, the day we walked around the lake. "You must get warm. We will not be near a fire for hours."

He agreed, and we were soon sitting side by side, wrapped together in my cloak, his wet cape lain aside. The clay floor held the cold but at least was not wet. The slant of the floor of the small cave kept the rain outside. Roots from the trees on the hillside grew inside, and it smelled of wet earth and the animals that used it as protection in the past. We had arrived first, and most animals would avoid us. I hoped.

He said, "I am glad you knew of this cave. It would have been a difficult ride back."

"I know the land around us. My favorite place is a waterfall in the small river near here. I find peace there."

Lovern shook his head like a wet dog and drops of water flew over me and across the cave.

"Stop shaking! You are getting me as wet as you," I said. "Let me dry your face."

I used the corner of my dress to dry his clean-shaven, carved cheeks and strong chin. I gazed into Lovern's eyes. His hot breath mingled with mine. He smelled of wet wool, leather, sweet bees-wax, and acorns. I had never smelled that combination before. Harailt had an odor of the oil from the sheep he tended, and Uncle Beathan the pork he loved to eat, but this… This was new. I wanted to stay here and inhale this scent forever. When I touched him for the first time not in anger, there was quickening, new to my body. Heat started in my loins and rushed up my neck to lodge in my face.

He broke into his crooked grin, his eyes crinkled at the corners, and their deep blue lightened. I became motionless, not wanting to allow anything to interrupt this connection.

"I can see we are both warming. Even in this light, I can see you are blushing," he said.

Questions blurred my thoughts. I had never felt this way about a man before, not even Harailt. I became embarrassed and eased away from him.

"What do you carry in your bag?" I asked, wanting to fill this awkward space.

Lifting its strap from his neck and shoulder, he untied the drawstring at the top of the bag and tipped it upside down. Three white crystals, as large as sheep's eyes, tumbled into his upturned hand.

"Hold these and tell me what you feel." He reached over and gently placed them into my hands.

They were warm. More than his body heat, they carried warmth of their own. Looking at them in the dim light, I had the impression that the milky, bluish white color was swirling inside the stones. I caressed them, and was not surprised when a feeling of love and respect emanated from deep inside the stones.

"These crystals," I told him, "are your link to your family, your life. They carry memories of who you were, who you are. They should be held near your heart."

His hand reached out and I opened mine to drop the stones into his. The words I had just spoken came from my heart, not my mind. They were out of my mouth before I thought of them. This was new to me. This and my earlier vision at the well had never happened to me before. It was unlike my passage dreams. I did not know what to think. Did I speak incorrectly? I searched his face.

Lovern smiled. "Oh yes, you have gifts from the goddess. You did not know of my stones, yet you told me what they mean to me. Your gifts will become stronger as we work together."

He took the stones and held them in his right hand, and rolled them together with soft clicks. "I received these on my naming day. Conyn, my teacher, gave them to me and told me they represented the three goddesses, Morrigan, Macha, and Bodb, the triumvirate of Queen Morrigna. He told me that I was to be tested, and I would need these to give me strength. I think he knew about the battles and my journey. He often told me about events before they happened."

Lovern's eyes stared out the entrance of the cave but seemed to be looking much further than the rain would allow me see. His eyes turned back to the stones. "I use them for meditation. They bring me closer to the goddesses and memories of my family."

He laid the stones on his lap, reached into his bag again, and drew out a piece of red fur. Fox fur. After caressing it with both hands, he handed it to me. His eyes held mine. As I took it from him, I remembered my first passage dream of him. The air around me crackled with excitement, and carried the strong smell of blood.

"Oh, Mother Goddess! This is from the fox I watched you kill! I was there!"

"I knew the fox I killed that day would mean more to me than just my naming animal. I kept a piece of its fur with me.

Yes, you were there," he agreed. "It is through our connection that we will work to find a way to protect your clan. We must, or what happened to my people will happen to yours," he prophesied. He slid the crystals and the fox fur back into the bag. "This bag is all I have of my home."

I wondered what had become of his family and why he was so frightened of it happening here.

The rain pulsed down outside the cave. The sky was bright with lightning and peals of thunder vibrated the air. We both whispered prayers to Toranis, the thunder god. Lovern reached for the cloth wrapped mistletoe and extracted a small sprig.

"Mother Morrigna and Father Bel, protect us from the storm." He touched the mistletoe to his lips and forehead. "I pray in your names for protection of this clan, this village who offers me a life renewed."

He reached across me, his arm brushing my breasts, and laid the mistletoe just inside the entrance of the cave. I wanted him to stay in that position. I looked at his lips and wondered what they tasted like. I had never thought that about any other man. He sat back against the wall. I hope he had not seen how I reacted to his touch. I had to do something, so I asked a question.

"Lovern, why did you come here, to my village?"

He sat silent. I began to wonder if he was not going to answer. Then, in a quiet voice, he told me his story.

"I passed nineteen seasons in my mother's village. She raised my two sisters and me, until I went to live with the druid. A wild boar, when I was but five summers old, killed my father. My mother, alone with three small children, knew times of strife and hunger, but we survived. But the last few years were beyond any we had ever experienced or dreamed of, filled with war."

His head hung, eyes to the floor of the dark cave as he continued.

"My queen, Boudiccea, fought to overthrow the invading Romans, but she lost. As punishment, her daughters were murdered. She could not live with her failure and without her daughters so she took poison. The Romans raged and went on a killing and raping quest. They wished to destroy all of her loyal villages. We had escaped notice but then our chieftain decided to raid a Roman camp. It was a decision that cost too much. After the battle, the Romans came to our village. My mother was killed, sisters raped and taken as slaves. My teacher was also taken. I do not know if they live. Of my village, only I escaped."

We have not had any of our clan taken as slaves in my memory. My mother told me stories of when our clan villages were at war with each other constantly.

"One of my uncles was taken," she told me once, "and sacrificed at Beltane by another tribe. Beathan has called a truce with the local clans and we do not have to worry the way my grandmother and mother did."

I had no memories like his. I could not compare his pain with any I felt. After a pause of ten heartbeats, his eyes looked into mine, and a spark of life flickered in their depths as he continued.

"Before the last battles, Conyn told me that he had no more to teach me. He arranged to send me to a nearby village to learn more about treating wounds, to the healer Kinsey, well known in our land. He claimed he could heal all wounds except those that separated the head from the body. His village was spared the Roman raids. They brought their wounded to him, so great was his skill. The Romans needed him. I learned much. Then, news came of the raid on my village, the home of my mother, sisters and teacher."

"Why did you leave? Could you not stay with Kinsey and be free?"

"The day the story of my village's attack came, I ran home. Ashes and bones filled my home and the homes that were my village. I walked and cried for one whole day, looking for anyone left alive. One man, a farmer, had been hit on the head and fallen into a hole filled with animal waste. He had escaped the fires. He groaned and I heard him. It was he who told me what had happened to my family and teacher. I had carried and laid him under a shelter. I gave him drops of water to drink.

"Then, a small band of Roman warriors came back to search for any left alive. The farmer told me to run as he scooted under some straw. I jumped into the hole I had pulled him from and pretended death. No Roman would crawl in after me. They found the farmer, killed him and threw his body on top of me. I did not move. I hid in a hole in the ground that stank of shit and death for one day. It was during that day I decided I could not stay.

"That night, deep in darkness, the careless Romans asleep, I ran. The tree and star gods guided my feet." His fist tightened around his memory bag. "Away from those murderers, the Romans. I will never forget the smell of my village. I dream of my sisters' cries.

"It took me three moon cycles to walk here. Months filled by hiding, eating berries, leaves, small animals, and stolen food. Three months of walking away from death, to life. To you."

He hesitated, took in a deep breath, and again sighed. I leaned forward, fascinated by his tale.

"I came to the bank of the fast, narrow stream and waterfall –"

My waterfall! I thought.

"– hidden in the copse of birch and alder trees, near your village and I sensed I had finally come to a place where I would be safe." He seemed to slump in a release of tension with these words.

"I had decided the gods would bring me out of the forest when they knew it was safe. I had no desire to move from the spot by the stream.

"While resting, I heard twigs break and leaves rustle. A strong odor of sheep floated in the air, and I knew a farmer watched me. I decided not to attempt to talk to him unless he came to me. I sat by the rushing sounds of the rapids and breathed in the peaceful clean smell of the nearby trees, meditated, and waited. The farmer was gone. My stomach rumbled from a lack of food, and I was dizzy from the lack of sleep. I wanted, *needed* this journey to end. I did not have long to wait. The scent of the pony came next."

He turned to face me with a smile tickling the corners of his mouth. It made me happy to know he finished his sad story and now was in a better place. He straightened his legs and wiped his nose as if he smelled the pony again.

"A large form shaded the sun, and then I saw a warrior's spear under my nose. It was poised ready to plunge. Its tip broke the skin on my chest as it cut through my clothing." Lovern reached up, and touched his chest where the spear point had left its mark. "The pressure was enough to tell me my life was in danger if I moved quickly. After many heartbeats, when the spear did not plunge deep into my heart, I respectfully looked up and saw him. He was a tall warrior whose feet hung low on his war pony."

Lovern's chin lifted as if he were looking at the warrior now. "The hand not holding the spear was holding a short sword. His hair hung to his shoulders. His eyes impaled me from under the brush of his eyebrows. His tight mouth and set chin, almost fully covered in a thick beard, signaled me not to move."

That was how he met our chieftain, my uncle Beathan. I visualized this encounter. What a difference in this story of the two men meeting for the first time.

"The warrior's stern voice, as well as his weapons, caused me to listen carefully. 'Where are you from?'

"I told him I was a druid healer. I came from the south, escaping invaders.

"He told me that the gods looked with favor upon him that day. He introduced himself as Beathan, chieftain of his – your clan. He pulled back the spear that had raised blood on my chest, sheathed his bronze-hilted sword, and called his dogs from the copse. Two of them came, each almost as big as his pony.

"He told me to give him my dirk until we reached his lodge. I would ride behind him, weaponless. With the threat of his spear and the dogs at his side, I obeyed. Beathan then told me, 'Our druid is dead. Our gods directed me to you. You will perform the Samhainn ceremony on the morrow.'"

When Lovern mentioned the Samhainn ceremony, Sileas's face and the promise I made to her came to mind. I needed to remember to tell Lovern about Cerdic's illness.

"Beathan reached under my arms and lifted me off my feet," Lovern continued. "I was deposited on the pony as if I were weightless. The sun was in the sky at mid-afternoon, glistening off the damp autumn leaves. We rode for an hour with no conversation between us. I observed as we rode. It was *foghara*, the harvests were in, and the fields were empty. We passed farms with generous stacks of hay and cornstalks that shared the stables with the ponies and sheep. The harvest was good; the goddess was happy. I heard pigs screech and smelled the blood of butchering float on the air. It was time to prepare and salt meat for the cold days. As I bounced on the pony's back, I filled myself with thoughts of the ceremony. Samhainn, the time that lies between summer and winter, light and darkness, the new beginning to the year. I silently prayed to the gods and goddesses, asking them to honor and protect the people of this clan. In exchange, I would light the giving fires and perform sacrifices. I also prayed that this would end my journey. I hoped I could stay with this clan, and again be a healer."

Pausing, Lovern reached above his head, pushed against the roof of the cave and stretched. My legs were beginning to cramp so I stretched them also. The incessant pounding of the rain had lessened.

"We came to the fort and the pony carried us up the hill to the enclosure's open gates. I remember how loud his voice was when Beathan called others to come to his lodge as we entered the hill fort.

"All the lodges we saw, the farms and the homes on the hill, could have been from my own village. The ride took us past the corn-drying kiln and your well. Dogs ran through the center courtyard and Beathan's dogs took off yelping in chase. The odors of peat smoke and cooking meat made my mouth water. I heard women calling their husbands and children to dinner along with a clamor of goats, ponies, chickens, dogs, and pigs, living together in the fort.

"Men came to him, all wearing capes of the same plaid as their chieftain. They yelled greetings and raised their empty mugs in a salute.

"His pony stopped in front of his lodge. Beathan lifted his leg over the pony's withers and slid off. He turned and encouraged me to do the same. I slid off and fell to the ground, weak with hunger and lack of sleep. Beathan laughed like a coughing bear in the spring."

"He snores like a bear in winter, too!" I said.

"I know, I sleep in his home now. Sometimes I cannot sleep through all the noise." Lovern shook his head and smiled.

"Beathan carried me inside his warm home that smelled of smoke, and cooked meats–life. You served me and I ate, my strength returning. Then I watched you dance and heard your voice. I grew weak again.

"When you walked me to the stables and told me your name, I had to grit my teeth and use all my strength to stay standing. How could it be, in the entire world, that I would finally meet you? You were as real to me as my mother, yet I knew you only through two day-dreams. Strange incidents that seemed real yet unreal. I had felt safe and secure during the events, never in danger or helpless. I was connected to you, in my heart. I was named Fox because I know to follow my instincts, and when my life was threatened, I traveled for months, never doubting my journey or the path it took. Now I know it was to find you. I am home."

Here, he paused, twisted towards me, and cradled my face in his gentle hands. "I do not know why you dreamed of me, but I do know that we are fated to be together. The gods, and my heart led me here, and now it is up to us to find out what we are destined for," Lovern concluded.

"But what is our future?" I asked. "Why did it take the loss of your family to bring us together? It saddens me to think that they are gone in such a horrific way."

"I have learned that the gods reveal their plans at their will. We do best if we do not question them. We must go, it is late and your uncle will send men after us if we are too long."

The rain slowed to a drizzle and we left the cave. Droplets gathered on my eyelashes, fell to my face and I blinked in the muted light. We reached the tethered ponies. He came up behind me and turned me to see his tender eyes. The warm fingertips of one hand lifted my chin and the others traced my cold face, from one cheek to the chin and back. His damp body still smelled of bees-wax and acorns. His hands had touched my face and heart.

I fell in love with him at that instant. His breath was sweet when his lips touched mine. A contract was sealed. I felt a shift in my life and future with that kiss. The old druid Ogilhinn's vision for me had come true.

My path was now clear. No longer would I weave wool.

I would weave love and, unknowingly, acceptance of death.

CHAPTER 5

April, 2005

Jahna first came to me when I was ten. I don't mean she knocked on my door and asked me to come out and play; I mean she slipped into my mind. My first waking dream. I was awake but it almost seemed dreamlike.

I'd heard adults use the term "invisible friend" and chuckle when talking about their children. My own Mom and Dad used it when I tried to ask them about what had happened to me. She'd come to me when I was studying in my room. At first, I was a bit disoriented, maybe dizzy. Then it was as if I had an echo in my head. I didn't know how else to explain it.

I looked through my eyes at the normal mess in my room and it was familiar, yet unfamiliar. I was off-balance. It was like I had never seen the room before but I knew it was mine. That was until I looked at the hand-mirror my aunt had given me the Christmas before. It had been framed by wood that'd been painted copper and made to look very old. I – she seemed to recognize it.

Just before she left, I heard her whisper a word in my ear: "Jahna." I thought it was her name; at least, that was what I called her. As I remembered it, I wondered why I wasn't afraid. I would be today, if it happened to me for the first time. I'd be sure I had a brain tumor or was going crazy. But back then, I felt calm, and at peace, when she left.

I was okay with it until I started asking around to find out if anyone else had ever felt this way. Mom put her hand on my head to feel for a fever and Dad and Donny laughed. I asked my best friend at school, but never mentioned it again when she made up a hurtful rhyme and teased me in front of the boys.

Jahna came about once a year after that. She never spoke to me except to whisper her name. A few pictures came through but usually it was just feelings. I was wary of the visits at first and then came to look forward to them. She stayed for just a few breaths and then left me with a longing to know her. She seemed to glean thoughts from me and even prompted questions. I think she helped find my career.

I'd developed my hunger for history early. My aunt was the keeper of the family papers and she'd shown me a letter that she said was hundreds of years old. After reading it, I decided to trace my family line. I also knew I wanted to hold ancient things in my hands, and study archaeology.

The second time she stayed for more than a second was the first day in my class on Ancient Celts in Great Britain. It was my favorite class at university. Marc was there, sitting next to me, and I'd felt an excitement on that day that I hadn't felt about any other period of history. The moment Jahna was inside me, the era seemed as if I had lived through it. The pictures in my text were familiar. I knew I would specialize in that period.

From the beginning, she seemed to be about the same age as me, a child at first, but now I saw her as an adult. It was as if I were reading a novel, putting faces on the characters. I'd done that for Jahna. In my mind, she looked like me. I could almost see her face as I searched for her in my mind. Were our faces similar? Did we share my straight-as-a-stick coal-black hair, my hazel-green eyes that I always wished were blue, my round face and big mouth? Was she tall, or short like me? I had never seen her, only sensed her, but she was a part of me.

When I married Brad, she stopped coming. Jahna was one of the many things I thought I'd lost through my marriage. Then she came back last year while I was working with Marc on the chieftain's tomb. A weight had lifted from my heart.

Now, Marc and I were back in Scotland. He'd gathered a crew of students and had come to help me get my site started. We were settled into a country inn, not far from the farm where the hill was and were ready to start work tomorrow.

I thought all was fine until Marc had come into my room five minutes ago. He walked straight to my only chair and sat down. I moved some clothes on my bed so I could sit. He began complaining about the lack of funding for our project. I knew I was walking a fine line with my relationship with him. I desperately wanted to be friends, but he seemed to be pulling away. We both tried very hard to be civil to one another, but I realized now how tired I was of defending my desire to dig on the hilltop. It was a hard decision to make, I understood that; however, he had promised to give it a try.

Suddenly, tonight, with Marc in my room, Jahna's smoky, peat scent was in my nose. Very faint this time but there. My eyes closed involuntarily. I hunched my shoulders and shivered, and the skin on my neck tingled. Shaking, I covered my face with my hands as I whispered, "Not now, Jahna, I want to be alone when you come."

"What's the matter?" Marc asked. "Headache?"

"Yes." I almost added "you." Taking my hands from my face, I reached behind me to arrange the very hard, small pillows on my bed into something comfortable to lean against. I didn't quite accomplish the cushioning I wanted for my back. This wasn't going to be a comfortable night.

A shrill ring made my heart stop and I leapt up, almost falling off the bed as I grabbed the phone. Startled, I answered. "Aine MacRae. Yes, he's here, just a second." I sighed as I stood and carried the phone to Marc, trying not to trip over the cord. The burning peat scent was gone. Jahna delayed her visit.

"Marc Hunt. No, my mobile doesn't work here. Scotland, the bloody Highlands. What do you need? Really?" He looked at me with a big smile on his face. I became alert.

"We could be there in two days! Let me talk to Aine. I'll call you later, bye." He handed the phone to me, and I set it back on the water-stained and scratched nightstand.

"That was Doug. He had some incredible news," Marc said. "I need to have something more concrete to keep me here, now. He said we could be in Wales working on the Roman digs. They need all the help they can get. Once I tell the team we have the job, they'll want to leave, too. It's only April, we could have a long summer digging and then the winter to do the cataloging."

I didn't want to have this conversation again. I turned my head to avoid his eyes. It took me five months to put this project together. Two months went into begging the farmer to agree to let us on his land, and then three more months to acquire a little funding, the license and to get Marc to agree. All this was about to be compromised.

I said, "I can't leave now!"

"I would rather be in the field than in the classroom. You know that. I've precious little time digging and I have to go back soon." He had been on sabbatical for almost a year; this fall he would return to university.

His face began to brighten as he explained, "The extra money I make in Wales will help me retire early. I might even get a post on the project and be able to leave university altogether." His dream was to do research. With this offer, he could see that in his immediate future.

"So you're asking me to stop this project?"

"Yes," Marc said. "It's just a hill, nothing else. When we finished the tomb last summer, we decided not to come back to the Highlands. Remember?" He was starting to sound desperate. "All you have to support your argument is the single bronze blade the farmer found, years ago. You know that anyone walking through here at any time might've dropped it. We don't have any other artifacts, this site isn't on a GIS map, and the money isn't enough to let us stay more than two weeks. We can barely set up a good camp in two weeks! Drop this and come with me to Wales. We can still work together there."

My jaw tightened as I tried to recall why Marc had been so attractive to me in the first place. At forty-five years old, his five foot-ten inch frame was still thin. His collar-length red hair and full beard was now streaked with silver. His eyes were clear and dark blue, even through his glasses. He smelled like the ground we dug in. I felt comforted when near him, even though the relationship was strained right now. Damn it, he reminded me of someone. Who was it?

"Yes, I remember saying that I didn't want to come back here. And you have to remember what was happening in my life at that moment. I wasn't thinking straight. Brad was behaving like an ass, and I said I wouldn't come back here because I didn't want to be near him."

I shook my head so hard my hair stung my face. I walked to the small table by the window, picked up a photo of my hill, and ran my fingers across its glossy surface. "I've a strong feeling we're supposed to be here." Turning to look at him and waving the picture, I continued. "There is something here."

How could I tell him my heart pulled me? I had to be here, it was time. How could I tell him this when I didn't really understand it? I walked this whole countryside last November. Something or someone called to me. I had to stay.

I laid the picture on the table. "We can go to Wales next week if this doesn't work, Marc. We don't have to sleep out there. We can be comfortable here, with real beds," I said sweeping my arm around the small but adequate room. "We can get a good start and at least get through one layer of soil in a small quadrant in a few days. Let me choose where we start digging, and then if we don't find anything you can go with my blessings. But I can't quit, not now!" A headache formed just above my neck. I rubbed my shoulders.

"Aine, I don't know. So far, we've only spent a little money on these rooms and transportation. The team is here as a favor, and we could back out of this without much loss. I really don't think we should stay." Marc leaned over, reached into his pocket, and removed his mobile phone. He flipped it open as if some miracle had occurred in the last hour, and it now worked.

My heart sank and my hands fell into my lap. I knew I would have to tell him. There was no other way to keep him here. I'd kept my secret for so long, I didn't know if I could find the words.

I never told anyone about her visits after the first one. Not Brad. Not even Marc. That was one of my many mistakes in my relationship with Marc. I needed to start being more honest with him, even if he didn't believe me. I tried to tell myself that I didn't care if he believed me but I did. I needed his help now and his friendship.

My stomach started churning but I knew I couldn't escape this time. I looked straight at him with exasperation, took a deep breath, and said, "Marc, do you remember the bowl?"

"Bowl? You mean the bronze we found in the tomb last year? Yes, I do. It was a lucky save," he said as he was looking through his phone list, trying different numbers, cursing when nothing connected.

I turned away, head lowered. With little breath left, I said, "No, it wasn't luck. It was Jahna."

"What?" I heard impatience building in his voice. "What or who is Jahna? There wasn't anyone named Jahna on that job," he countered, still fiddling with his phone.

I crossed my arms and sat on the edge of the bed, feeling very vulnerable. "All right. All right. I'll tell you about her." I stopped, took a deep breath, and continued. "I don't understand who she is, but her name is Jahna. I sense her thoughts."

I watched Marc. He stopped dialing his phone and stared at me, wide eyed.

Looking down at the floor, I tucked my unruly hair behind my ears, folded my hands in my lap, and began. "This isn't going to be easy. You're going to have a hard time believing me. I would. Just listen, please.

"I was ten years old, doing homework, when I had my first awake dream. That's what I call them. I wasn't asleep. I pinched myself and left a bruise. I was awake."

I held my hand up and looked at it. "I could see the pencil in my hand. I could hear the wind outside. But it was as if I were looking out of someone else's eyes and my eyes at the same time. I felt as if someone else were listening and watching, not–not outside my head but *inside* my head."

I recalled the odor that came before her visit, burning peat. "Everything in my room looked different," I continued. "I distinctly remember looking at my mirror, and thinking it was the same, yet not the same. She whispered her name in my ear, and then she was gone. I had several visits like that, short, with little or no information exchanged, until I went to university and took my first Pre-Roman Celt class, George's class. It was as if I lived then. Déjà vu, if you like. That class seemed to allow Jahna to come through easier. We didn't have real conversations, but as close as you could come. Like channeling or ESP. I've had a few vivid scenes pop into my head, like the placement of the bronze bowl we found. She showed me where to look."

I stopped, glancing at Marc to see his reaction. He was leaning back in the chair, arms crossed, smiling, and looking as if he were waiting for a punch line.

"Don't you dare laugh. I'm serious."

My room's radiator rattled into existence. It was already too warm in the small room for me. Small rivulets of sweat started creeping down my sides and under my breasts. I reached over, turned the radiator valve to the off position, and jumped when Marc's chair legs hit the floor with a sharp bang. His arms were still crossed but his face now wore a look of disbelief.

Staring at me, he said, "Aine MacRae." He shook his head and continued. "You can't expect me to believe we found that bowl through a ghost! We're trained investigators. We use science and scientific tools to find artifacts. Are you trying to tell me that a ghost pointed to the bowl? Am I to believe a ghost does all your research for you?" He looked at me, waiting for me to refute all I had just said.

"Yes. I mean, no." I paused and regained my composure. "So far it's only been the information about the bowl that I've been able to prove." Palms up and beseeching, I said, "She's real to me, Marc. Just because you can't see or hear her doesn't mean she isn't real. Jahna isn't a ghost. Well, maybe she is but…. I think she was alive then." I got up, crossed the small room, and anxiously rifled through a box in the corner. "Here it is," I said, finding my notebook.

"I knew we were leaving something behind. The rest of you were ready to say the grave was empty, that we'd found everything, and then, on that last morning, I moved the rock and found the bowl. I knew just where to look. Here, look at my notes. I wrote down the feelings I had from Jahna the night before. I saw the bowl under the stone and when I went back to the tomb, I went right to the rock."

I held my notebook out, turned to the page I had been looking for. Marc, with wrinkles of doubt on his face, wouldn't take it.

"This is a drawing I made. The design is on the bowl I found." I shook the notebook. "Jahna came to me and told me about it and showed me where to look. I'm not crazy, Marc. She is real to me."

He looked at me with the hooded eyes he wore when he disagreed with or, worse, disbelieved someone. I slammed the notebook to the bed. I was determined to get Marc to understand. I took a deep breath and stood tall, all five feet-two inches of me, ready to defend my story, ready to fight for what I knew was the truth. I knew it in the deepest reaches of my soul. I stood in front of his chair, fists and jaw clenched, looking down into his skeptical eyes and declared in a controlled voice, "I believe Jahna and I have a shared history. I think she is an ancient ancestor of mine. I believe my family, the MacRaes on Skye, can be linked back to her somehow and I want to try to prove it. That's one of the reasons I became an archaeologist." I could feel my defensive instincts catch hold now and I continued, arguing, "Now, I'm where I should be. It all feels right, as though I am home. All the digs before were rehearsals. I cannot leave!"

I walked to the window and leaned my forehead against the cool pane of glass. I looked out into the dark night and tried to see the hill I'd captured in the picture. "I think she wants me here, Marc," I reflected. "She wants me to find something."

"Okay." Marc's voice was laced with mockery as he stood up, stretching, filling the space between the chair and the bed. "So, you're telling me you have regular conversations with dead people, and now, I suppose, we're going to start digging tomorrow with spirits in tow. Well, I need some spirits, now."

I cringed at his tone and pulled back from the windowpane. I turned just in time to see him reach into my suitcase for my bottle of Lagavulin he knew I kept there. "Hey! Stop!" I said, just as he was touching the bottle. "If you want a drink, go get your own." I never let anyone else drink my scotch. I always had a bottle of Lagavulin with me, and no one dared to touch it without an invitation. I first offered it to him after we found the bowl, but since we arrived here, he'd been helping himself without my objection. Until now.

I was angry. I wanted him out of my room. He brought back feelings I thought I'd buried with Brad. "If you think I'm strange, then go find a normal person to be with. I don't want you here right now," I snapped. When he paused, I continued, "I'm not kidding. I am going to bed, and you need to leave. Now." I'd told him about a part of me that was sacred, and he'd made light of it. I felt sick to my stomach.

"Wow. All right, I'll go. Aine." He paused. "I'll have to think about this. I don't know what to make of your story. I've known you too long to know you wouldn't make something up like this, but it's so hard to believe," he said, shaking his head. "I need to talk to the team before we make a decision."

Marc pulled open the heavy door. He turned to look at me, confusion in his eyes. "We'll be downstairs if you want to come and join us." He walked out of my room, into the hall, and closed the door. He left me staring into my own reflection in the full-length mirror hung on the back of the door.

"Bloody hell! That's the reason I've never told anyone." I stared at the closed door. "Why did I let him get to me like that?" I took a deep breath and sighed with a release of emotion. "I don't care what he thinks. I knew it would turn out this way if I told anyone about Jahna." I searched the mirror, and said, "Jahna, I need you now. We are so close. I'll work this site alone if I have to. I'm counting on you, so don't let me down." I turned, lifted one of the heavy tumblers on the bureau, and poured myself a drink. Neat, no ice.

The first sip brought me its lovely, medicinal flavor and I calmed down. I let my thoughts drift back to Skye, to when I was thirteen. Had it really been twenty-nine years since Aunt Peggy had shown me the letter?

It was almost three hundred years old, and an ancestor of mine, a member of the MacRae family, wrote it. The yellowed parchment had been addressed to a British Colonel at Fort William and my aunt had it preserved amongst other family heirlooms. It described how the son of Dubhglas MacRae, nineteen-year-old Hamilton MacRae, could be identified. He was at Glen Coe in February of 1692, with the MacDonalds. They assumed he was dead after the massacre and his family wanted his body back to be buried on Skye.

"...his Body is short, not the tall, large Bodyes that are the MacDonalds. He also has Raven Hair and Beard, not red. His Eyes are Green, not Blue. It tis the Second Toe, on each foote, after the Great Toe that is greatly longer. It is a sign of the family for many years. I beg the return of his Bodye to his Mother for burial.

Signed today, the Fifteenth of March, in the year of OUR LORD, Sixteen Hundred and Ninety Two by Dubhglas MacRae, Father of Hamilton MacRae."

"We have traits in common, you and I, old Hamilton, our toes and hair and eye color." I looked around to verify no one was listening. I didn't want to be heard talking to another dead person.

Finished, I set the tumbler on the nightstand. I put on my comfortable, flannel nightgown and woolen socks. I knew she had something to show me. We'd find it soon, together, Jahna and me. I climbed under my down comforter and snuggled into the warm nest of my bed, yawned, and wondered if she would try to come back tonight.

I tossed and turned for an hour, and examined the conversation with Marc again and again. I finally slept, without dreaming, until the knock on my door the next morning.

CHAPTER 6

JAHNA

73 AD February

Harailt's father, Cerdic died.

With his dying, I found my life's work.

Our harvested mistletoe hung on the support posts of our clan homes for protection, and, to bring fertility, in the animal pens and stables.

I passed my days with Lovern, either in Beathan's lodge or my home when it rained, or outside in the meadows and woods when the sky was clear. He repeated chants, and recited the recipes for cures, and I prayed with him to learn the prayers. We mixed potions and medicines and distributed them to the women on the farms. He possessed knowledge of how to stop winter itching and fevers that beset babies and children, and more. A contented smile was my constant companion.

"Jahna, you are like you were when the spotted lamb followed you as if you were its dam," said Mother.

"Oh, Mother. I remember him." The lamb needed me to care for it. Uncle Beathan said it would die, but it lived for many years. "With Lovern as my teacher, I hope to learn and be able to care for the injured and ill people of our clan and not just lambs."

"I have thought on his being here," said Mother. "I was not in favor of his staying at first. I have seen how he made a potion I had not heard of before that calmed the stomach illness. He is making you happy. I still wonder why the gods brought him here and what could be following him, but Beathan tells me that he is good for our people. I have decided to leave the decision in the hands of our goddess Morrigna."

Lovern told the men and warriors at Beathan's evening table why he left his home. All agreed that he could stay. I had not told mother that Lovern was the boy of my passage dreams or that now, if he left, I would follow.

I had much to learn. I absorbed his information about medicines, spells, and how to treat the injured and sick. I remember the Druid Ogilhinn only spoke with the tree gods and asked for help. Lovern made potions that chased away the bad spirits. Lovern was a druid and a healer with the hands of the gods touching him. We were fortunate to have him here.

But, together we could not heal Cerdic.

It was Imbolc. Darkness came early on these days. We lighted our oil lamps before our evening meals. Again, the season brought labored breathing to Mother. One night, as I followed my mother into the cool night air again, Sileas' plea rang in my ears. I told Lovern about her request, and the next day we went to see Cerdic.

Cerdic, Harailt and Sileas lived in the home together. Harailt's sisters were married and gone. Sileas and Harailt were outside feeding dried corn to their hogs and chickens when we arrived, but urged us to go in.

Cerdic sat on the floor near a low fire. His hands grasped the edges of a blanket that covered his shoulders. His head low, he was folded over his chest as if to protect his heart from the dampness and smoke that filled the home. An oil lamp flickered a sickly, yellow shadow across his face. His neck stretched forward and jaw jutted open. His eyes were squeezed closed and his brow furrowed with lines of strain. His deliberate breaths escaped his body in liquid groans. I kneeled next to him and Lovern in front. There was no recognition of us in Cerdic's haggard face.

"Cerdic." I touched his shoulder, but he did not open his eyes. "Cerdic. Why are you up? You should be lying down," I asked.

"Can." He stopped to inhale between every word. "Not – breathe – lying –down."

A groan turned into an explosive cough that shook his body and sprayed blood to the dirt in front of his crossed legs. The floor was sticky with this spit. While he coughed, I rubbed his back, not knowing what else to do. I looked to Lovern. He watched Cerdic's spasm. When the coughing eased, Cerdic reached one arm out from under the blanket and wiped the frothy blood from his lips, his eyes still closed with the concentration of his breathing. The fresh and dried blood on the sleeve of his tunic scared me. I turned to Lovern, silently asking him whether we could help. He nodded, his eyes never leaving Cerdic.

The room echoed with Cerdic's ragged inhales and rough exhales along with the soft pops and hisses of the peat and dung fire.

"Cerdic, you know you are dying," Lovern said.

I looked from Lovern to Cerdic my mouth open in surprise.

"How can you say that? He is a strong man, he may live through many more Samhainns," I argued, not admitting what I had witnessed. Cerdic's fingertips and lips were blue and stained with blood. His white face was slippery with sweat and pulled from the struggle of living, neck ropey with the battle for breath and his head bowed as if surrendering to the war for life that was being waged in his body.

"Yes," said Cerdic, "soon."

I looked at Cerdic, not wanting to believe. Where was the strong man I had known all my life; a farmer whose sheep produced wool that my mother and I wove? A man who was a valuable member of our clan and the father of Harailt? I did not recognize the coughing shell of a man, readying himself to cross to the spirit world. His once proud eyes did not leave the floor of his lodge.

Sileas and Harailt stepped through their doorway. I stood and moved next to Sileas, my arms around her. Harailt took my place on the floor next to his father.

"He has been this way for three nights," said Harailt. "We have not slept, but stayed up to give him comfort. How can you help?" he asked Lovern.

"I cannot help him live. I can help him die," said Lovern gently. He turned back to face Cerdic. "I will try to ease your breathing, to ease your crossing."

Harailt grasped his father's shoulders with white knuckled fingers while Sileas stiffened in my arms with an "Oh."

Death was not unexpected nor feared by us. Our fear was a difficult passage to death, or dying alone. While we all traveled this path, no one wished to die helpless, with great pain, or alone.

Cerdic's passage promised to be difficult. He would not give up his soul easily. He had been a stubborn man in life and I knew he would be a stubborn man in death.

"We need to move him outside. It is easier to breathe in the fresh air," said Lovern.

I recalled my mother's trips into the cold nights, searching for relief.

We created a fire pit outside his home, in the protection of the corn drying area. The thigh high, three-sided walled space opened into the yard of the farm. Thatch-roofed and wind-protected, it allowed Cerdic the breezes and fresh air he craved. We built a small fire to bring warmth to him. He did not need it as much as we did; his body was hot with his struggle. Wrapped in heavy cloaks, dried grasses stuffed into our shoes and hands tucked under our arms to stay warm, we sat with him day and night.

Word spread that Cerdic was dying and our neighbors and friends came. For the two cold, damp, grey days he was outside, all who had known him, hunted with him, and traded stories with him said goodbye.

Beathan's father and Cerdic had grown up together. Cerdic helped Beathan's father become our clan chieftain. Beathan honored Cerdic by singing songs of the days when his father and Cerdic were boys. A smile crept across Cerdic's strained face.

Lovern went to our sacred pool with a jar and returned with some water. He asked Sileas for a dried apple which he cut into small bits. He put it in a pot, brought the water and apple to a boil, added wild garlic and the *lus mor* we gathered several days ago. The mixture was cooled and then held to Cerdic's lips to drink for relief. When he was too weak to swallow, I dripped it from my fingers into his mouth, the way I had fed my lamb. We laid mistletoe on his chest, a piece of salted pork over it, and bound a cloth around him.

Lovern's low murmurs and chanting were constant. He appealed to the gods of the Otherworld to make this passing, Cerdic's dying, a kind one.

After two days, his breath came in short, torturous gasps and Lovern told us Cerdic's death was close. Cerdic, lying on his left side, faced east, toward the sunrise and the door of the

Otherworld. He could not talk. Lovern sat, touching Cerdic's forehead. Sileas and Harailt were seated, holding his feet. I laid down behind him so my body was next to his and hugged him to me with my hand over his heart. I felt the struggle in his rapidly beating heart and shallow rising chest. I whispered in his ear over and over, timed with my calm breaths,

"Breathe in for life,
Breathe in for death,
Breathe in,
Breathe."

Cerdic struggled less, but he still lived. His worn soul, stiff with resistance, still refused to pass. We sang and prayed to our god of all nature, Cernunnos, and our goddess of the underworld, Cerridwen.

"Oh great horned one.
Oh Cernunnos.
Oh moon goddess.
Oh Cerridwen.
Cedric is traveling to you.
Help him build his boat;
He will cross the water.
Allow him into your lodge.
Seat him next to your fire.
Share food and mead with him.
Promise him successful hunts.
Show him the treasures of your abode.
Help him make this crossing to the next world,
To his next life."

"Cerdic. What stops you from crossing?" I whispered. He was growing restless again. My own breathing grew labored, matching his. I forced my mind to follow Lovern's labyrinth. It was one of the things Lovern taught me. I wanted a way to ease Cerdic's crossing of the river of death. I had never seen it done but in my heart and my mind, ideas came to me. I knew I could help. Just follow the labyrinth's path.

I whispered, "Cerdic. Who do you want to see on the other side?" All the animals in the farmyard quieted as if to hear his answer. Even the birds in the trees were silent.

I prayed to Corra, the goddess of the underworld crossings, and a vision came to my eyes. At the end of the labyrinth's path, Cerdic stood at the edge of the rushing, black river, looking to the other shore. He saw darkness. He was afraid. No one was there to meet him. In my vision, I brought his wife into my mind, Machara, as I remembered her when I was young. She stood on the opposite shore of the river. Whispering to him, I gave the vision to Cerdic.

"Open your mind Cerdic. Breathe and open your mind. Let me in to show you." I felt a small release in the tension of his shoulders. "There, Cerdic, she is there. Machara is waiting for you. She will help you across the river. It is safe for you to go now. Go with Corra and Machara in peace. You will be well there and breathe with ease. You will be young and in love again. You will own many sheep and have many cups of mead to drink. We who remain here will sing your song and remember you in our stories. You are free to go, Cerdic. You are free to follow Machara."

His struggle softened, then his racing heart stopped beating under my hand, and welcome tears of relief fell from my eyes. A few moments after Cerdic stopped his struggle for breath, Lovern came to me and helped me up. I was drained. It was as if I had carried Cerdic across the river myself. Lovern carried me to a cot to rest while Harailt and Sileas took care of Cerdic's body.

"You have done well, my love," said Lovern. "You have found your gift."

Lovern, Sileas and Harailt later told me Cerdic smiled just as his soul passed.

The hogs began to root again. The sky grew dark with another rainstorm.

Cerdic, buried with the others of our clan, lay in a meadow below the sacred pool.

Soon after Cerdic's death, Harailt and Sileas had gone to Beathan during a clan council, and asked that they be released from raising sheep.

"I will give my sheep to Crannog, my neighbor, in exchange for food for three years," Harailt said. "He has a good pasture and they will do well. The clan will still get their wool. I have told him he can use my land to grow food for us and corn for his hogs. We will have no time to work it now."

"WHAT?" I was sure Beathan's bellow was heard across the lake.

Sileas stood proudly next to her husband Harailt, and in a quiet tone said, "I had a dream, my chieftain. I dreamt that Cerdic came back. He stood next to our firepit and looked around the home where he raised his children. I was in bed but sat up as I saw him standing there. He looked at me and there was a spark in his eyes. He spoke with me."

"*This is to be the place all in need will be carried. For those who require healing and for those who are dying. Our gods and goddesses will be close here, ready to offer their spirit. The druid will be here. Jahna will be here. You and my son Harailt will be here. All will be doing the work of the gods and goddesses. There will be no more sheep raised here, only praises to the otherworld. Lovern will heal and Jahna will aid the eventual passing of all. Bel and Morrigna send this message. It is through this work that our clan will be allowed to carry its bloodline into the future. Heed this message or all will be lost.*'"

"We must do what he told us or Morrigna and Bel will be angry. The morning after this dream, a flock of crows, at least one hundred strong, came into our yard. Many saw them circle our abode and land in our trees." There was a murmur of agreement from the people at the council table.

"They sat quietly," she continued, "for a short time, while Harailt and I looked out our door at them. We fully expected them to eat the corn we stored for our hogs but instead they sat and stared at us as we watched them. I finally understood they were waiting for our answer and I yelled out our doorway for them to take the message to Morrigna that we would do as she commanded. As they all lifted off at once, a wind was raised that carried the smell of new cut grass. I knew we had done what was asked."

Beathan looked at Sileas and Harailt as if the crows had just landed on their heads. His face grew red and his hand clenched the short sword lying in front of him until his knuckles turned white. Beathan turned to Lovern and I as we stood listening. Harailt had bidden us to be with them while he and Sileas made this request. It must have been because they thought I would bring favor to them, being Beathan's niece. I wondered if this was a safe place to be at this moment, Uncle or not.

The dream was not an easy task, and one filled with hardships. I understood the call of a dream, however, and knew this one we had to follow.

"How are we to allow a farm that is one of the largest of the clan to go fallow and not produce? How do we just turn it over to the gods? Druid, is this your doing? What am I supposed to do?"

Lovern laid his hand on Beathan's shoulder. "It is a calling we must follow. The future of our clan depends on it. So say the gods. The fields will not lay fallow, Crannog will plow and harvest them and raise the sheep. There will be no change in the wool or food supply, we lose one farmer but gain a home for the sick and dying. If we are together we can be better at easing their struggle. I ask you, no beg you, try this plan for one year. If it is a hardship and you do not see that it works, we will go back to our old ways."

"Druid. You can talk milk out of a bull," said Beathan after running his hands over his face and beard for several minutes. "I will give you one year."

And so Lovern and I lived and slept with my mother but worked with Harailt and Sileas in the abode that became a hospice.

73 AD April

The winter darkness had passed, the fields were sowed, and the harvest was expected to be good this year. Many farm animals were with young and of the clan only Cerdic died. We had no threats from neighboring clans. The dark season, *Geamhradh,* was gone but had been kind.

To celebrate the spring, the coming of new life, Lovern and I asked Beathan to hand-fast us.

At the feast for the hand-fasting, I wore my green dress, Lovern's favorite.

"Jahna. You create a fire in my soul," he whispered during one of the few moments we shared alone. "Our lives will be joined by the gods and we will travel our path together. As I stand here tonight, I promise my life in trade for yours, at any time the gods ask it of me."

I could ask for nothing more, yet I felt a need to not let go of him. I knew our journey would not last long. I craved a vision of our grandchildren, of Lovern teaching them about the plants and gods of our land.

I could not say what the future held for us but only go through each day working with him and the gods and goddesses.

We were strong in each other. For now, I kissed him with a love-filled heart.

As he turned to take greetings from others, I noticed he had recovered from his travel here. He had gained muscle and carried a look of calmness in the corners of his eyes. My mother cut and stitched his new clothing. She also gave him a light cape of our plaid. She welcomed him to the clan with this gift. She told him he should burn his old clothes for luck, but he folded and stored them.

"There are too many memories woven in them," he said.

Lovern had given me a gift before the ceremony, a sacred drilled hazelnut strung on a leather cord to wear around my neck. With it came his acceptance of my knowledge of the Otherworld. I saw myself reflected in his deep blue eyes, as a woman and mate. I sighed with content. I was not a girl trying to find her way. Through the help of Lovern and the gods, I found my new life. I was now an *immrama*, a soul friend.

At the feast, we danced and drank Beathan's mead. My mother baked my favorite, salmon in eggs and herbs. All who came brought food to share, a cup of milk from a white goat, or a hog to be slaughtered and roasted. Kenric played music on his pipe. Hundreds of feet danced with us, even Mother's. Lovern spun me off the floor and I laughed.

"I bind the three threads of unity around your wrists. With this hand-fasting I ask that Morrigna, Bel and Lug bless you. Now go into the community and all will know you marry in one year," Beathan said as he tied the three strands of yarn around first my wrist and then Lovern's as we faced each other. "Druid, it is good that the plan you had for Jahna worked. She remains my niece, my sister's daughter and I will still hunt you if she comes to harm in your care," he said. His eyes were fierce.

"Her soul has been promised to the gods but I will protect her while she is on this earth," said Lovern.

I stood in the center of the circled clan. To be here as Lovern's colleague and hand-fasted with him as his life partner was an honor. The clan accepted me as a healer, and at the same time Beathan acknowledged Lovern as a clan member. We moved into our future.

Beathan invited both Lovern and me to his evening meals where we shared stories, music, and food. I did not serve any more, and I did not allow my mother to serve me. She sat beside me with honor. Grumbling, Beathan made do with one slave to serve his meals.

Lovern taught me much about healing. We gathered the plants and herbs that had been available in the cold darkness of winter, but we were ready for the plants that had been hiding to burst through from ground and reach for our hands to harvest. My mother's home, now our home too, became our storage and drying shelter.

We decided to make our abode larger to accommodate and store the herbs, plants, and other supplies we used and gathered more of each day. We traded with Straun, our neighbor. He built our room and we promised to care for his family's health, with no more recompense, for one year. It was a good trade.

"Straun. Our doorway must have this lintel and I wish it to be installed before we re-enter the house," said Lovern.

"Of course," said Straun.

Lovern crafted the lintel from yew and hazel and carved it with druid letters. He read it to me. "May our love invite health, good spirits and peaceful dreams." Peaceful dreams. A shiver slid down my back. The heavy feeling in my heart would not be eased. I knew not what the gods asked of us in the future but knew we walked to the end of our own labyrinth.

"Here will be the shelves to store the dried plants. We can keep a box of the stones we need for healing, here. And over there we can hang the mistletoe," said Lovern as he walked through the space that Straun would be enclosing with our new wall.

Straun had opened up the back of our home, breaking the stone wall out and stacked it nearby, ready for reuse. The outline of the room pushed out to touch the wall of the fort behind us. Straun dug three more support holes. The walls and the new thatched roof would be done in a few days, if the weather held. Mother, Lovern and I were sleeping at Beathan's and would be glad for an enclosed, weather-tight, quiet abode again.

"Yes," I agreed. "I can see it in my mind." In my mind, I also prepared our marriage bed. It would be here. I would gather the pine boughs for freshness and cover it with dried grasses and heather for sweetness and softness. Over it I would spread my best woolen covering and our blankets, the ones I wove last year. Three threads, one each of blue, red, and yellow, would have three knots tied and then all three braided around three small twigs of oak. I would say prayers to Lug for fertility, and place the small bundles where our heads would lie.

Lovern walked over to the first of the three holes and stood looking back into our home. "I am where the gods want me. I am here to live and die. I wish my memories to be new from this time on. Yet, do not want to give up my old ones. Jahna, please come here."

Startled, I came back to the present.

He turned to face the hole as I stepped next to him. I looked into his turned down face. His red hair fell over his eyes. They seemed to look far away as he stared into the hole. He shrugged his labyrinth bag from his shoulder, untied its leather string closure and it fell open. Turning the bag on its side, he shook it until the three sharp crystals fell out into his smooth hand.

"I have created a new life. These stones helped me arrive here safely, and they will protect my new abode and family." He handed me one and again it was warm in my hand.

"Place it in the hole."

I looked to him in bewilderment. Was he going to bury his stones?

"It will be a part of the support of our home," he said. I kneeled to the earth and placed the first of the three stones in the hole. We did the same twice more.

I stood and brushed the dirt from my knees. Lovern upright and tall behind me placed his hands on my shoulders, his fingers softly entwined in my hair. I laid my hands on top of his solid, protective hands, grateful to have shared this moment with him. I heard the ravens in the distant trees. Our powers were strong together.

"Great goddess Morrigna, protect us," prayed Lovern. "We are here now to live as you and Bel request. We shall follow the path to which you have led us. Create a peaceful and healthful abode in which we can teach our children to praise you. Grant us the knowledge to help the clan in any way you demand. In return for our lives, we ask for good memories to be made here."

Straun watched our ceremony from a respectful distance. After our completed prayer, he took three flat river stones and laid them inside each hole, on top of Lovern's crystals.

"These flat stones were from the sacred pool and will protect the crystals from the weight of the posts and the roof. The stones will protect the crystals for the life of the house," said Lovern.

My breath caught in my throat, and I knew the crystals would be here much longer than our home and the other homes on our hill. The crystals would be here for many moon and sun rises. Longer than our clan would inhabit the surrounding fields. Only our love would live longer. My body sagged with this knowledge, and I leaned against Lovern, my strong post supporting my future.

CHAPTER 7

JAHNA

74 AD April

I awoke next to Lovern before the cock's crow. In a deep sleep, his chest raised and lowered with each breath. He wrinkled his brow, and I wondered what he dreamed of.

I refreshed our peat fire and sat a small pot of water next to it. I sat, bundled in my cape, waiting for the sun to rise, and held my slate. I had found the piece of stone on the mountain trail behind our hill. It was two hands wide, and a small finger thick. I worked its imperfections into pictures that surrounded the labyrinth I had painted on it.

Since seeing Lovern's memory bag in the cave, the day of the storm, his labyrinth fascinated me. We grew closer during the time he taught me how to follow its path. The morning hours of our first days together were spent tracing it. When I knew I should continue the meditation on my own, I found my stone and began to paint my own labyrinth. Its course, a double spiral, was painted in the colors I loved, the red and blue I used to dye the clan plaid. The surrounding drawings were of the nature around my home, the mountain behind, the trees around, the sky and birds above us.

I did not like to let a day pass without at least touching the stone. I could create it with my eyes closed and follow the blue and red lines with my fingers. I often created its image in my mind when helping a person cross to the Otherworld as I had for Cerdic. It smoothed the way for my thoughts and the visions of the Otherworld, if they chose to come.

I tested the water in the small pot. Finally warm, I slipped off my nightdress, rinsed my face and arms in its comfort. As I ran my hands over my body, I wished they were Lovern's. I vibrated with the sense of the touch of his hands lingering on my breasts last night and the lovemaking that followed. The memory caused my nipples to become sensitive. My heart swelled with joy and wonder at the knowledge that we could be together for years to come.

My thoughts rambled in a confusing tumble this morning. Lovern and I were hand-fasted one year ago today. We had not yet approached Beathan for permission to marry. There was no reason for this lack of action; time just flew by too quickly. A year had passed. I knew I must speak on it soon. Beathan is not one to be patient; he would want this day observed with a decision.

I carried different feelings for Lovern than I had for any other man. When I accepted marrying Harailt, I expected no more than performing normal chores, and cooking his meals. With Lovern, my life was a partnership. He did not treat me like a servant. He and I discussed how best to heal and help our clan. He listened as well as taught me and often took my advice to his work. We were free to go where we wished, when we wished, yet I often followed along to learn from him.

I knew I would be doing this work for the years left in my life. I wanted to do it beside Lovern. But if he decided not to marry me, I would continue to be a healer and helper of souls. That was the gift the gods had given me. Lovern helped me learn how to use it. And I loved him for it.

There was a fear in my gut. We made love frequently, and I still was not with child. Usually, after one year of hand-fasting there was a child to consider. Lovern and I did not have that tie. This thought crept into my mind many times and now, as before, I sighed, shook my head, and released it. I must allow the will of the goddess be done. I will give birth when it is time, when I am ready. As Lovern says, when the goddess is ready.

This morning, as I followed my labyrinth, I prayed a silent thank you to Bel and Morrigna for allowing me to follow their way. I also prayed, while my finger traced my labyrinth, for a sign to help make the decision we faced.

Mother and Lovern were still sleeping. Lovern had come in late last night from a visit with a sick child. His day ahead was full, and I wanted him to rest as long as possible. I listened to the rhythmic inhale and exhale of his sleeping breath behind the hanging wool blanket, there for privacy, and to keep the sometimes messy and odoriferous preparations of our medicines as far away from my mother as possible. Smoke and some odors worsened her cough. A spoonful of a brew made from bog bean and the bittersweet nightshade, three times a day, along with the heather tea and sour milk helped. She seemed to be sleeping better.

We stored our plants and herbs used for the very ill at the hospice. Our small room here filled with treatments for the clan's common illness.

Hospice. The word sometimes still made my tongue stumble. Some of the clan would not use it and referred to it as Harailt's home. It was Lovern's word. He used it when he was learning the healing arts in his other home. Before he came to us – to me.

We tried to take care of our own in our homes. However, some of the ill required more watching than the family can provide. The hours of the day filled with the care and feeding of our animals, the sowing and harvesting of our crops and the raising of our children. The ill sometimes pushed families beyond their limits.

Harailt and Sileas slept in the home given to this dream, the hospice. Lovern worked there, and when a clan member was close to death, I stayed, too. It was my wish that our friends and neighbors would live long and useful lives with times of work and joy to share. But when the end of life was near, I helped create an easier path for the dying. I did most of this work at the hospice.

After I washed, I was cold and pulled on my tunic and peplum. The nights were still damp, and a breeze ushered in the early hours. I placed two small pots of clean water near the fire, one to boil barley and one for mint tea.

While I prepared our breakfast, I listed in my mind my chores for the day. There was no one ill at the hospice. My morning was free.

I would to go to the river and gather some blackthorn. Its leaves were just coming, and its white blossoms still were stark against the black bark. I harvested the berries in the fall; even the dried ones we now have help stop the bleeding in small wounds. There were many children with raw throats. A wash of its leaves and blossoms steeped in boiling water and then cooled would ease this pain. I wanted to gather enough to boil in a large pot and distribute the tea tomorrow.

I also wanted sweet heather, pungent juniper branches, and green ivy to freshen our bed. The ivy would keep lice away while the smell of the juniper and heather helped us sleep. I thought of lying next to Lovern on our newly freshened bed and smiled. I prayed the day was not too busy for us to lie in it tonight, together.

While the barley boiled and the fragrant tea simmered, I heard Lovern stir. His lithe, sinewy body slipped under the hanging blanket. His trousers already on, he pulled his tunic over his head and shook his copper hair loose. His belt, a cord for his hair, and his memory bag hung from his teeth. After he tied on his belt and slung his bag on his shoulder, he leaned over and kissed me on the top of my head. He tied back his long hair into a red tail.

"May the goddess bless this day," he said as he stepped outside, into the cool haze of a new spring day to carry on his morning routine.

Mother awoke, her cough softer this morning. This pleased me. If her cough was deeper, I would have changed my earlier plans and gone to harvest and start her on a tea of fresh *lus mor*. The plant was available year-round and we used it to ease the bloody cough. Mother had not yet coughed blood, but I knew she would. It was the progression of this illness. She cleared her throat and, after combing her graying hair into the thick plaits she wore on top of her head, came for breakfast. Lovern returned. We ate and discussed the day ahead.

"I am going into the woods to see if I can find him today."

Lovern went in search of his namesake, the red fox, every year at this time. He often sat for a full day near a den, waiting to see the foxes.

"If I find one, I will do what is necessary to please the gods."

"Good hunting, my love," I said.

He ran his hand over my hair and stooped to kiss me in a gentle goodbye and left.

And so the day of our marriage began.

I survived the sharp and hidden thorns of the blackthorn tree; boiled the infusion and stored it in small jugs, ready to be used by those with sore throats. The heather and juniper were fragrant in our bed. After giving Mother her medicine, it was time to go to the hospice to see if word of new patients came this morning. Sometimes people stopped by to tell us that someone in their family was ill and to ask us to come treat them.

I arrived at the hospice and greeted Sileas with a hug.

"Harailt and I have used this morning to sweep the house and lay clean bedding for the next patients," she said. "There was even time to go to the river and eat my midday meal. The sound of the waterfall and its peaceful surroundings renewed my spirits."

"I often wonder, do you and Harailt ever regret turning your home over to the sick? Do you miss the farm?" I asked.

"No. We have never looked back. Remember, it was not our decision. Cerdic commanded it through my vision. I have enjoyed being useful in ways other than farming. I am fulfilled with my work here and never regret it. Harailt tells me that his father's spirit has come to him in his dreams, smiling," she said. "We will never be unhappy with this choice."

She stepped back from the simmering pot, lifting her dress out of the way of the fire. We hugged, happy our lives would continue this path together.

Harailt and Lovern sauntered through the door, heads together, deep in conversation. Harailt hefted an armful of wood for the fire. Lovern carried two hares and his bow.

Handing the hares to Sileas, Lovern said, "There they were sitting in front of me, asking me to bring them to you. I agreed, and now they are yours."

"Thank you," said Sileas. She took the hares from Lovern, lifted them to judge their weight, and said, "I think it will be a good hunting season this year. It is early, yet these are a good size. The grasses are growing fast to feed them."

Harailt took the hares from Sileas. "I will skin, clean them and return them to you. But I must know, Lovern. How many did you see? Is there a concern that we may lose many of our chickens? If it shall be a good year for the foxes, then I must be sure to keep our fowl in a safe place."

"I saw three yearling males. Each was on the prowl for mates. I am sure there will be females for them close by." Then Lovern smiled. "I also saw a vixen with four kits. I am always glad to see them. I know Arimid is pleased as long as I continue to have my foxes around me."

"Arimid," Harailt said. "She is a demanding goddess. She expects much sacrifice by us to keep the foxes alive."

"Yes," said Lovern. "She is the one who gave me my skills for healing and sacrifices must be made to her. I cannot work if the foxes are not here. But I do not worry this year, they are here and well."

Harailt said, "I have heard your foxes are doing well. There are many farmers missing chickens and ducks. They blame the foxes and would trap them, but you have forbidden it."

"There will be many young kits for the vixens to feed this year. I will help you build a hut to keep your hens in. They will need protection."

"But you know many farmers will not be able protect their animals in this way. They will lose food."

"Yes," Lovern said. "It is always so. We will pass the word that if they are losing livestock to a fox, they may trap it. If it is a nursing vixen, let her be, but they may kill every other adult male. If that does not work, then come to me. I will help them build protection."

Harailt nodded, picked up a skinning knife, and walked through the door into the sunshine with the rabbits.

Sileas followed him. "I want to make sure he cuts the skin in a way that I may use it for a winter hat," she said. "I will return soon."

I touched Lovern's tunic. "There is too much blood here for just two hares. Did you find him?"

He reached his long arms around me, and pressed his face into my hair. "How is it you always smell of lavender?" he asked, inhaling deeply.

"It is the same as you always smelling of acorns and beeswax to me. It does not matter what physical work you have done, even after sacrificing a bull, I still find that scent on you, just under your skin. It is you." As comforting as it was in his arms, I pulled back to see his face. A questioning look came into his eyes. I repeated, "Did you find him?"

His face relaxed into a smile. He took a deep breath and said, "Yes. He was there. He was in the same glen as last year. He was sitting on a warm rock. His fat tail was wrapped around his body. He saw me before I him, yet he stayed. I was able to use one arrow to capture him and thrusted once to kill and bleed him. It was a clean sacrifice."

He reached into his tunic and brought out a leather packet, holding it at arm's length for me to take. I took it from him, unwrapped one soft corner, and revealed the red tail of a Forest Fox, Lovern's totem.

"The gods be praised. It is fine," I said as I ran my fingers through its long red fur. I wrapped it, handed it back and Lovern tucked it into his tunic. It was to be displayed above the door of our home, one to be added each year.

"I buried his heart near the sacred pool," he said in answer to my unvoiced question. "I stopped there, near the water fall, to pray and wash his blood from my arms.

"I understand the farmers' disquiet," said Lovern. "However, we must all make sacrifices to the gods in trade for our lives. For me to stay here, I must have the foxes nearby. I cannot have them killed, or I would leave. They bring my dreams," Lovern said. "Conyn told me they bring the art of healing to me. They are my namesake, my sacred symbols," said Lovern, with an earnest face.

"Lovern, do not be concerned about your sacred foxes. We will protect them. Our clan heeds your words," I said, my hand on his shoulder. "I, myself, will go to the den and raise the kits if something happens to the vixen."

Hearing a flurry of commotion, we turned and watched as a stout, red-faced man I recognized as Aonghus bolted into the room, carrying his weeping boy Torrian. His heavily pregnant third wife and gaggle of small children followed him.

"Please!" His appeals were directed to Lovern. "Torrian fell and hurt his leg."

We gathered around the big man carrying the small boy, parting the crowd of children to reach them.

Aonghus admonished Torrian as Lovern took the crying boy into his arms. "If you would do what I ask, the gods would not punish you in such ways. You must learn that you should get your work done and then go off chasing clouds."

"We will see what the injury is," said Lovern, "and treat it the best we can. Harailt, hold the boy's leg, keep it as still as possible, while I lay him on the cot."

"We cannot stay at home to care for him," said Aonghus. "We are lambing and have to get crops planted. We are needed in the fields."

Torrian cried out in pain as Lovern and Harailt laid him on the cot.

I saw Aonghus' brow crease at the sound of his injured son. "I sent him to clean the goat pen, but as usual he ran off. He never does what I ask. We always have to look for him. He runs off chasing butterflies or bugs. I heard him yell and found him lying on the ground under a tree. Can you help him?" He looked at Lovern with pleading eyes.

Sileas and I kept track of the children as well as we could. Some of our pots contained poisons. "Aonghus, take your children home. I will come after Lovern has done his work and tell you of the results," I said.

Aonghus controlled his children. He left with them and his wife trailing after him like a father goose with his goslings.

Lovern placed his hands on the boy's body to determine the injuries as I sat down next to him and held his small, trembling, dirt-encrusted hand and sang a lullaby. Torrian calmed his crying to a whimper. His tears slowed in the paths cut through the grime on his cheeks, and he answered Lovern's questions.

"The branch broke," Torrian whimpered. "I was trying to catch the bluest bird ever! That branch held me before. OUCH!" Lovern touched the swelling bruise on his leg.

"Is my father right? Is this the gods' punishment?" Torrian whimpered.

"Do you hurt anywhere other than your leg?" asked Lovern.

"I bumped my head and landed on my wrist but my leg hurts the most," the young adventurer replied.

I watched Lovern's face, deep in concentration as he inspected the boy's other injuries. He ran his large, gentle hands over Torrian's blond covered head, and down to Torrian's hand where he looked over his wrist.

Lovern's face softened when he spoke with the boy. "The gods do many things to teach us right from wrong. It is good that you are interested in the nature around you and want to know more. But the gods say you must obey first your chieftain, then your father and mother before you think of yourself. You should do your chores before exploring."

Torrian nodded in agreement.

"When you get better," Lovern continued, "with your father's permission, I will take you into the forest and teach you more about nature. After your work is done."

Suddenly, all my doubt left my heart. In my eyes, the hand of my own child replaced Torrian's small hand in mine. I would give birth. I did not know when but I knew I would have a baby. Silently, I thanked the goddess.

The boy nodded, his whimpering eased, and his tears stopped.

I was worried about the boy. His left foot hung out of its normal position. A red, angry blood-swelling raised one half the distance below his knee and above his ankle. Regret for a young life to be lived as a cripple washed through me. The result for this injury was at the least a very bad limp or maybe no use of his leg. I have seen some die.

"You have broken your leg," Lovern said. With a stern look on his face, he continued, "This will take three full moon cycles to heal, and you will be restricted in your movements during that time. The bone inside your leg, the thing that makes it stiff so you can walk, has broken. Like this," Lovern said. Lovern reached down by the fire, picked up a small piece of kindling, and snapped it.

The sharp sound made both Torrian and I flinch.

"But look, how the pieces go together." Lovern pressed the broken ends of the stick together. "This piece of wood is dead, but your leg is alive, and the bone will grow strong again. We have to put the pieces back together, like the stick, and keep them there for three moon cycles to give your leg a chance to mend straight. If you do not follow my instructions, and go off chasing a bird again, you may not walk with this leg or you will badly limp," lectured Lovern.

"Can you help him walk again?" Sileas' face was pursed in doubt when she asked this question. She voiced my silent concern.

Memories of the damp smell of the cave and the sound of lightning came into my head. The night he told me about his journey, he also told me he studied with Kinsey, the healer who could make people walk again.

"Lovern can do this," I said with confidence.

"Harailt, please find four strong, straight *caorann* branches, the length of his leg." Lovern said, in his teaching voice. "Sileas, we need four long strips of cloth to use as binders. Jahna, boil some barley, thick, and mix it with honey. Add some of the dried *meacan dubh*. We will lay the bone-set mixture on the broken bone."

We rushed to complete our assigned tasks while Lovern comforted the boy, told him stories of the gods' battles with giants, and dripped the juice of the red *meilbheag* onto his lips. The poppy juice was bitter and the boy made a face. After he swallowed, I knew Torrian would sleep and not remember the pain.

Harailt came in with the rowan branches, still removing leaves and berries from the gray bark as he entered. He laid them within Lovern's reach. Sileas appeared with cloth ties. I brought the still warm poultice of barley, honey, and comfrey.

"Harailt," said Lovern, "settle his head in your lap and hold his shoulders." He then asked Torrian, ""Are you a still a little boy or are you now a young man?"

Torrian's shoulders straightened, his brows knit in defiance and in a proud voice replied, "I am a man. I have my own goat to care for."

"Ah, I thought so. A little boy would be afraid of this injury, but I can see in your face, you are not. This will be painful, but you will sleep. When you awaken, you will lie here in this bed for seven sunrises. We will bring you food, drink, and care for you in all ways. Only then are you allowed up with an aid for walking until your leg heals. If you do not heed this bargain with the gods, your leg will not heal straight. Do you understand me?" asked Lovern.

Lovern spoke in his straightforward way. He instilled confidence in those he treated. He always spoke the truth, and the people of our clan trusted him.

"Yes," whispered Torrian.

Torrian's face, set in a determined grimace, seemed to get younger as Harailt settled his head and shoulders into his lap.

"Open your mouth." I inserted an oak stick soaked in vetch between his teeth. "Now bite." The taste would distract him from what was about to happen.

Lovern grasped Torrian's foot and ankle firmly, and pulled until the leg straightened. Torrian screamed and fainted, as we expected. I folded the poultice around his bruised leg while Lovern and Harailt positioned the branches and, as fast as Sileas could hand the cloth to them, tied them into place.

Sileas went to the fire to prepare the boiled *lus* for Torrian when he woke up. The wort would calm him and stop the bleeding in the leg.

"He must have mistletoe tied in red thread under his head when he sleeps. The gods will look on this with favor, and his blood may not poison. Feed him ground, boiled apple, and be sure he has a few drops of the poppy juice in his water," said Lovern. Sileas nodded and went to find the red thread and dried apple.

A large shadow darkened our doorway. I turned and saw Beathan, our chieftain. He had not come into this dwelling since Harailt and Sileas gave it to the clan in honor of Cerdic to be used as a hospice a year before.

"Tell me what you are doing." Beathan's deep voice shook the still air in the small room. "Why did I hear a scream as I came into this yard? Is the boy still alive?" His eyes found mine with his last question.

He gave Lovern and me the stern looks of a disapproving father. He was taking our measure.

I think he felt the loss of the farm, but I knew the sheep that moved to the neighboring farm in Harailt's trade were giving more wool than before. The clan did not lose but gained in this deal. He would not admit it. He was my uncle and I respected him as a father, but I was always ready to defend our work if he questioned it. His silence was worse as it hid his thoughts.

"Good afternoon, Uncle. It is good that you have come to see what we do here," I said, smiling as I walked over to the towering man. I took his huge paw that dwarfed my hand and proudly guided him to where Torrian lay sleeping.

"Lovern has given this boy a chance to heal and walk again. Torrian has broken his leg. Before this hospice, Torrian would have been in his bed, at home, alone, and in a fever with little treatment. He probably would have died. Or, if he lived, he would not have the use of his leg.

"Because of what Lovern accomplished today and the treatment he will get in the coming days from Harailt and Sileas, this boy will live to be a free farmer or warrior for the next chieftain of our clan. He will outlive you, *bràthair-màthar*, healthy and strong."

Uncle Beathan grabbed me in a bear hug and lifted me off the floor.

"Ah, I see you still have the tongue of a brat," Beathan said. "I am glad you have not grown out of that. You must cause Lovern many gut-aches with your insolence." He turned to Lovern. "Well, do you still want to marry this *meanbh-chuileag?* These midges can make a man very angry. Or have you changed your mind and found a pleasant quiet mouse to warm your bed?"

"Put me down, Uncle," I whispered, though Beathan's laugh probably woke up Torrian. "You are crushing my ribs, and what do you mean a quiet mouse to warm his bed? Do you expect him to follow your example of not marrying and trying on all the single women of the clan? I will not allow it."

"Not allow it?" asked Beathan, seriously. "Not allow it? Who are you to not allow it? Are you married? How can you not allow it if you are not married?"

Still in Beathan's grip I heard Sileas and Harailt begin to laugh and saw a grin break out on Lovern's face. Why was he grinning? Did he think it was a good idea to have all the unwed women of our clan to warm his bed?

Lovern stopped laughing and answered. "Ah, Great Chieftain. You are *mo chraid.* But, I would never be able to call you more than friend if I did not marry her. I wish to call you uncle. I have never had an uncle, and to have one as great as you would be a good thing."

"Unh," Beathan grunted as he lowered me to the floor, my feet regaining my body's balance as he let go.

Lovern came to me, leaned over, his face close to mine, and embraced my cheeks in his hands. My eyes looked up into his as he said, "There are no others, *a ghaoil.* My beloved, I want to marry you because you complete my soul. You healed my broken heart. I traveled far and outran many dangers to find you. I know that without you I would not be able to do the gods' work, my work. I wish to make our union permanent and marry you."

My heart swelled with love at his words. Standing next to him, I smelled acorns. I laid my arms on his chest, my hands on his shoulders, and said, "Bel and Morrigna sent me a vision today. I will have a child. I will marry you to complete us. I will marry you because I love you. Without you, I could not have finished my labyrinth." My cheeks were wet with tears. His thumbs wiped them away with tenderness.

I pulled him to me and when our lips touched, I felt a release of the tension of the day. In its place was an excitement for this night in bed as well as the years, no matter how few, ahead of us. I did not want this kiss to end. When we broke apart, we turned, arm in arm to Beathan.

"Uncle," I said. "I feel this is an auspicious time. We must marry now. We should not wait any longer. There is an ancient oak nearby." I turned to Lovern, "May we be married under the oak?" His hands squeezed mine.

"Yes," said Lovern, his eyes sparkling. "I agree. It should be now."

"Lovern," I said, "go to the tree, and wait. I will get Mother. Then, Beathan can marry us." He nodded as I turned and ran out of the hospice.

"Is it twelve moons already?" said Mother.

"Mother, let us start down the hill. You can talk to me as we walk. They are waiting for us, and we do not dare keep Beathan waiting too long."

"Bah. He thinks he is so important, but I knew him when our mother chased him all over the hilltop for teasing our hens. He was made to do his chores and mine when Mother caught him. Sometimes I would tease the hens and blame him so I could go off and be with my friends for a day." Mother chuckled. "He would get his revenge, though. I often found small animals or insects in my dress. He never admitted it, but he would wear a big grin when I found them and screamed."

We were through the gate and halfway down the hill, me impatient but gently tugging on her arm, her taking one deliberate step at a time, and she continued, "Twelve moons. That is how long it took your father and me to decide to marry. He was gone on one of his trading journeys for two moons. When he returned, he told me he had decided to marry me. I laughed. There was no decision to make in my mind. We were to be together. He was a part of my life and I a part of his. When he told me, I remember, he swung me up in his arms and kissed me. Then we walked to your bed. You were three months old. He picked you up and cradled you. So gentle for such big arms," she said with a far away look. "He looked into your eyes, the reflection of his, and promised to take care of you for all your life."

She stopped walking and coughed. "We did not know how short a time we would have together. But the time we had together was good. He was a good father and husband. I missed him for a long time. Enough of the past." She waved me on as if telling me to walk faster. "Let us go celebrate the future!"

We approached the tree where Beathan, Lovern, and Harailt stood waiting. Torrian would sleep a while longer so Sileas was there, also. I waved, but before we walked closer, Mother pinched my ear and brought me close to her mouth.

"I have doubts about your marriage to him, Jahna. You are not with child. I can tell. Is it best to be married to this man? Should you look for a man who can give you a child?" she whispered loudly. "You have been sleeping with him. I hear you. But there is no baby."

Taking a deep breath to calm myself, I answered, "Mother. Today, a sign was given to me. This is what the goddess wills. If it is to be, you will live to hold a grandchild."

"I hope to live to hold many, Jahna. I want many grandchildren. It is the right of a mother to want grandchildren."

The oak was near our sacred spring. We used the water under the oak to wash our feet and hands in purification rituals. Lovern and I used it when mixing our cures. It was a favorable place. It was a blessed place to be married. It temporarily eased my mind of the shadows of doubts about our life together.

We gathered into a circle, Beathan in the center. The trampled grass's fragrance wafted through the air. Flowers nestled in small clumps around the tree trunk and above us the birds sang. The sky darkened. A cloud of ravens flew over without a sound and landed in a willow. A shiver rippled down my back. We were being watched. Morrigna was there. My hand quivered in Lovern's strong hand. His grip tightened; he smiled, reassuring.

Beathan spoke, "That you wish to be married does not surprise me. Do not think the longing looks you gave one another at my dinner table escaped me. I knew you were eating to gather strength to tumble through the night," he said gruffly but with a twinkle in his eye. "It is about time. I was beginning to wonder if I would have to make a demand for this to happen! When you first came, Lovern, I was unsure, wary of you. But you kept your promises."

Beathan turned his head to look at me. Did I see a bit of moisture reflect the sunlight on his eyelashes?

"Jahna. My sister's daughter. You grew to be like my own and pestered me as you would have your own father. But, I am proud of you. You are a fine woman and healer. I thought I was losing a skilled weaver, but you now weave a path for our souls to follow."

He now faced both Lovern and I, his hands palm up in front of us. "You teach us in the ways of our gods. Our clan is better because of your partnership. I have seen your work today and say this is good for our clan."

At this, his arms, the tattoos of our clan around his wrists, rose over his head, spread in declaration. "I call the attention of all the gods and goddesses. I allow this marriage in my name. I join Lovern and Jahna. They will live under my protection as long as they keep the clan laws. I declare this and will proclaim it to the clan. May the gods and goddesses bless this union with many good years and healthy children!"

Surprised, we stood in silence. This was the longest speech I ever heard Beathan give.

"Well, Sileas," asked Beathan. "Why did you carry out the red thread? Have you forgotten its purpose?"

"Oh. No, O Chieftain, no," she stammered. Flushed, she lifted and tied Lovern's and my clasped hands with red thread, wrapped three times around. Lovern kissed me deeply. I could do nothing but smile, my heart laughing. And so we married.

A lusty, rejoicing whoop split the sky, caused me to duck and the ravens to rise in somersaults and caw in escape. Beathan's yell and bear hug enveloped us all.

My mother kissed me and then Beathan on his bearded cheek. "You have done well with your life," she spoke into his ear. "I often wondered what would happen to you when we were children." His belly shook in laughter.

Lovern tried to hug everyone in return but our tied hands restricted his movements.

"See, Priest?" Beathan said. "She has already a hand on your freedom!"

"I do not see it as a restriction, my friend," Lovern said with a smile at me. "I see it as a promise to each other. A promise we made many years ago."

I knew he referred to my first passage dream with him as a boy. Beathan's forehead wrinkled. He did not know about the dreams. He did not know Lovern and I touched our minds long ago.

With a shrug of his mighty shoulders, Beathan said, "Now we go to eat. Invite all as we go. It will be a big celebration at my home tonight. I killed a hog yesterday. Let all bring food and drink and we will sing and tell tales all night."

"I have two hares to give to the pot for the dinner," said Sileas. "Harailt can pick them up on his way. I must stay with Torrian tonight."

Harailt gave her a kiss and her arm curled around his waist as they walked back to the hospice. A flash of memory came to my mind. Harailt and Cerdic walking away from Beathan's after he ordered Harailt and I to be hand-fasted. Harailt's head hung, and he shuffled away. He loved another. He loved Sileas. All came to pass as it should.

We sat as honored guests at Beathan's table. Many came and more still as Beathan announced our marriage. He gave Lovern the honor to carve the roasted meat. Lovern transferred the knife into our bound hands and we both carved. Cheers of congratulations rang out. The night was long and filled with mead, peat smoke, poems of bravery, love songs, and music. We danced, kissed in the shadows, and laughed, our hands held with the red thread of our promise. The celebration lasted long past the moon's rise. Lovern and I stumbled home long after mother.

Lovern used his teeth and we both used our free hands to untie the thread's knot. We were forbidden to cut it. He put the thread into his memory bag.

I crossed my arms and grasped the hem of my tunic, lifted it over my head and Lovern came up behind me. He wrapped his arms around my waist and nibbled my neck, just under my ear, causing my knees to grow weak. Chills ran down my body and my nipples stiffened.

"I cannot get ready for bed if you do not let me go," I said.

"I am here to help you undress," he whispered into my ear.

His strong arms enveloped me, carrying his scent of honey and crushed acorns. No other person smelled like him. No other man could make me want to be surrounded by him forever. I fell into his arms, and he turned me around to face him. My breath came faster as my heart danced in my chest. Heat rushed up from my toes to my face, and my breasts ached, waiting for his soft fingers to caress them. My body ached with desire. I buried my face into his chest, wanting his scent in my nose forever.

"Jahna. When I think back on the time I did not know you, I wonder how I could have thought I was alive. I need you. I am strong with you near me. Now, with this contract, we will be together forever. You are now my family. You are my life."

"It is for you that I have waited so long," I said. "I have taken no man before you. You are the one who taught me that to love is to feel the presence of the gods. My life will be lived as your partner, your wife. I will love you through this life and all we have hereafter."

His gentle blue eyes misted. Then one of his hands left my waist and encircled my breast. My nipples hardened even more at his touch, and I gasped. I stood on my tiptoes, and pulled his lips to mine.

When our lovemaking was over, I lay next to him, weak, and rolled to him so my nose was against his ribs, inhaling his scent. His fingers combed through my hair; then his palm rested on the back of my head. We whispered promises of fealty. This night burned itself into my memories. It would be there until my death.

We spent that night in a bed that smelled of sweet heather, in each other's arms.

The day of our marriage ended.

Tomorrow I would follow my labyrinth.

CHAPTER 8

 AINE

April, 2005

I had been given ninety-six hours to find her.

Marc talked Lauri, Tim, Kendy, and Matt into staying for four days. They'd still have time to pack up the tent and equipment and go on to Wales if we didn't find anything in the time they gave me.

I called the farmer who owned the property, Mr. Treadwell, and told him we were coming up today. As he hesitated, thoughts of him telling me he'd changed his mind ran through my head. I reached for my antacids.

"Just be sure to close the gate when you come up," he said. "It wouldn't be good fer me cattle to roam the roads, unattended."

I thanked him and assured him we'd close the gate.

There was little conversation between Marc and I at first. The unpaved farm road was rough and full of ruts and I was glad we'd a Range Rover and a sturdy van for transportation. I decided not to ask any questions on the ride up about the discussion of their staying here. I was in the Rover with Marc and the rest of the crew was in the van behind us. Marc convinced the crew to stay, but I didn't know if I wanted to find out how much he told them about our discussion last night. I hoped he'd been discreet about Jahna.

The morning fog kept the dust down. It was also obscuring our view of the hill. I'd seen the hill and taken pictures of it last fall, but could hardly make out anything in this blanket of cold and moisture. Thankfully, I had my map coordinates out and the GPS in hand or we'd have driven right by it.

It wasn't a large hill, and it blended in with the landscape of pastures and surrounding hills. It also backed into the mountain just behind it, and was just tall enough to see the countryside, making any defense of it by ancient people easier. I knew they'd been here. Now I needed to prove it to the crew and Marc.

We parked at the bottom and gathered around the van to unload our little bit of equipment. I asked for a few minutes to walk up to the hilltop to find the first spot I wanted to excavate.

"I'm only going to get one chance at this and I'd like to make sure I pick the right area to start."

Marc looked at me with concern, sighed, and nodded while the rest of the team demurred and then agreed. The fog started lifting but the ground was damp and the air was still cold. The Rover's heater was on the blink, so the crew got back into the van to wait. Marc went with me.

"How'd you get them to stay?" I asked as he and I followed an old trail to the top. Oh Lord, I could tell I was having an attack of what my mother called "run of the mouth." I couldn't stop talking. It sometimes happened when I was nervous or happy. She could slow me down by holding her finger up, but she wasn't here. So, without any reason to stop, I continued, "When you knocked on my door this morning, I thought it was to say goodbye and please drop off the Rover when I was done. Then I opened the door and there you were, standing with the trowel in your hand and a smile on your face. I was quite taken aback! By the way, did you have Mrs. Dingleberry pack us a big lunch? I didn't have time to eat breakfast, as you know." I ran out of breath.

Marc shook his head and chuckled.

We reached the top of the hill. Sunlight and warmth filled the last steps of the trail and we surveyed the scene below. The valley was still invisible and I imagined this is what Noah saw after landing on Mount Ararat. It was a sea of grey, nothing but the ground we stood on and the mountain behind us visible.

"It was fun to see you so flummoxed," said Marc, "and I've never seen you speechless before. You certainly are back to normal. When we were dating, I barely ever got a word in edgewise. Anyway, last night I explained the job offer in Wales. Then I said to think of the opportunity of finding a new location in Scotland. I told them to imagine being the first team on a new dig and all the exciting things that could come of it. Finally, I asked them to compare it to being one of many on an established dig in Wales and getting paid. They of course, being of sound minds, chose Wales. I then implored and finally retreated by offering them £500 each if they stayed for the rest of the week. They said they'd stay four days. No pressure on you or anything but something had better come up out of the ground fast."

Looking over the edge of the hill, I asked, "Where are you going to get £2000 to pay them with?"

Marc reached out and touched my arm. I turned, not knowing what to expect and still feeling the possibility of loss in my stomach. His eyes were the lapis blue I remembered from our university days, the color I saw when, together, we made plans for the future, plans to conquer history. The feeling of loss was replaced with something else. Confusion. Why did it feel like I'd been standing beside him, in this place, forever?

"Aine. I've almost enjoyed this last month, gathering the crew together and getting here. I'd thought of it as a challenge."

He paused, shuffling from one foot to the other, his hands deep in his pockets. "And I have to admit, a way to get to know you again." His hands came out of his pockets and ran through his hair. "I'm sorry I was such an ass last night. Doug's call took me by surprise. Why don't we call a truce and see what the next few days bring? I thought it over after we talked in your room last night. I spoke to them," he said, pointing down the hill, "after I'd already decided I'd stay for a week. I told myself, 'just pretend it's a small vacation.' God knows I won't get one for a long time if I go to Wales. So I'll just sit tight and let the youngsters do all the hard work and I'll man the computer. The money will either come out of the grants you'll get from this dig or you'll sell everything you own to pay them," he said, looking at me with a sly grin.

"Oh God. I'm already in debt up to my armpits. Oh well. If all goes like I know it will, we won't have to worry about anything anyway. And you won't have to go to Wales. We'll have all the money we need."

Suddenly serious, I asked, "Marc, will you be unhappy here?"

"I had doubts earlier and still have a few, but I made the choice to stay. Heaven knows why, but I'm going to make the most of it, even if only for a week."

Marc and I walked around the edge of the hill. I stopped every so often and bent to touch the ground. Then I could smell peat fires around me. I heard animals in their corrals and felt the vibrating footsteps of people. This was where I was supposed to start. I turned to Marc. "We'll start digging here."

The fog cleared enough to see the bottom of the hill. We waved to the van and they came tumbling out and grabbed the little equipment we had: stakes and twine to mark the quadrants, and spades, trowels, brushes, and sifting screens for digging.

After trudging up the path, Tim marked the area I pointed to with the stakes and twine and asked me why I'd picked it. "It just felt right," I answered. I didn't tell him a warm feeling came over me as I felt the ground, a feeling that raised the hair on the back of my neck. Jahna had touched me.

After marking the quadrants, we started removing and sifting the first layers of topsoil.

We found the first pieces of pottery just before we left for the day. We were using hand trowels to remove the soil at that point but the ground wasn't difficult to dig in after we cut through the sod with the shovels. The sun hid behind clouds and we stayed cool even though we worked hard. We'd been digging for several hours and found nothing when I decided to take a short break to watch the sifting.

Matt balanced our square-frame screen on his hip. On the other side, it was supported by pieces of lumber attached to the screen frame. The soil that was going through the screen created a pile at his feet. The rocks that came up were tossed to the right of him and anything that he felt needed a closer look was laid to his left, in a bucket. So far, the bucket was empty. I watched as three small pieces of pottery emerged from the debris and lay on the screen along with the larger pebbles. Matt stopped shaking the screen and looked at me with anticipation. The pieces were dirt-covered and might have been overlooked by an amateur. With experience, you get an eye that searches for anything that looks as if it were man-made. I picked them up and looked for signs of age.

"They are coil pots," I observed, brushing off some of the soil. I walked them over to Marc and handed them to him. He looked at them and said, "Yes, this could be good news. I don't think we should break out the champagne yet, though." He handed them back to me and said, "I hope there's more. Lots more."

That night, back at the inn, I asked Marc to call and ask George Wyemouth to come while I was on the phone looking for more money for the project. I now had employees and tests to pay for. With George's connections to labs he could get our items carbon dated quickly. Without his help, it would take months to get results. I didn't have months.

In the second of my four days, we found a bronze blade similar to the one the farmer showed me last fall, more pottery, and two postholes. I was giddy after the postholes became visible. "This could be the reason to open a bottle of champagne!" I laughed. Marc stood next to me and I pulled myself up on tiptoes to kiss him. As I started to go back to level ground, he grabbed my waist, looked into my eyes, and said, "Congratulations, Aine. You may have a viable site." He let me down and shrugging his shoulders said, "And I may have to stay another week just to see exactly what is here."

I don't usually notice sunsets while I'm working. At that time of the day, I am in the tent, helping sort all the items we'd exhumed during the day. This one, however, pulled me into a whorl of feelings. I noticed the pink colors floating around me while I was walking from the tent to the Rover to get my coat. I glanced up at the sky but I wasn't expecting the grandeur that overcame me. The daytime scattered alabaster cumulous, and steel gray nimbus clouds wore edges of cyclamen pink. The sun was just sitting on the cusp of the three hills across the pasture.

"Everybody, come see this! Wow!" I said.

Lauri and Kendy came out of the tent and looked around. Kendy said, "It's beautiful. Sunset is the best time of the day. I use these colors in my art at home all the time. They are so peaceful."

Lauri continued, "Ohh. It's wonderful. Whew, just look at those clouds on the horizon, though. I'm sure glad we covered everything. I think we may have a gusher tonight." Tarps, weighted with stones, covered our working area.

Marc walked over, and I shivered in the cooling air. I snuggled into the warm curve his arm and shoulder made as he opened up his coat and gathered me into it. I sighed, knowing I could get into trouble with this man all too easily. I felt a stirring of interest in his body vibrations and wondered what he was thinking.

"I don't think I've taken the time to see one of these in a long time. It's pretty good," Marc said. He turned to take in the sight behind us. "Look! Up on the trail. There's a last bit of sunlight hitting that pile of rocks. It looks like a beam from a ray gun on a spaceship! Kapowie! Rocks and bad guys, gone! Hey, is there a good movie playing in town?"

The mood ruined, I said, "I swear I'll never get used to you guys and your lack of romance. Just go and let me look for a few minutes." I shoved him off with my hands. He left his coat on my shoulders and walked to the Rover to get CDs to use for a backup for his computer.

The sky went from a light blue to a smoky-lavendar in about two minutes and the clouds from rose to mauve with it. I was enjoying every moment and turned back to the mountain behind us to look at the trail where Marc's imaginative laser beam was pointed. The light was still being concentrated on the spot through a trick of the clouds, but a few shadows were beginning to creep up. Suddenly, I knew I needed to go get a closer look at that pile of rocks. No big revelation or scene in my head, just the certain knowledge that I was going there tomorrow. If it did rain, I hoped the weather cooperated and the rain would stop early in the morning. I didn't want to climb it in a storm, but there wasn't a question of going; I was going. I memorized the rocks and boulders nearby, and knew I could find it in the morning.

Back at the tent, the team was talking about the latest sci-fi movie they'd seen and the one they hoped to catch tonight. "Aine, we're going into town for dinner and to catch a movie. Coming?" Marc asked.

"Sure, this may be the last good night out I get for awhile," I said, knowing my evenings would be taken up by deciphering the day's work the further along we got. I wanted this dig to be perfect.

"Let's take the Rover and the van so we don't have to cram into one car," suggested Marc. "Put the box of pottery and the blade in the back of the van and Matt and I'll take it to Mrs. Dingleberry's. Tim can take the rover with Aine, Kendy and Lauri and we'll meet you there."

We got into Fort William about an hour later and found a café next to the movie theater that was showing the film we wanted to see. It was one of the Ring movies, and we were all excited to have a night off to enjoy it. Marc and Matt arrived thirty minutes behind us.

"Marc," I asked, "how long until the registration of the site is done, and when is George getting here?"

"A few days, and tomorrow. The Scottish Historical Association will process our request for listing on the monuments list, and George will get in on the morning train. I thought you and I could wait here tonight and bring him back to the dig in the morning. He gets in around eight," said Marc.

A chorus of catcalls and laughter went up from the rest of the team at that suggestion. The other customers in the café looked at us, and found a noisy group of disheveled friends.

"No wonder you wanted to bring two cars. We thought that was a bit extravagant of the tight Scotsman in you, Marc," said Lauri. "A night in town with a lady!"

"No, no!" Marc said. "I was thinking of your comfort! Tim is always complaining about not having enough room for his 6'5" frame and size 13 feet!"

"Now don't you go pinning this on me, Marc. I can fold up nicely when needed," said Tim.

I listened. Heat climbed up my back, around my neck and infused my face at these remarks. "If Marc and I decide to stay, it will be in separate rooms. There is nothing else to it, and I will thank you to stop this!" I said. "Anyway, I didn't bring clothes or anything else for overnight so I probably won't stay."

Marc said, "Don't worry, there's a small shop where we can get whatever we need."

That encouraged them, of course, and when we got into the movie, I was upset with Marc for putting me into this position. I angled my way around everyone else until I stood next to him as we slipped into our seats. "What was that all about? What've you been saying to them that has them thinking we are a couple?"

I wondered if I wanted us to be a couple. What would be wrong with having Marc as my lover? *No, I don't want anything permanent now. I've work to do to get my career on track. But just one night, what could that hurt?* I searched through my pockets for my antacids.

Just the truth," he said. "I told them we enjoy working together, that I respect your knowledge and decisions and would follow you to the ends of the earth if you asked." His eyes told me he was teasing.

I turned to slap his shoulder in response, and he gently caught my wrist. I tried to twist it away and was surprised by his eyes. They sparkled. They actually sparkled in that dim theater light. He smiled and kissed my fingertips. I gasped, then, unasked, my fingers touched his lips and my eyes welled with unshed tears. The movie started, and he held my hand through to the end. I don't remember the plot.

The exiting crowd escorted us outside. "Thank heavens the rain hasn't started. I hate driving on these single lane roads in the dark as it is. I can't imagine doing it in a storm, too," Matt complained.

"What? Driving in London is easier? Don't be a bloody galoot! Just pull into the turnouts when you see headlights and wait for them to pass. The Hielans will appreciate you not trying to race them through the straights. Too many tourists try that and lose so let's keep the natives happy, right?" said Marc, reaching into the van and pulling out an overnight bag. *How unfair that he packed for tonight and I didn't.*

"Yes, we Highlanders use our road kill in haggis, remember? So do take care on the lo-o-ong road back," Matt said. I laughed. They climbed into the van and waved as they left.

"I have reservations at the Caorann Inn for us. Come on let's walk. It's a few blocks from here."

"Right. I'm glad it isn't raining. It'd be a mess to work in the morning if it were. I've something I want to look at, and I wouldn't want to do it in a storm." *Here I go again. Why do I feel the need to talk? I know. Being alone with Marc is making me nervous. I want to be here but what do I expect?* "I'm glad George is coming. I know we'll find something great and I want him here to see it. He's helped me all through my career, and even before, in school. I appreciate him."

"Aine!"

"Yes?"

"Shut up!"

We walked quietly the rest of the way to the inn, watched over by Ben Nevis, the air smelling of the expected rain.

The inn was built with the magpie construction that was so popular, trying to look historical. It was modern inside, and I was glad to see the farce wasn't carried any farther than the exterior. Marc had reserved one room with twin beds.

"When I called, they were full except for this room. We've shared tents before so I figured we could share this room.

I thought of calling somewhere else, but I've stayed here and liked the location, the view, and the name of this place. So...."

As I walked to the window, I noticed the room smelled like Mrs. Dinglberry's inn, lemon wood wax. I lifted the curtains and said, "There's a gorgeous view of the mountains, even with the clouded sky. But the name? *Caorann*? Rowan? Why do you like the name?"

"It's the wizard tree. I thought I could use a bit of magic to get you to stay here tonight. It is my favorite tree because of its magic. Wizards, witching wands and such."

"Hmm. Well, here we are," I said as I turned to the hospital-cornered beds. "Which bed do you want? These are longer than the beds at our inn. I'll bet your toes hang out over the end of those elfin beds," I said, chuckling. "This will be a treat for you tonight. Well, I need to go to the store to get the things I need for tonight. Where did you say it was; close by?"

"Not too far, but I don't think you'll need much," he said as he picked up the overnight bag, opened it and dumped it out on the bed. Out fell his change of underwear, toothbrush, and shirt, followed by my undies, bra, shirt, and shampoo. He'd even remembered to bring my toothbrush and hairbrush.

Surprised, I went through the items. "Wow. You take big chances, Marc. How'd you know I'd say yes to staying?"

"I knew you couldn't resist helping me pick up George. Here," he said, unzipping a side pocket of the bag. "I hope you won't be upset by my touching it without your permission, but I hoped you'd share a bit with me tonight." He pulled out my precious bottle of Lagavulin, wrapped in a towel.

"Oh, thank you, this is perfect. A dram of the lovely will hit the spot right now. Would you pour for both of us, please?"

We made ourselves comfortable in the overstuffed armchairs that crowded the room, sipped our drinks, and discussed the day. "We'd a bit of good luck finding more pottery and the set of postholes today. The pottery should be able to give us a date. The postholes are a sign of inhabitation. We may have a hillfort!" I said. "My name will finally be first on an excavation report. I've been waiting a very long time for that to happen."

"Yes, I agree, it looks as if there might be something here. Let's give it a bit more time before we start claiming what it is, however. It could be a simple travel hut for a hunter, and we won't find anything else. We've only been digging two days. You should've heard the story I told George to get him to come here! You're going to owe me for a long time. We'd better find something big soon, or he may disown you as a friend." Marc smiled. "But don't worry. Yes, your name can go on the report first."

Suddenly, a flash over-filled the room with light followed by a loud, rolling, rumble reminding me of boulders being tossed in a flooding riverbed.

"What the–? Oh my gosh. It must be pouring," I said as I got up and walked to the window. It was covered in rivers of water.

I'd been standing there but a few seconds when Marc came up behind me. I felt his body heat. *Oh, please touch me,* I thought. My breath left my body in a rush. I loved this man, I was just realizing it again after so many years. My mind was spinning. After Brad, I swore off love forever. Marc kissed the back of my neck.

That did it, any resistance I'd had was gone. And he knew it. I melted against him and he caught me in the circle of his arms. He smelled like the ancient earth that we were digging in today, full of mystery and truths. I turned to face him on tiptoe, barely reaching his Adam's apple, and kissed him as he leaned his face down to mine. His beard was softer than I thought it would be, and I inhaled the fumes of the aged Lagavulin on his breath. I reveled in the sense of protection I found next to him. His hands came up into my hair and cradled my head. I was enchanted. Yes, Caorann was the right name for this inn.

We broke apart, breathless. I looked into his eyes. "Marc. Where did this come from?"

He wrapped his arm around my waist, and said, "Aine, I loved Darlene. I'm glad I'd those years with her." He paused for the length of one breath. "But, you were my first love. I was working up the courage to ask you to marry me when Brad stepped into the picture so many years ago. It killed me to watch your career fall by the wayside, and I thought you were out of my life forever. I tried to tell you that he wasn't doing right by you a long time ago but couldn't."

"You knew and just stood back and watched?"

"You needed to find out on your own what a loser he was and fight it on your own. That was the only way you'd be free from him," he said.

Memories slammed into me, and I tried to catch my breath as he said, "Look Aine. I was disturbed when I left your room the other night, but I figured I've known you for a long time and you've made some stupid decisions in your life but you've never seemed crazy. I don't owe you anything. Hell, you owe me. You left me for Brad."

I cringed when I heard the pain in his voice but kept my eyes on his. There was nothing I could say in the face of the truth of his words.

"I went a bit crazy for a while. I decided that I'd never love anyone else. I was really messed up. I followed everything that you and Brad did and watched you as he took your life away. Don't get me wrong. Darlene was wonderful. I'm glad she was a part of my life and I never cheated on her. I loved her and she still has a place in my heart but she never took your place. You had a hold on me that I can't explain. I never seemed whole. Now, maybe we've another chance, and even though I am scared of getting hurt again I don't want to miss it."

I stood rooted to the floor, not able to move. I was petrified and humbled. He was trying to forgive me. Tears stung my eyes. "I am sorry, Marc. What I did was so wrong. I've no excuses. But I think I paid for it."

"Yes, I guess you did." He circled me again, with his gentle bear hug, lowered his head and used his mouth to cover mine in a deep, long kiss. I tasted the tip of his tongue. Feelings of order, of things being right in the universe, came over me. I'd not felt this way since he and I were together in college. He was my life partner, my teacher, and my love.

"Aine?"

"Um, yes?" I answered, breathing fast.

"I wanted to do this right. Is this romantic enough?" he whispered into my ear.

"Shut up."

One of his hands came down from my hair and settled in the small of my back and pulled me closer.

We didn't want to let go of each other and waddled to the closest bed. I began to laugh, and Marc covered my mouth with his and gave me something else to do. Oh my God, it'd been years since I last made love, wanted to make love, and I'd feelings I thought were gone forever. My heart tattooed against my chest, my breath was ragged, and my conscious thoughts were gone. I'd one thing on my mind, and from his reactions, fast breathing, drumming heartbeat, and one noticeably hard item, I knew he felt the same way.

We sat on the edge of the bed and Marc's hands began to explore my back. He grabbed my tucked in shirt and began to pull it out of my pants. We were still kissing but without the earlier panic. We knew we'd be here for each other and time didn't matter. My shirt was above my waist, and his warm hands touched my cool skin. Fire and ice. I melted even more. His hands crept up under my shirt and came to my bra. I knew one truth: if he stopped for any reason, I'd die. I prayed he knew how to undo this bra. He did. His fingers cupped my breasts, and his thumbs circled and gently pinched my nipples.

I pulled back from him, unbuttoned the top two buttons on my shirt, and pulled it over my head. He let my bra slip to the ground.

"Aine. You're perfect. I knew you'd be. Beautiful," he said as he lowered his mouth to a nipple, licked and sucked it. My back arched to meet his mouth and I gasped.

Now, I wanted more. "Let's get your shirt off," I said. I reached over and started to unbutton it when he jerked the shirt off, popping a button across the room. "I brought another shirt for tomorrow, don't worry," he said, and grinning, when he saw my surprise.

He turned the lamp off, and the only light in the room came from under the bathroom door, just enough to let us see what was necessary. We pulled off the rest of our clothes, climbed under the down spread and started kissing again, his tongue exploring my mouth and mine teasing his. His hands were velvet, rubbing all over my body. He explored tender spots not touched in years and I was ready to explode. I brushed my hands down his furry chest, into the curve of his taut waist. His stomach began to vibrate and heard an intake of his breath. I slid my hands down his thighs. This time he arched and groaned. We were together in lust and love.

When it was over, I cried tears of completion and happiness. I kissed his neck and shoulders as he lay on top of me. He wasn't heavy. I wanted to be covered by him, still have him inside me, kissing the top of my head for a very long time. When he rolled off, I rolled with him and snuggled. "The world seems right when I'm with you," I said. "I think I'll need a lot of this."

"Me too. Do you think we stand a chance?"

"God, I hope so. I hope you can forgive me. I'll try to make it up." I kissed his hairy cheek. "I want another drink. Do you?" I scooted out of bed, found his shirt and put it on against the coolness of the room. I poured two fingers of scotch into our glasses. Sniffing the pungent odor of iodine and peat mixed, I handed the tumblers to him to hold as I climbed into the bed. I piled my pillows against the headboard, and retrieved my drink. He balanced on one elbow, took a swallow, and looked at me.

"After I sew the buttons back on, I think I'll give you that shirt, it never looked like that on me," he teased.

"Humm. Cute. Sounds like a beach romance."

Suddenly, I smelled a very strong scent. "Do you smell it? Do you smell the smoke?" I asked, sniffing and turning to Marc. I saw the confused look in his eyes and said, "She's here. I smell peat smoke. Get me some paper and a pen. Quick, from the desk drawer, hotel stationary, anything. Just get it." He brought them back as I sat my glass on the floor. I took the pen and paper from him just as her thoughts started running through my mind.

"Who is here? What's wrong?" demanded Marc.

"I'm fine. Just let me be quiet for a few minutes and then I'll tell you."

Jahna was here. I closed my eyes and let her thoughts put pictures into my head. She stood in the spot on the mountain where the sun shone at sunset. She was there with someone, looking back at her village. Several homes stood on the hilltop, farms in the surrounding valley and three hills in the distance. I could feel her happiness. She loved this spot and she shared it with those she loved, a man and a child, their daughter. I could feel the two standing beside me. I saw her home, the one closest to the gate, with the unusual small alcove. Something was heavy in my hands. She looked at a bronze bowl. It wasn't the one I found last year, this one was different. A big, red forest fox ran in across the path in front of them. My mind went blank. The pictures were gone. Jahna was gone. I wrote down what I could remember, although the scene seemed burned into my head. I wrote about the sights and feelings that ran through my mind and drew a picture of the bowl. I sketched three ravens as I saw them on the outside of the bowl. When I was done, I slumped in exhaustion, and the paper and pen fell to my lap.

Marc leaned over and took me into his arms. "What the hell was that? I thought you were having some sort of seizure or something, and then you started writing. What happened?"

"I'm sorry, but Jahna came. I felt her touching me several times today and wanted to get everything she told me on paper so I didn't forget it. I saw the hill-fort, Marc. It's there!"

"Your ghost? Your invisible friend, Jahna?" he asked as he leaned back on his pillows. "Did she show you where to find some money to pay the crew with?"

I remembered the invisible friend poem my girlfriend made up when we were kids. I picked up my glass of scotch, put my folded notes in my pants pocket so I'd find them tomorrow, and went into the bathroom to take a shower. I didn't say a word.

I had just stepped under the hot spray when the bathroom door opened, and Marc walked in. "All right. I'm sorry. I promise to try not to make fun of you about this again." I thought about his apology for a nanosecond, accepted it, and invited him into the shower with me. He kissed me and we made soapy love again under the warm spray of the shower.

The next morning we rose early, breakfasted, and walked to the train station. The rain stopped about an hour before we went out, but the air still hung heavy with the ozone from the lightning storm. The gutters were full of fast-running water as we crossed the streets.

We arrived at the train station by seven-thirty. People were milling everywhere waiting for the train from London to arrive. Some waited to greet lovers and family and others with luggage were ready to start an adventure. A loud din surrounded us. I glanced up at Marc as he looked out over the crowd. I grasped his arm to keep him close, and he leaned to hear me. "I know what happens to me is very hard for you to believe. It would be hard for me to believe except I'm living it. I've never told anyone else, not even Brad, and I want to keep it that way. Please don't mention it unless we are alone."

"Okay. I haven't and won't tell anyone until you do. By the way, do you get warnings when this is going to happen? Does it ever happen when you're driving?"

"Yes, I smell peat smoke. Sometimes just a whiff and sometimes it's thick. Last night it was heavy and no, it's never happened while I was concentrating on something, like driving. I need to be relaxed."

"Good. Let me know when you smell it and I can get a drink and turn on the TV so you two can converse in peace," he suggested as he continued to survey the crowd.

Pulling on his sleeve to get him to look at me, I asked, "Marc, all this must seem strange to you but you're still here. Why? Most people would've run at my first mention of Jahna. I couldn't believe you didn't go downstairs and tell the team about her. I was surprised the next morning when you weren't on your way to Wales and you're still here after last night. Why did you stay?"

He pursed his lips and nodded as if deciding to answer my question was difficult.

"Okay. Here's my confession. I don't know if I believe in ghosts, but I've an aunt in Ireland who talks to the dead, or so she says. My uncle says she got bored with him and wanted to bring some excitement into their marriage. She says that isn't true, but she does love being fey. My uncle doesn't fully believe her but says it doesn't harm anyone. No one else admits to it although my cousin seems a bit strange at times. Of course, that could be just because she lives in Ireland. They seem happy. And, ghosts are a big part of this island. They're woven into our history. And who knows, this may be that one piece of information that will lead us to our pot of gold under the rainbow," he said, shrugging his shoulders.

Thank God for his Irish aunt. I decided I'd have to meet her someday.

The train arrived in all its thunder and confusion. We watched for George among the detraining passengers, me jumping up and down trying to see past the bodies of those around us, Marc calmly looking over the heads of the crowd.

Then Marc waved and yelled, "George! Hi! Over here!"

CHAPTER 9

JAHNA

75 AD MAY-JUNE

The oak fires of Beltane were cold, the home fires cleansed and restarted. The proper sacrifices were made and rituals observed. Lovern had seen his fox vixen with two new pups this spring so all was well in his mind. Mine was dark with foreboding. In it lay a heaviness that did not allow recognition.

Twelve bloody moons had passed since our marriage. I slept with mistletoe under my head, and making a sacrifice to the god Lug often crossed my mind. Lovern had not voiced any concern about my not being with child. He told me what the gods wanted to happen would happen in their time. I was the impatient one.

My mother requested – no, demanded a grandchild. I hoped to give her one before she died. My mother, at forty sun cycles, was one of the last of her generation. All her childhood friends were gone and she bemoaned it every day. Gray now streaked her bronze hair, and her blood cough caused her to lose strength. She wasted, eating only soup. I worried that I would not be able to ease her pain.

She had coughed blood last month, even with our treatments. I knew from the experiences of the others that we could not stop the course of the illness, but I hoped we could slow it. We made her comfortable. I was selfish and did not want her to go before she held my child. I used this to explain the darkness in my mind.

Beathan passed thirty-eight sun cycles, and was now the oldest among his warriors. He swore he had not lost any strength. However, he walked slower, and sometimes could not count hogs in a pen at a distance the way he used to. Streaks of white ran through his beard. He had shades of gray near his ears he tried to hide when liming his hair.

The *seanmhair* of our clan was almost sixty sun-cycles and revered. A grandmother many times over, she revealed stories of her youth during our festivals.

"My father and brother died in battle against other clans. My first husband's head hung off the rail of an enemy's war chariot, the fourth summer we were married." She always started her tales with these sad memories. "You complain of hardships but you do not know of those we suffered when we were young." The snowstorms in her youth were fiercer than ours and the stream flooded every year. "Beathan's peace has made you soft. You may come to regret not having to stay fit by fighting every day," she told us.

She could not walk. Carried to the festivals, they said she was as light as a seed. She ate food that someone else chewed. Her breasts hung to her waist, and her face was lined with the tracks of many sorrows. Her hair, still long and plaited on top of her head in our fashion, was the color of the wispy clouds that came before a rain. Goddess be blessed, her mind was clear. She and I spoke often. She had in her memory many cures from the old times. Sometimes when we were together, she sat and stared at me.

"Why do you look at me so, *Seanmhair?*"

"I see no age in your face. It is the face of a youth. No age lines like mine. I see no age lines in your future," she said. "Always be at peace with our gods. You will not live long."

I shivered. I have lived through nineteen growing seasons. How many more would the gods give me?

A dal was called after our last Samhainn. All the valley clans attended the meeting. Lovern and Beathan represented our clan. It was there Lovern learned that the sea grass harvest on the coast brought in several rare kinds this year and that the tradesman who brought these to us died on his last trip. Lovern wanted to go gather the sea grass. We had many uses for it, such as thick-neck, aching of the joints, sick stomach, aches of the head, and the expelling of afterbirth. There were healing quartz stones on the beaches as well.

"I have not seen the sea from this coast. I would like to go and gather as much as two ponies can carry. If I stay long enough to dry it before packing, I can bring more home."

"I cannot go," I said. "Mother is not well and there are the plants that are ready to harvest here that I must take care of. The winter rains stopped early, and we will lose the plants in bloom if not gathered now. We need the seaweed. You must go. I ask that you take Braden with you for companionship and another sword if needed. I am afraid. The Romans are beginning to cross the line they have not crossed before. It is true, you will be headed away from them, but you do not know who might meet you in the dark."

"My wish is not to fight, but you are right. It is auspicious to have three go. I will ask Beathan for Callum to also accompany Braden and me."

Beathan was reluctant to let another warrior or pony leave his stable. He asked me whether I foresaw any battles in our clan's future that might require the warriors Lovern requested.

"I dreamed a badger was overtaken by a bear and two wolves. The dream ended with much blood, but the badger lay dead and three ponies were on the trail leading to our clan," I responded. I saw the future more often now. I accepted it as another gift from the gods.

"Unnh," said Beathan. "There will be a fight. But, if you saw the badger taken by a bear, then good, I am the bear. I never lose a battle. My sons and other warriors who live under the sign of the wolf will be here. Braden and Callum have other signs. They can go, Druid. Take three ponies. Use your own backs to carry supplies or find a way to trade for another pony," he growled and lumbered away to attend to the clan council.

"To cross the mountains, gather and dry the sea grass, you will be gone at least three moons. You need something to trade for food and supplies. Take the blue dye and iron pin I use for tattoos. Copy the patterns and the spirals from our labyrinth that I tattooed on you, Braden and Callum. The symbols will be unknown where you go." I traced one up his arm. "Warriors and others will want these and animal symbols. If you tattoo a chieftain or high warrior you can trade for a pony and come home faster."

Bags filled with dried pork, barley, and bitter vetch to quell hunger, barely gave room to sit on the three smallest ponies from Beathan's herd. When I saw the size of the ponies, I went to Beathan. He told me that Lovern was lucky to get them and if I complained again, he would find even those small ponies lame and unable to travel.

"Uncle, you are a very stubborn man. We have done much to help your clan, our clan. Lovern is going on this journey to gather healing plants and yet you do not wish to make the trip easy. If you become ill in the middle of the night, remember that I sleep deeply and will not get up until the sun does!"

I slammed his door as I left. His laughter and "I never become ill!" followed me.

Braden, the warrior I fawned after like a puppy in my youth, and Callum gathered at our door at dawn on the next morning. I studied Braden and compared the differences between him and Lovern. Braden was much thicker around his waist now, and his nose was always red. These were signs of much mead every day. He was noisy and was always fighting. He was a good warrior but not a good husband.

Lovern had passed twenty-three sun cycles. His body was still lean. Quiet, he often meditated. He drank mead sparingly, and ate lightly. He and I kept many long hours, but our energy did not lag. He was the perfect mate for me.

The sun peaked over the top of the mountain behind Lovern and his hair glistened with the red gold of its light. I handed him the small jug of blue woad dye, stoppered with a piece of oak branch, and my sharp iron pin. It was threaded into a piece of my plaid.

"Keep these near your heart. They will remind you of me through the long nights you are gone."

"Ahh, Jahna. I have traveled before and have never forgotten you. Do not my homecoming nights, wrapped in your arms, prove that? My body sometimes remembers even when I should be thinking of other things. This is the longest time I will be gone, but I will return to you."

I smiled, my throat catching my breath, not allowing me to speak. I swallowed my tears.

He pulled a small leather bag from his tunic. "I made this for you. You will have our labyrinth with you always. Your stone is beautiful but too large to carry," he said smiling.

It was fashioned after his memory bag; its labyrinth was smaller but more detailed than his. I clutched it close to my heart and bit the tip of my tongue, tasting blood, so I would not cry and spot it with tears of loneliness.

I drew my dirk, raised it to the hair that fell around his shoulders and cut off a curl. A lock of my own raven black hair joined his. I mixed them together until his gold sparkled amid mine. I kissed it and then handed half to him. We opened our memory bags and placed the precious token inside.

"We will be near each other always," I said.

He gathered me into his arms; his nose buried in my hair, my head filling with his scent and whispered, "Your hair smells of the heather in our bed. If you need me, I will feel you. Dream of me, Jahna. Ask me and I will come. Just dream."

He mounted his restless pony, turned, and said, "Do not be at odds with Beathan. He is stubborn, like you, but he is my friend and he has given us much."

I nodded. He rode to the gate where Braden and Callum were waiting and the three trotted down the trail, away from me.

Lovern had been gone one full cycle of the moon. Twenty-eight sunrises. I counted his absence by sunrises because each greeted me after another restless night without him. I worked hard to pass the days.

Sileas told me we needed to re-supply our meadowsweet. The deceptive meadowsweet, cursed in my memories. I could not smell or think on it after this day without gagging. Its creamy blossoms, though sweet scented, released a strong odor when crushed. It was used to relieve headaches, fevers, and pain. The flower was blooming in the meadow near the creek at the edge of the forest. I had been there often but never ventured farther. It was a full day's ride from the hill.

Beathan gave me the use of one of his older ponies, a mare that gave birth to many strong colts. I was not in a hurry, and her gentle ride would help the time pass. I was ready to spend the night there, alone, and ride back the next day. If Beathan had known I was going alone, he would not have allowed me to go.

I told my mother I would be home for the next day's evening meal and put some dried pork and bread in my pocket. It was a warm day. I did not take my cape, but dressed in the green dress Lovern said turned my eyes mistletoe green. I smiled at the thought and slung my memory bag over my shoulder.

At the meadow, I tied the pony on a bush near the creek. There was long grass for her to nibble.

The day was beautiful. The harvested flowers gifted the air with the aroma of cleanliness. I filled and tied my cloth. Finches flitted from branch to branch on the edge of the meadow in a great chorus of feeding. My pony joined in the sounds of nature surrounding us. She gave a soft, contented whinny. I arched up, my arms stretched over my head to the blue sky, and took in a deep breath. The warmth of the sun filled the air. Overhead, I followed the hunting glide of a falcon. Sometimes I likened my passage dreams and visions to being able to fly like a falcon. When I had passage dreams, I was out of my earth body and able to go great distances unencumbered. I gave thanks to Morrigna. I had one regret: I wished to share this day with Lovern.

When my right leg gave way, I fell to the ground. Not understanding what happened, I looked at my leg and saw an arrow piercing my thigh, from back to front. How did it get there? Swift pain took my breath and senses away, and then I smelled him.

The rancid stench of rotting eggs and piss blanketed me, and I vomited.

"Bitch. That is no way to greet your master."

The first time I felt him there was more pain; he grabbed my long hair and jerked my head back. He stood above me, the bow and unused arrows in his other hand. I had a quick view of a short, unkempt man. My last sight before I fainted was his black-bearded grimy face, broken with a sneer.

I woke to the jolting gait of my mare. I was loaded across her back, and tied ankles to hands under her belly. I groaned as I tried to move my head around to clean air. My leg burned as nothing I had ever felt before. I saw blood dripping from my foot and knew my wound was bleeding.

"Shut up, bitch. Do not cry out. It will not help you."

I felt a sharp pain behind my ear and then nothing.

The sickening, rocking motion had stopped. I was off my pony and lying on the ground. I smelled the earth as well as the foulness of the man. I tried not to move as I slowly opened my eyes. The light was dim, but I could see a hollow under an overhang of a hillside. He had built a wall of branches and logs. I looked further and saw I was alone, so I tried to move. My leg pounded, and I had an intense thirst; my mouth was sticky.

The arrow was gone from my leg. I had treated a similar wound in a warrior's leg who had been shot while hunting. The arrow was not difficult to remove. He lived. I had hope.

My bone was not broken, but I could not move my leg without the risk of fainting from the pain and restarting the bleeding. It was wrapped in a dirty rag. I prayed blood poison would not take hold, but in this hut, poison thrived. A thought ran through my head. *I might not live long enough for blood poison to be a worry.*

My hands were tightly bound in front of me with a braided cord, tied to an iron ring and attached to a peg in the ground. I tugged, but it was secure. Startled, I watched as the corner of the wooden wall lifted and the man crawled in.

"You are awake. Good. I want you to feel what I do to you."

I tried to roll away and fold my knees into my belly, but I cried out at the sharp stab of fire-like pain. I watched in horror as he came closer.

"Don't worry, bitch, you will not need to move. I will move for both of us," he said with a yellow grin.

The dim light filtered in through the wooden wall, but it was enough for me to see him. Long, greasy, mouse-brown hair covered his head. The angular bones of his narrow eye sockets jutted out above a beard that hid the lower part of his face. His lips were barely visible through the tangle. His pitted and scabbed nose ended in a point. He panted through his open mouth and I saw the holes of missing teeth. I smelled rot in his breath as he drew closer. He used his gnarled and filthy hands to drag himself across the dirt to me. He carried my small dirk clasped in one hand and the other, open on the ground, had only three fingers and thumb. The first finger of that hand was missing, gone at the joint. I recognized that sign. He was a slave.

"You are mine. I am owed," oozed out of his mouth.

Burning bile rose into my throat as he crept closer, like a venomous snake.

Never before was I this afraid. I had no way to protect myself and would become his victim. I knew the deep fear of feeling lost-the fear of a soul dying alone.

He was on me. I could not move. His filth-encrusted body rose to half-sitting as he reached over and cut off the green dress that Lovern loved. I screamed and writhed and he hit my face with a closed fist. His rough hands covered my breasts.

"The bitches at the camp were not like you. Dirty camp followers. They gave themselves to who ever had money or food. Not loyal to anyone. You, I will not share."

His mouth covered my breast, and I screamed as he bit me.

He struggled to get his ragged tunic above his waist and when he had it tucked into his belt, he forced his knees between my bare thighs. The only covering I had now was the filthy bandage around my wound. I could see his swollen penis, as he held it in his hand, ready to force it into me.

"No! No! No! Morrigna, protect me!" I cried and tried to squirm away. My tied wrists and his body weight stopped me. The goddess must have been sleeping; she did not come. His full thrust into me and his weight on my wound pushed me into oblivion.

It was dark when I became aware again. I heard him snoring in a corner of the hollow. The cave filled with the acrid smell of his piss and rotting teeth. I rolled to my side and vomited again. Only bile came as I had not eaten nor drunk for many hours. I had no hunger, but my thirst was overwhelming. I knew it came because of the loss of blood. My swollen hands and joints began to ache from not being able to move freely. I was desolate, without hope. Abandonment, thoughts of no rescue, fueled the fire of my fear. I had no idea how far we were from the clan and did not know whether my blood left a trail to follow.

Then I remembered my labyrinths. Both my stone and the bag Lovern gave me. A hollow feeling of loss twisted my gut when I realized I might never see my memory bag again. If I stayed at this level of consciousness, I feared I would lose my mind. I had to escape. I brought my painted stone into my mind. I pictured the red and blue path surrounded by nature as I had painted it. I placed my forefinger on the path and followed as it led to the center, back out, and then in again. My breath calmed, and my muscles relaxed. Sudden wavelets of fear ripped through me, but I was able to contain them, to allow myself to fall into a light sleep. I had some control over myself. He had taken my body, but he could not capture my mind.

The sun rose. I was still alive. He sat near me, drinking from a flask.

"Please," I croaked, my voice dust in my throat. "May I drink?"

He threw the flask to me, and I grabbed it with my swollen hands, barely able to hold it. Two swallows of water were all he gave me.

He laughed and again crawled to me. I screamed as he bit my other nipple.

"I can have you at any time. I am as good as those cursed Romans and their whores," he said as he lifted his bare buttocks over me. He was ready and groaned and pushed into me. His thrusts were uneven and shallow at first but as he continued they became faster and deeper. His weight crushed the air out of me and caused my leg to pound. My eyes closed, and I tried to fly like a falcon. I begged the gods to let me escape.

When he was done, he lifted off me, his penis small and drooling. He rolled back to his corner and sat up.

"Please, more water. My wound. I need to drink," I whispered.

He lifted the corner of the wall that was his door and left. In a few minutes, he brought back the flask and gave it to me. It was full, and I drank it all. I vomited.

"Gods curse you. This place is small enough without your messes." He untied the cord from the iron ring, leaving it attached to my wrists. He tugged and I crawled, forced to move like a worm, leaving the tatters of my green dress behind. He was unhappy at how slow I moved and when we were outside, was angry.

"You are not worth all this trouble. I will kill you soon and leave. The Romans are not far away. They will find me if I stay." He tied me to another iron-ringed peg pounded into the ground near the cave entrance.

"If my clansmen find you first there will be nothing for the Romans to find."

He stood and kicked me in the stomach.

"Shut up, bitch."

I vomited again and fainted.

He was on me when I awoke. Finished, he rolled off, stood and pissed. I don't know why he told me bits of his story. I hated his voice and wished he would choke while he talked.

His voice was gravel in my ears. "I was once a great warrior for Queen Boudiccea." *Lovern's queen,* I realized. "When she killed herself, I tried to escape but they caught me and cut off my finger."

Was his story supposed to make me feel sympathy for him? It did not. If I could have reached my dirk, I would have cut his throat and drunk his blood with no regrets.

"I shoveled Roman horseshit. Me, a warrior! I hate them. One night, the guard drank too much. I got hold of his dirk, slit his gut, and ran. I have been running for days. Hunting and eating when I could. I built this shelter. I was hunting when I found the best game of all—you. Now it is time to go. I will not like leaving you but you will slow me too much. Pity. You are beautiful and a good fuck." He was done pissing but started to rub himself. He was getting stiff again.

I forced myself to think. Something echoed in my head. He would not stray far from his protective cover to hunt. We were not far from the meadow. There was a chance of discovery. My soul lifted. I knew now I had a chance to live. Hope began to rekindle.

He laid on me again and I bit his ear. The metallic taste of his blood heightened my thirst. He pressed my dirk next to my cheek and threatened to slice my eyes if I did it again. He pushed into me and I traced my labyrinth in my mind.

The second night, I started shivering. Still outside, I lay on the cold ground. The skin near my wound was red streaked. Blood poison. My body was heating from inside. My goddess was warring with my soul. I concentrated on my labyrinth and Lovern. I must not cross the river of death yet, but I would die if I did not get away soon.

My mind, deep in meditation with the labyrinth, allowed the shivering of my illness to take over my body. The third day he gave me just enough water to keep me alive, nothing more. My soul came to the top of my body, to cross the deep and fast river, twice.

To let go and cross the river of death would have been easy.

"No!" said the goddess. "You cannot go. You have more pain to live through for me. You have more to sacrifice. I will not let you go, yet," she told me.

My blood poisoned pus odor mixed with his putrid fungus smell, and gagged me as I inhaled. I flew into my passage dream with the stench of rot in my nose. Three small ponies stood shuffling their feet on the sand. Callum and Braden packed bags of dried seaweed. Then I knew. I was in Lovern! Morrigna granted me one last wish. Startled by my visit, Lovern hesitated, and sat on the beach with his eyes closed. It was different this time; I gave him my message. I sent him my fear. I relayed my anguish. I begged for his rescue. I cried for his return. My pain tore through his heart and when he opened his eyes, I heard him tell Braden and Callum, "Go for the ferryman. We must leave the island, now!" He ran to his pony. I left his mind. Lovern knew. My dream was over.

Time stopped.

On what I learned later was the third day, a vision appeared. A giant bear stood tall over me, growling. His fangs glistened. He dropped to all four feet, and called my name. How could a bear know my name?

"Jahna, do not speak. I am here to take you home. You are safe," the bear said.

My mind was not clear. Who was here? Beathan? I remembered the man telling me he was going hunting and would be back soon. My voice would not come. There was no moisture in my body. I could not speak more than a frog's croak. Beathan's dirk slipped under the cord tying my hands and the sky behind him exploded.

Sound and motion rushed in, and Beathan, caught on his knees, twisted away from me into a man who would kill him. Beathan fought using the dirk. He lunged forward. His dirk plunged into the triangle between the man's legs, cutting the tool that had done so much damage to me. I screamed with the pleasure of seeing the blood and pain of this animal that had tortured me. The shrieking man straightened and raised his sword. Beathan tried to stand and stumbled. He was half crouched when the sword swooped down. The world fell silent for a breath. Then a victory screech tore into my ears.

Beathan's blood washed over me. His body fell to one side and his head to the other. I stared into his eyes as his soul crossed. For an instant, I was without thought. How could our chieftain, our *ceann-cinnidh*, my brave Uncle, be dead? But he was. I closed my eyes and prayed.

"Cerridwen. Take our *ceann-cinnidh*. He was brave in battle. Make his crossing easy." I could not think of more to say.

The trees around me came to life. Our clan war cries, branches, and blood rained down. Finlay and Kenric were here. They sliced the man into small pieces before he fell to the ground. His blood mixed with Beathan's on my body. His dead eyes stared into Beathan's. And my world changed.

When I awoke I smelled puffball fungus. A clean, healing smell. Its spores fought blood poison in wounds such as mine. I was laying on a bed in our hospice, Sileas bent over me. Tears coursed down her face as she raised my head to sip the tea she held to my lips.

"Drink, it will help you sleep. It is what is best for you now. Do not remember, just sleep."

"Beathan," I whispered after I took a sip of the warm elixir.

"He thought he alone could rescue you. He told Finlay and Kenric to wait. It cost him his life. But he died in battle. His head was buried with his body, so his soul has crossed. He is at the Long Table of Chieftains, ready to fight for the right to carve the joint and drink his fill of mead," she said, crying as she spoke.

My eyes closed, and his dead face filled my mind. "May you find peace, Beathan. I owe you my soul. I will honor you," I prayed. "My memory bag?"

"Here."

She put it in my hands. I trembled as I opened it and slipped my fingers inside. Our hair still mingled. I pulled it out, and the light picked up the bronze glitter of Lovern's hair.

"He is coming," I said and smiled, my heart beating fast at the thought.

She helped me get our tangled locks of hair back into the bag, and I held it close to my heart.

She bade me sleep. I held my bag up to see the labyrinth. This pattern kept me from leaving my body and dying. I followed its trail with my finger as every muscle in my body relaxed, aided by the drink. One small vision appeared before I slept. I held my baby up to the skies. I heard her cry. I prayed, please let it be Lovern's child.

Do not let the monster leave a mark.

CHAPTER 10

JAHNA

75 AD JUNE

Spirits haunted me day and night. I was afraid to be alone.

With Sileas and Harailt's care, my body was healing. My mind was not. My blood moon came. Thank Morrigna. I was not carrying his child. I hobbled, walking aided with a stick, while my leg wound healed. I spent most of my time in Finlay's smithy or his home with Eiric, his wife. I needed to rest where I blended into the background. In the house, Eiric managed their five children. She seemed to always be in motion. Her four girls helped with the chores and watched the baby boy. Now ten moons old, he was beginning to walk. I tried to hold him, but he wriggled out of my arms faster than I could move to catch him. He made me smile when it hurt to smile.

The toddler, Broc, looked like both his mother and his father. His father's sky blue eyes sparkled with the laughter that bubbled out of him, and his mother's blond hair was just becoming thick enough to be seen on his head. Whenever Finlay came into his house, he would smile and rub the boy's head as if making sure he was still there. After four girls, he finally had a boy child and I saw his pride.

"I will make his first sword and take him hunting," he said. "He will make a fine warrior for the chieftain. My girls will marry warriors and hunters. I can ask no more from the gods."

Kenric, my other cousin and Finlay's older brother, was now our chieftain. I spent little time in his dwelling. He and his family had moved into Beathan's home. His wife, Caitrin, managed the two boys, the feeding of the family and all the warriors and others who came to eat with the chieftain. I could not help as much as I had earlier, and I felt underfoot.

There was another reason I did not go there. Beathan was in every corner and I saw blame in the eyes of the men who were now Kenric's warriors.

I did not have the energy to work at the hospice. Sileas, Harailt, and I would discuss the illnesses, injuries, and treatments. They followed what I suggested in Lovern's absence.

I was also unwilling to sit and weave with my mother. She wore the grief of losing Beathan in her eyes, but even worse, I saw Lovern in our home. Lovern was at the fire, mixing medicines in our room, and drinking mead at the table. I could not sleep in our bed. His scent was gone.

Most nights I trembled in a corner by the loom, the putrid smell of the badger filling my nose. In my mind, I went back to the hut, wondering if I could have stopped him in some way. The gods did not give me an answer to this never-ending question.

Confusion, always nearby, reigned over me. Mother spoke of Lovern coming home. She missed the druid and his medicines. I prayed for and dreaded his return. My passage dream had alerted him, and he was coming, I was sure. But when he arrived, how could I tell him that the man who had taken me also beheaded our chieftain, his friend Beathan? Even that seemed a small concern when I worried about how he could still love me after my taking. Another man had used me.

The idea of Beathan's gift had started the day I sat near Finlay's stone workbench on a small wooden stool. Buckets of water stood ready for dunking the hearth-heated metal. Pieces of leather used to work bronze were lying on the bench. Tools hung from the beams or lay on the ground near the hearth. Here, Finlay had crafted the small oak pins that Beathan declared represented our family. He had honed and engraved Beathan's swords on this workbench, the blades now buried with Beathan. He made plows and sharpened knives here. I felt safe. The heat, the smell of charcoal, and the rush of work in the smithy wrapped around me like a woolen shield.

Finlay had started work on a bronze bowl the day before. I watched him hammer the metal into shape and pictures drew themselves in my head.

"What will it look like when you finish?"

"I have no design in mind." Finlay stopped hammering and reached for a mug of mead. "How would you decorate it?"

"I would use an oak tree and its acorns." I picked up a stick and drew it in the dust on the floor. A shaft of sunlight streamed through the hole in the wall of the smoky room to the center of my picture. "There are strong branches, able to carry many responsibilities. Here, acorns, ready to grow into adults, and finally the heart of the oak, pure. It burns with the fierce heat of bravery." As I traced the tree, I cried for the first time. I cried for Beathan. I cried for the loss of my life as it had been.

Finlay put down his mead, walked around the workbench, and sat beside me in the dirt of the smithy floor. The alder charcoal fire in his hearth was hot on our backs. My tears mixed with his sweat as he hugged me, his heavy leather apron stiff against my face.

"I am sorry for Beathan's death. It was because of me. If I had not gone out that day, Beathan would be here." I sobbed into his shoulder.

"Beathan died saving your life. But remember, Jahna, he died in battle, as a chieftain. He is in the next world, on the council, making decisions for others. You are the one who reminds us that we all die. Some go easily in sleep, some go with a difficult sickness, but we sing songs about those who die in battle."

I looked to his face, his misty eyes belying his words of strength.

"I have started a song for Beathan that will keep his memory alive for many generations," he said. "Our clan will remember him as long as we are a clan."

"A s-song," I stuttered. My tears stopped. I wiped my face and nose with my dress. "A song for a brave warrior." Finlay stood up and shook out his tunic, lifting the wet spot I had created on his shoulder away from him. He nodded, and I continued, "I would like to decorate this bowl and take it to Beathan. Will you teach me to work the metal?"

"Yes, I will teach you. The tattoos you design are good. The tree you drew in the dirt will give honor to the bowl and be a fitting gift to Beathan." He picked up the bowl he was working on and said, "I promised this one to Darach. He is giving me woven wool so my girls can make new dresses. They grow too quickly. It is a gift from him to his wife for the son she gave birth to six moons ago."

He walked over to a storage chest and lifted out a bar of metal. "I have just enough bronze to make another bowl for the honor gift to Beathan. You will engrave it, and we will take it to Beathan's tomb when you finish. Here are the tools I use for the fine work," he said and opened a leather packet.

Out rolled small iron, copper, and bone tools. There were hammers, and sharp picks with different shaped tips.

"I have a copper bowl that has no engraving. I use it for washing. You can use these tools to practice on that bowl. Learn how each moves the metal and leaves its mark. Learn how you can make them different." Our last smith had fashioned a large copper bowl that Finlay brought to me. Picking up several tools, he demonstrated. "Hold this one like this and gently tap. Do not pierce the bowl or you will be hammering it back into shape." He laughed.

I turned the bowl over in my hands, feeling every bump and wrinkle. I said a prayer to Dagda, asking for the energy to create my picture, and began with one small tap. Small nicks and scratches happened at first, but I got used to the way of the tools, and became sure of myself. I worked without lifting my head, lost in the bowl.

Several days later, Finlay lined the second, unfinished bowl with a piece of leather and used small taps to create a finish that reflected shards of firelight around the room.

"It is beautiful," I said, holding it in my hands gently, as if it would break. I gave it back to him.

He laid it on his hearth. He went to his small altar, near the hearth, and knelt to say a prayer to the smith's goddess, Brigit. I kneeled beside him and prayed to Bel to inspire me with the skill to complete my work, to Brigit to thank her for the bowl, and to Morrigna to ease my panic and fears. We both rose and Finlay carried the bowl back to the workbench. I brought over the two nearby stools and we sat.

Finlay picked up the copper bowl I had practiced on and looked at it silently. He turned it from the scratches I had created in the beginning to the design covering the other side. "What is this? I have seen it on the bag the druid carries."

"It is a labyrinth. See how it leads to the center and back? It is a path from the center of the earth to the gods. Lovern brought it with him from his home and he taught me to use it." I stopped talking for a moment, and remembered my finger tracing the path in my head. "It helped me escape most of the pain of the taking." I did not tell him that I had not been able to use it since.

Reminded of my trials, he searched my face. Was he looking for signs of lunacy? As if reaching a decision in my favor, his face relaxed and he nodded.

"Hmm," he grunted. He put the copper bowl aside and picked up the bronze. "I know you will create an honorable design. We can make the trip to place it in his tomb when you are finished."

In two days, I engraved the design of the oak onto the bowl. I tapped leaves on the strong branches that spread around its circumference. I scratched lines on the acorns. I carved my heart into the heart of the tree. When I stopped to look at it, memories of Beathan flooded my mind. I remembered when he brought food and peat to my mother and me when the snow was deep. When I was small, he lifted me to his shoulders to carry me through the mud. He helped repair our loom when it was overused. I gave thanks to the goddess that Beathan had been a part of my life. Now the bowl honored his life as a caring *ceann-cinnidh* of our clan as well as my uncle.

Pleased with my work, I turned it over in my hands. It was time to show Finlay.

He was fitting a new buckle to Kenric's war chariot's leather harness. Kenric wanted all Beathan's harnesses for his ponies and chariots repaired. Beathan had worn them to breaking.

My breath held in anticipation of what he thought, I walked over to him. He cooled the buckle in a bucket of water. Hot steam rose, and he cautioned me to wait. He went to the labyrinth bowl, washed his hands, and walked back to me, wiping his hands on his tunic. He raised the hem of his garment to sop the sweat from his face. As he raised his shirt, his strong belly muscles rippled. A picture flashed through my consciousness. Lovern's smooth belly and chest. Gripped with a longing for him, I inhaled through closed teeth and silently begged him to hurry. Come home to help me heal and, I prayed, to forgive me.

Finlay took the bowl and looked at it, for what seemed to me, time enough to grow a new beard. He turned it over and around, carried it to the door, used the sun for light, and came back to the workbench. I could not read his face. He picked up a piece of very soft leather, a bucket of water and a small jug of fine creek sand. First, dipping the leather into the water, he touched it to the sand and began to polish the bowl.

"Use a gentle circle movement." He handed it to me, nodded, and said, "It is a good and fitting gift for Beathan."

I was proud and pleased.

"Can we take it soon?"

"If Kenric allows. Tonight I will show it to him and the warriors. I will ask if others want to accompany us to Beathan's tomb to place it."

I heard the music and laughter echo through the lodges, late into the night, from the evening meal's gathering. Just before dawn, Finlay knocked on my door. I was awake. I opened the door, and he stood, swaying, silhouetted by the moon. He spent his night drinking and singing his song, regaling Beathan's heroic deeds.

"I heard you sing your new song repeatedly last night. It must be liked by the men."

"Yes, I will teach it to you on the journey. We will have plenty of time. We are readying to go to the tomb."

The tomb. *We will make the trip today,* I thought.

"There are four of us including you," he said. "Kenric is coming and bringing his son Logan. He is old enough to leave his mother now. We are loading the ponies. Come to the stable soon."

"Be sure to take food," my mother whispered into my ear. "All those men will bring is mead. They must always be reminded that there are things that satisfy a hunger other than mead," she said with a smile and then coughed blood.

I described the bowl to my mother last night before she slept. Her eyes misted, and she said, "It is a good gift to take to my brother. His spirit is walking at night. I see him, sometimes, in torment. I think he is disturbed at the way he died. He holds his head in his hands and tears fall from his eyes. Maybe this will comfort him." She nodded and mused with her fingers resting on her lips. "Yes. It is good that you are doing this."

Her agreement did not take the heavy guilt from my back.

Finlay, Kenric, little Logan and his wolfhound Mialchu were at the stable gathered around the impatient, stomping ponies. Logan, at six sun cycles, was Kenric's oldest, and looked through his father's gray blue eyes. His mother's blond hair was tied back with a short piece of leather. His feet were in one place, but his body bounced all over the stable. I stood and watched, amazed at how he could move yet not move. Small boys were to be watched and kept from harm, but not understood by adults.

Kenric asked whether Logan could ride with me. He was too small for his own pony on such a long journey. Our supplies, Kenric's and Finlay's swords and shields were strapped to the rumps of their ponies. There was no room for Logan.

"I will be honored to ride with the grandson of Beathan. I will tell him stories of his grandfather," I said.

I wore the leather pouch decorated with the labyrinth Lovern had drawn. I tied my dirk to my belt, and a short sword that had been Beathan's hung across my chest. It was a gift from Kenric when I walked again. It had hung in Beathan's lodge. Kenric told me to use it for protection. It lay well balanced and not heavy in my hand. With it, I would kill the next man who hurt me.

Finlay handed me the bowl, wrapped in soft doe's skin, and I slipped it into the bodice of my dress. My corded belt held it in place. I used a small stool to mount the pony, and swung my leg over its back with a grimace. Logan was boosted up. I hoped for some peace as he began to wriggle and grope for a place to hang on. We rode, one in front of the other, down the trail to the lake.

Logan was unsettled so to quiet him for a few moments, I started a story. "I remember, when I was your age, your grandfather, my uncle, would throw me into the air. I loved it, but Mother hated it. She was sure he would drop me. I would cry until she gave in. He would throw me one more time and catch me. He then kissed my mother on her cheek and told me to run and play with Kenric, your father. He was a good man, your grandfather. We are a stronger people because of him. That is why we make this journey."

Logan told me his stories of when Beathan tossed him into the air, too. His mother had reacted the same as mine.

"I miss my grandfather," said Logan.

"Yes. So do I," I said.

Beathan's bowl began its journey.

CHAPTER 11

April, 2005

George's thick white eyebrows lifted in recognition when he saw Marc waving. He waved back, and then his hand fell to his balding head as if to straighten hair he'd remembered he used to have. He wore his uniform of khaki, multi-pocketed pants and a tan, long sleeved shirt.

"Good," he said. "I was hoping both of you would be here."

He leaned his tall, work-stooped frame just enough to kiss me on my upturned cheek. I smelled coffee on his breath and saw crumbs of his breakfast on his shirt. His rough hands brushed my cheeks. He hated wearing gloves when working, always afraid of missing something. Time had created a road map of capillaries on his face that was new since the last time I had seen him. He also looked tired.

"How are you, my girl?"

He was a trusted friend of my family. He knew my dad when they were younger and my dad made him promise to watch over me at university. Although my father died years ago, George still looked out for me.

"I'm fine," I said. "I'm so glad to see you again. It's been far too long."

I put my arm through his and noticed he seemed a bit thinner than I remembered.

"How have you been?" I asked, patting his shoulder.

"Oh, you know, all the aches and pains that come with age. But I find, now that I'm retired, I have more work to do than ever, so I don't dwell on my problems."

He retired three years ago, but was still invited to most of the digs in Great Britain as a consultant. We were lucky to have him.

Marc picked up George's bag and we climbed into the Rover. We dropped his bag off at Mrs. Dingleberrie's and were on the hilltop by mid-morning.

"We've only been here two days but have part of a domicile excavated," I said. "I'm expecting to find more very soon. I'm really excited about being here."

I immediately saw the look I dreaded from his class when I would go to him and ask for an extension on my papers. I could never get them pared down to the page number requirement.

"You're always trying to make something bigger than it really is, Aine. Well, we'll see. I needed a small vacation for a day or two and then it's back to my report. It's worth the trip just to see you both on a job together," he said, smiling.

"Yes. It's been enjoyable so far." Marc said, looking at me with a smile. He winked and I blushed. "We have a small crew, but all hard workers."

We stopped at the edge of the excavated area where Matt and Tim were on their knees, trowels and brushes in hand.

"Did it stay dry?" I asked, changing the subject.

Tim and Matt stood and shook George's hand.

"We had to use a bucket to get some of the water off the tarp before we moved it, but it's dry enough here," said Tim.

"Good. I see standing water in places. We could have been up to our knees if we hadn't covered it," I said.

"It is a good thing the tarps worked," said Marc. "We probably don't have enough money to get a pump and generator if we flooded. We'd have to break camp. We may have to do that in a day or so anyway if something more doesn't show up."

"I really don't think we'll have to worry about that anymore, Marc. I feel it in my bones," I argued.

"As nice as your bones are, they could be mistaken," Marc said.

I gulped and had no answer to that truth. My stomach was back on its nervous roil as Marc and I walked George around the site.

"You must have trusted Aine's instincts somewhat," George said as he reached over, tucked me protectively under his arm, and gave me a hug while we walked. "You called me and I'm glad you did. I'm happy to be here for her, even if only for a few days. I'll help in any way I can." He smiled at me. "You were a great help when my Sophie died. I'd've had a hard time of it if you hadn't come and helped me. I'll look around. If I think it is warranted, I know where we can get some funding."

My hope leaped at this bit of good news, but the pressure was on. All I had to do was find something in the next few days. *Jahna, I need you now, more than ever.*

We were back at the tent and Kendy showed us her drawings of bits of pottery and the bronze blade we found yesterday.

"Marc, I'm going to take a hike up the mountain a bit," I said. I couldn't wait any longer. I had to get to the trail to see if I could find the spot Jahna had shown me last night. I located the area the sun was shining on yesterday while we walked around.

"I'll take my camera. I think it would be valuable to have some photos of the hilltop and the surrounding area from above." I pointed up. "The sky looks as if it might rain again, and I want to go before it starts." From the way the clouds were forming, I figured I had several more hours before we had to pack it up and go back to the inn. I couldn't waste time.

George agreed. "There might be some ancient trails that show up in photos from above. I think that's a good idea. It might give us an idea how popular this hill was. Wait. I brought some new toys, walkie-talkies. Aine, why don't you take one? They're supposed to have a range of over two kilometers. This will be a good test. I've not had to use them this far away before. When you get up there, call and tell us what you see."

I grabbed my pack, put in my camera, the walkie-talkie, a bottle of water and started to the mountain that flanked the hill.

I skirted around the standing water and mud puddles on the hilltop and found the trailhead. I hopped over ruts formed by rivulets that had run down it last night. The mountain was picturesque. Greenery of all shades was starting to show in the spring warming. Grasses and small brush surrounded granite boulders that seemed to burst out of the mountain's side. It wasn't a big mountain, but a respectable one in one's book of mountains, I thought. The trail led me in a zigzag fashion, the way animals would clamber up. I followed it without much difficulty, stepping carefully to avoid slipping in the mud.

The larger exposed boulders partially hid my view of the hill below. About halfway up the trail, I stopped. The boulders opened up, and I saw the valley and hill clearly. The hilltop was just large enough for a few dwellings and the accompanying animals. We had uncovered the first sign of habitation and I visualized the rest of the fort. The depression that would have been the defensive wall followed the shape of the hill. I imagined people walking in the courtyard and animals in the stables.

Looking out over the fields, I saw the bog where Mr. Treadwell let some of his Highland cattle feed. There might have been a lake there at one time. On either side, now surrounded by stone walls that were centuries old, lay other fields that looked as if rows of ancient cultivation were plowed into them. They were now pastures for cattle.

As I turned back to the hilltop, I had a dizzying feeling of déjà vu. I had been on this spot last night. I looked through Jahna's eyes with this view filling my vision. The spot now being excavated was where she saw her home in my awake dream. It was exactly where I decided to start digging. I knew she had come here to look over her home, happy with her life. There was nothing else I wanted more than to know her at that moment. She was happy, and I would have loved to see her and talk to her at that point in her life. She had given me a gift. Jahna allowed me to feel her joy.

I turned to go on, but something looked strange from the corner of my eye. An unusual slab of stone, actually a large piece of slate, was set into the mountain. It was out of place. This was a granite mountain, and didn't have slate running through it naturally. Earth partially covered the slab, and a mound of dirt directly under it must have come off in the rainstorm last night. On its left was a trickle waterfall from last night's rain. The soil was saturated.

Suddenly, I was depressed. My shoulders fell forward, and sadness filled me. I almost fell. I put my hand against the slate as a brace and sat down to catch my breath. The peaceful feeling was gone. I couldn't understand the grief that replaced it. For a moment, it seemed all my dreams had vanished, that there was nothing left to live for.

I sat with my back against the slate, unable to see the hilltop below me. Dark shadows filled my eyes. I closed them to gather my strength to stand again, and felt the slate grow warm against my back. It was as if it were sun warmed, but the sun hadn't cut through the clouds for hours. I leaned forward and, still seated on the damp trail, scooted around to face the slate. It was dark, the color of the damp earth around it, and large, about one and a half meters across and over a meter high. I traced it with my fingertips and found the outside edges buried in dirt. It was a huge piece of slate that should not have been there. Someone must have placed it for a purpose. I had to know who placed it and why it was here. Starting to try to dig around the stone with my fingers, I remembered the walkie-talkie. I pressed the button and said, "Hello George. Would you get Marc for me please?"

"Sure. I'm walking over to him now. Where are you?"

I stood up and waved my arms. "I am about halfway up the trail, and I've found something I'd like Marc to come see."

"Hi, Aine. Oh, there you are, I see you waving," said Marc. "What is it?"

"There's a slab of slate up here. It looks human placed. Could you bring up some of our tools so we can take a look?"

"Should I get a pry bar from the Rover?"

"Yes, I think we might need it," I said.

"George says he is coming too. He suspects the view from up there is good."

"Tell him he won't be disappointed. I'll take pictures of the stone and the surrounding area until you get here. You should also bring a tarp, the ground up here is very damp and we don't want to be sitting on it for long without protection," I said and wiped some of the mud off the bottom of my pants. "Bring Kendy along. We should get some grid sketches before we try to move it, too."

"OK. We'll be there soon," Marc said.

While I waited, I took pictures of the surrounding valley, the hilltop and the stone slab. I put my hand next to it to give it a size comparison and pulled out my notebook to make a sketch. I wanted my own record. I knew this was important.

As soon as they arrived, we spread out the tarp. Kendy sketched the hillside and the slab. We used GPS readings and measurements to get its exact placement.

Finally, Kendy said she had enough information and Marc and I started cutting the soil away from its edges.

"It sure looks like it was covered originally. Either by humans or an early slide," said George. "Last night's rain must have loosened the soil just enough. The topsoil here looks a bit unstable so be careful. There is a shoulder of earth just above you that looks as if it could cause some trouble."

I looked up where he was pointing and said, "Then we need to get it excavated so it doesn't get covered up again. I don't want to lose it. I have a feeling this is very important."

"Okay," Marc said. "We have it as far as we can go by hand. Grab here while I use the pry bar to loosen it a bit on this side." The stone started to lean back and let light behind it for the first time in, I was betting, centuries.

"Stop," I yelled. "There's an opening. It looks like a cave. Let me take some pictures before you move it further."

Marc and George held the slab in place, while I took pictures of the stone and the hole behind it. Kendy was furiously drawing. A minute later, we had it moved to the side and the mouth of the cave exposed.

I stood trembling while Marc, using a flashlight, peered into it. "It seems to go back a bit but I can't see a lot through this small opening," Marc said.

I got down on my stomach and crawled to the edge of the opening so I had a direct view into the cave. "This was dug by someone. It's short, about four meters. I can see the end of it. And about a meter or a little more high and wide.

I can see more slate lining its bottom and sides. There is a box of some sort toward the back," I said, excitedly. "I'm going in."

"Wait, Aine," George and Marc said together.

"Do you think you should be going inside? This looks pretty water logged and could be dangerous," asked George.

Marc continued, "We don't have the best equipment to get anyone out if it collapses while someone is in there."

"I'm willing to take the risk," I said. "We need a big find to help fund this project, Marc, and this could be it. This cave is man made and is lined with slate. And that box. What could be in that box? I don't have time to wait. I'm the only one who will fit in that hole. I am going in now."

On my tummy, camera in one hand and flashlight in the other, I inched forward like a worm. I tried to keep the flashlight focused on the box and took pictures as I slid myself further into the dark cave.

"I'm at the box! Oh my gosh! Its sides are pieces of slate, balanced against the sides of the cave and each other. There is a larger piece that is the lid. There isn't room in here to do anything more than lift the lid so here goes."

The stale air made me sweat. I lifted the lid, slowly. The front and back sides of the box fell inward and banged against what was inside. I held my breath, and hoped I hadn't broken anything. I laid the lid to the side, and saw a faded design painted on it. I couldn't see what it was. I expected to be able to look it over more carefully outside, but now I longed to see what was behind the rest of the slate. I pulled the front side down and my flashlight highlighted a raven design. Three ravens intertwined. There, in front of me, was the bronze bowl I had seen in my dream last night.

"Oh my God! Oh my God! Oh my God!" I screamed. "There's a bronze bowl in here. Marc, I've found another bronze bowl!"

"Wow!" said Marc.

"Take pictures!" said Kendy.

"Be careful," said George.

I snapped about thirty pictures, still unbelieving what I had discovered and said, "I am going to pick it up and bring it out." I laid my camera and flashlight down and wrapped my hands around the bowl. I glanced up and noticed a shadow at the back of the cave. Something was on the floor, just beyond the bowl. I was drawn to it but first I wanted to get the bowl out.

"OK. You'll have to help me. I have my hands full and can only use my elbows to move." I felt myself being tugged by the hem of my pants. I inched backwards and my shirt bunched around my waist.

Finally out, I handed the bowl to Marc and stood, pulling my shirt down.

"There's something inside," said George. "It looks like cremated remains. It could be a burial bowl. We can send it to Glasgow for testing."

I gently liberated the bowl from Marc's sweaty hands. It was the size of a large grapefruit with three ravens engraved on the outside. As I held it, I felt the same heavy grief I had felt before. My shoulders slumped as I realized these must be Jahna's ashes. I had found Jahna's remains. I didn't want to let it out of my sight but I realized it should be studied. "Okay. Yes. Send it to Glasgow. There probably are human remains in the bowl. Let's see if there are enough remains for it to be sexed."

"Good idea," said Marc. "It could be another chieftain."

"Could be," I said. "Could be." But I knew he was wrong.

"Kendy, would you walk it down for me?" I asked. "I need to go back in and get the camera." George placed the bowl and its contents into a large, plastic bag, keeping it upright.

"Please be extra careful, Kendy. The trail is very slippery," I said.

She started down saying, "I'll guard it as if it contained my mom's ashes." I watched her until she was halfway down and said, "I have to go back in. I left the camera and flashlight and I saw something else in there."

"OK, but be very careful and don't stay long," said Marc. "We should get down and start the paperwork on the bowl to get it sent off."

I kneeled down, crawled back into the hole and inched forward until I reached the camera and flashlight. My hands stretched the last few inches and touched what had created the shadow. I had to make a choice. Do I carry out the top of the box or the unidentified lump that attracted me? I made the choice. I would come back to retrieve the slate. The lump was going first.

With the lump of metal in one hand, and camera in the other, the flashlight would be left behind. I could get it and the lid next time.

"I'm ready. You can start tugging."

I was out up to my waist, when it happened. I heard a rumble and "Watch out!" simultaneously. Everything went black, and I couldn't breathe. The whole mountain was on top of me. I tried to scream but choked. Someone whispered, "Do not let go of the acorn. Do not let go of my acorn." I don't remember anything else until the clinic.

When I woke up, a woman in a white coat hovered over me. Marc, George and the rest of the crew pressed their faces against a window, looking in. Machines buzzed and blinked and tubes of liquid ran into my arms.

"What happened? Where am I?" I asked.

"Hi, dearie," she said.

Usually I hated to be called "dearie," but I didn't mind this time.

"It is sure good to see you awake. My name is Susan. I'm a nurse. You're in clinic. Your friends brought you in. We're waiting for an ambulance to get you to Fort William so you can have further tests. Do you remember what happened?"

I shook my head.

"Can you tell me your name?"

"Aine MacRea."

"Yes, Aine. Good. Glad to have you back." She smiled a teacher smile at my correct answer.

"Well, you were buried in an avalanche and when they uncovered you, you weren't breathing. Someone had to breathe for you until you started on your own."

Over her shoulder, Marc's dirt streaked face broke out into a wide grin. I lifted two fingers and waved, felt a sting in my arm and then everything was gone again.

The next time I woke up, George was in the room alone with me. "We're at hospital in Fort William. You've been asleep for about twelve hours."

"What happened?" I croaked.

"You were almost out of the cave when the ledge that I was worried about gave way. It triggered the whole cave to collapse. Marc and I scrambled out of the way and when the dirt stopped falling, we got back on our knees and dug for our lives. Uh, for your life. It seemed to take an eternity but I guess it was only a couple of minutes before we had you out. You weren't breathing and Marc started CPR. After about two rounds you started coughing and breathing. We got you to the village and helicoptered here as fast as we could. Fortunately, you only have torn muscles and deep bruising but no broken bones. We were all very lucky!"

"Marc?" I whispered.

"He went to get a cup of coffee."

"Bowl?"

"It's in Glasgow."

I silently thanked God that it was ok.

"Camera?"

George broke into a smile. "Ah, the ever present scientist. We recovered the camera and the pictures are perfect. We had to pry open your hand to retrieve the piece of metal you went back in for. It seems to be two items that have become welded together over time. We'll decipher them later."

Marc came into the room with two steaming cups of coffee. "Sleeping Beauty is awake!" He handed the cups to George, came over to my bedside and took my hand. "God, I was scared. I don't want to ever have to do that again. No more caves for you." He leaned over and kissed me gently on my lips.

"Awakened by a prince," I said and smiled. "When do I get out of here?"

"We can take you home to London tomorrow if we promise to give you proper time to recover," Marc said.

"No! Not London, the inn. I don't want to leave the site."

A stormy look covered George's face but Marc said, "Okay, okay. Calm down. I'll call Mrs. Dingleberry and see if she's fine with it. After all, you'll be under her feet for a while. That way I can watch over you, too."

"Tomorrow?" I asked.

"Yes," said Marc.

"Good."

I thought about the bronze bowl, its contents, and the whispered order to hold onto the acorn. I knew there was no way I could prove who was in the bowl to anyone else, but I knew. I had found Jahna.

What other secrets did she have hidden? The mountain almost killed me but I knew Jahna had more for me to find.

CHAPTER 12

JAHNA

75 AD July

An ache settled deep in my leg. Dusk hazily descended as we sighted the meadow through the trees. Depths of hopelessness filled my heart and sank into my gut. I wanted to vomit as we rode into the open space and started across what was once a place of beauty for me.

Meadowsweet's potent odor rose from the green, marshy lea, crushed by the weight of the ponies. I looked around. There, near the bend in the stream. Was I standing there? Yes. I was gathering the blossoms, reveling in the sunlight of the summer day, remembering a night of love with Lovern, when the arrow crippled my leg.

Panic caused my belly to fill with fire and pull against my backbone. The memories of my taking haunted me, but here I felt the fiendish presence of that man. My hand rested on my short sword, ready. I would never let myself be taken again.

The ponies entered a stand of alders just on the far edge of the meadow. This hot-burning, hard wood became charcoal for Finlay's smithy. He whispered a greeting to the fire god, Bran, as we passed from the meadow into the cover of the trees. What god was I to thank for my despair?

The size of my world had increased, not by my choice, and would never be the same again. This line of trees was where, at my taking, I once crossed into a world of the dead. The grass trampled by the hooves of the ponies smelled sour to me. The sweetness of this formerly tranquil place had disappeared. Everything I had known beyond this meadow led to the battle of my spirits and the death of Beathan. The blood red setting sun and shrill call of the birds in the forest set the scene in my heart. Tears welled and fell onto my white dress, spotting it with grey grief.

"*Piuthar Jahna*, why are you crying? Why are you not excited like me?" queried the small Logan as he shifted to pat me on my back with both small hands. He rustled behind me as I leaned forward in pain, both from my leg, and the heavy burden I carried.

"Quiet, pup. Let her be. Your aunt is grieving," admonished Kenric. Kenric and I had been riding side-by-side, exchanging glances. We did not need words for our conversation. In the meadow, his eyes sympathized with me, and seemed to say, *I understand. Here, you were gathering the herbs. It was from here we followed the blood trail with the dogs.* Feelings of fear and suffocation were dredged from my memories. I choked back my tears, not wanting to frighten Logan.

"Do not make me unhappy we brought you along, little nephew," Finlay said, following us. "We will be camping soon. Then you will hear the song of how Beathan captured the Autumn Bear."

Logan began bouncing up and down in anticipation, almost knocking me off the pony.

"Sit still, *meanbh-chuileag*. You are as troublesome as the spring midges," I teased as I semi-emerged from my cocoon of self-pity. Logan giggled with young exuberance. I imagined the size of his sky blue eyes and smiled as I realized I was jealous of his innocence.

My back ached and I groaned as I lifted my sore, swollen leg to allow the feeling to come back to my foot. I did not know whether I would be able to stand when I slid off the pony.

"Here is a good place to stop for the night," said Kenric, in a small grove of rowan trees.

Logan slid off the pony to the ground and began to run as only a child can after a day on horseback. Finlay slowly lifted me down. My legs trembled as he supported me until I could feel the ground with both feet. As the men and Logan gathered wood for a fire, I hobbled and kneeled at the roots of the sacred rowans to pray.

"O Sucellus," I called and knocked on the tree bark. "God of the Forest and Trees that are sacred to us, we thank you for the wood we use tonight. You, who ferries the dead across the river, be aware of Beathan. He was a mighty warrior and Father of my clan. I ask you to protect us, this small group, as we honor our dead. Keep us from the evil spirits who walk the night." I searched my soul for a prayer for Morrigna. I asked only two things. "Take this panic from my heart and return Lovern safely to me."

Mead flowed from my flask as a gift to the gods mixed with my tears. I was unaware of the roughness of the tree bark as I ran my hands over it, rubbing my prayers into the pith of the sacred tree's heart. I pulled my hands away and small droplets of blood formed in my wounded palms. I grasped my chest. The dark crimson stain covered the bodice of my white dress, and I fell over, deep in the arms of Mother Earth. My heart could not continue to beat carrying this weight.

Kenric gently lifted and carried me to the fire, his eyes wise in a way I had not seen before. Sadness showed in their creases. He bore the weight of his family and our clan now. The air around him vibrated, a sign of a life filled with burdens of others.

"He will return. I have no doubt Lovern will return," he assured as he laid me on my cloak near the fire. Logan was holding dried pork with both hands, pulling off bites with his small, white teeth. The deerhound, Mialchu, was peacefully curled up next to him, waiting for falling scraps. Finlay laid a large log on the fire and then spread his cape on the ground next to Logan.

"We have dried meat and bread for the meal. There is plenty of mead," said Kenric. He handed me a full skin.

"Eat, and then we will sing of Beathan and the bear and the time he found a druid in the forest," coaxed Finlay. "You can add words for the dance you did the night the druid came to our clan. Do you recall?"

I nodded, reached for the mead and was grateful I was with my cousins on this lonely night.

The next morning's ride was uneventful. We traveled along a river, down into a valley littered by small grey boulders and few trees. Large and small stones lay scattered in the heather and bracken. The valley's surrounding hills shook the stones off like water drops off a wet dog's back.

Just after midday, Kenric stopped and unstrapped his shield and long sword from his pony's rump. Remounting, he laid the sword across his lap and hung the leather and bronze shield from his shoulders. Finlay did the same. They readied themselves to fight as warriors, if needed. We were closing in on the village. My hand was on my short sword.

"If we have a reason to run the ponies, hang on tight to my dress. Do not fall," I warned Logan.

A cleft midway down the valley was our goal. When we turned in, there stood four structures built using scattered stones. The slate-roofed lodges stood in a semi-circle around a central well.

"This is the clan of Beathan's wife, Gavina," said Kenric. "My mother. They are the *Mathan Sealgair* Clan. Beathan's song contains a verse that tells this story."

Finlay began to sing. "While hunting one fall, a young chieftain, Beathan, stopped to rest here and fell in love with a maiden, Gavina. To marry her he fashioned a truce with her father, the clan chieftain."

The verse ended and we were silent remembering the times Beathan and Gavina laughed together. It was a good marriage. Now they are together on the other side.

"Beathan told me he loved coming here," said Finlay. "Even after her death. It was a place he could be at peace. He drank mead and sang songs. The memory of Gavina, our mother, as a young girl made him smile. That is why we decided to carve his tomb nearby."

After my rescue, Kenric and Finlay had carried Beathan's body and me back to our clan. The next morning, while I lay unconscious, Kenric, and Finlay took Beathan to be buried. They had stopped at this village on their way home after they performed the ritual of entombing him.

At that visit, bringing news of Beathan's death, Kenric swore to uphold the vow of peace Beathan fashioned with his wife's clan. Clan Chieftain Haye, pleased they came, honored Beathan and the agreement of peace with a feast. It was here Finlay first sang Beathan's death song. With the renewed vow of peace, Kenric had the bargaining tool that challenged our council to vote him the next chieftain of our clan.

Now, Kenric, Finlay, Logan, and I rode in among women grinding meal, boys feeding pigs in a small pen, and dogs chasing chickens. The tantalizing smells of evening meals floated on the air along with the sounds of the families gathered in shared lodges. My mouth watered as I followed the smell of fresh baked bread from this direction and roasted fowl from that. Our ponies paused in the center of the village; people stopped to watch, rakes or vegetable baskets in hand. I heard the laughter of children. Mistletoe and pine boughs hung in the doorways and lay in the windows. Respect for the gods and nature was visible. Alertness ruled the air. We sat at ease but with our hands on our weapons.

Kenric sat up straight and spoke loudly. "Kenric, mac Beathan is who I am. I am the *ceann-cinnidh* of my clan, son of the last *ceann-cinnidh*. I have come to honor the tomb of my father, Beathan. We ask for hospitality this night."

I heard a murmur, a rustle of clothing, and then I watched a young warrior bend to enter the largest stone dwelling. Mialchu stood, hackles raised. All of us were unsure what the tone of the greeting would be.

A man stooped as he came outside and stood in the doorway. His shield was corded and laid across his back to allow him quick access, a long sword in his right hand and a spear in his left. He was the tallest man I had ever seen. Limewater stiffened his long black hair, and serpent tattoos crawled up his muscled bare arms. His tunic covered broad shoulders, and a wide, woven leather belt encircled his waist. The cloth they all wore as breeches and dresses was a simple weld yellow but a cape of dark blue wool hung from his neck. His skin was the brown color of working outdoors.

Behind him stood a blond woman holding a wriggling tawny-haired child, Logan's age. Though tall herself, she was shadowed in the man's height.

From behind the house stepped four warriors, arrows aimed at us, ready to shoot if commanded. Their chieftain, Haye, his face alert, addressed us in a deep, demanding voice.

"Good eve, Kenric mac Beathan. We have watched you ride through our valley. You have asked for a night's hospitality? Tell me why we should give it."

"Because you will honor the peace my father Beathan arranged and I renewed, Haye," said Kenric. Our ponies did not know these people and were anxious, flickering, and sidestepping. We held our reins tightly, and he continued. "We will not stay if you do not wish us to. We are making a journey to honor Beathan's grave. We will pass good words to his spirit if you let us bed here tonight. It would please him if you give us food and mead."

"Hhhach," growled Haye. "If there is a spirit I wish to please, it is Beathan's. He would be a difficult one to appease if angry. Now, get off the ponies before they step on a child and I have to kill you!" He ordered the bowmen, "They are friends, let them come."

Haye laughed as he took two steps and covered the distance that would have taken Kenric four. Kenric and Finlay bounced off their ponies and were instantly embraced in a bear hug. Haye then noticed me and turned to Finlay, his eyebrows raised.

Finlay answered the unasked question. "She is Jahna, the mate of our druid. She is carrying a gift for Beathan. He died during her rescue. She wishes to honor and thank him."

Haye's booming voice was directed to me. "You will stay the night. There is boar to carve and good, strong mead. Come."

I handed Logan to Haye's wife, the smiling, tall woman from the door.

"Logan, go with Mialchu and make sure he has food and water," I reminded him as he scampered off to be with Haye's son and the other children. I heard Logan's words tell them that he was on his way to see his dead grandfather, the bear fighter. His giggles and Mialchu followed him, and they made quick friends as children and dogs do.

Kenric and Finlay, with Haye's hand on their backs, went into the large stone dwelling. The men of the clan followed, and the women gathered the children to help carry the prepared food. There would be stories and songs tonight for everyone in the clan.

A bent woman led the ponies into a stable next to the chieftain's lodge. I followed. In the waning light, I noticed she wore the wrinkles of many years. Though small for this clan, she was four fingers taller than me. Her hair was not grey like my mother's and other older women I knew, but long, white, and worn free. I stared at her. She noticed and laughed as she brushed her hair away from her face.

"I see you have noticed my hair. I have a long story about how it became white."

"I have only time and would be honored to hear your story, wise lady," I said.

"I will get a brand and light this space. We will talk when I return."

She went into the large dwelling and returned with a torch while I stood outside the door of the stable. She entered and put the torch in a niche in the wall. We gathered some dried grass and fed the ponies. I made sure there was water in their buckets. She pulled a rope gate across the doorway to stop the wandering of the animals.

I rubbed the ponies' backs and thanked them for carrying us this distance. I laid my cape on some of the sweet dried grass piled in a tiny alcove of the stable and sat down. All was well. I was warm, had water to drink and was ready to hear her story. She sat beside me and began in a soft, far away voice.

"It is not a story sang around the fire. It is the story of one life traded for another. Similar to the way the warrior Beathan's life was given in trade for yours."

The torchlight created long shadows as she leaned her body to rest on the wall. She groaned and straightened her legs. Her knees cracked as she stretched.

"Aooow! My knees ache all the time now, not just in cold. I cannot walk the distances I walked as a youth. My body sounds like rocks falling down a cliff with all its bangs and gurgles and clicks. Forty-three winters have worn this body down."

I knew our world was filled with lives as tragic as mine, but I could not understand someone else surviving the same guilt I carried since Beathan's death.

She wriggled her rump as if to soften the hard ground. Her long fingers ran through her hair and she started her story.

"It has been this color since I was a child. In the beginning, it was the color of Haye's. Black. Not black like yours. Yours reminds me of a glimmering raven's wing," she said, touching a strand of my hair, lying on my shoulder. "No, my hair had ribbons of copper in it. Mmm. But, I stray from my story.

"When I was young, my parents died in a village three days' ride from here. Raiders from the sea destroyed it. Only a boy and I escaped. Everyone else was killed by them."

"Oh gods," I said, beginning to understand.

"No, no, child. Do not be distressed. It was long ago. I am at peace with it now."

She took a strand of white hair and began twirling it around her finger.

"We heard they were coming. A man ran in from a neighboring village. They had just been raided. My father decided to hide me in a hole he had dug in the field behind our home. As he lowered me, he saw the boy run by and grabbed him. My father ordered me to take care of him."

She sniffed and rubbed her face as if to rub the memory away. "I did not want to take care of the smelly, wriggly boy who lived with the tanners. My father covered the hole with sticks and leaves. The dust fell through and got into my eyes." She looked up as if looking for the roof of sticks.

"He finished the covering and told us to be very quiet. 'Do not come out until I or mother come back to get you,' he told me. Noise exploded around us and the ground shook with running ponies. We heard many screams, then one last woman's scream. She called for her husband. Early in the raid the boy was in tears, and I feared he would cry out. I covered his mouth with my hand. He tried to break away from me, but I was bigger and had a tight hold on him. I was so scared we would be caught. My father told stories of the sacrifices of people caught in raids like these, and I did not want to die. The boy was struggling so I-I stuffed the hem of his tunic into his mouth and sat on him."

I grew cold with a premonition of her story.

"After a few minutes he stopped struggling. Later, I heard the ponies and the men as they left our village. Father had not come yet, so I did not think it was safe to climb out. We stayed through the night. I fell asleep, sitting on the boy."

She looked at me, her brows creased in concern and said, "He could still give us away, and I could not let him do that. When the sun came up the next morning, my hunger, my need to pee, and the ache in my legs would not let me stay in the hole any longer. I stood up, pushed the sticks off the top of the hole and turned back to the boy. The sunlight streamed in on the body that I had sat on all night. He did not move. I had traded his life for mine." She stopped at this and murmured a short prayer to Bel.

"Now, I was alone," she said. "I climbed out of the hole and walked to the front of the burned lodges, calling for my father and mother. I found them, the parents of the boy, and all the rest of my village. I found the bodies. Their heads were gone. My mother and father's blood dripping heads now hung on the raider's walls. I was the only one alive."

As she spoke, a shadow came over my eyes. The smell of food and sounds of happiness around me were gone. I heard only the sword as it passed through Beathan's neck and smelled Beathan's blood as it poured over me. I steadied myself against the wall; I did not want this horror to overcome me. "No, no, no," I whispered to myself. When my vision cleared, I saw that she noticed my distress. Nodding, she continued her story.

"I stayed there for two days, in shock, wandering around and eating what I could find. But, the need to live is powerful. I went into the forest to find food, eating grass and worms until I learned to trap small animals. I ran from anyone who came close, until the druid found me. He talked to me for days. I came to trust him. I told him my story. He and I lived together as husband and wife for fifteen sun cycles until his death." She sighed. Her hand touched her hair, stroked it as if in memory, and confessed, "It turned white the first full moon after my parents' death. He loved my white hair. He loved me."

I nodded. She understood. She lived through a horror as great as mine. A sense of relief and perception filled my heart. My grief was lighter. I raised my hands to my face and tears came to my eyes. I could almost believe Lovern would continue loving me. I stopped crying and looked up to see her watching me with kindness.

She awkwardly rose to her knees and with a smile said, "As much as I enjoy the company of my family, sometimes we just need to be with quiet animals that cannot sing, talk or drink mead." She leaned over to me and touched my chest where I had wiped the blood from my palms. A surge of energy came through the tips of her fingers to my heart. Her green eyes burned into mine, and her thin mouth broke into a grin.

"You are a healer," she said. "I saw your decorated leather pouch. We are sisters. I am a healer too. My name is Rhona."

"I am Jahna. Thank you for your story. It lifts a burden."

"Life goes on, my child, life goes on."

She walked to the opposite wall of the small stable, stretching as she moved. "We hunt bears and they are many this year. I know there are hardships to endure. The gods and goddesses have wars to fight, and we often are caught up in them. For now, my family is not in the sight of angry gods. I pray that it may be so for a long time."

I shivered with the thought that came. "The slave who took me told me the Romans were coming our way. We can prepare for them and fight until they leave," I said with hope.

"Sometimes, all the preparations we make cannot help," she said as she handed me a skin filled with a liquid. "This is from my healing spring and is pure. Wash and drink. I will bring you an infusion I make from a plant brought from the seaside. It never fails to bring sleep."

"If that is true then I will be in your debt," I said, bowing my head in respect to her. "Thank you. I will stay the night here." The loudest noises were the ponies munching their dried grass, a sound more inviting than the laughing voices I heard emitting from the dwelling nearby. "I do not want to seem inhospitable, but I do not think I can sit through the music and laughter in the chieftain's lodge. Will you tell my whereabouts to Kenric and Finlay? Will Logan be looked after?"

"Yes, I will speak with your men, and the boy will have a place to eat and sleep," she responded. "I will leave you here to make yourself comfortable, and I will bring food and the drink."

"Thank you."

She left. I heard the soft neigh of a pony and an echo in my ear.

"Sometimes, all the preparations we make cannot help."

CHAPTER 13

JAHNA

75 AD July

I readied the dried grass under my cape for sleep, Beathan's bronze bowl next to me. Rhona brought back a small roasted fowl, bread, and two containers of drink on a wooden plank. A mug and a small cup of clear liquid sat balanced next to the food.

"Here is mead to quench your thirst and the infusion for sleep. I used only a drop of the oil as it can also cause death."

"What is the name of this plant? There are many that cause death but few that will also allow sleep," I asked as I ate.

"Hemlock. Tales of ancient use come with it. Drink it after you eat and are ready for sleep. It will come soon. The oil is bitter, but I mixed in honey to sweeten it."

She pointed to the package on my cloak. "Is that the gift you take to Beathan?"

"Yes. I adorned it for him," I said, handing it to her. "The oak was the tree he adopted for his family."

She nodded as she unwrapped the soft leather. "It is a good gift. One that will honor him for all time."

Rhona stayed with me as I ate and drank the bitter infusion. I laid down, enveloped in the odor of the ponies and the peat smoke from the dwellings that surrounded me. It was but a few moments until I fell asleep and dreamed.

I stood watching from a distance and saw the stone dwellings, the homes of Haye's clan. People moved quickly. Gathered food lay in bundles, and weapons glinted, tied to the backs of ponies. Men and women were readying themselves for battle. Loud shouts rang from dwelling to dwelling. Haye's war chariot stood outside his lodge with two ponies throwing their heads in impatience. Haye stepped through his doorway and behind him came his son, Eanruig, and Haye's wife, Nairne. Eanruig was older than when I saw him today, but not yet an adult. Both he and his father were bare-chested, and their faces and bodies dyed woad blue. Limewater stiffened Haye's black hair. Bronze and leather shields, swords and dirks were strapped to them. I felt excitement and fear.

Hayes spoke. "The King has called us. We must go quickly, Nairne. I must take those who can fight, and I chose you to guard the children of those who go. We will come back when the battle is done. We will have a celebration to honor Morrigna, may the Goddess protect us. We will chase the invaders off the land and will be rewarded by our king. Be glad we go!"

In the shadows I saw the white hair of Rhona, Haye's mother. I turned to face her. Bent in grief, she cried out, "Have I not given enough of myself? Must I lose also my son and grandson?" Many ravens flew overhead, and I shivered.

No one answered her. The stone dwellings were empty. Moss grew on the fallen rocks that were once walls. Roof slates fell into the centers of the lodges. Heavy dust covered the fire pits. A cruel winter wind blew Rhona's white hair around her face to catch itself in her tears.

I woke with the bitter taste of the infusion in my mouth. I had not had dreams of the man I knew and feared but instead, I had a vision of a future I did not want to know.

Rhona sat near me, touching my shoulder as I sat up, the dawn's light just reaching the village.

"Your face twisted with a dream," Rhona said. "I am sorry. I thought you would not dream of the man who haunts you."

I could not tell her that I dreamed of her son's death.

"Rhona, do you know where Beathan's tomb is?"

It was still dark as I wrapped my cape around me and picked up the bowl.

"Yes, I have visited there. He was a man I respected in life and in death."

"Will you take me if we both ride my pony? I am ready to go now. I do not want to wait for Finlay and Kenric. They will come later."

We rode a trail that was steep at times, but my pony never faltered. I was seated behind Rhona. We spoke no words; we communicated by touch. The sun rose hot on our backs, and we stopped at a creek to wash and drink. We would eat after the gifting. Bracken and blooming heather surrounded the trail. Crossing a moor, I could see the hills that were the feet of the stark mountains behind them. The hillside where Beathan's body lay buried was a mountain foot. Covered in creeping juniper and blue harebells, color filled the spaces between the quartz-filled granite rocks and boulders strewn about the ground. The clean smell of recent rain was in the air.

Rhona sat holding the pony while I slowly climbed to the entrance of the tomb. The side of the hill was steep and covered in loose shale. I carried the bowl, a small piece of peat, a coal from last night's fire and a live pigeon Rhona had given me. I finally came to the ledge in front of the entrance of Beathan's tomb. I stood, caught my breath, and leaned on a large boulder that had been rolled to block its entry. I could not get in but that was not important. I would leave the gift outside the entrance. Beathan could see it from the Other World.

I dug a hole using my hands and small sword. As I lifted the bowl to the sky, it caught sparks of sunlight and reflected the color of Beathan's hair. He was watching. His hand was warm on my shoulder.

"Beathan. A gift to you for the gift of my life. You exchanged your life for mine. I honor you and say you will be in my heart forever. We sing songs about your bravery and drink toasts made in your name." The last tears I cried for Beathan fell as I continued. "I offer this bowl to bring you happiness. May you drink mead from it. May you dip honey from it. Watch over us, your clan and the clan of your wife. I feel unrest is coming and we will require the help of the gods. Please make them aware of my request," I called, remembering my dream.

I tucked the bowl, wrapped in my cape, and the soft leather snuggly into the hole, covered it with dirt, and rolled a large stone over it. The entrance looked undisturbed.

After gathering small twigs, I retrieved the live coal from the moss it was nestled in and blew on it until it and the twigs caught fire. The peat began to smolder. I laid hemp on top, and the smoke began to writhe around me. I unwrapped the pigeon and held it securely in my left hand. I lifted my dirk to the sky and called to Andraste and Caswallawn, the Goddess and God of war.

"Hear me, O God and Goddess. If we must fight, make us victorious. Help us defeat our enemies. Help those who die in battle cross the river easily." My dirk found its way to the pigeon's heart and blood began to drain from its body, covering my uplifted arms. The smell of the blood, the mixture of the sweet hemp and acrid peat smoke carried me to a passage dream.

I looked through Aine's eyes at Beathan's open tomb. To be able to see it through her and know our life story continued was a blessing from Morrigna. Beathan would be remembered as a warrior and chieftain. Tears came to my eyes with this understanding.

I willed her to find my bowl. I took her to the stone and watched as she lifted the bowl from under it. She saw the oak tree I had engraved. She held the bowl I made up to the sun. It reflected the color of Beathan's hair. I knew then she would help keep Beathan's memory alive. My heart filled with peace. I paid my debt to him, and Beathan was a fair man and would forgive me my guilt. Now, I could forgive myself.

"Jahna. Jahna, are you well? We awoke before daybreak and found you gone already." Finlay and Kenric knelt next to me on the ledge and spoke at the same time. Logan was slipping his way up the hillside. My fire was out, and the pigeon blood dry on my arms. My passage dream was gone.

"Yes, I am well. I pleased Beathan." I smiled at them both. "Thank you. Thank you for bringing me here. We can go home now."

Logan clambered up to the ledge just then and touched the stone covering his grandfather's grave. He turned, grinning at his accomplishment and was ready to go down, just as fast. His quick slide down was followed by our evenly measured footsteps. We spent another night with Rhona's clan and continued on our way the next morning before daylight.

Arriving at our trail, I looked up at the gate of our hill fort. There stood a sentinel waiting for us. The sun was in my eyes and I could only see that he stood like a warrior, tall and straight. The hot summer breeze wore the smell of crushed acorns and bees. My heart lurched in my chest. I gasped—I knew who the man was.

I could not go up the hill. I slid off my pony's back. Kenric leaned over and scooped my pony's reins and Logan. He and Finlay rode on. They stopped at the top of the hill for a moment. The tall man and Finlay exchanged words. Kenric nodded to him.

Mouth dry and moist hands, I waited. Lovern turned and walked to our home. I followed, limping up the hill with trembling legs.

I had forgiven myself for Beathan's death, but could Lovern forgive me?.

CHAPTER 14

May, 2005

I jerked awake, knowing I would have to fight my way out of here. I'd behaved and was a good patient for a week, but I'd decided to rebel and was itching to go. Marc had been restricting my movements but no more; I was vacating this inn today.

George had received a grant for us several days ago. It was enough for us to stay for the rest of the summer. Things were changing at the site, and I wanted to see it. I'd been cooped up here too long.

My room was littered with clothes; jeans and button up shirts were strewn across the floor and bed, all too hard to put on. I finally surrendered and, with great trouble, pulled on sweatpants and a t-shirt. I couldn't even get a bra on. It hurt too much to twist and reach behind yet.

Marc walked in just as I finished dressing, carrying a cup of steaming coffee.

"Aine. What are you doing?" His forehead creased with concern, his tone gentle, yet impatient. "You're not supposed to be going anywhere. The doctor told you to rest. I think you should be inside at least a few more days."

"Yeah, Marc, I know. But I have to go to the job site. I want to see it. It seems like weeks that I've been away. That coffee smells delicious. Can I have a sip?" I took the hot cup from his outstretched hand and sniffed the adrenaline-starting steam. "Mmmm. How can someone who doesn't drink coffee make it so perfect?"

"Well," said Marc, "you aren't a coffee gourmet and she makes it strong, just like you want it. If you stay here one more day, I'll have her make you coffee all day long."

"No, even that isn't enough to keep me here. If you make me stay, I'll tunnel out. I really want to see what you all have done to my dig."

He compromised. "Ah well, okay. But promise me, if you feel the least bit tired you'll let us bring you back."

I endeavored to finish dressing but couldn't lift my arm over my head without pain. I tried to hide my grimacing face in the sweatshirt. I didn't want him to see how much it still hurt to move. "Oh, damn it. Marc, can you help me, please?" I sighed and stopped struggling. "I'll be careful. It's been seven days, and I can't stand the inside of this room or any room in the inn anymore. I promise not to do anything strenuous," I said, sweatshirt piled in my lap.

"I hope not, even your feet were bruised. I don't know how, the cave-in didn't bury them. It must have happened when we pulled you out. You were complaining about them the first night in hospital so I slipped the sheet off and saw that they were bruised. Then I saw your toes. You know the super long second toe? I remembered teasing you about that when we were at university."

I looked down at my bare feet and waved my toes in the air for him to see. "Yep. The MacRea toe. Pretty neat, huh? It's in the family genes. Or should I say on our feet?"

Marc grabbed my sweatshirt and lifted it so I could get my hand inside. It slid on and I gently eased it over my sore shoulder.

"Thanks. Finally, real clothes. I'm surprised they still fit. Mrs. Dingleberry must think that to feed is to heal. I've probably gained 5 pounds." I could see Marc's keen, blue eyes peruse my body. Chills ran up and down my back and other places. I had to concentrate on getting outside, or we wouldn't be going anywhere, even if I were still sore. My body wanted him and a debate was going on in my mind.

"Nope, I don't see anything that shouldn't be there. You look just as tempting as before," he said as he kissed me gently on the tip of my nose and then my ear. I closed my eyes and wished he would continue, but after taking a deep breath my resolve strengthened.

I slipped on my loafers and ushered Marc to the door. "Have the results from the urn come back yet from Glasgow?" I gingerly followed Marc down the short hall.

George had called Jim Cowley, an osteoarchaeologist and friend, when he realized I was going to be okay. He paid for a helicopter to pick up the bronze bowl and what we hoped were human remains while I was in the hospital in Fort William. They were flown to the Scottish Universities Research & Reactor Centre in Glasgow for Jim to analyze.

"No. We put in a rush order. The lab's been running some recalibrating tests. They haven't started any new work and won't for the next week. I called yesterday. Jimmy told me the remains would be tested as soon as they're done."

"A week? Another week? Oh, bloody hell. I don't think I'm going to be able to wait that long. God," I said, shaking my head, "am I glad I wrote down my impressions after the awake dream I had when we were together. I reread them yesterday. I had forgotten so many details since the accident."

"That shouldn't be a surprise, Aine. Your injury was deadly serious." Marc stopped on the landing of the narrow staircase and turned to me. "I would have been just sick if you had been critically injured, or worse, Aine. You have to promise me to be more careful. I don't ever want to feel so helpless again."

I slipped my arms through his and hugged as well as I could with the still-bruised ribs. "I know, Marc. I'm sorry. I'll try not to put you in that position again. I like having you here. This week would have been a lot worse if you hadn't been here to play Gin Rummy with me and tuck me in." I pecked his cheek with a kiss.

"You know, I'm glad you talked me into staying. And I'm glad you found the bowl, even if you say you had help from a ghost. I'm happy to be here, with you."

My heart raced at his comments. He was happy to be here with me. But bringing up Jahna, even in that teasing mode, gave me chills. She was waiting for me and getting impatient. That was one reason I had to go today. She had something else for me to see.

He paused, as we made our way downstairs. "Oh, we did date the pottery."

I stopped and turned to him, hoping for the information I had been praying for.

"We got a date of 80 AD plus or minus fifteen years," he said. "I know you were looking for a pre-Roman site and it looks like we have one. Remember the lump of metal you went back into the cave for? It looks like it's a bronze clasp or pin with the head in the shape of an acorn and a bronze bracelet. The pin was probably a cloak clasp."

"WAHOO! The year is perfect!" I gloried briefly in the moment and grinned at him. Oh yes, this was going to be a very good day. I could feel it. "Is there any food left? I need breakfast," I said and walked as quickly as my back would let me.

My back ached, and I hung onto the glossy, oiled balustrade for balance. Marc trailed behind.

Mrs. Dingleberry had insisted I eat breakfast and dinner in my room; it had been days since I had been in the dinning room while food was being served. My mouth watered as I entered and smelled the bacon and coffee.

This was Mrs. Dingleberry's heaven. Cooking and cleaning was her forte; nursing was not. I had eaten well while recuperating, but she just barely tolerated having me around all day. Guests weren't meant to be here unless it was mealtime or bedtime. I'm afraid I caused her some schedule upset. Today she would be rid of me for most of the day, and I could imagine her oiling and polishing to her heart's content. I smelled the lemon oil along with her delightful breakfast.

"George! Good morning! Hi, Tim, Lauri. Good to see all of you."

"Aine!" they chorused as they twisted in their chairs to see me. "Congratulations on the funding! Good to see you out of bed."

"George. You're my savior. Thank you for talking to the 'powers that be' and securing the money. Marc told me you were also using some of your grant money to fund us. We'll pay you back. My heart is touched by your trust in me."

"You're welcome. But the news that brought University money to you, of course, was the Raven Bowl. My influence hardly played a part in the decision."

"The Raven Bowl?" I asked looking at Marc.

"That's what the press is calling the bronze bowl you found. We don't know what's in it, but the beauty of the bowl is enough to bring attention up here. The lab started spreading the word," Marc returned.

"Wow. 'The Raven Bowl.' It's good. I like that." I knew Jahna would have liked it, too.

George stood up, walked over to me and kissed my cheek. His nose was perpetually wrinkled from keeping his gold, rimmed glasses on. He was balding; it seemed more since my accident. He ran his hand over his head as a nervous habit, and it looked as if he had rubbed most of his hair away. He was rubbing it right now. "I was wondering when you were going to get out of bed. Are you going to stay downstairs today? I have some reports you can read to catch up. There is a great reading chair in the library."

"Actually, George, Mrs. Dingleberry and I have already walked through every room here in the inn that I am allowed into. She wouldn't let me alone until she was sure I wouldn't keel over in her parlor!" Mrs. Dingleberry scurried in at that moment with a tray of warm scones and scowled.

"Do you see that puzzle set up on the table over there?" I pointed across the room. "I've been working on it for two days while you were at the dig. I even helped Mrs. Dingleberry dust the furniture! She wants me out of here. She's had me walking up and down at least two sets of stairs and three rounds of the rooms for two days, now, to strengthen my legs. I'm going stir crazy. I *am* going to the hill today." I noticed Mrs. Dingleberry quivering, probably with happiness at having me out from under foot.

She turned from the buffet she was loading with more food and said, "I must go down into town today and was going to ask one of ye to stay with the lassie. She's fine."

George looked at me, then Mrs. Dingleberry, and then turned and looked at Marc. "What? You've gone and jumped over the gunwales on this one! This injured woman can't go to the site!" He harrumphed.

I tried to calm him. "I've already promised Marc I wouldn't do anything to get in your way. I just want to walk around and see what you've found."

Lauri reached in front of me to get the butter for her warm scone. "We've found some more postholes and a fire pit. We have a coal layer, and we think we are in the center of a dwelling," she said, ready to take a bite of her scone. "It's near the southern walls, next to the double gate."

I looked at Marc with raised eyebrows. "Is it a domicile?"

He nodded slightly. We were so close. I could feel her. My neck tingled. I thought that the feelings and dreams would end when I found where she was buried but yesterday, as I looked out the window toward the hill, I had a feeling that I had to go to the site today. I couldn't shake it. My gut was telling me that it was urgent that I get to the hill. My shoulder was aching, and I could feel my back trying to spasm, but dammit, I was going.

"Mrs. Dingleberry, your coffee is perfect this morning. Thank you. Marc, would you please pass more of those wonderful currant bannocks? Oh, and the butter?" I asked.

Marc watched me eat with an amused grin. I could swear he was waiting for me to burst out of my clothes.

After breakfast, they jumped into the jeep and I eased myself in, over George's protests. "OK, George, I'll a take a pillow to lean against. I think Mrs. Dingleberry will let us take the rose patterned one in the dining room."

As we bounced along the farm road, me sitting against the rose pillow, I remembered the last time I came this way seven days ago. The dream was in my head from the night before. I could feel Jahna at my elbow, directing me. I had found her tomb that day, and had almost found mine.

We arrived, and I felt as if I'd come home. I was amazed as I looked around the site. George and Marc had called in more workers and there were fifteen people here now. I was involved in discussions about the increase back at the inn, but was not expecting to see them here yet. It reemphasized how long I had been gone.

There were several people on the east side with sonar equipment, looking for disturbances deep in the soil. To the west, I saw surveyors staking plots for further digging. On the trail, a crew worked on the cave where I had been trapped. A larger tent had been raised for meals and laying out artifacts to photograph and catalog. It also contained a stockpile of supplies, snacks, and water. It looked as if we planned to stay awhile.

I inhaled the odor of freshly overturned earth, the intoxicating smell of my work, smiled, gingerly slid out of the jeep and limped to Kendy and Matt. Marc and George had registered the site with the West of Scotland Archaeology Service. That meant the news would spread. Matt and Kendy had volunteered to be on site at night. The world around a dig tended to start coming to look and take anything that isn't nailed down once a site was registered. We would hire security guards as soon as I could afford it and I notified the local police. They couldn't make a regular stop but were aware we were here. When the security did come – soon, I hoped – Matt and Kendy could go back to sleeping in a real bed. The looks on their faces told me they really wouldn't care where they slept as long as it was together. I wished I could be that young again and have a fresh start to my life. Although, I have to admit, my start so far with Marc was pleasing. I smiled with the memory of our one recent night of lovemaking.

"I see the press is here," I said and nodded toward the tent. "I want to avoid them.

"Oh, no problem," said Matt. "They stay inside, protected from the always expected showers. We hardly ever see them."

The reporters were as anxious about the carbon dating and material composite results as we were and would send the results to the local papers and the archaeological societies. Bronze bowls were news in both circles. I was pleased, even with the extra work and money spent on guards, that news of our find, *my* find, was making it out to the world. I wondered how many cameras would show up if there turned out to be a cremated human body in the bowl.

Matt laughed. "Aine, you are looking good for being so close to becoming one of our artifacts!"

Kendy poked him in the ribs and frowned at him. "Seriously, Aine, should you be here? You look as if you still hurt a bit."

I tried to wave her comment off, but George looked at me with his "I told you so" look and then walked away.

I shrugged my good shoulder. "I have to admit that I'm not feeling as good as I was a week ago, but wild pigs couldn't keep me away for another day. Wow! We look legitimate now. It's amazing what an increase in funding can do!" I turned to Kendy, who was still standing near me. "Kendy, please show me what you have. I haven't seen your drawings for at least seven days."

Tim and Matt picked up trowels and sifters and stepped into the ever-increasing hole. Marc trudged back to the jeep to get his computer and George was off to direct the surveyors, I'm sure to their dismay.

"I'd love to! It's so much fun being here at the beginning of things. We've several structure outlines already plotted, and I've had a bit of fun with them. I needed something to do while Matt and I were stuck out here." She grinned crookedly at me. She opened her sketchbook. As she leafed through it, I could see the drawings she'd made before my accident. She had different views of the cave the way it looked before the slide. My mouth went dry with the memory of the mountain falling on top of me. My bruises seemed to step up their demand to be noticed. Then she turned the page. They had found more postholes and she drew them just as they looked in the excavation. But there was more.

"I drew this one for fun, to give us an idea of what this side of the village might have looked like. It keeps me motivated to remember these aren't just holes in the ground, they were homes and places of work."

The drawing was a composite of the total excavation site, the structure in front of us with the fire pit in the middle, other structures that were being uncovered, and those we might uncover later. She superimposed a half sphere built with a short, circular, stone wall about fourteen inches high, continuing to the roof in wooden planks and mud or wattle and daub for each of the excavation sights. The roofs were thatched. It looked as if she had been sitting in the courtyard of the fort while it was being lived in. And it looked familiar.

"Oh, did anyone tell you that we found pieces of quartz in three of the postholes that are at the back of this structure?" she asked absentmindedly. "We found the stone from the walls scattered all around, as you would expect. We were charting, and removing them when I noticed one of the postholes had a flat stone in the bottom. I lifted it to find a piece of white quartz under it. It looked deliberate enough to raise my curiosity. We found the same flat stones in two other holes and with quartz under them, also. The flat stones look like river stones but the quartz isn't found around here. They seem to be an offering to a god or goddess. Have you ever seen them before, Aine?"

My legs went wobbly but not from my injuries. I grabbed the back of a camp chair that was near the edge of the excavation and sat down.

"No, I've never seen it before in a dig." *I've seen it but I can't tell you where,* I thought, *or you'd think I was crazy.* "Go get that chair and come sit beside me," I said pointing to another camp chair to the side of the tent. I looked at the actual excavation, and back to the picture. There it was. The pattern of the postholes and the stone wall of the structure led to the defense wall and touched it. It wasn't a round circle. It created an alcove, of sorts. That and the quartz made it jump out at me. *We are in Jahna's home*, I thought. We had found her home.

Trying to sound calm, I said, "Kendy, look at the postholes toward the back of the structure." I pointed to the excavation. "They don't go all the way around, but in this picture you have drawn them in as if they do," I continued, handing her sketchbook back to her.

"Yes, I see that. I was supposing the rest of the holes would be uncovered, maybe today."

"I'll bet there won't be anymore holes uncovered for this structure. I have a feeling. This structure didn't stay round but took this jog to join with the fence. Look. It could create a private alcove by hanging a blanket. One of the first private bedrooms in Scotland!"

"Well, Aine," she said looking at me out of the side of her eyes. "No one should ever say you don't have a good imagination!"

I smiled at her and looked back at the drawing with déjà vu.

Mr. Treadwell walked up to Kendy and me just at that moment. "Good morning," I said.

About 5'6" tall, I was sure he had been taller as a young man. But now, age and hard work had caused his body to disfigure with arthritis. He still carried the rugged look of one who has worked outdoors all his life. His white hair tufted just above both ears, and he was clean-shaven. His watery blue eyes had seen too many days in the sun, and deep lifelines creased his face. His muddy boots were least twenty years old and he smelled of tobacco and scotch. His voice lilted with a strong Highland mark, and it made me feel as if I were home on Skye.

"Good mornin', lassie. I ken ye were here. I would appreciate it if ye did not scamper into any more caves. I would like not havin' anyone kill't on my land." I noticed he was serious.

"Kendy, would you mind if I spoke with Mr. Treadwell for a few minutes? I'll look at the rest of your pictures later," I requested.

"No problem. I have to get back to work. You can find me here when you're ready." Kendy looked relieved as she picked up her drawing pencils and notepad and slipped down into the dig near the newly excavated fire pit. She proceeded to start drawing the layers Matt and Tim were uncovering.

"Mr. Treadwell, I hope not to have to go into a cave again for a very long time," I replied, knowing in my heart I would go into another one in a heartbeat if I thought something was there. "Would you give me a hand up, please? I would like to take a short walk with you."

Mr. Treadwell extended his arthritis-bent hands, and I took one as gently as I could. As I started to pull myself up, I began to twist my back. "Ouch! Oh that hurts!" I sat back down into the chair, tears just squeezing out of the corners of my eyes.

"Ach," said Mr. Treadwell. He dropped my hands as if they were on fire and backed up five steps.

Marc heard me, quickly stood up, and put his computer on the table. He walked over, but before he could say anything, I frowned at him to show my determination. He faced me, grasped my upraised arms and helped me stand straight up. Much better. I saw a frown returned in his eyes. "Thanks for helping me, Marc," I said with a grimace I hoped looked like a smile.

Plainly concerned, he quietly said, "Aine, you need to go back. I'll have Tim take off and drive you. I told you it was too early for you to come here."

"No, I promise not to do anything that strenuous again. I just want to take a short walk with Mr. Treadwell," I said and leaned against him until I caught my breath.

"OK, but only if you promise not to go off the hill unless one of us is with you. We don't need any repeats of last week."

"Scouts honor, I won't. I am a big girl, Marc. I can take care of myself."

Looking worried, he countered, "Yes, but I can still worry."

His strong arms supported me and I was comfortable and secure in them. *This is where I should be.* I hugged him as well as I could without wincing and with my cheek against his, I whispered, "Marc, I owe you my life. I love you. I wouldn't do anything to hurt you, but I can't live my life in a bowl. I promise to be as careful as I can."

I turned to Mr. Treadwell, who watched the conversation with a humorless face. "Mr. Treadwell, let's take a stroll." I offered him my arm.

Marc watched with concern as Mr. Treadwell and I limped off, Mr. Treadwell's arm protectively under mine for support. I wasn't sure who supported whom. I looked back at Marc to tell him I was in good hands. He stood there watching us, shaking his head.

As we walked, we looked out over the pasture where several head of long-haired Highland cattle were grazing, and then at the mountain. I stared at it, not breathing, for a long moment. That mountain almost took my life. I shook my head to shake the memory of the accident away, and turned, searching the surrounding skyline. I noticed three tree-covered hills. They were alone, standing as if they were sentinels.

"Do those hills have a local name?"

"Aye. They are the Ben Rien. They are the three Celt goddesses that become one. It is said the hills remember the uald Picts."

"Ah, the Queen Hills, named for the queen goddess Morrigna. The goddess of fertility and war. Interesting combination, wasn't she? Her favorite was the raven." I looked up into the blue sky, empty except for the scattered, cotton ball clouds. I seemed to remember it peppered with ravens.

"Aye, ravens roost in the trees on those hills. They're here at harvest. They're lucky for us. Like the ravens in the Tower of London. We say our town will have ill luck if the ravens don't come back every year. We look for them to come."

"I know what you mean. We need all the luck we can get these days."

I noticed a depression in the middle of the pasture just below us. There were trenches cut into the pasture.

"Are you cutting peat, Mr. Treadwell?"

"Aye, lassie. I use it in the longer winters when fuel prices are dear."

To position my self in the memory of my awake dreams, I turned to look behind us, to the place on the hill where I thought the gate would be in the defense wall, then turned back to the pasture. "Mr. Treadwell, was there a lake here once?"

"Oh, aye. My father said my great-grandfaither drained a wet-land to create a pasture, bad as it is. It was called Loch Dubh or Black Lake." He paused. I imagined his ancestor standing on this hilltop we were now excavating and looking at the area, deciding how to drain it. "Most of the year the ground is still wet and full of sinkholes. I cannot let the cattle run in it but a few months of the year. The few I have there now are sure footed and will be canny of the bogs. There's a story about it if you're interested, lassie. 'Tis a ghost story. Would ye like to hear it?"

"Yes, please. I would love to."

"There was a grand battle between the Romans and the Picts near here," he said, using his chin to point in a faraway direction. I figured he was referring to the battle of Mons Graupius of AD 84. He continued, "They supposedly sacrificed a druid near here to keep it from happening. It's told he still walks here."

He turned and studied my eyes with a look that chilled me. "Lassie, ye must swear never to speak of this."

I raised my hand and promised.

Quietly, as if he were in a church, he went on, "I saw him one November morning, kneeling at the edge of where the loch used to be. He was praying, or at least I took him to be a praying. His arms were raised to the sky. The tartan was on his shoulders and he had a proud, straight back. A figure in the corner of my eye. When I turned, he was gone and a big fox was sittin' there, right there where the man stood. He ran off when my eyes caught his." His whole body shifted closer to me as he whispered, "Others would laugh, but that's what I saw."

"Mr. Treadwell, I believe you. I've seen ghosts, too." He looked back at me with understanding in his liquid blue eyes.

I suddenly had the most overwhelming feeling of dread. It felt as if the air around me were filled with water. I could barely breathe and began to double up. I couldn't stay on the hill anymore. After arguing so hard to get here, I had to get away.

"Are ye all right, lassie?"

"Yes, please; let me lean on your arm to the jeep, and then if you would let Marc know I'd like to go back. I think I need to get out of their way for the rest of today. Mr. Treadwell, I am very glad you came up here today. Thank you. Thank you very much for telling me your story. You don't know how much it means to me." I leaned on him and felt strength belying his age as he walked and supported me, limping, to the jeep.

Tim drove me to the inn, trying to avoid the bumps in the road. All the way back I thought about Mr. Treadwell's ghost and wondered why I'd had that reaction at the telling of his story. Just what I needed, another ghost in my life.

The ghost of a man that turned into a fox.

Chapter 15

JAHNA

75 AD August

Lovern waited outside the door to our dwelling, his eyes filled with questions. After treading slowly through the gates of our village, my head full of doubts and fear, I stopped in front of him, not knowing how he would receive me. He gently took both my hands into his, raised them to his lips, and kissed my fingers, his tears wetting my knuckles. His right hand moved to my head – I leaned into it – and his left hand to our doorframe; he prayed a blessing on our home and me. His hand then rested on my shoulder. I looked into his deep blue eyes and saw an immense relief and then deep concern. Dread replaced my temporary happiness. I did not know how much he knew of the events that led me here.

"I arrived home several days ago," he said, "after you came to me in the passage dream. We rode as fast as we could, stopping only to sleep a few hours and feed the ponies. You were gone when I arrived. I learned of your taking and of Beathan's death from your mother."

I bowed my head, unable to look into his eyes any longer.

"I thanked all the gods for sparing your life," he said. "I wanted to ride after you to comfort you and heal your spirit. I craved to hold you in my arms and assure myself you were well."

"Yet you did not come," I whispered. "Why?" The heat of his body touching my skin made my stomach burn. I drew into myself, unclean, not worthy of his touch. I felt his arms fall away, and air moved as he stepped back. In my mind, I knew he smelled the stench of the badger, the man who took me, which I carried in my nose continually.

"I could not leave your mother. We have taken her to the hospice. She was not eating when I arrived two days ago. She is very ill."

Startled at his news, I said, "My mother? My mother is not here?" I had prayed to hear her healing words on my arrival home. Disturbing news of my mother's progressing illness was not in the vocabulary of my dreams. My stomach turned inside out, and my world began to tumble again. My reunion with Lovern, curative moments of talk and love, would have to wait. The forgiveness I felt at Beathan's tomb was far away in the depths of my heart.

I lived in routine. I rose early, after little sleep, and saw after Mother's daily needs. Sileas and I would make medicines and complete chores while Lovern and Harailt went around the village to visit the injured and ill.

Lovern and I had not slept together since my return. I made my bed at the hospice because of Mother, and he at our home.

We had not spoken about my taking, although Lovern tried. Once, while alone in the yard of the hospice, he turned to me, holding a bucket of water he had gathered from the sacred spring.

"Jahna, drink from the god's water. Let it rinse the gloom from your soul. Let it wash away your memories." His hand dipped in and offered me a drink. The sun was too bright for my eyes and the birds too shrill.

"You cannot want me," I said. "I am impure. You are a healer. It will cause you to be ill." Pain filled his eyes, but I could not stay. His glances were licks of fire on my skin. His touches caused unseen bruises. Nausea rose violently in my gut, and I ran away. To find a path of purification was a constant prayer of mine. My days were long and nights longer.

The gods called me, even in my time of distress. Death in our clan required my attendance during this time. Braden was the cause of another heaviness in my heart.

Braden and Callum had ridden hard with Lovern from the seaside. On their return, they had gone back to practicing daily as warriors and hunting. They both decided to chase an old boar that had lived in our forest, fattened on acorns for several sun cycles. Running ahead of Callum, Braden slipped, and the angered animal split his gut with its long, sharp tusks.

Callum ran into the hospice with Braden cradled like a baby in his strong arms. "I told him you would heal him, Lovern. I said you have the god's ear." He laid Braden on the cot, who was breathing fast and bleeding from his midsection.

Lovern and I prepared the meal of boiled onions we fed to those with such wounds. It told the severity of the damage. The smell of onions came from Braden's belly. It was then we knew death would come soon. There was to be no miracle here.

Braden died the hard death of a gut wound. For two sunrises he was brave and tried not to show pain, but the third day gave way to his deep groans and cries. I sat and talked with him, trying to capture a vision to help him cross the river of death. He strongly resisted.

In a low voice, tempered with a smile, I recalled the times we played as children. Braden always seemed to attract trouble. His father was strict, yet always forgave. Together, we remembered the day Beathan watched Braden prove himself as a young warrior. He won a contest as he practiced fighting with the other young men of the clan. Impressed by Braden's strength and skills, Beathan called him to be one of the chieftain's guards. He was among the bravest in the band of personal protectors Beathan had around him. It was during that time I imagined him to be my first choice of a husband.

"Braden, my friend," I said. "I am sorry for my being captured and forcing Beathan into battle without you. You might have been able to save him. Thank you for protecting Lovern on your journey. Braden, be in peace. We will sing songs to your name. You will be in my mind as long as I live. When you cross the river, you will be at the hand of Beathan. Go. He has need of you there."

Braden slipped into the deep death sleep. My labyrinth guided my thoughts to his river crossing. Through the fog of a light vision, I helped him into Death's boat. Braden's sucking breath rattled and stopped.

It saddened me to see the hero of my youth pass.

After this death, I realized it was time to tend to my own life. I had tried to wish the guilt away, but it hung over me like a black cloud and hid the warmth of my friends and Lovern. I took a deep breath and decided to try to perform the necessary rituals to cleanse myself and prepare for my mother's death.

My mother's dying happened in small stages. I attended her evening meals. She could eat tiny spoonfuls of wild carrot and rabbit stew with encouragement. Questions arose in her eyes, sunken into her thin face, as I fed her, the answers out of my reach.

Among other rituals, I prepared hazel memory sticks for my mother. She and I recalled her life story, and she chose a remembrance for each stick. There were ten. Among them were the days she spent with my father, three sticks to record the day she met him, the day they married and the day she came to believe he would not return. She told me she believed that in whatever way he died, he went calling our names.

"His love for you and me kept him returning from his travels. He would not have stayed away willingly. Now I will join him," she said with a far away look in her eyes.

Three more sticks stood for memories of hers and Beathan's childhood: their mother's love for them, times she and Beathan enjoyed playing and later hunting together.

"The days of play did not last long. Beathan knew early he was to become our chieftain and started the necessary training before he was ten. It sometimes made him insufferable to live with, but I was proud of him. The day he became chieftain was a very good day for our family. He was a brave and fair leader of our clan. His death was not in vain and he will be remembered long after I am forgotten."

After I took a deep breath with my eyes closed in Beathan's memory, I said, "Mother, you will be at his table to remind him of his family. Carry our love to him. In this you will be remembered, also."

The last four memory sticks were for my birth, her only child, and events around our life together.

"The day you were born, your father gave me this bronze armlet." She shook it from her bag, her arms too thin to wear it. "It is one of the first pieces Finley made with decoration. Its spirals symbolize the continuing of our bloodline. I want you to have it now, Jahna. It is up to you to carry on your father's family. I also want you to wrap me in my plaid cape when I die. The day Beathan took the plaid you created and declared it to be the clan plaid was a good day in my life." She paused to cough. Blood now colored the cloth she used to wipe her mouth. I brought her a cup of warm brewed chamomile to calm her. "Good. That is very good. It is in the Goddess's light that you are now working to help our clan in healing. And to assist our spirits cross the river to the Otherworld is a path that will take you straight to the Goddess's side when it is your turn to go. I am proud you are my daughter. Your marriage to Lovern will bring only good to our family, I am assured."

My mind was buzzing like a hive of bees with the memories we had discussed. Her pride for me was an emotion she had not expressed before, and I was humbled. I grasped her hand and held it to my lips, my tears falling into her palm. My heart knew she would to be in a strong body when she crossed, but my mother would also be gone from my everyday life. The calming words I said to others at this time seemed difficult to believe right now.

At day's end, on the thirtieth day after I arrived home from Beathan's tomb, we burned her hazel memory sticks, bundled in one long, red thread. Holding the bundle, she kissed it three times, said goodbye to her past, and slipped them into the fire. Lovern, Harailt, and Sileas reverently watched. A tender smile filled my mother's eyes with calmness, and she slowly nodded in approval.

The vision that came to me as that fall night's air filled with peat smoke began with the god Cernunnos. He wore the head of a Red Deer, and pointed to a peak covered in clouds. As a hawk, I flew over the peak, down under the clouds, to see Bel and Morrigna drinking from a single cup. The battle for my soul had been waged and was now over. Both had hands on the cup as they raised it to the knot of tall rowan trees, our sacred trees of healing and life. A White Stag stood under the tree and stared at me, the hawk, and lifted its head in greeting. The splendid white animal tossed its head as an invitation, and I perched on its mighty antlers. Blood, dripping from an arrow lodged in its heart, splashed on the ground under its breast. My wings carried me down to the pool of warm blood. I watched his life slowly leak away, shadowing his eyes. When he nodded to me, no regret radiated from him.

Without warning, brilliant blue butterflies rose in a silent flutter from the forest floor and filled the air around us.

Certainty filled my heart. I used my wings to carry me to the air currents and rose above the scene. I looked far below and burned this location into my memory.

In my bed at the hospice, I awoke to silence. The ravens that had been harshly cawing in my ears every moment since my taking were gone from my head. My shoulders were at rest, and my neck's tension was lifted. The weight of guilt was gone from my body. I knew what I needed to do to be purified and be able to go back to Lovern's side as his life partner.

Mother was tranquil, as calm as the cough would let her be. She smiled and seemed to sense a change in me while she sipped a small amount of broth.

"Mother. I must go for a few days," I said. "Lovern and I have a quest. I have found what I need to continue my life, to mend my spirit."

Her words filled the spaces around her coughing. "Go. I have been sad to see pain in your face. This is the first day I see light in your eyes. My daughter, you must find the way to bring Lovern back into your bed. I still ask a grandchild of you! Sileas will care for me. I will not die before you return. Go."

I packed bread and dried meat in a cloth, filled a skin with water, went to fetch a pony from Kenric's stable and walked it to our lodge.

Lovern was at home. I could not go in but stood in the doorway and called out to him. I was pleased as I looked around. He kept the fire area clean; all the cooking dishes were in the right places and the ashes swept from the ring. This showed respect for our dwelling. The blanket that separated our room from the rest of the home lifted and he walked quickly out.

"Jahna. Are you home to stay?" Joy filled his face until he saw me shake my head. "Oh. I was coming to the hospice soon. Is your mother...?"

"Mother is as comfortable as possible this morning. Bring your bow, arrows and short sword. We go to hunt the White Stag. I have seen where it lives. It waits for us by the rowan trees."

Lovern stepped forward and laid his palm on my cheek. "You have had a dream. The gods are coming to help us. We will recover our lives and live together again. I have prayed for this day." He ran to our room and returned, his bow strung across his back, balancing the bundle of arrows under his arm as he strapped his belt on and slid the sword through it. His dirk was already in its sheath; he was ready to hunt. He stood in front of me waiting for an explanation of my request, his brows resting under the lines on his forehead caused by his concern. I looked into his face and noted that all the vestiges of the young boy I had seen in my passage dream were gone. His face wore the lean look of a man. I stepped back as he reached for me. I was not ready to allow him to touch me again, still working to overcome the weakness his scent of honey, acorns and, today, leather gave me.

"Jahna, tell me about your dream. The White Stag will bring many blessings to us and our clan if we find it," said Lovern. "Cernunnos will bring game and Morrigna will be pleased if we capture it for them."

It was in Lovern's heart to think of the clan as well as me. I bit my tongue to keep my selfish reply hidden. The White Stag was mine, not a sacrifice for the clan.

"In the form of a hawk, I flew to the Stag. I stood on its antlers and was covered in a blue light. Blue butterflies, Lovern. Butterflies. It means my rebirth as a pure woman. It foretells my return to be with you. I need to be a part of your life again, and this is the path we must follow to achieve this end."

"I have waited for a sign," he said. "If the gods say we must capture the White Stag to allow you to come home to me, to lie in my bed again, then we must go, now. There has been too much time apart. We cannot live like this any longer. I will do what is asked of me if it means that I may reclaim you as my partner, to love you and caress you. If it is not to happen, then I will leave this hill fort. I cannot stay without you by my side."

He jumped into the saddle of the pony and reached out for me.

"First, I must tell you that we do not go to capture the Stag," I said. "I agree it would be a trophy worth much if we could bring it home, but the gods told me it must be sacrificed. Its life is in trade for mine. No one else may be allowed to wish upon it. No one else may be allowed to see it alive."

He frowned and thought for a moment while holding the prancing pony's reins. "If the gods have sent you this message, I will abide. Our gods speak with you as well as me. If it is to be a sacrifice, it shall be. Let us get started." He grasped my arm and easily pulled me up behind him. I shifted, clutching his narrow waist under his bow and over his belt as we started downhill.

"Go to the mountain trail that is in the morning shadows," I whispered in his ear and tightly held on. I pressed myself against his straight back, buried my nose in his hair and took deep breaths filled with the scent of him.

"Jahna, I have missed you," he said turning slightly to me.

"Quiet. We must be as your fox on this journey or the Stag will flee. We will talk after, I pledge."

His slight groan and flick of the reins betrayed his impatience.

I followed the trail I had seen from the air as a hawk. We went without a stumble around large boulders and across very narrow, washed out parts of an animal path for the rest of the day and into the night. We were guided by the gods but tired as humans. Stopped to rest, we ate dried meat and drank water from the skin. There was neither a fire nor words between us. The rocky ground did not allow an easy night's sleep.

Confusion clouded my thoughts. I prayed to be on the right trail. I thought about my mother. I remembered my childhood, so many memories dredged up with my mother's memory sticks and Braden's death. The ever-present smell and hideous thoughts of the time I was taken slipped between the happier moments, as much as I tried to erase them. Lovern traced his labyrinth. In the light of the moon, I brought my labyrinth into my lap and ran my finger over its lines. My fast breath of unease slowed into measured calmness. In my mind, understanding the scenes were not real, I was able to relive my taking. I was on this path for redemption, to be allowed to purify myself and I had a need to fully remember why. The tension that was always present during these times of recollection was gone. Lovern sat near me and we were here to wash this evil spirit from me with the blood of the Stag.

The night escaped as dawn's light streaked over the top of the mountain. Luminous pink reflected from the granite boulders on the mountaintop allowed me to recognize this place. We had arrived without my knowing. We were in the clearing of my vision.

"The Stag is here," I whispered to Lovern, cautioning him not to speak.

Crouching in the grassy edge of the trees, we crept to the copse of rowans, their leaves beginning to turn the gold and red of autumn. The proud buck stood just beyond the perimeter of the trees. His thick neck lifted his fine head to sniff the morning air, and he took a step forward. His muscles rippled just under his snow-white pelt, and his tail flicked at an annoying insect. He stretched his neck up, becoming taller than Lovern, to eat the higher, more tender leaves. The sun continued to climb in the sky and enveloped him in a golden light as we watched.

I counted ten points on each side of his antler crown. Here stood a legendary creature of the forest. His carriage was one of a virile, tested bull. One at this age had given life to many young. His proud bloodline assured, the gods would let us take him. Breathing quietly and seldom, we crawled on our bellies to cross the distance between us. The underbrush provided cover. He seemed not to hear us.

Lovern notched an arrow to his bow. My body trembled, and I fought not to close my eyes as Lovern slowly stood, pulled the string of his bow and took careful aim.

"Give me the permission," prayed Lovern in a whisper, "and strength enough to kill this mighty animal of nature with one arrow. May it be accepted as my sacrifice." I prayed for Lovern's straight aim and crouched, prepared to give chase after the arrow was shot.

The Stag's ears twitched, and he looked over his shoulder, away from us, into the depths of the trees. He snorted and took in a breath that rattled the nearby leaves. He seemed to be giving us the chance to take his life while not looking into his eyes.

Lovern let lose the arrow.

Hearing the twang of the bowstring, the Stag turned to face us. His intelligent, black eyes bore into my heart with the knowledge of his demise. I begged for his forgiveness just as his ears cocked toward me. As if he heard and understood my need, he stepped into the arrow's path. His head rose, carried his eyes to the heavens and opened his heart for the iron point of death.

Pierced, he jumped and snorted; his antlers vibrated with the shock. The arrow sank deep into his chest, and he fell to his knees unable to run. We raced to his side just as his noble head settled to the ground. I knelt, touched his forehead and gazed into his eyes as he took his last breath. It sounded like a sigh of relief. Then, as if released from this difficult world, his inner light extinguished. Another trade, another life for mine. A life so my bloodline would continue.

Together, Lovern and I rolled the magnificent animal to its side and Lovern pulled his dirk from his belt to open the Stag's neck veins. The red blood ran down its white neck and spilled onto the green mat of grass. My cupped hands captured a few drops, and I sipped. I tasted the smell of Finley's smithy – hot metal. Lovern drank and then we wiped our hands across our faces. Lovern's cheeks were streaked with the crimson fluid that had been the White Stag's life. I felt the stickiness on my face and watched it drizzle crimson down my arms in spiral trails. They ran under and copied of the design on the armlet my mother gave me, the spirals of life.

Lovern jumped up, droplets of blood spraying through the air. "Jahna! Look! Behind you — quickly, look!"

Thinking the mate of the Stag may be on her way to take her revenge, my breath caught in my throat as I twisted to look in the direction his blood covered finger pointed.

Out of the corners of my eyes I captured movement, a rush of blue flickering and floating on the air. Facing the trees, my eyes wide, I watched clouds of small blue butterflies lift to the sky. I accepted the scene from my vision. The blue butterflies and the White Stag were here in this copse of rowan trees to heal the relationship between Lovern and me. I did not question our presence. We were here by the grace and wonderment of the gods.

A song came to my lips.
"Anaman   dance on air and color to bring life
              and blessings from the gods;
              purify our spirits,
              bring change and rebirth;
Anaman   alight, blue mysteries, and heal me.
Anaman Anaman Anaman."

"O Morrigna," sang Lovern in his own prayer song. "Shown in the form of Cernunnos, we welcome you. The King of the Forest rests at our feet. In him, we seek fertility for ourselves, our forests, and the animals within. Bless us so in your name we may continue to teach others to bless you. Blessed Cernunnos, we will be forever grateful for your blessing and allowing us to sacrifice the White Stag to Morrigna and you."

"I will be there until I am free," I said and pointed to the edge of the small meadow where we spent the night. "I will come to you when I feel my soul release."

Lovern nodded. I picked up my cape and walked a small distance away.

Lovern continued singing just out of reach of my ears. Birds in the forest around me twittered, their songs sweet again.

Lovern stripped off his clothing. I admired his tall, lean body and the muscles that worked as he shoved the Stag's body into position. Lovern's penis, hanging limp between his legs, did not show his true virility. He was my lover and I tingled with memory.

I kneeled and wrapped myself in my cape, my labyrinth bag in hand. I thought on the reasons we were here. Through the rest of the day, I relived my first meeting Lovern in Beathan's home.

Lovern went into the forest and returned with a short log. After he reached in and cut out the Stag's tongue, he placed the log just under its chin, raising its neck off the ground. He placed the tongue on the grass nearby. He lifted his short sword into the air, bringing it down repeatedly until the Stag's head separated from its body. He grasped it by its antlers and sat it on its neck, facing his work. Then, he rolled the Stag's body to its back and cut a deep line down the belly with his dirk. He cut again at the joint of each leg. Grasping a corner of the pelt, he pulled and cut under the skin to separate it from its body.

I remembered falling in love with him as he taught me how to heal and find my life's path.

Midday saw the pelt completely removed and set aside. Kneeling, covered with blood, Lovern carved large pieces of meat off its shoulders and haunches. As if called, a small red fox walked to Lovern's side; its sharp nose dug into Lovern's arm to announce its arrival. Startled, Lovern looked down and laughed at the brave copper-colored animal. Its white-tipped red tail slowly swished back and forth. Lovern crawled on his knees, not rising above the small animal more than necessary, and reached for the Stag's tongue. He laid it just in reach of the fox. The fox sauntered over, sniffed, bit into it and tried to lift it. It was too heavy so the fox snorted, gave in, and dragged his prize back into the forest from whence he came. Lovern watched in silence and bowed his head to the empty air left by the disappearing, sly fox.

After quenching his thirst from our water skin, Lovern reached into his labyrinth bag and retrieved the red thread we had been handfasted with. It fell in tendrils from his fingers as he brought it to his lips and kissed it. His penis became partially erect. I wondered if he was remembering the night of love that came after that ceremony. He tied the thread around the antlers of the Stag.

I recalled our marriage and the night of love we shared. My loins moistened and readied for entry.

Using his sword with both hands, Lovern dug a hole. He finished it just as the sun started on the down side of the day. He disappeared into the forest again.

My throat closed, and I grew weak with memory of the fear of my taking and the death of Beathan.

When he returned, he piled the logs he carried into the hole along with twigs and small branches. He pulled and rolled the body, with difficulty, into the hole. The King of the Forest's head balanced on top of its body. Lovern laid his short sword near the hole and reached into his bag again for his firestones. He lit the tinder and wood under the Stag. Soon, wood and fat fed, red and gold flames jumped into the air and the fire's smoke rose to the darkening sky. The body of the White Stag, King of the Forest, was consumed by the purifying blaze. His spirit flew to the forests of the gods on the smoke.

Lovern stood to watch for several breaths, then reached down and picked up the white pelt he had removed earlier. He walked towards me. I could hear his voice. Holding out the white pelt, he prayed, "Morrigna. Bel. Hear my pleas. Forgive my wrong-doings. Give me the power to heal and protect. Give me guidance to bring back into the true line of our nature the love of my life."

I grew stronger with the sound of his voice. I watched him declare his love and need to me through his actions and prayers to the gods. I knew the gods gave us this love we shared, and I would continue to honor it into whatever future we held together.

"Lovern," I whispered with a dry throat, "help me rise. I am free. I am purified."

He came to me. His hands strong under my arms, he lifted me to stand and raised his head to heaven singing thanks. I turned to stand behind him and dropped my dress to the grass. I took a step so my back was against his, my hot skin absorbing his sweat. My head rested under his shoulder, and I entwined our fingers. My legs were growing weak with relief and need of him when I felt his body quiver.

I released his hands, and we turned to face each other. "Are you chilled?" I asked this as I trembled with my need.

"No," he said as he pulled me tightly against his body. His head dipped to kiss me and I felt him, fully erect, pressing his hips into mine. Our bodies reacted to the prolonged absence of each other.

"I have missed you so," I wept and reached my arms around him, my face buried against his chest. He lifted my chin and looked into my eyes. I saw tears in his, reflected in the waning light.

"Jahna, as my wife you should not have had to face the trials you did. It is my job to give you protection, and I failed. Before I left, you implored increased protection for me and I failed to do the same for you. Your taking and Beathan's death should fall on my shoulders, not yours. I ask your forgiveness. I ask the gods' forgiveness."

"We are both purified with this hunt and sacrifice," I said. "We must now follow the path of our future."

We kissed, our tears creating clean lines through our blood-covered faces. Lovern eased me to the ground, the white pelt under us for protection. I cried in pleasure as his mouth and hands found my breasts. I lifted my legs around his slender hips, and he groaned as he entered me. We moved as one, searching for the most important truths in the entire world. The love of a man and woman. The urge to create new life.

I screamed into the night with my release, and he cried out my name. We clung to each other, loving again and again until the sun rose.

"The fire is out," I said as I lifted my head to look over his shoulder. He still lay atop me. "I am hungry. Is there dried meat and water?"

"Later, I will cook the meat I removed for this purpose. You need to eat well from now on."

Looking into his face and seeing his grin I realized he would know, even as I did, that I was with child. His child. Our child. A child of this night.

"Yes, I will take care of my body and soul for our daughter. She will carry our blood into the future."

"I agree, but now we will take care of us. I need you again, Jahna. My body will never tire of yours, even when you are too big to walk!"

"Mmmm. It is pleasant to have you inside me. But I have enough hunger to eat a pony."

"Quiet, woman. I will feed our souls first and then your stomach."

Later, we ate meat from the Stag, climbed onto our pony and traced our path home. We stopped only to wash our bodies in the waterfall of the sacred pool. There, we loved each other again.

My mother was awake when we returned to the hospice. I knelt by her and whispered, "I am with child. A girl child."

She laughed, and for a few days we made plans. She spent her last days with smiles on her face and hope in her eyes. At the end, she kissed me and said she would be with me at her granddaughter's birth. I was to look for a sign. "Teach her to weave the clan colors. They must be carried on."

"I will, Mother. She will learn to use your loom as I did."

"Jahna, you will be a good mother." She blessed me with the highest praise a mother can give a daughter. My heart filled with pride and sorrow.

She died in her sleep during the next full moon. Lovern gently cradled me in his arms while we mourned our loss. A large owl, my mother's sign, made its resting place in the tree outside our door after hunting.

She watched over me and mine for the rest of our time. She still watches over my blood.

CHAPTER 16

JAHNA

76 AD May

My mother had blessed me before she died, and the time the baby grew in me was easy. I slept in our bed, our home protected by Lovern and our crystals, comforted by his warm breath on my neck and arm over my shoulder. This was a time of peace and recovery for my body and mind. Passage dreams were not a part of this life, nor were visions, until the night before Crisi's birth, ten days after the Beltane ceremony.

Our Beltane festival was good that year. Our animals were healthy, many carried young, and our crops grew fruitful with an early warm spring. Lovern and the clan members, satisfied with the graces and blessings the gods had given us, knew we would have enough food for next winter.

Sleep had become precious to me and I did not get enough as the size of my belly grew. When I did sleep, it was for short times. The night before my birthing pain started, I settled next to Lovern, trying to get as comfortable as possible on my side. I realized I had to pee and groaned.

"What is it? Have the pains started?" Lovern was as ready for our daughter to be born as I.

"No. I must pee. Again. And I will take a small walk. The moon is full, and I want to sit under it, alone, for a time. When the babe is born, I will not have any time alone."

Lovern pushed against my back to help me get my unmovable body up. The baby, a small boulder's weight I carried in my belly, threw my balance off. It was difficult to rise out of bed without help. I would not only welcome a healthy babe but my body back as well when the time came.

Outside, on a stool near our well, I sat for a few moments in the light of the moon, envisioning our home with a small child in it. My body cooled, I shivered, and rose to go in. On my walk back, a flash of light caused me to look up at our home. It had disappeared. In front of me was the framework of an unfinished lodge. Gazing around, I saw it was the house Lovern and I now lived in. Where I grew up. Instead of walls, rooms, and a fire pit, only the support posts and cross beams for a future roof were standing. The room we built, where his crystals laid buried under the posts, was part of the shell that was outlined by the timbers. This was strange; we added that room after he came to live in my mother's home. I stood, turning and staring deep into the unfinished abode. I searched for something precious to me.

I walked into it and paced around the uneven floor. A picture dropped into my mind, and I realized I was looking for a baby. There, crying, lying on the cold dirt, was a newborn girl child. She was naked on the White Stag pelt. An owl, my mother's sign, was perched on the floor next to her in a protective stance. The owl hooted and watched me intently as I walked to the baby. I stooped to the floor; the owl grew quiet, and the baby stopped crying. I picked her up and saw my eyes studying me from her face.

The goddess whispered her name into my ear like a spring breeze. *Crisi.* Her eyes looked deep into mine with the knowledge of all newborns, the knowledge we forget as we grow. Her hands waved in the air in front of her face. I reached for them. She grabbed my finger in a strong grip. I looked at her feet, raised above her nakedness. Lovern's second toes on each foot were longer than his large ones and she had toes like her father. He said it was a family mark from his mother. This child, Crisi, was a child of ours, a mixture of our families. This was our baby. I cradled her gently as I lifted her to the stars to display her to the gods.

"This is my daughter. This is Lovern's daughter. This is Crisi, the one who will carry our blood into the future."

A pain brought me back, seated outside my home in the dirt, empty hands lifted to the sky.

When told of my vision, Lovern discerned that we – he, I and Crisi – would be the start of a new blood line. The lodge in my vision represented our family, and we were the beginning frame for it. The next generations would continue to build, creating a secure family line, establishing a safe home.

The next day I worked between the pains with the help of Sileas to ready our home for a baby. We cooked, stored water and wood. I renewed the mistletoe in the window and juniper branches under our bed. Energy ran through my veins. I did not want to sit down. Lovern was underfoot, trying to get me to settle, so I chased him out to gather herbs in the gardens around the village.

He returned for the evening meal, and Harailt joined us. The pains were strong; I knew our daughter would come soon.

"Our baby should be born by the sacred spring," I said. "We can give her the taste of its cool water with her first breath. She will carry it with her all her life, its protection, and its memory of this home."

All agreed.

"Harailt, go check the ill," said Lovern. "Tell them I will be there in the morning. Tonight, I tend my wife at my daughter's birth." He turned to me, smiled, grasped my hand, and kissed my forehead. My love for him was never stronger. He was my protector, my baby's father.

Our owl followed us to the grove near the spring where the waterfall's spray was lifted to us by the evening breeze. Of the birth, I remember Lovern's strong hands supporting me while I squatted and Sileas's gentle hands rubbing my back. Crisi was born with the taste of her home on her lips, her grandmother watching over her, and surrounded by love. Clean and wrapped in the protective White Stag's pelt, she did not cry until the next morning. She grew healthy and strong.

79 AD May

My adult life had contained the many fears and visions of war and early death. Since Crisi's birth, many of the fears were resting. I did not know whether they were gone or asleep like a bear in winter.

When Crisi had passed three springs, she, Lovern and I hiked up the mountain trail behind our fort. We often looked there for flowers used in healing. I was in a peaceful place in my life and watching her play brought back memories of her birth.

She was a peaceful baby, easy to care for. Even now, she would rather laugh and play than cry. I often took care of other children of our clan, and at this age they had become willful. Crisi had shown some stubbornness (I told Lovern it was from him) but usually she listened to us. I saw a wisdom in her eyes I had not seen in other children. I liked to think that she was the best child in our clan. I was sure, however, all mothers thought this way. I had heard and joined in when mothers bragged about what their children had done, but none sounded as smart as Crisi.

It seemed the goddess, Morrigna, would only bless us with one child. I prayed and made pilgrimages to the waterfall for sacred water, and done all the other things a woman must do to have a baby. But, as Lovern said before, the gods act in ways we do not understand sometimes, and I had no more children. Not even a whisper of one. I had not given up, but learned not to hope so much. Now, when my bloody time came, my heart did not cut with longing and I did not hear a ghost babe cry in the night. If it happened, I would rejoice.

This day echoed with laughter as we came around the mountain. When we saw our home, I asked Lovern to stop.

"I want to spend the rest of the day overlooking the hilltop and the valley beyond," I said. "Our lives are very good. I wish to say thank you to the goddess Morrigna for this time of my life and my family."

"I have a block of peat, I can start a fire," said Lovern.

Crisi played and hid in a small cave nearby. The peat was damp, and the fire's smoke curled around my head. I slipped into a passage dream with Aine. She was with a man. I felt in her heart she loved him and I was glad for her. I guided her eyes to look through mine. I wanted her to see my family and home. She looked through my eyes at the hilltop fort and the dwelling Crisi grew up in.

"Aine, know that I am satisfied. Here we are happy. Here life is good," I said in my mind to her.

This was the first time I had been able to direct the dream, the first time I could pass along a message. Many things in my life changed when Crisi was born. Maybe this was one. Maybe our future was another. For the first time in many months, I had hope.

81 AD August

We attended small *dals* every season, but every third season was a large *mor dal,* a gathering of many, and this year, Crisi was old enough for me to take her. Six of us journeyed: Kenric and Logan, now ten seasons old, Lovern, Crisi, I, and a warrior,

Daimh. Daimh was a young buck who had proven himself in the practice arena and as a hunter for the clan.

"Finlay will be the appointed chieftain while we are gone," Kenric told the clan before we left. "He will have all the rights of judgment he needs to settle small disputes. If something larger comes before the council then it will wait until I return."

Agreement set the meeting place at the intersection of many clans. Some had far to come, and some lived close, but no one crossed the land of their enemies.

The land we traveled was beautiful. A few purple and yellow field flowers waved in the breezes along with long grass for our animals. We brought two ponies to carry our shelter and cooking tools and a few goats to milk. Logan rode rarely, but Crisi rode often as her short legs could not keep up with us and, although small, she was heavy to carry. We tied her to the pony when she fell asleep on its rocking back.

Crisi carried on long conversations with the pony. She tried to draw its attention to the birds in the sky and other animals we saw on the trail. She was very good at naming the animals and had some knowledge of the plants and trees. She was still quite young, but Lovern and I wanted her to know the land and nature she was a part of. The gods demanded it of us. He taught her much as they were together often.

We hiked through the area where running water froze in the winter, and I was glad we brought our cloaks as well as our heavier blankets for sleeping. The nights were getting cold. When we stopped for the night, Lovern set up our shelter, several large pieces of cured leather sewn together with tallow rubbed into the seam to slow the rain. I gathered pine branches to keep Crisi and me off the cold ground.

For the meals, we had handfuls of barley at dawn, dried pork at midday, and whatever animals Daimh and Logan had been able to kill during the day for the evening meal. Lovern and I added the herbs and greens we had picked along the way for flavor to the stew.

We were never hungry. We rationed the barley and dried pork, not knowing how many sunrises we would stay at the gathering or how long the trip home would be. We brought plaid cloth and bronze pins for gifts and trade. One or two of these could go for food, if needed. After a few days with so many people in one spot, all the easy game would be gone at the place of the meeting and the hunters would have to make longer trips into the forests if the meeting lasted several sunrises.

We walked for three days before we arrived in the great glen. A large hilltop fort was perched above us, and we spread out on the plain under it.

"Crisi," I said. "Do not run off. If you get lost, I may not find you. Stay and hold my hand." My armlets jangled against one another as I reached for her. One was the spiral bloodlines my mother had given me. Lovern gave the second to me at Crisi's birth. He had Finlay fashion it unbeknownst to me. He asked that a raven and a fox sit on either side of each other with a knot tying them together. The armlets never left my arm. Crisi said she could find me anywhere because of the jingle sounds I made.

"But Mother, Father says I have the sense of an owl. He said I could find my way home from the woods by myself now. Am I right, Father?"

"Yes, little bird, I did say that," said Lovern as he picked her up and set her on his shoulders, pride showing in his walk. Her long, autumn-colored hair mingled with his bronze locks. "I meant you know your way around our woods very well now as you should. But you have never been here before and there are many other people from neighboring clans. If you walk around unescorted, you may be mistaken for a slave, picked up, and put to work in a house. I know you would not like having to stay inside all day, would you?"

"No, Father. I would climb out the window and run away if I had to stay in all day."

"As you have done at home," I said. "Now stay with me as we go to find Rhona and the others. If you do not cause me to worry I will find you a piece of honeycomb and bread for your mid-day meal." I smiled up at my beautiful daughter. She giggled and pulled on her father's ears. She had grown so, and at five summers it was difficult to keep up with her energy.

A *mor dal* was a time for order and agreement, not a time for battle between clans. Chieftains from many villages and forts attended. It was a time to exchange the legends of each clan during the evening fires, different cures for illnesses and injuries that worked, and mock battles among the warriors who had come as protectors of their leaders.

Many druids attended. I was anxious to see Rhona. We had been in contact each year since I traveled to Beathan's tomb and had grown to think of her as a grandmother to Crisi.

Haye stepped into view and I knew Rhona would be at his heels. Haye was chieftain of his clan, but she was always close by his side to take in the events and trials and give advice. He appreciated having her near. As his clan's druidess and his mother, she had his ear often.

"Chieftain Haye," I called. "It is a pleasure to see you."

"Ah," said Haye. "I see the Fox and his family are here. Lovern, have you renewed your fox skin yet this year? If not, I can cut a strip of bearskin from my coverlet and you can convert to my guiding animal spirit."

"I could not let you take a piece of fur, even a small piece from the tiny skin you took from a cub this year. I wager it is the only bear you have seen in years. I hear you have grown too slow to hunt and are sending out your son to do your work now."

Haye stood two hands taller than Lovern and his shoulders were almost twice the size of Lovern's. This was evident as he towered over Lovern at this moment, frowning.

"Your ears are not working correctly, Red Dog," Haye said. "I have taken three full-grown bears this summer alone. One could step on a fox and eat it for a morning meal."

At this, I saw Daimh ready his hand on his sword if the words came to blows. I stepped to him and rested my hand on his arm.

"We will have no need of this now," I said, "but if conversations get heated after the mead tonight, I will ask you to step up. Please do not drink more than two cups at the evening meal." He nodded in agreement but gave me a look of unhappiness. He had eagerly awaited the drinking at this meeting and had not expected this request.

"No one would go with you to hunt these legend animals?" said Lovern. "How do we know you did not come upon them after a war among themselves for a female, having already killed each other? My fox would out run them and be safe in its den before your bears would understand that something ran between their legs. Phhh, it is not a fair contest.

"I have my new fox skin," boasted Lovern, touching the band on his arm, the skin of a red fox, his guide. "I took only the oldest to leave the young ones to tickle your bears."

At this, Haye reached around Lovern and laughed, as he picked him and Crisi, still on Lovern's shoulders, up off the ground.

"Kenric," Haye said looking over his shoulder, "do you not control your druid that he is allowed to insult a fellow chieftain?"

"Ach. He insults me continually. He says it makes me stronger. I want that he eat the evening meal at your side tonight and give me some peace!"

After the greetings by the men were completed and Eanruig, Haye's son, and Logan had wrestled their hellos, I felt that it was safe for me to step up, retrieve Crisi safely from Lovern's shoulders, and ask about Rhona. I did not see her in the trail of the dust that floated in the air around us.

"Greetings, Jahna," said Haye, dipping his head to me. "Rhona is in the tent of Chaim. It is the large one near the central oak tree. The druids gather there. Fox, take your wife and your cub and go find out what they are brewing. Kenric and I will walk and talk about hunting large animals worth risking life and limb for and teach our sons about women."

"Yes, I will go and if the gods be willing I will see you tonight for the meal." Lovern touched Haye on the shoulder in friendship and then took my hand. They walked away as we headed to the tent.

"It is good to see he is well and his family is healthy," I said.

"Mother," Crisi said, "I want to go with Logan. He will play with Eanruig, and I want to be with them."

She thought of him as her big brother. She had spent much time with Kenric's and Finlay's families. Their children all were older yet seemed to have taken her in and treated her like a sister, a sister to be loved, tolerated and taught. In turn, she had developed love for them. Especially Broc. Finlay's son was now seven seasons and Crisi followed him like a puppy. She would be with him all day and night if I did not ask her to come home for meals and sleep. Eiric, Finlay's wife, accepted her too and fed her along with her own when I was busy with an ill clansman. We had all become close through the loss of Beathan and my mother.

"Crisi," Lovern said, "Logan is to be with his father, our chieftain, and Eanruig is to be with his father, his clan's chieftain. It is not a time to have a small girl along getting in the way of men."

She was holding my hand but at Lovern's statement pulled away. "No. I am not a little girl. Logan gets to stay outside. I want to stay outside and go hunting with them. You are going to talk with Rhona, and I will have to sit still. I do not like that and want to go with Eanruig and Logan."

I smiled, and my heart swelled with love and pride when I looked at her. I saw so much of my mother in her when she was like this. She tilted her head to the left when she was angry and crossed her arms. Mother did the same when she called me in from playing. She was angry that I was not inside weaving, as I should be. And I saw in her Lovern when flashes of light came from her eyes as she smiled. Her hair curled around her chin in the same rust-colored waves his did. I was there in the way she picked up injured animals and cared for them. She was our daughter, my mother's granddaughter. She was our blood.

"Come with us and I will find the honey and bread I promised," I said. "There will be other children there to play with. Logan must be with his father right now." At the mention of the honey, she ran ahead and called for Rhona.

A crowd had gathered in and near the shelter. It was rigged so it had three walls and a roof to protect us from the rain. The hole in the center of the roof let out the smoke of the blessed oak fire that burned for the duration of the gathering. This was the meeting place of the druids. The chieftains had their shelter and we met for evening meals.

After Crisi was fed and settled with other children under the eyes of the older girls, I followed Lovern into the shelter.

The smoke was thick, but I saw him near a group of white-cloaked druids I quickly assessed as druids I knew.

Rosston was young, a finger taller than I, and had hair the color of a meadow mouse and wide brown eyes. When I looked at him, I thought he was always just out of reach of the owl who was chasing him for dinner. His teacher had recently died. He was living with a clan near ours and was often asking Lovern for assistance or for his opinion. As Lovern had said, "At least he knows what to ask."

Uilleam was attending his second *mor dal* from a clan north of the meeting place. His look was of the mountain hare. Something on his body was always moving; fingers drummed, or nose and ears twitched as if he had seen an eagle. He didn't speak until asked and then took the side of the greater number of the group.

Moroug and Coira were partners. Coira was a healer. They brought to mind river otters. Playful and sleek, both with brown hair worn back in leather ties. They never tired of smiling and were hardly ever out of sight of each other. I saw a crying child raise a smile to Coira's face just in the delight of having a child nearby. I had never heard Moroug speak, but Coira often spoke for him. They lived with a clan near the coast.

Rhona had the look of a mother while she watched Moroug. She touched his arm often. "He has golden light around his body," she said. "The weight on my shoulders is less when I am near him."

Nathraichean, the wolf from the east, was speaking, using his hands to emphasize points in the conversation so the others had to step back. Something must be exciting him. I walked closer to hear. He was taller than Lovern and most of the rest of the group surrounding him. Long, straight grey hair cascaded over his shoulders. His matching eyes roved over the attending group. His waving hands covered a great distance. I stood to the side of Lovern, away from Nathraichean's long reach.

"There are no traders coming from the south any more. We are losing the ancient paths we have walked forever. My friend from the land of Boudiccea has not been seen for two years. In my heart, I know he is dead, but it was not a natural death. My gut is uneasy, and there are words that are passed to us from that part of the land. Slaves. Many are taken as slaves or killed."

The conversation around us grew quiet. The mention of slaves brought fear to all our hearts. Lovern's body was locked stiffly next to mine, and he clenched his jaw. His sisters were slaves if they were still alive.

"What are the floating words, the rumors?" Lovern asked. "What do you hear?"

"The wall is being crossed and there are battles every day," said Rhona. She spoke softly from behind us. As we turned to see her, she held out her hands to me in greeting.

"Good day to you, sister," she said.

I walked to her; we wrapped our arms around each other and kissed. Her shoulders were still as strong and wide as the first time she gave me support on my trip to Beathan's tomb. "Good day to you. I hope your family is well." I remembered my vision and silently wished her many more years with them.

"Yes. We are all well. I noticed Crisi outside. She is graced by the gods."

I smiled and hung my head in agreement.

"Good day, Rhona," Lovern said impatiently. "What do you mean the wall is crossed?"

"The floating words say the Roman wall is crossed by Roman warriors trying to take our land sheep by bloody sheep, Lovern."

"No one here has seen them, have they?" Uilleam asked. "Do we know they want our land or just the few miles near the wall?"

"You are right," said Coira. "Maybe they will not come to our clans. If we stay away from them and keep to ourselves, they may not war with us."

"I hear the timid voices of the untried warriors," Nathraichean said.

"I agree that we must not let them come near our clans," said Lovern. "I know what they leave behind, only dead and missing. But I do not want to bring them here, either."

A murmur of agreement ran through the crowd. "We will talk with the chieftains and decide if there should be a plan for the protection of our clans," said Nathraichean in his deep, calming voice. "We must be ready if they come."

The tension in the air eased and we went to other conversations. Lovern followed Coira, talking about the illness that vexed him the most, the fever that took children by closing the throat passage and choking. They are always trying new treatments. I prayed for one to work, fearing for Crisi. Rhona and I went to watch Crisi and talked about children until the evening meal when we rejoined our families.

The evening meal was a great, noisy, song-filled event. The hunter–warriors, who followed their chieftains, had killed two bucks that were now being spit roasted. Each had its own man to turn it and keep it from scorching. The fat from the meat dripped into the fire and created a smoke that caused us all to hunger. The mead ran freely, and even Kenric rose to sing our clan song about Beathan. Kenric created a new verse every *dal* and now the song had Beathan killing ten warriors with one blow. I laughed when I heard this and knew Beathan laughed too, on the other side.

I took Crisi by her hand and motioned Logan to follow. At our shelter, Crisi crumpled to her blanket and fell asleep instantly. Logan and I laid next to her for warmth and I fell asleep, the children's sweet breath on my cheeks.

Daimh, Lovern and Kenric returning awakened me.

"Yes, the talk at our fire earlier was about the Romans," said Kenric. "There is concern about the lack of trade coming from the south. Even with the wall, trade could continue, and has for many lifetimes. It has diminished greatly this season. We have not decided what to do about it yet. It will be discussed again tomorrow. This is a time to bring the druids and chieftains together, I believe. We have to plan our future tactics if we decide to alter the Roman advance."

"Yes, after the morning prayers, I agree we should gather," said Lovern.

Both men became quiet as the night around us fell silent except for the snoring of others asleep. Cuddled between the two warm bodies of the children, I tried to calm my breathing by tracing my maze in my mind. My visions and foretelling of a great battle seemed too close to us now. A *nathair* with a sharp, deadly bite coiled inside my belly and never left me from this time on.

In the morning, I sat stirring cooked barley and goat's milk for Crisi and Logan. Lovern came to me from his solitary walk and morning prayers.

"I heard you talking last night as you came in," I said. "Even the chieftains are hearing words of the Romans."

"Yes, we are all to discuss it today." Crisi was sitting and playing, drawing pictures in the dirt with a stick. He reached down and picked her up, wrapped her in his cloak and sat down next to me.

"Good morning, Father. I am going to look for a honey tree with some of the other children today. We talked about it yesterday, and we are going as soon as we eat."

Lovern looked at me with concern.

"The older children have this planned and asked the younger ones to go," I said. "Logan and Eanruig are going."

"Ah, little bird, *m'eudail*. Is there a honey tree nearby?"

"If not, I will call the bees and we will make one. We want honey for our mid-day meal."

"You are in woods that you are not familiar with. Do not stray from the others when you go." Lovern tousled her hair and hugged her. She jumped from his lap and sat down to finish her drawing.

Lovern did not turn from her but stayed watching her movements.

"I will not let anything come to harm her." He turned to me. "Or you."

The snake in my belly hissed.

The children left in an adventurous noise, and then word that the druids and chieftains would meet together today was passed from lips to ears.

We stood around the fire to sing praises to Morrigna. All hands were raised in praise of her when a thunder of hooves and chariot wheels disturbed the start of our day.

I turned just as the assembly of riders came to a stop at the outer edge of the crowd.

Three warriors slid off their ponies and moved with practiced fluidity into position. Each bore a spear, a shield, a bow, and arrows. They wore capes of brown wool and loin wraps to protect themselves on the ponies. Their arms and legs were blue. This was a custom of the men who lived far north. The woad, taken there by traders, was used for body color more than for dyeing cloth. Two stood to either side of the ponies that pulled the chariot and one on the ground to the side of the man who stood in the chariot. Their eyes measured the crowd, watching, their bodies tense and ready to protect the man they were guarding.

The man in the chariot reviewed our gathering with sharp, dark eyes. His naked, fully dyed blue body revealed a short but very well muscled warrior. His long nose hung over a mouth that was set in a grim line. He wore his golden hair swept back and stiffened with lime, his yellow beard trimmed. His only protection from the weather was a cloak of deep green. On its collar was a row of feathers from a sea eagle, a bird that watches all, bearing talons of surprising strength to hunt and kill for its family.

In the chariot next to him stood a woman. She wore a sun-whitened wool dress. Her cloak was the color of undyed wool. She wore strands of yellowed boars' teeth around her neck. Her rust hair, braided in many rows, hung to her waist. A sea eagle feather was woven into it and hung over her left ear.

The man lifted his arms and looked as if he were ready to fly over us. He did not shout but spoke in a tone that caused us to lean forward. We concentrated to hear.

"I am Calgacus. I am *ceann-cinnidh* of many clans in the north. We pray to Scotia, the fierce mother goddess of our land. We have come together to prepare for the coming war. We know the Romans are coming to us. We have won and lost many battles with them before and have slowed their progress into our realm. Hope was never abandoned, as we are many and hidden in the most secret and sacred places. Because of these places, we have been shielded as the most distant dwellers upon this ground. Our remoteness and obscurity have hidden our name from their lips. We are the last of the free. The Romans, in the name of peace, will rob, slaughter, plunder, and enslave those left alive. It is so in the lands they now live. They have wiped our kind from existence there and we alone are left to carry our bloodlines to the future. There is nothing beyond us but waves and rocks, yet they still come.

"Nature teaches us that every man's children and family are his dearest objects. We have seen these torn apart by death and slavery. Some are left to farm, to feed the slaves that were once members of their families. Can you raise grain to feed your daughters who are raped by the Romans daily?"

A loud "No!" rose from the throats around me. Lovern wrapped his arm protectively around my shoulders. Heat radiated from his body. His eyes did not stray from the speaker, and a low groan escaped from him at the mention of rape. The face of the man who took me flashed like lightning across my mind. He was a Roman slave. He was once a proud warrior, but they turned him into an animal. This could not happen to us. I grew resolved not to allow it.

"There is one Roman who comes our way with warriors," Calgacus continued. "Agricola. He is the chieftain we must kill. It is his army we must defeat. His men are ignorant. They do not know our sky, our sea, our forests. They have no wives or children to kindle their courage, or parents to goad them to battle. They are lost in our land; the gods have delivered them to us.

"Behind him lie unmanned forts guarded by the old, our mines of ancient times, and many slaves who will welcome a release to freedom.

"They cross the wall and are coming. What say you, chieftains? Others that I have spoken to have agreed. If you say yes, then you will train your warriors and wait for my call."

All the chieftains in attendance gathered into a knot of men. After a conversation the length of three breaths, Haye and Kenric stepped forward.

"We agree," said Haye. "We will train and await your call."

Instantly the vision I had in Haye's stable was brought to mind and the snake in my belly bit me. I was poisoned. I knew of Haye's death. Fear was fastened deep inside me now.

The woman next to Calgacus stepped down from the chariot. Her path was straight and the crowd split to allow her progress. She came to Lovern, laid her hand on his forehead, and said, "This man is one who will work well for us. He can speak the tongue of those who live on the wall. He will bring us what we seek. The goddess Scotia picks him for herself."

The woman's beautiful face melted away and became the face of a hag. Her already long nose became sharper. Her sky blue eyes turned to iron. Her well formed mouth hung open to reveal black, jagged teeth. I imagined her breath to smell like the inside of an unclean stable. Her hair writhed about her head. I shook my head at the sight but the hag's face remained. She slowly looked down to the ground and when she looked back up her face had become beautiful again.

Lovern stepped to her as if drawn by a cord. His arm fell from my shoulders and, in my spirit, I knew our relationship would never be the same again. She had stolen part of his heart.

"Firtha," said Calgacus, "is my druidess. She tells me she has dreamed of you. She said you could go where the Romans live and bring back information. Her visions tell me that we must have this information. We must know how many they are and when they come."

Lovern answered, "You ask me to leave my family and my clan to take a journey that will last at least three moon cycles."

"I do not ask, I order," Calgacus said. "Go in the spring. After Imbolc. They will not come in the winter. Go and come back to me with this knowledge. With that information, we will be prepared to go into battle. We must not lose to become slaves of Rome."

Lovern's shoulders rose as he took a deep breath and turned to me. "My mother died at their hands. My sisters and teacher are slaves if still alive. I cannot let the Romans come here. I must go."

My body was losing its strength to stand. I wavered and would soon fall. Rhona stepped up behind me and laid her hand on the small of my back. Lovern's deep blue eyes begged me. I had no choice. We had to save Crisi. My soul cried as I nodded and whispered, "Yes, I agree. You must go."

The sea eagle and his hag won. My Fox was theirs.

CHAPTER 17

MAY, 2005

"Marc," I yelled. He was across the field, talking to Jack and walking slowly towards me. "Has Jimmy called yet?"

The work on the site was progressing. Along with George's grant and the one I brought in last week, my small amount of money had grown to a modest size. Marc's team was still here along with a few other young, freshly graduated archaeologists I'd hired through the available students listed on University website. All were working in various stages and places around the site. I took care of the finances, budgeting and paying the workers and bills with advice from both George and Marc. But this project was mine. My name was on the account, and I was signing the checks. I paid Marc's students a stipend, and to save money we moved from the inn to a rental in Fort William. The four members of the ground-penetrating radar team were still residing in Mrs. Dingleberry's Inn.

I'd hired a security company who had someone on site all the time, but I still wanted someone I knew there, especially overnight. Kendy and Matt were not the only ones who slept there now. To give them a break, we all took turns spending the night.

The sun was overhead in its rise to its zenith. We were in short sleeves, taking advantage of the unusually warm air.

I shaded my eyes to see Marc. He stopped talking to Jack, the head of the ground-penetrating radar team, and waved to me. Jack and his equipment were here for the rest of today only. We'd been able to use the GPR longer than usual because George called in some favors, but it had to go. I couldn't afford it any longer. Both Marc and I felt the urge to work until exhausted, trying to get as much of this sight mapped as possible.

The underground scanning followed a spiral grid system. The outside edge of the hilltop fort was charted first, and then we followed the spiral to the center, where we assumed the village square would be. We'd located the site we called the smithy, a building with large fire pits, and started excavating it as soon as it was mapped. One fire pit contained small pieces of charcoal that had been burned in intense heat. When we picked them up out of the clay that now held them, they almost turned to dust. I knew the smith had worked both bronze and iron from the heat of the fire that it took to make this charcoal. I believed the bronze bowl containing ashes that I found in the cave, the Raven Bowl, was fashioned here.

If I were given one wish, I'd want to meet the villagers who lived here. What did they say when they got up in the morning? I tried to envision the women who came to the well and wonder if they gossiped like me when I met friends at a coffee shop? I often picked up a handful of dirt and imagined who'd walked on it and who they loved. Maybe, just maybe, Jahna, the man she loved and her child had left footprints here. It was such an honor to be allowed to see through her eyes occasionally, but oh gods, how I wished I could speak with her. I had so many questions.

"Jack says they'll pack up about four this afternoon," Marc said as he walked to me, brushing his hair from his face.

His full head of copper hair has a bit more white in it, I thought, smiling to myself. *I'll have to remember to tell him about it tonight.* It was our turn to sleep in the tent.

"They've got one grid left to map and found the edge of what looks like the wall of a large building."

"Super," I said. "It might be the chieftain's lodge. I'd hoped we'd find it before they left. How probable do you think it is that your tomb's chieftain lived here?"

Marc turned to me with a look of incredulity. "What? That tomb is several days away in their mode of travel. Why do you think they would bury him there? No, Aine," Marc said, shaking his head, "I don't think there was much chance of that. What gave you that idea?"

"I was thinking about the bronze bowl I found here and the one I found at the tomb. She led me to both, Marc. Jahna led me to both."

"You want me to tell you that my tomb is now part of your site? No. There is no connection. Just because you had a dream? No way. I said I understood that you believe in your dreams, but, dreams or not, I don't think they could be connected."

"Okay, Marc, okay. I was just wondering, talking out loud. You're a bit testy today. What's wrong?"

"Nothing." He turned to walk back to the tent and without looking at me said, "By the way, Jim's office called and he'll email you his report this evening."

My breath caught in my throat. Now I'd have a date and finally know what the contents of the Raven Bowl were. I knew in my heart what or who it was, but now I could see my beliefs validated, even if only in my own mind. It was good enough for me right now.

"Wait, Marc! Did he say anything? When did he call? Why didn't you tell me he was on the phone?"

Only a few steps away, he stopped walking, pivoted and faced me, his face dark. After a deep sigh he resignedly said, "Actually, I didn't get to talk to him. His office called. About an hour ago, while you were indisposed. I'm sorry I forgot to tell you, but I've been busy here, too. I knew you'd check your email later so I guess I figured you'd find out."

"How can I check my email later? You and I are here tonight! I wouldn't have seen it until tomorrow."

"Oh crap. I forgot we were out here tonight. Well, it wouldn't have been a disaster. You've waited this long, a few more hours wouldn't have hurt much. Now, I suppose you'll want to go into town tonight. Since it was my fault for not telling you Jimmy's office was on the phone, then go. I can stay here alone."

I stepped closer to Marc, and he took a step back. "Marc? I've been on pins and needles waiting for this report. You know that. Why are you acting this way? Are you angry about something?"

"I got a call from the University and have to go back for the next term. I want to go to Wales and look in on that site. Doug said they've found coins from the early first century. That means it's a site where the Romans had a fort during and after the time of Queen Bouddicea."

"How exciting! Exactly the time period you love. No wonder you want to be there."

"I should've been there for the discovery."

There it was, a load of bricks on my back. He blamed me for not being there and that's why he was angry. It was my fault.

"Marc, I asked you to stay in the beginning but we aren't connected at the waist. I can handle this now. We've had fun getting to know each other again, but if you really want to go, then go! Gods. You're sounding like such a little boy!"

His face turned red. "I'm up to my shoulders in a dilemma and don't know how to dig myself out. I don't want to go back to the University, but I may have to. Don't make this more difficult than it has to be. Oh God, Aine, I've said things today that I really don't mean. I'm sorry. I wish I could rewind the day but I can't, and right now I have a decision to make."

He quickly walked away. What had just happened? Stunned, I watched him go. Words wouldn't form in my head, but I knew I didn't want him to go. I wanted us to continue with our lovemaking and falling back in love.

I wanted... I wanted this site. I had to stay here and finish. I'd no choice. This was my life now. *Get a grip girl. Remember that.* I liked having him around, but I didn't need him. *Okay, then why does it feel like the bricks on my back are now in my heart?*

I wanted to go download the report so I ran to the van and then remembered the team would need it to get into town tonight. I slipped into the tent to get different keys, hoping not to run into anyone, but Lauri was there. She had a look of pity in her eyes as she handed the keys for the Rover to me. "Don't worry, Aine," she said. "He's tired and angry with the University. He'll calm down. I'll bet all will be okay by tomorrow."

Great, everyone heard! I nodded and ran down to the car before anyone could see my tears.

The next day, Marc packed up the few things he had in our room. "I've decided to go. I've loved being here with you and want to be with you all the time. You are on my mind all day long now, Aine. But you won't leave here, and I can't stay."

My heart stopped beating. I guess I was hoping for a miracle, but the real world stepped in and he was leaving. His equipment bag was already in the Rover.

"Did Jimmy email you his report?" Marc asked.

"No, I called and he'd wanted to finish one more test but I talked him into sending what he had today."

"Good. Look, no one came to the site last night. I left everything in good condition with Tim. Lauri, Tim, Kendy and Matt decided to stay here and work for the next few weeks.

They have to get back to University for the next term, too. I've given them leave to stay so you won't be short-handed, but you should hire a few more people soon. You want to get as much done as you can before the end of the season."

"Thank you. I'll go back online and see who comes up."

Outside, Matt waited to take him to the train. Marc threw his bag in, slid into the passenger side of the car and looked at me expectantly.

Christ, is he waiting for me to give in and ask him to stay? Why doesn't he give in? My pride's as important as his. After Brad, I couldn't be the one to cave here. I couldn't give up my independence and ask him to stay. Not after all my work. Not now.

"Thank you for all your help here, Marc. It was invaluable." There, just enough to tell him I couldn't have done it without him but not gushy. It was hard saying that over the lump in my throat.

"Call me. I want updates," he said. "I'm sure my mobile reception is good in Wales. And remember, I'll be glad to help in anyway I can."

A clean goodbye. No regrets from either of us. No promises made to be broken later. *Am I ever going to be able to breathe again?*

I nodded. There was nothing more to say. Nothing would change where we were right then. I began to miss him as I waved goodbye and the Rover pulled away.

Three hours later, the report was on my computer, a full description of what we'd found, what I'd crawled into the cave and almost died for. I pored over it for hours, marveling at the pictures of the cleaned bronze bowl. The raven was in the center of the group of animals, flanked by a fox standing on its hind legs against an oak tree. I saw the outline of a smaller bird in the branches of the tree. Beautiful, absolutely beautiful.

George knocked on my door about 9 PM. I hadn't come out of my room –Marc's and my room – since Marc left.

"If you're wondering," he said, "Tim volunteered with Luke to stay tonight. The site is guarded."

"Come in George. I'm sorry I'm being such a stick in the mud. It's just Marc…."

"I know, dear. I know. I heard part of it. We all did." I grimaced as he continued. "I brought you back some curry if you're hungry." He walked in carrying a plate of food. I'd not eaten all day.

"Please sit down, George." I pointed to an empty chair. My room, filled with a table, the double bed Marc and I shared, and two chairs, was cramped. I was working; my laptop and the pictures we took of the cave were scattered around the top of the table. He scooted a few pictures aside and set the plate down.

"Mmmm. Smells good. I didn't think I was hungry," I said and nibbled at the curry.

"You know," George started, "you'll still be able to do you want to do, work this site. You have your hands on everything here and are doing well, just like I knew you would."

"Oh, George, I know that. I just thought, well…. You know. But I have to be so careful after Brad. I need to finish this job to prove I can work. I need to prove it to myself and everyone else who doubted me. Not you, of course."

"If it's meant to be then it will happen. Just don't let your pride stand in the way. So many hearts are broken because of our silly pride."

Those two words marched through my head. *Silly pride, silly pride.* I swallowed a dry piece of chicken and slid my laptop around so he could see the screen.

"Here's a picture of the slate that was lying on top of the bowl in the cave. They were able to clean it up, and look how bright the colors are."

"It's a double spiral labyrinth!" said George. "How beautiful. It looks as if its maker painted symbols on the slate around it. Did they say how old it is? I have several at home, but none like this."

"The report says the contents of the bowl – now we can officially call it an urn – are human. They put it at around AD 80, give or take fifteen years. Jim said the quality of the bronze bowl is superb. The bowl itself is very good quality and was engraved by an artist. He said it reminded him of the bowl Marc found in the chieftain's tomb. Huh. The bowl *I* found, he means. Anyway, Jimmy said he's trying to sex the remains. The cremation fire was extremely hot but there may be enough left to try. He'll let me know. It's really exciting news."

I stopped for a minute, put my face in my hands, and massaged my temples. "George, I should be happy! But, earlier I remembered what day it is. Donny was killed three years ago today."

"Oh my, I'm sorry. I hadn't remembered either."

I stood up and leaned to the cupboard where I kept my Scotch. "Do you want a drink?"

"No, thanks."

I was a bit surprised, as he was the one who introduced me to Lagavulin, but the thought quickly left my mind. I was in the mood to be selfish and not think of others that night. I poured myself a double.

"My aunt sent me an email. She is pretty good with her computer now. She is in a group that actually plays bridge online if you can believe that. Anyway, she says she went to the graveyard and put flowers on the family today. Even Mom and

Dad. She figured they'd like them too. She said she put yellow roses on Donny's grave."

I sat back down at the busy table, facing George. "I still don't understand why he had to die in such a horrible way."

I remembered the speech given by the colonel when we buried my brother. He stood at attention over the hole my brother's body was now in and had said, "Major Donald MacRae gave his life in protection of the men under his command in Afghanistan. He laid his body over the grenade when he saw it thrown so the four men around him could live. There is no greater sacrifice than giving your life so others may live." At this, my mother collapsed and had to be taken home.

The colonel came to me after the ceremony and privately told me that he was recommending Donny for the George Cross. I laughed and asked whether he thought he could replace my brother with a ribbon and a piece of metal. I told him I didn't understand why Donny was even there and to die there was unforgivable in my eyes. How could he leave Mom and me? And his wife and kids, Craig and Tira?

"How could he do that George? Why didn't he just stay in his vehicle? He was coming home the next month. Why did he die?"

"Some things are never going to be understood, Aine. Donny had a reason. We may never know what it was. Sometimes a man has time to think about his sacrifice, but usually it happens instinctively. Donny was a brave man. The men he saved have gone on to lead good lives. One has even become a member of the clergy. And through Donny's children the family blood will continue."

"Oh, bloody hell. You sound like Dad would if he were alive. Even Donny's wife's came to terms with his death and has taught my niece and nephew that their dad was a hero. I just miss him." I finished my drink in one gulp and coughed as it burned a hole in my guts.

"Well, I'm sorry," said George. "Let me take the plate and go now. It's late and I'm tired." He kissed my cheek and picked up the still full plate he had set down in front of me.

I didn't sleep that night. The bed was too empty, the room too quiet and ghosts were rumbling outside.

Two days later, George bought train tickets to go to London for a physical check up. He had leukemia but had been fighting it, successfully as far as I knew, for two years, but he looked more tired than any time since he'd gotten here. I was worried but he reassured me.

"Just a regular thing. I'm sure I may only need to adjust some of my medications. No need to worry."

"George, I'll always worry about you. You're my rock. I look to you when I'm floundering. Pass your check up with flying colors and come back. Please."

It was Sunday and the station bustled with noise and motion. People were coming home from holidays and leaving to go back to work. I heard laughter, loud hellos, and sobbing goodbyes. The rolling suitcases everyone seemed to have now chased, passed by, and almost tripped me every time I took a step, but I felt alone. Crazy. There were lots of people working at the hilltop. The house was full at night, and I'd already started looking for more people to come, but I felt lonely.

George put his arms around me, pulled me close, and kissed the top of my head. "Thank you for calling me. I knew you were trying to restart your life and was hoping you'd find a place to fit in. I think you've done it here. I'm glad to have a small part in your success."

Suddenly, I felt a hollow pit just under my stomach. This sounded more like a goodbye than an "I'll see you later." What was he saying?

"Aine, do me a favor and don't crawl into anymore caves unless you have a crew nearby, okay? I don't want to have to worry about you."

"Okay. I'll be sure I have plenty of rescuers around next time." He walked to the crowded train car door, turned, lifted his arm high and waved.

As I waved, the music slipped into my ears. Somewhere, someone was playing "Amazing Grace" on bagpipes. A chill came over me and tears ran down my face. This piper played it just like the one at my brother's funeral. George's train pulled away and I hunted for a tissue.

Snuffling and blowing, I shook off the feeling of dread that had come over me. Enough of my ghosts. I had ghosts of others to find.

I retreated to my fort.

CHAPTER 18

JAHNA

82 AD January, February

Lovern was distracted and spent little time with Crisi. After we returned from the *mor dal,* he took her out as before. As his leaving grew closer, though, he preferred to go to the hills and forests alone.

Our lovemaking was infrequent, much less than I wanted and hurried when I broke through his curtain of concentration. He was not with just me; the king and the druidess were also in bed with us.

Since our return, the snake in my belly lay coiled and did not lessen its hold. I often forgot meals until Crisi reminded me. I thought it was because of my worry about Lovern. I promised myself to speak with Rhona when I saw her next.

Planning and preparing for the order given to him by King Calgacus had taken many of his waking hours, and now many of his sleeping hours as well.

"Last night, while I lay in our cave, the mistletoe cave, I dreamed of Imbolc. The gods requested more light than we have ever had before. This morning, I harvested many sprigs of the golden bough. If we conduct the Imbolc festival in the way the gods request, the mistletoe will bring a fertile harvest. We will need food if the Romans come. We must be ready to feed ourselves and gather extra if we must leave." Lovern paced, creating a worn path around the fire-pit, his hand running through his loose hair.

I stirred our meal, adding dried juniper berries to the stew. Crisi, now almost six seasons old, sat at her grandmother's loom. Her fingers worked the shuttle between and under the warp to create cloth. Not perfect, but still a good attempt, and it kept her still for a few minutes.

"We will have many candles for you to bless at Imbolc," I said. "Tell me, Lovern, have the gods given you anything that will make your trip less dangerous? Have they told you that you do not need to go?" I wished him to say "Yes, they told me to stay with you and Crisi." That was not what I heard.

"As much as I pray, I hear nothing. I still must go. I do not want the same fate to come to this land that visited the land where I was born. As for now, the gods have shown me an Imbolc filled with light and I must do as they demand."

Imbolc was the halving of our winter season. We prayed for the coming spring to bring fertility to our crops and animals. I prayed for Lovern's safety.

Imbolc dawned to heavy rain, too much for a ceremony outdoors. Lovern and I went to Kenric's home where Lovern lit the sacred Imbolc oak fire. His home, the chieftain's lodge, was filled with clan members, enough to bulge its walls. Lovern asked me to bring the candles we had gathered in the days before. We passed them out to those in the lodge and then I slipped on my cloak. White stag's fur lined my hood and reminded me of a time when Lovern was mine alone. It saddened me. I understood he worked to ensure the safety of Crisi and the other children of our clan, but I missed having him to myself. I gathered the rest of the candles with a heavy heart.

Lovern picked up a large-mouthed, empty pot and a small fire-brand. He turned the pot to hold over the burning oak log, protecting it from the rain. We lit three candles in every abode we visited that night. As I moved from home to home, the rainwater on the path behind us reflected the burning candles. I trembled when I saw the light behind us but darkness ahead.

Home, with Crisi safely in her bed asleep, we stripped ourselves of our dripping cloaks and sat on our bed, wrapped in our blanket. I shivered as I moved closer to him to garnish the heat of his body. He held open his arm and invited me to scoot closer to him. We sat skin to skin.

"Tell me how your hair always smells of spring flowers," he said with his nose resting against the top of my head.

"I have petals from last summer pressed into the soap I use to wash it with," I said as I snuggled deeper under his arm. "You always smell of honey and leather. I have found you in the dark by your fragrance."

"Jahna," he said, his warm breath tickling my ears. "We are traveling the path the gods prepared us for. I feel that this is the reason we were brought together. We are here to save our people, through healing and whatever the gods ask of us at this time. I do not want to go, to leave you and Crisi alone. I swore to you I would not go far again after your taking. But, I must break my promise. Crisi needs you and if I do not come back, you must ask the gods what should be done to protect the clan, to protect Crisi."

He stroked my hair as he spoke, and tears fell off my chin onto my bare legs. My head nodded yes; a fist gripped my heart. I understood, but I did not like it.

The lovemaking that night was like the nights just after our hand-fasting. We did not let go of each other. As I was falling asleep, he whispered into my ear. "I am going when this storm pauses. There has been a lessening of the cold and I think it will continue. I have a better chance of traveling unnoticed in the winter. Eyes turn inward, and I can slip past them." I turned to him, cupped his now bearded face in my hands, and kissed his warm, sweet mouth. I scooted even closer to try to get under his skin. I wanted to never have him leave me again, but I knew he had to go.

"Yes. I will ready your things."

After one more rain-filled day and love-filled night, he left at daybreak, under a clear sky.

Crisi needed little of my attention as she spent most of her time at Finlay's home now. She did not ask about Lovern. He had told her in his way what he was doing, and she accepted it. Harailt and Sileas treated the ill. I looked for something to fill my hands. At Finlay's, I asked for another bowl.

"Are you making anything that I may engrave for someone? I have a need to create something long-lasting."

"Ah," Finlay sighed. "I have a large one for the next *dal.* I would trade for a tiny bit of gold. I will lend you this bowl to work on." He hunched up his shoulders and said, "If it is good enough, I may get more gold for it."

I gathered his small tools and sat down at his worn, burn-spotted workbench. The bowl was smooth and heavy in my hands as I turned and rolled it to see what lived in the bronze. A picture was there. The fox stood on his hind legs, the front two resting on the trunk of a sacred oak tree, his tail fanned out behind him. In the tree rested a raven and, just below it, a finch with a crossed bill. The small bird had come to Lovern in a dream about Crisi. He told me its black wings had reminded him of me, yet the rest of the tiny bird's feathers were the color of Crisis' hair.

"It is small, lively, and twitters, like her," he had said, laughing. "It is her spirit animal."

On the other side of the bowl, I tapped out a standing bear with an owl perched on its left paw. It was my spirit family.

I worked on it for two moon cycles while Lovern was gone. When I finished, Finlay gave the bowl to me.

"No one would trade for a bowl with your spirit animals on it. The gods wanted you to have this one," he said. "I made another. I must have known of this end. I request flowers and braids on the new bowl. No animals." When I started work on Finlay's bowl the next day, my spirit bowl sat on the table next to me.

LOVERN

After our return from the *mor dal*, I spent many days preparing myself for the journey the king had ordered me to undertake. My mind seemed to be in three places at once. I knew I should be spending more time with Jahna and Crisi as well as the ill and injured, but the forest drew me in to meditate. I tried to interpret the message sent by the gods.

Sunlight hours passed quickly in the forest, and I often found myself there after sunset. The nights were cold and on many it rained, so I made it a habit to get to the small cave Jahna and I had protected ourselves in during our first storm together. I was safe in the small, weather-carved abode, and the memories of that first night we spent together were still fragrant in my mind. My heart and body longed for her, but I could not give in.

When I did allow contact with my family, I tried taking Crisi out as I had before our trip. She required more teaching; I wanted her to love the world around her as much as I. The trips stopped after she wandered off and I had not realized it until daylight was dimming. I spent many anxious breaths looking and calling for her before she stepped in front of me, giggling.

"Father," she said, her face as bright as the spring flowers in the meadows. "I have been following you. I sat as quiet as a fox, as you taught me. I sat behind a tree until you started looking for me, and then I followed you. I laughed so I had to cover my mouth, but I was still very quiet! I am a good fox, am I not, Father?"

I picked her up and squeezed her to me, whispering my gratitude to the goddess for keeping her safe.

"Yes, you are a good and quiet fox. I expected to find my little bird, flitting and singing, but you have learned to be a changeling. You have done well with your training. *M'eudail,* beautiful girl, I have loved our time in the fields and forest together." I had to explain why I would not take her out any more. I could not keep my mind on her and prepare for my journey. She must stay with Jahna now.

"The weather is too unpredictable. I do not want us to be caught outside in the rain. Your mother would be angry with me if I brought you home cold and wet day after day. You will stay with her and learn some of the art of healing and weaving. You should have skills from the forest and the home to live well in this world." I knew I would miss her being with me.

I was alone in the cave the night the god gave me the dream about our Imbolc ceremony. Kenric, our chieftain, had started the training of his warriors and it was becoming more and more vigorous. Words passed from mouth to ear to mouth among the clan. Worries were growing about the advance of the Romans; the unknown was causing fear, which grew in the stormy darkness of this season. I dreamed about a ceremony that brought light into every home of our village. I would bless candles, light them from the oak Imbolc fire, and make sure all families had three to relight their home fires from.

Jahna collected the candles and all was ready for the ceremony when the sky opened with its worst storm of our winter. We gathered in Kenric's home to light the ceremonial fire, and then she and I made our way out to the homes of those who did not come. We left light and words of encouragement.

Many came up to me and asked me to pray for their farms and families.

"Druid Lovern," one said. "Pray for fertility for our animals. We ask for a new calf this spring."

"Yes," I answered. "The prayer has been spoken. If the gods are willing, you will get your new calf and many piglets this year, Arden."

I must leave soon, I thought. I could not promise new animals to those who might have to go to war soon and may not come back to farm this land. I could not go on with my routines with the knowledge my family and others may be in danger. I had to go quickly – as soon as this storm calmed.

At home, wrapped in blankets to dry and warm ourselves, I held Jahna in my arms. "The winter will help hide me. I must go now. I will not return for several moons, and our people must be given time to prevent a war or to prepare for battle, whichever the gods will ask of us. If I wait longer, we may not be ready. I must break my promise to you and leave you alone. I ask the goddess to watch over you and Crisi."

"Yes," she sighed. "Yes, *mo dhuine. A ghaoil.* My beloved husband, I hate your going, but yes."

We became one repeatedly that night.

The next daybreak, Crisi noticed we were preparing my bag for travel.

"Father, where are you going? Are Mother and I going with you?"

"No, *eun,* I am going alone."

"But Father, I want to go. Are you going for a long time?"

"I may be a long time. You must stay here and help your mother. And you must help Logan learn his birdcalls. Remember, he did not know as many as you on our last journey."

"But why do you have to go?"

"Crisi, sit here with me." We sat next to the fire pit where Jahna was adding dried juniper berries to the soup. "Do you remember the foxes we watched this spring? The father fox came out of the den after the kits were born and started hunting. He had to protect and fed the mother so she could make milk for her young. For days, he would bring her small voles and mice, leaving them at the door of the den. On his last day, he brought a rabbit and seemed so proud as he carried and laid it at her door. Then the badger came out the bushes and attacked him; the badger wanted the kits. The father fox fought very hard, so hard that he wounded the badger bad enough and it left. But the father fox was also wounded. He crawled under the bush near the den and died."

"Yes. I remember. We buried him after you took his tail and made your armband."

"Yes, that is correct. The mother fox was alone and had to go hunt for herself. She had to leave the den everyday for food, or she would not have had milk for her young."

"Oh, Father. The badger came back and stole her babies while she was gone that day. I cried, but you said it is the way of nature. Sometimes the way of the gods is sad, Father."

"Yes, I agree. Nature can be harsh. Now think. If the mother and father fox had known if the badger lived close by, do you think they would have dug their den there?"

After a few breaths, her face in concentration, she answered. "No, Father. If they had known their babies were in danger, they would have moved. I wish they had. Next time, I will look for the badger and if it is there, I will leave the foxes a message not to stay."

"Ah, you understand. Sometimes, if knowledge is known before an event, we can prevent sad things from happening. I am going on a trip to learn some information that may help stop some bad things. The gods have asked me to go so they can protect us, their kits."

"Oh," she said. "Oh, I understand, Father. When will you come back?"

"I pray to the gods, soon. But, if I must stay away, I want you to remember how much I love you. And always, in your heart, know that I will see you again. I will never be far from you if you think of me."

I thought of a remembrance to give to her. My pipe. I had been teaching her to coax notes from it. She would practice while I was gone. I smiled at the thought that Crisi would also remind Jahna of me — I hoped not badly – when she played. I handed my pipe to her. "You have started learning to make music on this. I am giving it to you. I want you to become a good musician, so you must practice often." She started blowing into it, producing notes shrill enough to make my teeth hurt. "Crisi, I think it would be best to practice out in the stable and then when you are ready to play for your mother you may come in. For now, play only outside."

She had gotten over the sting of my leaving and scampered out the door to play the pipe. I watched, wondering how grown she would be when I returned. If I returned.

The next morning, I donned my oiled cloak over several layers of shirts and pants. Jahna had asked for boots from Finlay, whose feet were larger than mine, and lined them with otter skins she had been saving to make a hooded cloak for Crisi.

"These will keep your feet warm and dry. When you return, I can still use the skins. Do not lose these," she warned.

"My feet have never been so well taken care of," I replied.

"Your feet will walk a long distance. You must take care of them. If they freeze, you will not be able to travel. I beg you to get home, Lovern. I will look for you every day. I have something to add to your labyrinth bag."

I handed it to her. It would be the last thing I added to the pack I would carry on my back.

"I cut some of Crisi's hair. She is with Eiric, playing with her children. I hope she is not blowing that pipe you gave her. I am afraid we will her hear untamed music for the rest of the winter. She loves it so."

She opened my bag, took out the locks of hair she had mixed before I left to gather sea grasses and added some of Crisi's golden red to my rust-colored and her raven's-wing-black hair. I grabbed her hands and kissed the tears that ran down her cheeks. She retied the red thread and returned the precious packet to my bag.

"I will caress it when I rest, to think of you both. Jahna, I must tell you. You are a beautiful woman. When we married, you were a girl." My hand rested on her shoulders and I looked into her tear-filled eyes. "Now, the knowledge of helping those who are dying, and becoming a mother, have added lines of wisdom to your forehead and mouth. I will miss tracing those lines with my eyes and lips. I love you fully. It is because of you and Crisi that I take this journey."

She tied the hood of my cloak under my chin. I enfolded her into my arms but could not feel her body heat through my clothing. We kissed deeply. I turned, and through the fort's gate walked away from my home.

I was glad the tall mountain was behind me when I started. I did not want to climb it in the snow that covered its top. The hills that lay in front of me were treacherous enough. I stayed away from clans I did not know. Alone, I would be suspect and maybe killed. It was safer to walk a longer distance around them.

The weather was fine and clear for the first seven sunrises after I left. My progress was good. I did not know how far I would have to go, but reckoned to reach the village I lived as a child would take seven more days in weather such as this. I traveled faster than the first time I came this way. At that time of my life, my spirit was injured. Then, I hid during the days and traveled only at night.

After escaping the Romans who killed my mother and captured my sisters, I was not a whole person. Then I found Jahna. The gods had led me to the person who had spoken to me through her dreams, and we had created a life together. Jahna and I knew that our souls belong to the gods. I was now their messenger.

Rain fell for the next three days and I slipped and slid up and down the rocky trails that took me in the direction of the Romans. I slept under rocky outcroppings and in depressions of the earth and ate food from my travel bag. Water was not a problem. If I thirsted, I opened my mouth and rain fell into it.

Finally, the clouds emptied. I tied a snare, trapped a rabbit for dinner, and started a small fire, only enough to warm the meat of the rabbit and me. I knew I was close to the Romans, as I had seen trails and the spore of their horses. I was even more careful now.

On the next day's walk, I started across a gully. A small herd of sheep were scattered across the hill on the other side. *It is the wrong time of year for sheep to be pastured,* I thought. *Where is the shepherd?* Leaving sheep scattered and alone was leaving them open to become food for the wolves.

I heard a shout. Not knowing who it was, I crouched, my feet soaked in the frigid stream that ran through the bottom of the gully. Another shout led my eyes to the boy. I carefully looked around for anyone else. No one else was in sight, so

I started for the boy. He huddled in the middle of a pile of boulders that had rolled into the gully from the hillside.

His words were not ones I knew. They brought back the sounds that flooded my ears in my village that horrible day so long ago. The commands of the Roman leader were in this tongue. Bile rose in my throat. How had this boy learned this foul language? He looked to be one of our people, not Roman. I did not want him to know where I had come from, so I spoke with him in only the language of my mother. He was not moving. As I got closer, I noticed that his arm was trapped between two large boulders. He was a boy of about ten seasons.

"Shhhhh, boy," I said. "I will help you."

He stiffened, cried out, and lost consciousness. *Not good,* I thought. *I shall have to move the rocks, and I must have his help to get him out.* I pulled out my water skin and dribbled water on his lips. He woke up and opened his mouth. His thirst was great.

"Boy, I need to gather some things to use after we get you out."

He did not seem to understand. "I am going up the hill." I pointed first to me and then the hill. He shook his head rapidly. Although I did not know the language, I could tell he was scared and thought I would leave him. Tears poured freely down his thin cheeks.

"I will be back, boy. Shhh. I am going up here to find the best branches from this bush." He calmed and did not cry as much. He seemed to understand I would help him.

I walked over to him. "Stand here," I motioned, "just out of the way of the boulder. I do not want it to roll over you and create new wounds." He whimpered as he moved but bravely scooted as much as his trapped arm would let him.

"Yes. That is perfect. Do not move." I moved around the stone to the spot I had picked to push against the boulder that pinned him.

When his arm was freed, he fell unconscious again. I placed the branches on either side of his arm and wrapped the strips I had torn from my shirt around them. His arm was secure and would not move. If he were lucky, the bone would mend and he would still have use of his hand.

When he awoke, I gave him more water. We were near a bag that I assumed was his. I looked inside, and it contained a small amount of hard, black bread. "Boy, you have some food in here. Would you like something to eat?" I put my hand to my mouth as if eating and he nodded. He had some rough bread so I tore off a small piece and gave it to him. He drank a bit more and then fell back to sleep.

I captured a sheep and brought it near us. I tied it to the bush and nicked its neck with my dirk. I used the bread the boy had to soak up as much blood as it would hold. The sheep's wound closed, and I carried the bread to the boy. He woke again.

"Eat. It will give you energy." The bread was softer from the blood, and he chewed and swallowed almost all of it before he fell back to sleep. I sat until it grew cold and knew we should find a place to rest for the night.

I put his pack in mine, gathered him into my arms, and carried him to a copse of trees. We had shelter and I layered dry leaves to help keep away the damp cold. He sat on my lap, both of us wrapped in my cloak. I did not risk a fire, but we were warm. I thanked the gods it was not raining. We slept uneasily until daylight broke over the hills. His skin was hot, a sign the spirits in his body were fighting. I carried him toward my enemy.

At mid-day, I reached the top of a hill. Below us were tents. A Roman warrior camp. The air was filled with dust and noise. My breath stopped and my heart rose to my throat. I turned to go down the backside of the hill, but a man stood behind me. His glare and the sword in his hand caused me to stop.

The gods wanted me to meet the Romans now, no matter what my heart thought. With threatening motions and harsh sounding words, he ushered me to the camp.

CHAPTER 19

LOVERN

82 AD February, March

The Roman's sword prodded me in the shoulder and guided me to the edge of the encampment as I carried the unconscious boy. The soldier's words were the same sounds I had heard long ago but did not understand.

He pushed me into a tent that smelled of blood, smoke, and healing herbs. Relieved, I nodded my head in recognition as I tripped into the dark space. The Roman yelled something at me and then left. The sun let in through the open tent flap sent a quick shaft of light past me. Then, as it fell back into place, I stood in darkness holding the boy. I knew better than to try to leave.

In a breath's time, the tent flap was lifted again and a small, fat man peered in. Not a warrior, he wore a long, dirt-striped grey cloth I had heard called a toga. Before he came completely in, he reached up on his toes and fastened the tent flap up on both sides so sunlight penetrated the smoky room. In front of me, in the middle of the space, was a waist high table. Three low cots hugged the edge. A water bucket and a lit blazer were near the back of the tent. Tools used to treat wounds were laid out on the table in two rows. I recognized the iron needle used to pull the gut threads to close a wound.

The small man limped to the table and said something to me in the Roman language. When I did not react, he threw his arms up into the air, said a few words to himself, and pointed to the large table. He motioned me to lay the boy down.

I took him to be the Roman's healer, so I gently laid the boy on the blood-stained table and backed up until my knees were against a cot. I became a mouse and squatted just out of the man's sight.

To examine the boy's wounds, he undressed him and gently, but confidently, probed the thin body. The boy woke and cried. The bald man was able to quiet him and asked him questions. The boy spoke and pointed to me. The man turned and looked at me for a moment. He walked over to the bucket, lifted a mug of water from it, and opened a small chest. He lifted out a jar, poured a drop of liquid into the mug, and handed it to the boy. He motioned him to drink. The boy took a sip and spit it out, earning some harsh words. He looked at the healer, who stood with his hands on his hips, a stern look balanced on his long-nosed face, and swallowed. His face pinched from the bitterness of the liquid.

The man continued to inspect the splint I put on the boy's arm. He asked the boy questions. The boy answered a few but was soon quiet. *The medicine he drank must aid sleep*, I thought. The man took off the splint and examined the boy's arm. From where I sat, I could see the broken bone, a bump in the boy's skinny arm. I was not going to speak until I knew I could trust the healer.

"Did you make this splint?"

Startled, I fell off my heels onto my bottom. In this humbled position, I stared at the short man. If I had been standing, the top of his head would come to my mouth, but now I looked up. He spoke in words I could understand!

I pushed myself up off the ground.

"I asked you, did you splint this arm?"

"Yes," I said with caution.

"How do you know to do this? There are men who have been in many battles who do not know to do this."

"I am an observant man."

"Observant? Observant means you must have been around someone who knows this treatment. Do you also know how to set the arm so it will heal straight?"

If I answered, I would be admitting to being a healer. I had to find out if I would be safe telling the man who I was.

"How do you know my language? You speak it like one who lived in my village," I asked.

"I had a life before the Romans," he said. "I was a healer near the mines. I watched the sunrise every morning as a boy over the hills of my home south of here. I have traveled and learned the language of the Romans since Queen Boudiccea killed herself. I pray she is sitting at the tables of the kings."

I answered, "May she live in our minds and the memories of her daughters flow through our blood forever." I was relieved he was from my land, but still did not know if I could trust him. "Yes, I know how to set bones. I was in training when my home was raided. I escaped. I am a healer where I live now. I have set many broken bones on children and adults."

"Then come finish the treatment, while the boy sleeps."

We set the boy's arm, then padded and re-splinted it.

"Who was your teacher? I know of some healers who are now like me, living with the Romans," he said.

"You must swear that only the gods will hear my answer." I did not want to give names as they could place my home. If he swore, he spoke a sacred promise. If he lied, he would not be able to cross the river of death to be with his family in eternity.

"I speak with our gods daily," he said and leaned over the boy to see if he was still sleeping.

"My first teacher was Conyn," I said. "He sent me to Kinsey. I learned my bone setting from him. Have you heard of them?" I asked.

"Yes. It is said only the gods are better at healing than Kinsey." He looked into my eyes. "Now, I must ask, do you speak with the gods?"

"Yes," I said, swearing the same promise.

"Kinsey is required to be with the Roman general and treats him and his personal guard. We have a way to pass words to each other, and I have heard Kinsey is moving as much as I am. Always north. It seems that the Romans want even more land. Wait. Let me check the boy."

We had been sitting on one of the cots. He got up and looked at the boy who had begun stirring. The cup still had a bit of the mixture in it, and he had the boy swallow more.

"It will be good to have him sleep for the rest of today. Tomorrow, the spirits in his body may be uneasy, bringing him heat and illness. Sleep is good for him." He stepped back to the cot and sat down. "I am called Ofydd."

"I am called Lovern. The boy is fortunate to have you so close to where he had his accident."

"It is not a coincidence. He is the shepherd for this camp. He belongs to one of the soldiers. He warms the soldier's bed and watches the sheep. The Romans killed his family when he was very small and he has been with this soldier since. He had taken the sheep and goats out to get some fresh grass and greens between storms. He has been gone for three days. They were ready to send some men out to look for him. I am sure his owner will be here soon. We must make sure you are in the background when he comes."

"This boy is a slave?" I asked.

"Yes. Of course. The Romans bring only slave children on these assignments. Their own families are in their villas in the south or across the sea. This boy speaks only the Roman language. He has lost the touch of the gods. If he prays, it is to the Roman gods. We lose our land and our children to the Romans. We are becoming a lost people."

"Ofydd! Ofydd! Is that my boy you have in there?"

A soldier, in full wardress, sweaty from the practice field, came rushing into the tent. Ofydd indicated I should go the dark back corner of the tent and stay quiet.

"Yes, Centurion Candidus. He is here. He is sleeping, see?"

The man was not as tall as I. I could not see his full face in the shade of his helmet, but his nose was well beyond the size of any nose I remembered seeing before. He wore a grey cloak over his armor. The smell of his sweat filled the tent. Ofydd led the Roman to the table, staying between the centurion and me.

"Is he hurt badly? We move in two days. Will he be able to travel with us?"

"Tonight and tomorrow will be the telling time. He has many bruises on his body and was trapped for a day without water. If you let him sleep here tonight, I will watch him. I will do my best for him, Centurion."

"Tillius came to me and told me he had found a man carrying him? He said he guided the man to you. Who brought the boy in?"

"It was a local man, Centurion, not anyone important," said Ofydd. He did not lie; he did not know who I was or where I came from.

"Hmm. You must be wary of the local men. They may have more than the care of the boy on their minds," the warrior said. "All right, I agree. The boy should stay the night here. I have much work tomorrow getting ready for our move. We are going to the place where we build the fort in two days. The scouts have found a good hill that will be easy to defend from these savages. I will look in on the boy at sunrise."

The centurion's cloak swung in a large arc and his sword hit the table as he turned and left.

"Does the boy have a name?" I asked when it was safe to come out.

"Only 'the boy.' If he lives and grows he may earn a name, but one of the ways the Romans keep our children servile is by not letting them have any personalities."

I thought of Crisi and Logan. How could they live without names? *Our names are in our souls. They are as much a part of us as our animal spirits.*

"How do you stand this? How can you live in this way and watch this?" I needed to know how he lived with himself.

"If I did not, I would be dead. In this way, at least I am healing my people when I can. Yes, I treat the Roman soldiers. But, as with him," he pointed to the sleeping boy on the table, "I give him a chance at life. It may not be the life he would have had with his father and mother, but it is life! We cannot ask for more here. Overtaken and overcome by the Romans, we only exist now."

I heard his speech and my stomach began to sicken. I thought of all the people I knew in my clan and the other clans around us. All the druids I had met and worked with. I covered my face with my hands and remembered Jahna and Crisi. Their faces ran through my mind's eye.

"Oh, Goddess Morrigna, protect us. Do not let this come to us," I prayed.

"Quiet!" Ofydd said in a loud whisper. "Do not ever say those words out loud here! You will be slain in a heartbeat. It is blasphemy here to pray to her. Where do you come from that you do not know this? What is your story? Your words are the same as mine when I was a child. Why are you here?"

I told him pieces of my life. He heard about the attack on my village and my escape.

"I live in the north," I said. "We see a change happening. The traders who normally come have not for two seasons. We hear the Romans are coming north. I came to find out what I can. We do not want to be a lost people. We will stop the Romans. Our king decided to fight, and we will win. Then we can come down here and free the slaves of the mines and the villas. We can become a whole people again. I must tell my King that the Roman advance is real so we may prepare."

He slowly shook and lowered his head and was quiet for two breaths. He raised his face and looked at me with hope in his eyes. He took my hands and asked, "What can I do? How can I help?"

"Tell me how many Romans are here and when they are going further."

"Ah. This encampment holds eighty men. These men will build and hold a fort. It is one of a line of forts that Agricola, the general, is building. He finally wants to rid himself of the thistle your king has buried under his horse's blanket. The constant small attacks on the wall by the men from the north have angered him, so he advances. It is not a fast pace, but he is coming. He wants the forts built so he can hold the land and people as he takes them. He does not mean to let any Picts live free. That is the word that comes from Kinsey. I have heard there are many forts planned. You will need many good warriors, men and women, to defeat this fire. If you do not, it will scorch your land, burn you, and we will be slaves forever."

It was urgent that I start back. I had the information my king ordered me to find. Now my duty was to tell him.

"I am going outside to the fire," said Ofydd. "I will roast some meat and bring wine. Then you may sleep in here tonight. You will be safe; no one likes to come here. It reminds them of their mortality. However, you should leave before the dawn."

"Ofydd, you earn yourself a place at the table of the chieftains and kings. After the battle, I will look for you. Or we may meet again on the other side. I will sing thanks to you."

I left the encampment before the horses were up. Ofydd told me where the guards stood and I became like an ant and crawled by unnoticed. As I left the camp, I swore to myself and any gods listening, "My family will not fall to the Romans. I will not let Crisi grow up with no name or Jahna be taken again. I swear with all my life's breath and blood."

I stood on the trail above my home in the same spot Jahna loved to stand and overlook our valley. Women were trading secrets at the well, smoke came from the evening meal fires, and men lead tired ponies up the hill. The feeling was not of peace but of anticipation. We smelled war in the air, and I carried the truth of it in my heart.

There, I could just see her flowing, long black hair as she lifted it from her neck. Jahna was holding Crisi's hand and walking to Kenric's lodge. I choked back a groan of thankfulness and let my eyes feast on Jahna's walk and Crisi's playful jumping. My charge was to go to the king, but my wife and child would come first.

JAHNA

I lifted my heavy hair from my neck and said, "Crisi, I am not in the mood to chase you. I ask you to come calmly with me. You said you were hungry and the evening meal is ready at Kenric's." I had all but stopped cooking while Lovern was away. I was not hungry and now began to have pain in my gut more often. Earlier in the day, Sileas had commented on my thinness.

"You need to eat more, Jahna. Your cheeks are sinking, and I can almost see your bones through your dress. Do not let Lovern's absence stop you from your meals. He will not want to see you have not cared for yourself when he returns."

"Sileas, I eat when I can. It seems since the *mor dal* my hunger has grown less every day. I will be better when Lovern comes home. I miss his smell and presence. Do you know that I sleep with his old clothing? There is a small scent of him left in them, and I use them under my head at night. Yes, I will be well when he comes back. I will eat then."

Just before Crisi and I entered Kenric's lodge, I scanned the mountain trail as I had many evenings. Praying and hoping, but always disappointed. Tonight, habit lifted my eyes to the path. The setting sun was opposite, and the mountainside was golden in its ebbing light. I saw a figure stopped on the trail, a hand over his eyes to shade the sunlight. He looked at me. His eyes burned into mine. A rush of fear flooded from my body, replaced by gratefulness and tears. He was home. My arms lifted to him, and I screamed his name.

"Lovern! Lovern, you have returned! Oh, the gods are merciful!"

One moment I was alone in my realization that he was here, and the next all the people on the hilltop surrounded me. It seemed that I was in the middle of buzzing bees in a hive. Everyone went to meet him. He ran down the hill and when we all stood around him, he lifted Crisi in his arms, and gathered me as close as we could get with a squirming, laughing child between us.

"Let me be seated and eat," he said when all asked the same and similar questions of him. "I will tell you of my journey."

I could not let go of his arm, and traced his footsteps to Kenric's lodge. Sitting at the table, I snuggled my face to his chest just to reassure myself I was not dreaming. There was the scent of a man's weary body, but Lovern's sweet honey odor also streamed into my senses. *Yes*, I thought, *he is home. If even for a short time, he is with me again.*

Then, without bidding, my mind beheld our journey ahead. Lovern was to tell the king the Romans were coming. The druidess Firtha would be there. Her hag face appeared before me in the air. Venom dripped from the fangs of the snake in my belly.

CHAPTER 20

May, 2005

I was feeling sorry for myself, but time slipped by quickly that night. Jim Cowley had called. He'd finished testing the contents of the urn I'd found in the cave. The last test he ran on the contents of the bowl came up with results showing the urn contained ashes of a female. As I was yelling for joy, he broke through with another tidbit.

"Aine, remember I told you your bronze urn, the Raven Bowl, looked like the one Marc found? Well, I had an expert on bronze engraving look at it and compare them. She said it looked as if the same artist engraved both. She wouldn't put it writing, but I thought you would be interested."

"Flippin' 'eck!" I yelled. *Thought I would be interested? Calm down,* I told myself. *Breathe in. Breathe out.* "Yes. That's incredible news. I understand. Just to hear someone else with that opinion is enough for me. Thank you so much, Jim."

"I think you need to call in a Regional Archaeologist. Your site is becoming more and more interesting. I don't have names here but could research it for you."

I wanted more time to mull over his results before the rest of the world found out. As soon as I called in the government,

I would have the reporters on site. I also wanted time to get more people here for security.

"Jim, give me a few days before we release this news. I'll find out who the Regional is and make the call. I want to make sure I understand everything before the reporters from the publications inundate us."

"OK, Aine. Call me before you release. I want to be ready, too."

"Right, Jimmy. Thanks again."

I grabbed my bottle of Laguvalin, ran into the living room of our rented house, and realized all the others had gone into town. It was Friday night, our traditional night out. I vaguely remembered hearing them invite me before Jim's phone call, and my lack-hearted response, "No, not tonight, thanks." Now I was alone. Only me, myself, and I, to drink my good scotch. Oh well, more for me. I sank to the floor and poured myself a drink.

"Actually, I can drink with you, Jahna. No, drink *to* you." *Oh here I go, talking to my ghosts. Marc wouldn't like this. But, Jahna might be listening. I'm not crazy yet.* "Thank you for leading me here, for getting me through the quagmire of my life to get me to this spot. This scotch isn't the same as the honeyed mead you drank, but it's pretty good. So here's to you, Jahna." The alcohol quickly heated my stomach.

The next day I shared the news about the urn with my crew and was buoyed by the cheers. "Yes, I agree. We've found a treasure. I truly think there is more to find so let's go back to work. Be careful, don't overlook anything and if you have any questions please ask. By the way, I am going to call in a Regional Archaeologist. I want this site to be put on the schedule. I hope it is classified as a national monument, but we will have to wait and see."

About midday, I was down in one of the domiciles we were excavating. "Can we get some supports in this area?" I called to no one in particular. "The soil is shifting here and we may lose all the hard work we've done."

"I'll bring some timber over right away," Terry said. He was one of my new hires. He had arrived last night, and, on the job for the first day, he was ready to fetch anything I needed.

"Thanks. And can you get me another bottle of water? We keep them in the large tent, under the table. Thanks again."

The notification I posted on the University's web page last Monday morning was already producing results. Four post-grads applied; one was here– Terry, and another on the way this weekend. The other two decided to go to the site in Wales where Marc was. That site was sucking away all the available people in country. My disappointment was tempered by the hope that they were tripping over each other there.

Smiling, I shook my head as I watched the lithe, dark-haired young man leap out of the excavated depression. It would have taken me a few minutes and maybe even someone's hand to help me out of this hole. Oh God, how long ago had it been since I could move so freely? Now, my back and knees were always aching. It was the payment we gave to our profession – we traded our bodies for clues to the past.

I ruminated on the passage of time. The years since graduation were skimmed quickly – didn't want to spend any breath on them. But here, on my hilltop, I wanted time to stop. I loved it here. I was comfortable here. Despite my problems.

There were never enough daylight hours to get everything done, even with the increase of workers. I seemed to be needed in four places at once, continually. Both Marc and George had taken their supervisory skills with them, and I was still learning how to delegate. It was hard to not watch over the shoulders of everyone here. I wanted all the information I could get about the people who had walked on this square, brought water up from this well and lived in these abodes so long ago.

It was also hard to admit to myself, but I missed George, and, yes, I especially missed Marc. I missed him even more as I watched Terry run across the field to the tent.

"Stay strong, Aine. Stay strong," I whispered to myself. I was too busy during the day to have time to think, but the long nights and empty place beside me in the bed tempted me to call him. So far, I'd resisted calling for a whole week. I had a plan. Just get through seven nights, one night at a time, and then I could black out a week on my calendar. I already had one week blacked out, and one night crossed off on the second week. I was doing pretty well, in my eyes. As long as I didn't spend too much time watching Terry.

I sighed and kneeled back down to brush more loose dirt off the fire pit in the lodge we had started calling the chieftain's lodge. There were enough animal bones on the floor to indicate the serving of numerous large meals. It was logical; the chieftain entertained his troops continually. He loved the songs praising him. His warriors and hunters did most of the work and he demanded praise. *Just like today's men,* I thought. *Can't give credit where credit is due.*

"Aine! Aine, there's someone here to see you," Terry called from the tent. I had told him to call me Aine, not Ms. MacRae. When he called me Ms. MacRae, I felt at least fifty years old. I was close enough to that as it was.

"OK, Terry. Would you please bring the wood to Tim and help him with this wall?" I climbed out of the pit and walked to the tent. An old truck was parked in the field just below the trail. Someone had walked up the trail while I was looking at the deer bones in the chieftain's lodge fire pit.

I stepped from the sun into the tent, squinting to see in the shade. The tent was empty except for the dark figure in front of me. When my eyes adjusted, I saw his face. He looked like Mr. Treadwell would have looked at least thirty or forty years ago.

"Hi." He walked to me, his hand out. "My name is Steven Treadwell." Ah, a son.

I stepped closer and noticed that he had on new jeans. His blue button-down shirt seemed out of place on a farm but hey, if that's what he wanted to herd his father's cows in, then let it be. When we shook hands, I knew he'd done farm work in the past. His hand was strong but had lost the calluses his father's hands still wore. He was into some sort of bookwork now. This land had lost him.

"Hi. Is your father okay?" We were still on this land only by his permission.

"Yes. He's fine. He asked me to come up and talk to you."

I didn't like the sound of this. Why didn't he come himself? "Would you like a bottle of water?" I reached under the table and grabbed one for me.

"Sure, thank you."

We twisted the bottles open. I drank half of mine, and he took a sip.

"Well, what can I do for your father?"

"He asked me to come up and tell you that he has decided to put his land up for sale."

I was in the middle of another swallow and spat out the water in my mouth as I went into a violent coughing spasm. *Oh no. Oh no. Oh my Lord, no.*

He came up behind me and started pounding my back. Coughing, I pushed him away. He was hurting more than helping.

"Oh my, when?" I asked when I caught my breath. Now it became imperative to get started on my quest to have this site identified. Oh gods, I should have done it earlier. But I never thought….

"Da said to say that you can have this summer but a major hotel chain is looking to buy some land in this area and he wants to get his foot in the running."

"But we just found this village! We'll need to be here for a few years, excavating this hill fort."

"He said you wouldn't be pleased."

Not pleased? I was panicked!

"I'm here from Coventry. Dad called me in. He wants me to handle the sale."

His smile reminded me of a snake ready to strike.

"I am sure we could get you some excavating rights built into the contract. I'm sure you know that Scottish law allows development around sites like this. I mean, wouldn't a hotel like a new archaeological site on its land? It would be a draw to the new kind of tourists – what are they called? Eco-tourists. They love to come and 'do' things. They could help you dig!"

Gods above. I could see it now. Untrained people coming in through a turnstile gate, picking up their visors and trowels in the gift shop and creating potholes in Jahna's home. I sat down hard on a stool and almost fell over. He reached out to catch me as my arms started wind-milling.

"Oof." Oh gods, I had hit him right in the nose and it started bleeding. He backed away from me and I pushed myself up off the ground to look at his injury.

"Oh no! I am so sorry! Let me get some ice. Yikes, we don't have any up here. Oh here, let me put some pressure on it. No, don't lean your head back, the blood will go down your throat and make you sick."

"No," he said nasally, his nose pinched shut with his thumb and finger. He had his blue kerchief out, trying to wipe his blood from his chin and shirt. "I'll get it." He continued to back away from me and then turned to go down the path. "Actually, that's all I came for. I'm sure it will stop soon. If not, Da has ice."

He took off for his car at a trot while I stood at the tent door and watched. At the open car door, he reached in and grabbed a paper bag. "I forgot," he yelled up the hill. "Da found these in the peat the other day and thought you'd want them. I'll leave the bag here." He leaned over and set the small bag on a boulder by the path, obviously not willing to risk another encounter with me.

I stood rooted to the ground. I really needed to talk to someone. Someone with more experience running sites than I had. As my senses came back into focus, I looked around and saw everyone watching me. They had gathered around the tent, having heard the whole exchange. "Well, he said we have the rest of this season." I shook my head and shrugged. "From now on, I have one of two goals: either this site gets scheduled as a historic monument or we find a pot of gold. I think we have a better chance of finding that pot of gold right now. Terry, would you run down and grab that bag for me, please?"

He handed it to me and I stuffed it into my pocket. I wasn't ready to open it. Everyone shuffled back to where they had been before the bad news interrupted our good day. I walked to the opposite edge of the hill, overlooking the peat bog and Mr. Treadwell's long-haired Highland cattle. I spent a few quiet minutes thinking about my future. Who should I contact? Of course, Marc's name came into mind immediately but I really didn't want to call him until I had exhausted all my other routes.

I started to sit on the green grass lining the side of the hill to think over my options when the contents of the bag dug into my leg. "Ouch!" I dug it out of my pocket and opened it.

From the clanking, I could tell the clumps were metal, but I couldn't see any shapes. I dumped three pieces out of the bag into my lap and picked one up. Though centuries of bog grime covered it, I recognized it. I quickly picked up the other pieces and intently looked them over. Gods, they were bronze horse harness fittings! I could almost make out the engraving and could see a bit of color. This could just be the pot of gold we were looking for, the evidence I needed to sway a council. The bog would be included on the site map with the hill fort, the urn was dated, and contents identified as human. My site was important. It was as good as gold to me, and others, I hoped.

"Tim, Lauri, everyone! Come here!" I yelled as I ran to the tent. "Look! These were found in the bog!"

Kendy took them from me, her polishing cloth in hand. As we stood and watched her, the gleam of bronze that had not seen the light of day in centuries started glinting in the afternoon sun. Then we saw the engravings.

"We need to get these cleaned and dated," Lauri said, excitedly. "But they sure look beautiful right now! Should we send them to Glasgow?"

"Yes. Please catalog and wrap them. Bring them home and I'll take them to the post tomorrow. I am going to go find Mr. Treadwell and take pictures of where he found them." Normally, we'd map and take pictures of the objects on site but it was too late for that.

"Good afternoon, Mr. Treadwell." His son had answered the door at my knock and watched over his father's shoulder, protectively, as I spoke.

"Now, lassie. It will do no good to try to talk me out of selling. My lads want no part of my father's land excepting the money it'll bring. They tear my heart out but what's a faither to do? I've no other family to leave it to so I may as well sell and go live in Coventry. I don't know what I'll do there."

"Da," Steven said. "Shirley and me said you would be living near us in that new retirement apartment complex."

"Ach, aye. Maybe I can scritch a vegetable garden along the highway that runs just behind."

"Mr. Treadwell, I need to take pictures of where you found the things you sent me today."

He nodded and stepped out the door. "Stay here laddie, I wouldn't want you to get your nice shoes muddy."

He and I started through his fields. "I am sorry that your sons don't want the farm," I said.

"Yes. Well, there's little to be done about it. No use crying. My only hope was to be able to live out my life on this land. My da and his da and his died here. I wanted to do the same. Now I will die in the city." A deep sigh and shake of his head told me all I needed to know. He was not the one who instigated the sale of this land.

"Mr. Treadwell, there may be a way I can help. You've found some very important pieces in your bog. They're bronze harness fittings. I'm sending them off to Glasgow for cleaning and dating, but they may be just what I needed to get this property sale delayed. I can get your land on the Scheduled Monument Consent list for consideration. I'm calling in a Regional Archaeologist and we could have your whole farm listed. There isn't much money available for that, but at least your land would be preserved. If that's what you really want." In my heart, I was praying he would say yes.

"I'll tell ye. We have no real indication where the hotel wants to buy, but my son says he can talk them into coming here. He says maybe since we have been on the land so long, the hotel would be named after us! Can ya just see it? Treadwell's Inn. Ach, but Mrs. Dingleberry would have her knickers all bunched up, that's for sure." The smile on his face told me my chances were very small if existing at all.

We walked the rest of the way in the traditional Scottish silence. I was nauseated and he, I was sure, tired from talking so much.

The bog was wet; I was glad I wore my wellies. He stepped up to a recently dug trench.

"Here. I came out here when my son came two days ago, to get away from his constant talking. I cut a row and in the middle, about here, my spade hit the metal. Did you say they were harness bits? Why would they be throwing good things like that into a bog?"

"At the time the village on your hilltop was occupied, I think it was early in the first century, the people believed in many gods. They made sacrifices to these gods. We have found bronze swords and other items in bogs that were once lakes. Their priests, the druids, asked for valuable and personal items to be given to the gods. There were even human sacrifices at times."

He stood looking over the bog while I walked up and down the row, taking pictures. I thought he was imagining the history that had taken place here.

"He's been here almost every day, recently."

"What?" I looked up, and noticed Mr. Treadwell looking across the bog to the trees on the other side and turned to look myself.

"That fox," he said, pointing with his chin. "Lately, he's been here more than usual. What a creature. I wonder if there are many chickens missing around here? Mine have been okay. I keep them locked up at night since I first saw him. He's a big one."

Ravens erupted from the trees, flying into the sunset. The fox Mr. Treadwell referred to stood stock still just ten feet away, not taking his eyes off us, not blinking. Then he rose and turned. His long, bushy tail carried proudly behind, he strutted into a row of oak trees. The chills on the back of my neck made the fine hairs on my arms stand up. I had the distinct feeling of being judged. I hoped the verdict was favorable.

Back at the farmhouse, I asked Mr. Treadwell not to make any hasty decisions. "And please don't remove any more items. I'll call you as soon as I hear from someone."

"I'll no make any promises, lassie. We'll take it day by day."

I knew by then that I needed to go talk to George. He could guide me to the right people. Maybe even call in a few more favors and get the sale stopped or at least slowed.

"This is my mobile number. I am going to London for a couple of days. Please call me if there is any change or new development."

"Right." He took the slip of paper and tucked it away in his pocket. I hoped it wouldn't get mixed in with the receipts for cattle feed and other things in the farmer's pockets.

The next day, I stopped at the post to mail the harness bits to Glasgow. Tim was in charge of the site for the time I would be in London, with strict instructions to call me with any questions throughout the day and reports every evening. I didn't expect to be gone longer than two nights. I hadn't called George, but I knew he would be okay with my visit. He always had been in the past.

I found a Fort William paper to read on the train. One article interested me above all the rest. A local mall had been increasing the size of its parking lot and stumbled across a pit of bones. All construction stopped until the coroner determined the bones weren't human. They were the bones of what looked to be a stag. Before they paved over the pit, an archaeologist removed the bones. It was surmised that because of the positioning of the bones and antlered skull, the stag had been sacrificed. Interesting, I thought, as the train sped its way to London, but not unusual. Finds like that happened everyday in Great Britain.

CHAPTER 21

JAHNA

82 AD March-April

My body ached from our anxious and hurried lovemaking. We had fallen together as soon as we were alone.

"I must leave when the sun rises," he said.

His hand caressed my hair and my leg was strewn over his bare thighs. I wanted to never have the warmth of his body leave me again.

"You are just returned from a difficult journey," I said. "Must you go again so soon?"

By moonlight filtering through our small window, I saw a look I had never seen before on his face. His head seemed to sink in to his body and his brow creased. A light dimmed in his eyes.

"If it were in my power to change our world right now, I would make it stop here," he said, "with you in my arms, the smell of lavender in your hair and my need for you sated. I do not have those powers. I am afraid, Jahna. *Tha gaol agam ort*, and I will love you forever, but I am afraid I cannot protect you and Crisi. I have seen what happens to those captured. Our people cannot rest until our future is secure. We are going to be in a fight for our land and our lives. Our children's children's children's lives."

His heart raced under his breast as he clutched me even closer.

I felt his fear but after a few breaths, his heart raced for another reason.

"However," he said with a smile creeping back into his eyes, "I have a few moments to spare. We do not have to leave at this moment." His hands gently traced familiar paths on my skin, raising warm feelings deep inside me. "Let me remind myself of your body." His hands stopped on the side of my chest. "Jahna, I feel bones on you I have not felt before. Are you not eating?"

"I worried for you. It was hard to concentrate on my life when I was wondering if you still lived. I will be better now." I hoped that was true, for even now, with his hands, fingers and mouth at my breasts, and my breath quickening in anticipation of the coming pleasure, I could feel the serpent just under my skin. I arched to his fingers and thrusts, and prayed he would chase it away from me, if only for one night.

We left early the next morning. On the way out of our valley, we stopped to ask Rosston to join us. Lovern knew the druids would support and vouch for his truthfulness if the king questioned his story. Those who knew Lovern knew he was an honorable druid and man. Rosston gathered his things quickly and we went on to Rhona's, moving as fast as possible. The chieftains allowed their druids to take ponies. We did not have the luxury of time.

Rhona was waiting for us. "I have sent word to Moroug and Coira. They will join us on the way. We would have to double back if we went to their clan, and my grandson rides like the wind when no one impedes him. He carries my message and my ring. Their chieftain will let them come. My gut tells me we must make good time with this missive, Lovern."

"Have you seen anything in your dreams about this event?" Lovern asked. Rosston leaned in to hear her answers.

"I have seen a battle," Rhona said. "I do not know when or where but it is coming. We must hurry to the king with your knowledge."

We traveled quickly for the next three days. Nathraichean joined us.

"My mind has been unsettled for days. I could not wait at home without knowing so I decided to come without bidding to your village. It is fortunate we meet on the road." He turned to Rhona, his gray hair floating in the breeze. "The air itself carries tension," he said, his ever-moving arms swinging with his words. His eyes took us in and measured our response. We nodded in agreement.

We stopped only to rest the horses and hunt rabbits for our evening meals and spent most of the ride in silence. Conversation about the scenes of the countryside and treatments for unfertile animals seemed out of place to me. I concentrated on imagining what the king would do when he heard Lovern's news.

When words were exchanged, it was in a quest to find the best way to draw the gods and Morrigna's attention to us.

"We must have their ears turned to us now. The gods and goddess must not be allowed to carry on as usual," Lovern said. "We must decide the best way to get their attention this Beltane."

Rosston answered. "Maybe Firtha has a new prayer that will capture the gods' attention."

I closed my eyes at the mention of her name. I was not looking forward to seeing her. "We may have to cut all our sacred oaks to raise a fire that will reach the heavens," I said. I was so innocent of the gods needs.

We traveled to the end of the Great Glen and turned east, toward the rising sun. One more day in travel and we came to the valley of King Calgacus. Gray boulders were mounded to form a wall, topped with a fence of logs. We could not see over it, even sitting on our ponies. Through the partially open gate, I saw many lodges. Naked men, skin dyed blue, guarded the wall, ready to close the gate if needed.

Lovern rode up to the gate but was stopped by the tip of a sword held by one of the heavily muscled guards. "I am the druid Lovern," he said. "I am ordered by the king to come. I have a message for him."

"Wait," we were told.

One of the guards jumped off the wall and out of our sight. I listened in curiosity to the noises behind the gate. I heard people laughing and talking, all busy with the chores that filled our daily lives. I felt less like a stranger here, for they lived like us.

Dogs chased chickens and men laughed. Mothers called to children. Smoke rose over the wall, home fires lighted to chase the damp, chilled air. Noise and the odors of life floated around us. As word of our arrival spread, eyes peeked around the gate. I matched them to the faces of curious children. I inhaled deeply as I missed Crisi.

I was tired and sore from sitting on my pony for so many hours. I wanted to dismount. Sitting on the back of this beast was torture, as thin as I was. Although I wore several layers of clothing and my heavy cloak, I was cold and needed to pee. If the guard did not come soon, I would go into the surrounding woods and relieve myself.

Just as I stretched and leaned over to tell Lovern and Rhona that I would be absent for a moment, a chariot came crashing around the far corner of the fence. In it stood a wild man, long blond hair flying. His mouth opened to show white teeth centered in a face stained blue. He screamed the battle cry and waved his sword over his head while his driver and one other man stood behind him. Following him were nine mounted warriors, all armed and naked, bodies dyed blue. They rode close to each other in sacred groups of three.

My pony started but held. He wanted to join the race but obeyed my commands. My heart thudded like a festival drum at the sight of the king and his guard coming toward us at full speed. If his goal were to impress us, he succeeded with me.

They rode past, and just before they turned and slipped from our sight, they pulled up at the opposite corner.

After much cheering and jostling among themselves, one of the mounted men slid down and held out his reins. King Calgacus climbed out of the chariot and onto the pony's back. The rider he replaced stepped into the chariot. The king and two of the mounted guards came to us in a fast trot while the rest of the cadre and his chariot turned the corner towards the back of the village. As they came closer, I saw that the two guards behind him were women. They were so well conditioned – tall, slim-waisted, with muscled legs and shoulders – that their stained blue bodies blended in with the men on the charge. Their long blonde hair bounced on their backs in heavy braids. They carried the same shields, long swords and spears the men carried. They rode proud and I knew they would protect the King with their lives. I had seen female warriors, but none so strong and none stained fully blue. This display of the king's guard and battle practice gave me hope that the king would be ready to accept Lovern's news and go to war with the Romans.

The men on the fence who had joined in on the battle cry grew quiet as the king rode closer. I saw their respect in the way they stood tall before him. A lathered pony, chest straining with his breathing, was now upon us, King Calgacus on its back. His face was a study of concentration. His body glistened with the sweat of one who had worked hard. I admired him as he came closer. He had no extra flesh. Arms, abdomen and legs well muscled, and the look of health emanated from him. He peered into our group until he saw Lovern, and then with a nod of his head he turned and looked up to the top of the wall near the gate. I was surprised to see his druidess, Firtha, standing there, her face just showing from under her white hood over the top of the fence. She turned to face the back of the village, and the king kicked his pony to move in through the gate. His guards motioned us to follow.

Our ponies fell into step after theirs and started into the fort. I was last in line, and just before my pony crossed the worn path of the gate, I pulled back and stopped. Though surrounded by noise from all the king's people as well as the animals in the fort, I shivered as all sound was instantly gone from my ears. I looked through wavering air. Confused and not knowing what was about, I spun my pony around, ready to run out of the fort. A shaft of clear light shined on a scene in front of me.

In the front line of trees, across the road leading into the fort, I saw them. The oak was heavy with ravens. Its branches bobbed with their weight, and its new leaves fluttered with the stretching and unfolding of their many wings. They sat, quiet, and watched me with night-black eyes, almost invisible in their blue-black bodies. The sun glistened on preened feathers.

Why had my animal host shown itself to me in such a way? I watched for a moment longer, their eyes unblinking, when I saw movement on the ground. The pair stepped from behind the raven-filled tree. She was young and timid. Her eyes darted about, looking for danger, body tensed and ready to run at an instant. She carried more blond-colored hair than copper, accented with snow-white tips. Small, when she crouched in the grass under the oak, it hid all but her face and twitching ears.

He was royal. As large as a hunting dog, the male fox stopped, his body one step in front of his mate. He turned and nipped her gently on her neck; she nuzzled his fur. As he sat, he laid his white-tipped, flame-colored tail across her back, claiming her as his. His chest was not as white as hers, showing the yellowing of age and life in the forest. Sunlight glinted off the deep copper color of his back. He looked up at the tree filled with ravens and then back down at me.

I knew the king's foxes were large and not often seen. They were wary of men. I sat quietly, filling my eyes. Then, the male stood and barked, and the female disappeared behind the tree. He looked up into the tree, at one very large raven that seemed to be the leader, yipped, and then the sky grew dark over me as they rose together and flew over the rooftops of the fort. My eyes followed until they were out of sight. I turned back, and the fox faced me. He walked out of the long grass to the road and dipped his body into a long stretch, as if bowing to me. He took no notice of the people or noise around me and then calmly turned to lope into the woods, following his mate.

I sat in a prayer of gratitude while sound became normal around me again. It seemed no one else had seen what I had seen. Everyone carried on with what they were doing before. I shook my head in wonder. It was a powerful sign from the gods.

Following the direction my companions, I started my pony after them, my eyes still filled with the splendor of the sight. I passed a long row of lodges, all built in the round form as ours. Coming to the end of the row, my pony took one step around the corner and neighed to a group of ponies standing in front of a dwelling. Lovern's pony was among them.

A child reached up and took my reins as I slid down and walked into the lodge. Its main room contained three fire pits, all in use. Over one, tended by a small boy turning the spit, cooked the full body of a boar. The boy had to jump back often. The flames that shot up when the fat from the animal dripped into the fire came close to burning him. The other two fires had large pots stirred by young women. An older woman was making her way back and forth from one fire to the other, adding vegetables and roots to the pots and pinching the crisping skin of the boar. "Don't let this burn, boy, or you will be sleeping outside with the pigs tonight. Girl! Bring more herbs here, we need more flavor in this pot," she yelled across the room. Five large tables circled the room. All were in use, some where women chopped onions and herbs for the stews in the pots, and others where there were women who slid loaves of fresh, dark rye bread off baking planks. One table was piled high with mugs for mead. *Many are coming to this evening feast,* I thought. Many came every evening, as this looked like a well-practiced dance by all here.

Lovern and the others were standing in front of a large chair in the center of the lodge. In it sat the king, dressed in a finely woven, blue shirt and trousers. His clothing seemed to blend in with the woad blue of his dyed skin. A bronze pin fashioned into a large cluster of mistletoe closed his cape. The pin's painted golden-green leaves and white berries caught my eye. *Finlay would have loved this,* I thought. He would have asked the king if he could hold it to better look at its fineness.

The king spoke. "So, Druid, it is as I expected. The Romans are coming to us. Were you able to find out how long before we will see them trampling our fields?"

The noise around the room stopped, as if by an order from the king, all eyes focused on Lovern.

"They are building forts as they come," Lovern answered. "I was told their general, Agricola, wants to build a line that will not be crossed before he comes further. They may not come this far this year, but the Romans are coming."

"Hmmm. The news is bad, as I feared. We will have to stop him. He is foolish to think he will have an easy time taking our land. The only good news to come from you is that we have time to prepare. We have time to raise the army and move them to the spot I will fight," said Calgacus. "I have ridden over and mapped this country, and know the best mountain pass to take a stand. I have planned a long time for this. My druidess told me we would go to war. She has seen it often in her dreams. She has prayed for a way to capture the ears of the gods. We will be victorious over the Romans and will win and keep our lands free from all invaders."

At this, he raised his hand, heavy with rings on every finger, and waved one of his guards to him. "Call in Tearlach. I must talk to him. He will lead the training of all the warriors promised to us by the clans."

A tumult grew around us. All the warriors at the tables were standing on the benches or on the tables, yelling battle cries. Those coming in late were told the news and joined in the scene. It seemed some were looking at our little group with distaste. We were the harbingers of bad news and I began to wonder how safe we would be if they decided to come at us.

"I am here as commanded." The man at the door was two-hands taller than the king. His dirt-streaked face wore lines of the years of experience, and heavily-browed eyes took in the room at a sweep. He carried a spear, and from his belt hung a short and a long sword. The battle cries turned into a cadence of calling a name: "Tearlach, Tearlach, Tearlach!"

Tearlach raised his spear, and the hall filled with the roar of men ready to fight to their death for him.

"Warriors," he said. His voice was deep, but he deliberately did not raise it above the din. He waited. As men noticed him, they grew quiet. He continued. "We do not fear the Romans. We will go to war and win. We are stronger and fight for our land. *Our* land. It is *our* land, not theirs. They will regret bringing the battle to us for the rest of their short lives." He began pounding the butt of his spear on the ground and others followed by banging their spears or swords against tabletops. The walls around us began to shake.

The king raised his hand and the noise stopped again, this time by a king's order.

"You have done well, Druid," he said. "You and your companions are welcome at my tables for the meal."

Behind us, men talked again. We bowed, turned, and walked to a table close to the door. The king's men sat near him, the honored at his table. We sat where we could escape the long night's festivities, as we planned to start back home at sunrise.

The room continued to fill with people. "Look," said Rosston in a voice that spoke with inexperience. "That man – wearing a gold torque! The king wears only bronze, but his is gold!" We watched as a tall man, braided red hair hung over a red cape that matched the king's, walked to him and nodded his head. When he turned, we saw a similar pin of mistletoe closing his cape over his left shoulder.

"He owns many fields and sheep," said Uilleam. "That is Malcom. He has men who come to trade with my village. He is the brother of the king and carries the purse of the army."

"It seems," Nathraichean said, his hands strangely still, "he spends the purse of the king on himself as well."

"Be careful, Wolf," warned Rhona. "There are many who listen for words such as yours just for the pleasure of reporting them to the king and watching the beheading and mounting of the severed heads on the fence. We want to take all of you home on the morrow, not just your body, your head left to decorate the gate of this fine fort."

"The king would not kill a druid, would he?" Both Moroug and Coira asked the question in unison. I wondered if they often spoke as twins and finished each other's sentences.

"The king will do what is necessary to keep his warriors and people happy. If a druid must die, then a druid will die," said Rhona. A chill crept into my heart with those words.

They carried the roasted boar to the king's table where, with his sword, he separated the beast with one stroke, to the cheers of those around him. He took up a short blade to cut the smaller pieces, and filled plates with the meat as he carved. Also, wooden bowls of vegetables and mugs of mead

were passed around. Mugs of mead were refilled from buckets
carried around the room. As the overfilled platters of food
passed, we stabbed our portions and piled them on the table
in front of us. Everyone seemed to enjoy the food. The mood
was light even though the news we carried here could bring
death to many warriors in this room tonight.

Music started at the back of the lodge and two men
sidestepped those carrying food and mead to stand in the
space directly in front of the king's table. One blew into a
pipe, creating a tune, and the other beat a drum while singing.
I recognized a song about a battle long ago with a giant monster
of the land that Bel and Morrigna fought with. The monster
fled into a lake and it is still told that she raised her head and
became visible at times. Many have sworn to seeing her.

We sang the same song at home, we ate the same food, wore
the same clothing. Now we feared the same enemy. I prayed
our people would be victorious in battle. If we followed this
king and the gods heard our prayers, we would be victorious.
I believed it to be so.

The smoke in the room grew thick. Men added peat to keep
the fires burning through the night's festivities. I was tired from
the long journey, the ride, this day's events, and wanted to find
a quiet place where I could tell Lovern about the animals I saw
earlier. Foxes and ravens gathered in and around an oak was
a powerful sign for us. I wanted to discuss it with him until we
understood it.

I looked to the door, readying myself to leave to find clean
air, when the figure appeared. I started, unsure of what it was,
my eyes unclear from the smoke. Rhona was next to see it.
Nathraichean stood when Rhona touched his shoulder and
directed his gaze to the apparition. "Who are you?" he asked in
a voice that drew the others eyes to him and then to the white
hooded, caped man in the doorway.

"Firtha requires your attendance," the figure said.

"Whose attendance?" asked Uilleam.

"All who rode in with the Fox today."

We followed him outside. The night air was crisp and cool after the room filled with smoke and the body odors of men who worked hard. I took a deep breath. The newly green leaves and turned fields left an odor of spring. It was not yet Beltane; however, the signs were there, even this far north.

The figure led us to the back wall where a small opening let pedestrians through. I was a bit dizzy from the mead and lack of sleep so I hung onto Lovern's arm.

"Where are we going?" asked Lovern.

The cloaked man stopped and turned. "We are going to the sacred stones. Firtha has had a vision and she must share it with you. The way will be dark and rocky. I will carry a torch, so stay close." He picked up a torch from the guard on duty at the opening of the fence and we were outside the fort walking into the trees.

"This is the path of the ancients," he said. "The path we walk on and the standing stones were both placed by the gods. We hold our most sacred ceremonies there."

"I seem to remember a storyteller's song about standing stones in this area," said Coira.

"It is said the gods built them for man to use as a sacrificial altar for our ceremonies," said Moroug.

"Ouch, wait. I have tripped," said Rhona. "Nathraichean, please give me your arm to steady myself on these stones. I do not want to fall into the water."

We had come to a stream. The robed druid seemed to float across while we stumbled and bruised our feet as we clumsily walked from stone to stone to cross the shallow but cold and fast water.

The forest opened up to a small meadow and in the middle was a small circle of man-height stones. There was a large fire in the center, and I heard a multi-voiced hum coming from the stones. They seemed to move, waver in the firelight. We walked closer, and I saw eight swaying figures in white robes, just like the one leading us. The people in the robes held hands and made the shadows that seemed to give the stones movement. The robed figures sang the song I had heard.

Our guide stopped just outside the ring of stones and whispered into the ear of one druid. The circle broke, and he walked into the ring. He motioned us to follow. I got to the ring and again, just before I stepped in, I looked around the circle of trees behind us. I knew he watched. The fox I saw earlier was there and watched us.

Firtha stood in her white robe on the other side of the ring. The fire between us bathed her in an orange light. Shadows danced on her body, created by the moving flames. I had not seen her at the evening meal, and I wondered what would keep her away from her king, especially, when Lovern's news proved her right about the Romans. Now I knew. She had been here preparing this ring. Waiting for us to come.

She watched us come into the circle and bade us to sit on the ground around the fire. As we sat, her eyes took us in. Her loose hair, red in the firelight, hung below her waist; her hood hung down the back of her robe. The fire did not give enough light at that distance to see the color of her eyes. I remembered they were the blue color of water melted from ice. A band of beads circled her forehead and tied at the back of her head; her sea eagle feather was attached so it hung behind. She still wore the necklace of boars' teeth. I wondered if she were able to add to it from the boar that had become our evening meal.

An alder staff was in her hand, one long enough to touch the ground at her bare feet and rise above her head more than two hands high. Lessons from Lovern about this tree flashed through my mind. He made his music pipe from it. It gave different dyes for our cloth. Some druids used it to help call in spring. *Maybe that is why she holds it tonight. It is almost spring, almost Beltane.*

Unbidden, the memory came that it also called the soul of the sacrificed human to come back to aid the living. A *volunteer* sacrificed human. The little I ate at dinner laid unsettled in my stomach.

Small stones scattered on the ground dug into me. Uncomfortable, I shifted, hoping not to put a hole in my green dress. The hot fire burned my face, while my backside was cold. I shivered and Lovern put his arm around me. I was able to settle down, and when I looked around the small, seated circle of fellow travelers, I saw they all had their eyes on Firtha. Rhona lowered her eyes until she looked straight into mine. I saw a great strength there. I was glad she was my friend.

"Now you are here," Firtha said as she came closer to us. The humming stopped as soon as she started talking. Robed druids came closer to hear her words. "Tell me what you found, Lovern."

"As I told the king, the Romans ready themselves to take our lands. To make slaves of us or kill us. That is what they have done on the lands they occupy now. It is what they want for us. I stood in a camp of Roman warriors and have seen they have weapons and train to kill us."

She nodded. "It is what I have told the king for many moons. I have seen it many times in my dreams. It is because we are weak. Do any of you know why we are weak?"

Firtha slowly looked into the eyes of all present. No one responded.

"We are weak because the gods ask us to give ourselves to them. We have stopped obeying that command. Yes, we learn what we can about nature and healing and other magic, but we have not given back all we should, in payment, for many years.

My teacher was ancient when he taught me the arts. He told me we should never change them, but we have." She paused. "We have become soft and because of that we could lose all we have. Our lands and our families. We need to catch the ears of the gods again."

Her staff pounded the ground in her agitation as she paced, walking around us quickly. We had to turn our heads to follow her footsteps. "We must get back to the ways of the God and Goddess. They gave me a vision. A vision of victory. I was told that if we come back to them fully, we could have what we want. We can have peace."

She stopped pacing and as the alder staff hit the ground in time with her every word, I trembled.

I heard words tumble from her mouth but could not understand them. Voices from all those in cloaks around us uttered short, quiet sighs of agreement.

She raised her staff to the sky. "Gods and goddesses, listen to me. We will have a human sacrifice!"

A fearful rushing sound of unstoppable water and wind filled my ears. I closed my eyes and began to pray. My heart heavy with dread, I began to shiver. The snake awoke and raised its head in my belly again. Memories of my feelings, those that had told me of my shortened life, flooded my head.

I was afraid, so very afraid.

CHAPTER 22

MAY, 2005

Noisy London. I'd almost forgotten. Fort William's traffic was nothing like what flew by my little apartment above the bookstore. Arriving back late on Friday night, I fell into bed and slept until the din woke me at half past eight.

I tried to phone George's home, but got no answer. His office didn't answer either. I had called him a dinosaur because he wouldn't carry a mobile.

"Too damned intrusive," he'd said.

There was no answer all day Saturday so I finally decided he must be out of town.

Saturday wasn't a total loss; I did get to visit with some friends from MGC and decided I'd made the right decision by going to Scotland to chase my dream. Talking to them brought back all my old dreary, depressing thoughts about jobs in my past. Writing up reports and statistics didn't fill my life with any light. I ordered after-dinner drinks for my friends and I and silently toasted myself and my choice of a new life.

Sunday morning. The bookstore, closed and quiet, allowed me to laze around until ten in the morning, rereading my notes on Marc's earlier site. The chieftain's tomb where I'd found the first bowl, the first one Jahna led me to.

It was in the University of Birmingham's Museum of Ancients along with the other tools Marc found in the tomb. I leafed through the pictures I'd taken of the bowl found under the stone where it had lain so many years. Jimmy's words ran through my mind. *The same artist probably had worked on the bowl that contained the ashes I'd found in the cave.* Jahna. I was certain it was her. I'd never be able to prove it to the world, but I didn't need to. I was proving it to myself and remaking myself in the process. If Jahna wanted to help me along, who was I to dissuade her?

I called George's home again. Three rings—why hadn't I called before I left Fort William? I was about to hang up when she answered.

"Hello?"

"Oh. Hello. I hope I have the right number, is George home?"

"May I ask who is calling?"

"My name is Aine. Aine MacRae."

"Oh my, Aine. This is Meg." She sounded a bit dazed, not at all like her normal formal self. Meg Smyth was George's secretary while he worked at the university. Also Sophie's friend, she helped when she could while Sophie was ill. She'd retired at the same time as George, and now made sure George had food in the house and didn't get buried under an avalanche of his books and paper work. George paid her to stop by once or twice a week. She came more often as a friend. Her husband died many years ago, and there were no children. I often wondered if they were going to get married or stay in this strict relationship, stepping around their need for each other's comfort for the rest of their lives. "Aine, George is not here right now. He is… Well, could you come by?"

"Yes, I can be there in a little over an hour. Meg, is he in hospital?"

"No. Not in hospital. Aine, let's not talk on the phone. I'll be waiting with a bit of lunch for us. See you in a bit." Her voice was not jolly, not jolly at all.

My thoughts rambled while I rode the underground. She said George wasn't in hospital. A deep, dark thought about death sprang forward, but I quickly buried it. He must be on a trip. Yes, a trip. Why didn't he call me and tell me? He wasn't beholden to me. We weren't related. We were friends. No. More than friends. I considered him my uncle. But still, he didn't have to call me every time he left town. Why did Meg's voice sound as if she were holding a secret close to her heart? Why was I frightened? Now that I think about it, he really didn't look good when he got on the train last week. He didn't tell me he felt ill. And Meg said he wasn't in hospital.

All these thoughts swarmed through my head as I jumped on the tube at the Marble Arch, running up and down the stairs when changing at Trafalgar and then on to Waterloo. George lived near the Royal Theater.

When Sophie was well, they'd loved to go to the theater. Since she'd died, I don't think he'd gone once. He told me he didn't need to live through others' lives; his life was filled with his own memories to keep him company. I didn't think he read a novel or a work of fiction after her death. It was as if a door closed to a part of the world for him when she died. He lived buried in his history. The buried memories of others released through his archaeology. His life.

I knocked. Meg opened the door. She looked just as she had the last time I saw her several years ago, thin as a straw, grey hair so tightly pulled back into a bun at the nape of her neck it seemed to give her brown eyes an almond shape. Her strong, long fingered hands grasped my shoulders and pulled me into the house. Though she was severe looking, she was anything but. Every bone in her body was friendly. She wasn't much for powder or lipstick. It was to her benefit now, as powder and lipstick seem to gather in a woman's creases and wrinkles as we age. Rosewater. She always smelled like rosewater. Hugging me close, I could tell she still wore it.

"Aine. Oh, my dear. It's so good to see you! Come in. I've sandwiches and tea for us. Here, sit in the study. I'll bring them down."

I watched as her calf-length black skirt and sensible brown shoes marched up the stairs to the kitchen. I stood in George's study. Its dark, mahogany shelves overflowed with books and papers. I also saw labyrinths. He told me he'd been collecting them but there were close to fifty, of all sizes in here. Some on top of books, some standing propped by papers and others braced by little plate stands. There were even a few on the arms of the leather chairs. Some looked ancient and some new. It was as if he'd started his own museum of labyrinths. I picked up a bronze one with its own stylus in a hole in its side. A medieval Eleven Circuit pattern that looked like the Chartre labyrinth. Four quadrants walked and traced to meditate. Heavy in my hand, it looked as if someone had used it lovingly for many years. The edges of its grooves were worn.

"I see you found his pet."

I jumped. I'd not heard her come down the stairs.

"Pet?" I didn't know what Meg was talking about. I looked around for a small animal or bird. I was surprised, as George never liked animals underfoot. "What pet?"

"That thing. He carried it around in his pockets until he wore holes in them before he went up to Scotland. It is not a light thing as you can tell. He decided not to take it with him on his trip; 'too cumbersome,' he told me. He got it from a friend who found it in an estate sale in Ireland. He'd take it to the park before sunrise and sit on a bench, waiting for the sun to come up." She started pouring tea into rose-patterned china cups. Sophie's rose patterned china cups.

My mouth watered. The cheese sandwiches looked yummy and the steam from the tea smelled like Taylor's of Harrogate Scottish Breakfast. George's favorite.

Then she stopped and set the teapot down. My eyes moved from the teapot to her face, and I watched it fill with even more wrinkles as tears filled her eyes and slid down her cheeks, spotting her white blouse. I lost my appetite.

" And now, of course, he can't use it. Aine, dear. George didn't want me to call you. He told me to tell you he went out of town if you called or came by. But I can't do that."

I closed my eyes. Bad news was coming, and I didn't want to hear it. I took a deep breath and opened my eyes to look into her teary ones.

"George is in St. John's Hospice. He's been there for a week. He is dying, Aine, dying." Her hands covered her face and her shoulders bobbed up and down as she sobbed.

I stared at her, unbelieving. A week. He'd gone in right after he left Scotland. He didn't seem sick. *What does she mean he's dying?*

"Meg. If he's so ill why isn't he in hospital?"

"His treatments have stopped working now." She lifted a tissue to her eyes. "He knew this some time ago and made plans with St. John's before he left for Scotland. I didn't want him to go up there, I thought he should stay here and fight this thing, his illness, but…. He is such a stubborn man. I doubt even Sophie could have convinced him otherwise. Anyway, I have been told he is close to dying."

Death had visited me before. My father died before I went to university, then my brother Donny, and, soon after, my mother. But, I'd not grown used to it. Does anyone get used to death? Now George. I knew he was ill, but it was always in the distance. When I asked how he felt, he always told me he was fine. Looking out the window, at the road in front of George's home, I wanted to yell and stop the traffic. George is dying! But, the cars continued on their way. Life was the same for the people in them. George's death would not affect them.

I gently took hold of Meg's shaking shoulders until she looked up at me. "I need to see him. Can I visit? Is he well enough for a visit?"

"Uh, oh. Yes. Of course. Let me call and tell them you are coming. I'll be right back."

As I waited for her return, I picked up the labyrinth and held it. My trembling hands would have dropped the stylus, so I traced the grooved path with my fingers. Years of quests and meditations were recited over this piece of metal. It felt warm to my cold fingers. As I traced the path, I silently begged whatever powers that be to let George be well. When I got there, I wanted him to be standing at the door saying, "What am I doing here? Let's get back to work, Aine. There are years to uncover and mysteries to find answers for out there. Call a taxi and let's go!" Grasping the sculpture to my heart, I wished him to be well. I didn't know how to handle his death.

Meg walked back into the room. She hugged me and said the hospice was expecting me. The address of St. John's Hospice and cab fare were stuffed into my hands.

"But aren't you coming with me?" The thought of doing it on my own made my heart beat fast. I was close to panic.

"No, I can't. I have said my goodbyes. I have done all I can for him. I can't watch him die. I call everyday and tell the staff to pass along my hello. But to go and watch him die? No. I'm not going. They'll call me when he goes. Who else would they call? I'm all he has left. Well, you and me, Aine. I would have called you. After. He didn't want you to worry over him. But, I guess you were supposed to be here."

She picked up the tea and still full sandwich tray and started climbing the stairs in her sturdy shoes. "The taxi will be here in a moment. I took the liberty of calling. They'll take you there straight away." She stopped and turned her head to me. "Tell him I am praying for him and think of him. Please?" Her tears started again. She snuffled and climbed to the kitchen.

My taxi arrived just as George's front door closed behind me.

Light filled the reception area. Light and soft classical music. Never a music buff, I couldn't tell what music was playing, but it soothingly filled my ears. I expected the medicinal smell of a hospital, that sterile, antiseptic smell that permeates clothing and never seems to come out. I was surprised at the lack of any odor. No antiseptic, floor cleaners, or – what I dreaded most – death. I didn't really have an idea of what death would smell like, but I was expecting it here. Then as I stepped up to the reception desk, perfumed lavender wafted into my nose. The woman, Jane by her nametag, must have lavender lotion or a candle nearby. I preferred the scent of real lavender.

"Good afternoon. May I help you?"

"Yes. My name is Aine MacRae. I'm looking for George Weymouth. I mean, his room."

"Mr. Weymouth," Jane said, running her finger down a list of orders. "Yes. Ms. MacRae, I'll call and let them know you are here. They're expecting you."

Overstuffed chairs sat heavily on a blue linoleum floor and filled the reception area. Water gurgled over stones in a small table fountain. Doors opened and closed down the long hall to the right and left of the desk. I wondered if George would appear around the corner of the wall at any moment.

"Ms. MacRae, Sarah will be right here. Would you like to sit down?" I wondered if she wore that look of condolence for every visitor who came here.

"No, thanks. I'll just wait here."

Another door opened and closed, and a woman slipped around the corner, smiled at me, and then Jane, and at Jane's glance back at me extended her hand for me to shake. "Hello. Ms. MacRae? My name is Sarah MacDougal. I'm working with Mr. Weymouth. I'd like to talk to you for a minute before we go into his room, if you don't mind."

"Sure, and please call me Aine."

"Good. And call me Sarah."

She led me around the corner. We passed three rooms and then came to a door labeled "chapel"; she opened it and invited me in. The room was small; four pews left a narrow walking space between them and the walls. The wall at the far end was covered with a pleated, deep purple velvet curtain. An oak table sat in front of it with two brilliant yellow mums on it. The blossoms seemed to explode out of the quiet colors behind them. A golden chalice sat between the plants, simple yet spiritual.

We sat and she began. "Mr. Weymouth has asked me to explain a bit of what is going on in his room right now. He is actively dying. He may not live until morning." She stopped when she saw the disbelief in my eyes.

"I just saw him last week! He looked tired, that's all, tired! He told me he was just coming for tests. How can he be dying?"

"He stopped his treatment for his illness, leukemia, several months ago. He was about to come here when he left for Scotland. I was surprised he did as well as he did while there. When he got back home, he was completely depleted and very weak. An ambulance brought him here from the station."

"Oh my God. What can I do? Can I donate blood or something?" My hands searched my jeans' pockets in vain for tissues to stem the flow of my tears. Instead, my hand found George's labyrinth. I must have slipped into my pocket when Meg told me about George. My hand came out of the pocket empty. Sarah reached into her tweed jacket pocket and pulled out a handful for me. I thanked her.

"He has slipped in and out of consciousness the last twenty-four hours or so. Oh, and he sees and talks to Sophie."

"What? He sees Sophie?"

"Sometimes, the people we loved who have died return to us just before we pass. I consider it a blessing when it happens. When she is there, he smiles and looks into a far corner. The room fills with love." A slight smile and far away look came to her face and she sighed. Then she refocused on me. "We can go in now, if you like. He's ready for you."

I wasn't ready to hear this. I knew he was looking across the Celtic River of Death he loved to go on about in his classroom. A few of us were allowed this vision. It meant he was seeing across to the people who stood there to welcome him. Sophie.

"Will I be the only one in the room?" My mouth was dry. He was so close to death and I didn't know if I could be there alone with him.

"I'll be there. I'm staying until he passes or comes through this crisis."

I took a deep breath. The only other person I'd seen just before death was my mother. She was in the hospital, hooked up to what looked to me to be every machine in the building. I went into her room, but she was in a coma. Her heart attack was sudden and massive. She died that night, while I was getting coffee.

"What do I do? What do I say? Can he talk?"

"Yes, he's able to talk a little. The best thing is to just be there, hold his hand, and let him talk to you. What you need to say will come to you. Don't force it, but it is important to tell him goodbye." She squeezed my hand. "You'll become a part of this room very quickly. It's full of peace." She smiled, and I believed her.

We walked into George's room. Drapes of royal blue and forest green framed the bed. A deep green fleece lay on top of him, his body an irregular mound under the blankets. His head lay on a pillow wrapped in deep blue satin. I stood still until I saw his chest move. A small weight dropped from my shoulders and I started breathing again.

He looked so small. I remembered him as giant of a man. "Did he collapse because he came up to Scotland?" I whispered.

She took my hand and said, "No, dear. The trip didn't cause his illness. He's been ill for several years. Actually, I think the trip to Scotland did him a world of good. He would have been lying here, just waiting, if he hadn't gone. No one is to blame here. Death is a part of life. Mr. Weymouth wants you to know that what is happening is all by his choice. I am sort of a coach. I create a comfortable and peaceful death for those who ask me to help. He and I have been planning this for several days now. I have helped him create a place he feels secure in. And he has asked me to do certain things that help him feel like his work here is done."

I wondered if that included saying goodbye to his friends. Why didn't he call me?

"Aine," Sarah whispered. "Come sit here." She pushed a straight-backed, padded chair in line with George's chest. I sat.

She reminded me of my mom. When she spoke, her golden hair brushed the tops of her shoulders and she leaned her head to the right. About sixty years of experience softened her kind face. She seemed to glow, even in the dim light of this room. George's friend was an angel.

She leaned over George and gently tapped his shoulder. "George, Aine is here. And I am going to burn your memories now."

His eyes fluttered; his eyelids looked translucent. When he opened them, it seemed his intense blue eyes were pale and unfocused.

"Do you need another pain patch?" Sarah asked.

"Mmm. No." George's eyes found me and a light seemed to come on inside. "I want to be clear. Those things are wondrous, but they take me away." He looked at me, and I knew he was telling me he would stand the pain for a few minutes, for me.

"George. Do what is best for you. If you are in pain, treat it," I said.

"Aine. I'm fine. I want to talk. How are you?"

"George. You are not fine! Why didn't you tell me... or Marc? Does Marc know?"

"No. Marc doesn't know." His arm slid out from under the covers, and his hand lay palm up on his bed. I slipped mine into it. His skin was dry and papery, thin blue veins visible.

"Why is this happening? Why are you dying? I don't think I can take this, George. I feel like my links with my past will all be gone. Why didn't you tell me?"

"Well, maybe I made a mistake there, Aine. But I really wanted you to concentrate on getting your life back. And why am I dying? It is my turn, Aine. We all do it, just in different ways."

Sarah carried a stand topped with a bronze bowl to the other side of his bed. "I have the memory strips here, George. Aine, George and I have written some of his foremost memories on these strips of paper. Some are things he loved, and others are things he wishes to be forgiven for. Memories to release." She laid a small bundle of strips of paper, tied in red thread, in the bottom of the bowl. She dropped a lit match into the bowl, and the paper ignited, flashed, and was gone. No smoke or flame. I was shocked.

"How did you do that?" I asked.

"We used flash paper. No danger of fire," said Sarah.

Flash paper. A life gone that quickly.

"Sarah, thank you. I do feel better." George turned his head on his satin pillow and faced me again. "What do you believe happens after death, Aine? Do you believe we go on, pass over to another side?"

"George, I don't know what's on the other side. I really want to believe we cross over and spend eternity with those we love and meet all those who came ahead of us. Or maybe even come back someday, ourselves. But right now, I'm trying to understand why you are here. I'm not ready for this. I want you around for many more years."

"No. I am dying. I don't want to, but I've no choice. The only choice I have left is to die the way I want to." His arm waved around the room. "With ceremony."

He laid his arm back on the bed, and I took hold of his hand again, determined to hold it as long as I could.

"We do everything we can to stay alive, but we haven't found the eternal springs yet. So. We do what we can to make the situation better around us after we die. Do you think Donny planned on dying? Do you think he wanted to become a hero, a martyr? No. He would rather have lived to watch his kids grow. But life just didn't give him that chance. He did what he could at that particular time. He saw the chance to save his buddies and did the best he could with his life."

His other hand came out of its warm cocoon and rested on my cheek as he looked directly into my eyes.

"I am ready. I believe there is something else after death. I'm not a church-goer, as you know, but there's another place to go. I know it. I've talked to Sophie. She comes to me now, and I'm ready to go to her."

His hand fell from my face, and he grew restless. "Sarah, it's time for another patch."

She went to a table by the wall, entered something into a laptop and brought over a band-aid-looking patch. "This is morphine. He'll sleep soon." She further softened the lights in the room.

I remembered. Sarah told me to say goodbye. I pulled the labyrinth out of my pocket and gently laid it in the hand I was holding. "George. Here is your labyrinth. Meg said you love it."

His eyes grew moist. "Thank you. I've been dreaming about this today. I'm so glad it is here. After, when I don't need it anymore, I want you to have it. It brought me peace. I know it will help you."

"Okay." Now was the time to do what I was here for. "George, you know I love you. You've been so kind to my family and me. You took over for my dad in so many ways when he died. I'll miss you, but I know you want to be with Sophie. Go be with her, George; leave the pain here and be with her. I will be fine. You have given me all the skills I need to survive, and now your labyrinth for strength." I leaned over and kissed his cheek. When I straightened up his eyes were closed, his hand lying loosely in mine.

Sarah walked over to a tape player and turned it on. A voice came through the fog in my brain and I recognized it. Meg Smyth. Then, I understood what she was saying. She was reading some letters addressed to George. They were the love letters Sophie wrote to him while he was gone on his many projects. She couldn't go along, she was teaching, but they kept their love alive through these letters. Meg's voice wavered and hesitated often as she read them. I realized the sacrifice it took for her to do this. Meg loved George. She was sending her love to him for the last time by reading these letters to him. No wonder she couldn't be here.

Time seemed to stand still and rush by. George's hand was still in mine. Sarah brought me strong tea and buttered toast. I'd not eaten all day and was grateful. It was about midnight when George turned slightly to his left and whispered, "Sophie. Sophie." I looked and couldn't see anything. Was she really there? Could he see her?

Sarah took his other hand in hers and softly chanted, "Go George. Go with Sophie. You have been released George. Go with Sophie."

"Go with Sophie, George," I said. "I'll be okay. I'll find myself. Be at peace."

George sighed and stopped breathing.

After sitting with him for a few moments, I went to the brightly lighted lobby. No one was sitting in the chair behind the desk. I called Meg on my mobile and told her. She sobbed and hung up.

After a minute more in the glaring lights, I went to the chapel. *Oh God, I hope there's more. Another side. I have people I want to see again. My mom, my dad, my brother, and now George.* There was one more call to make. I dialed.

I heard a sleepy "Hello?" and then I cried out, "Marc! George is gone. He just died. I was with him. Oh, Marc. I need you!" I sobbed. "Please come to London."

"Aine? Oh, gods above. I'll be there as soon as I can. You'll be all right, honey. I'm coming."

Chapter 23

JAHNA

82 AD April

Firtha walked to a waist high stone, picked up a goblet with her free hand, raising it so all could see. The flames of the fire reflected off it as a golden halo. I thought I saw it vibrate in Firtha's hand.

"In this cup, I have water from the sacred stream. It will give strength to the one who will sacrifice his all, his soul to the gods. The one who drinks from it will carry our plea to the gods. That person will be resurrected in the gods' presence." She walked back to our small circle, goblet still held above her head.

"One of you will speak to the gods with our voices." With her statement, our eyes searched each other, waiting for the other one to say, "I am the one. I want to die for our people!" But no one spoke.

"We all must be ready to give one life," she said, "to keep the blood of our people from being lost for all time." Rhona's words rushed back into my head. I remembered her story about the boy who was sacrificed to save her life and continue her family line.

"The Goddess Scotia has demanded one earthly life for all. One life for our king and his people, our families. She has given me dreams of difficult battles and seemingly impossible times ahead, however she has also shown me that we will triumph in the end. But she grows annoyed. We have stopped following the ancient ways and we must act soon if we are to have the goddess's help. She wants a human sacrifice - one who talks to the gods from this side. I vow the one who dies will live on in our songs and memories, this life will not be lost to time. This sacrifice will live through the ages. Scotia has spoken to me and promised me this.

"I have seen the chosen one in my visions." She stopped behind and between Moroug and Coira. They held hands and stared into each other's eyes. I imagined they were saying to each other, "If it is me, I will not go without you."

"It is not either of you," Firtha said, keeping the goblet high. "You would not be able to deliver our message alone." She moved on to Rosston and Uilleam. Rosston smiled and looked up at her. Did he know what she was asking? Maybe not, he was so young. I doubted he had even seen a sacrifice in his village. Slaves taken in battle were traded, not sacrificed for many years.

Uilleam knew. I could see him start to curl up into himself, trying to make himself as small as a mouse and skitter away unseen.

She rested her staff against her shoulder as she stroked Rosston's cheek and said, "The gods do not want an innocent. One who knows nothing and cannot tell them stories of our world. You have not even begun to scrape the hair off your face, it seems. You do not know enough."

She turned and looked at Uilleam and said, "The one who goes must be brave. It must be a person who will not cower in front of Bel and Morrigna. You would try to find a place under their table, not in front of it." His shoulders dropped a fraction, as if in disappointment, but I watched the fear release from his eyes.

How could we just sit there, accept her insults, and then permit her to choose one of us? Did not the others understand what was happening? I grabbed Lovern's arm and tried to get him to look at me. I wanted to stand and shout, wait! You are asking us to leave our life here! You are asking us for the ultimate self, our souls. How can you so be cruel?

Then, as if a shaft of light fell on me, I understood. We shall lose our families, our way of life here if we do not win the battle with the Romans. All the way to this fort, we talked about the best way to get the ears, the attention, of the gods. How better than to stand in front of them and ask for their blessings? How better to save Crisi? Am I not ready to give my life for hers? Firtha must have the perfect messenger. "Yes!" I tried to say it under my breath, but both Lovern and Rhona looked my way. They gave me a nod of understanding. They had come to this conclusion long before me.

Nathraichean stood and reached for the cup. "I will give my life in this way. I am ready to speak with the gods."

"Ah, Wolf. I agree you are ready. But you will have to wait. I need you here, in my band. We will protect the king, and I need your life force with us during his battles. You carry the animals of the forest within you, and the voice of the wolves will rise, howling above the din of battle." He stepped back, a look of contentment on his face. He may not be the one chosen for this deed, but he knew his value was understood.

"Rhona," Firtha turned and said, "your knowledge and calmness will be needed in the coming days. Your life experiences and being a seer will be invaluable to the king and me. You will also stay here."

Rhona stood, took Firtha's hand, and said, "Yes, I have seen this, too. I know what comes to pass is necessary." Then Rhona sat down facing me.

It was to be me. Rhona was sitting in front of me to acknowledge that I was the chosen one. Breathing rapidly,

I closed my eyes, fingered my labyrinth bag, and calmed myself. I was ready to reach for the cup when Firtha stepped behind Lovern. I stood and tried to reach the goblet.

"I will take the cup," I said. "I am the one who already talks to the gods. I help the dying cross the river of death, and have seen people from the other side. I know of the path to the gods. I have had visions since I was a child. I am the chosen one. I am the one to go."

Rhona, standing now, gently guided my hand away from the cup. I looked at her in confusion. Why was she doing this? It was so right for the chosen one to be me. I was ill and would cross Death's river soon. Lovern would stay and take care of Crisi. She would need a strong protector. Why wouldn't Rhona give me my hand back?

"Yes, Jahna," said Firtha. "Your work is pleasing to the otherworld. You have helped many cross the river of death to eat at the tables of the gods. But Scotia has not chosen you. You will help the chosen one cross. You are the one who brought him to us." Pounding filled my head and I became unsteady on my feet.

She walked a few steps to my right, standing in front of the only one left in our group she had not addressed. Lovern. She raised her staff to the air, as high as the goblet still over our heads and said, "It is you." Firtha's voice cut through me. "The goddess Scotia has spoken to me. My dreams show me your face. I have seen it for many seasons, watched you grow and become a healer. I have seen you revere the sacred water and oak. You are the one with the colors surrounding your body, the colors of the rainbow. Scotia has chosen you to bring our plea to the gods."

"No! It is me!" I could not believe her words. I had to pull her attention back to me.

"Shh," said Rhona, trying to calm me. Wrapping her arm around my shoulders and leaning to my ear, she said, "I have also seen. It is Lovern."

Firtha continued. "Lovern, you were brought to us by the gods. You should have died by the Roman sword, but you fought and lived. You are the one to be sacrificed on Beltane." I watched as she gave him the cup.

He turned to me and said, "I do this because I love you. I have pledged not to let the Romans take us. If this will keep you free, I will gladly die in a sacrifice to Scotia." He gulped the contents of the now black goblet.

The roaring inside my head was subdued by the hissing of my snake. I understood now what I had seen from the beginning. The gods had given us a short life together on this earth. Too short a time together. All my fears were being realized.

Rhona's arms left me and I stumbled back to the circle of stones as all the druids gathered around Lovern, and the droning hum started again.

His voice rose above the noise of the druids. "I will speak to the gods for us but I ask one thing. I wish to go home. I want the ceremony to be during Beltane with my clan chieftain by my side. I ask to hold my daughter one more time. Pray to the gods to allow me to do this one last thing, Firtha."

Lovern held my eyes locked in his. I wanted to flee, to grab his hand and both of us run as fast and far as we could. We would go get Crisi and live in the forest, by ourselves. We could do this. He had done it before. But in his eyes, I saw he would not run again. Resolve and understanding passed through me. At that moment, I started to give him up to the gods, though it rent my heart into pieces.

I did not see him again for three days and nights. Firtha had received the answer Lovern asked for. We would go home. I did not remember eating, drinking or sleeping the time we were in the fort after the night of the choosing.

I watched him come out of the lodge and slipped through the druids' protective circle. When I reached him, I could not stop myself. I hit him. I beat him around his chest and shoulders. I was so angry I could not stop. "How can you leave? Why is it you? Why not another druid? Who is to protect Crisi? How can you do this?" I knew the answer in my mind. He was not mine. He belonged to the gods. I felt betrayed.

He stood still, his strength holding him upright. As I started upward to his face, he took hold of my wrists. I tried to wrench free, but although he did not have a tight squeeze on my arms, I was unable to break away. My breath ragged and my muscles weak, I leaned against his chest in tears, his hands caressing my hair, telling me to shush. When I calmed enough to lean back and look into his face, I saw tears running freely from his blue eyes.

"Do you not think I wonder every day why the gods chose me? Why it is me who must go to their table and beg for our lives? I remember every minute of our lives together. I can feel Crisi's weight as a baby in my hands. I hear her laughter. I long for the warmth of your body against mine, the sweetness of your lips, the velvet tip of your tongue. The last thing I remember at night is you. The last thing I will think about in death is the lavender scent of your soft, raven's-wing hair.

"These earthly things I will miss more than any man could ever know." He wiped his nose with the back of his hand and shook the tears from his face. "But it is not for me to ask why. I have been chosen. I am the one to go. You are the one to stay and remind the others to prepare. The gods will not make this an easy trial. Scotia has told us that we must fight to free ourselves." He slipped his labyrinth bag off his shoulder, held the soft leather in his hands, kissed it and handed it to me.

"Jahna, this is all I have of value other than you and Crisi. I charge you to care for it and pass it on to Crisi. I am not going to see you again until the night before the ceremony.

"You of all people, Jahna, know how to make my crossing smooth. I want you there. I need you there and will ask you for no more tears. No, I demand no more tears. I will spend my last night with you. I will give my body and soul to the gods willingly if it will save Crisi and the other children of our clan the loss of self I have seen in the captured children. I need you to be strong. I have begun my last journey."

His eyes bore into mine, pleading. I could not refuse his request, his demand. "Yes. I swear," I whispered. "No more tears. I will build a wall around my heart to dam them and keep them from falling. I will be with you and will make your crossing as easy as possible. I will plead for Beathan to be there to guide your boat across the river and my mother to meet you on the other side. She will keep you safe and go with you to the gods until it is my turn to come. We will meet again, Lovern. We will be together again for a time longer than this life on earth."

I slid his bag over my neck and under my dress to be warmed by my heart. We mounted our ponies. Our small company had grown. Firtha, her nine druids, and three of the king's warriors. The warriors were to return home as soon as we reached our hillfort. They were charged to stop at all the villages between ours and the king's to spread the word of the Roman invasion and gather proof of the pledges of warriors.

I had no memory of the trip home. Rhona rode with me and I slept only when she brewed her tea for me. The druids surrounded Lovern. They enveloped him in their ceremony. Beltane eve, the next time I would be near him, would come too quickly.

All came out to honor him. News of our journey traveled from village to village and clansmen and women stood in the roads, watching as we passed. Whispered words drifted to all ears about the upcoming Beltane sacrifice. If Lovern had been a warrior who killed others in battle, they would have cheered. But on this ride, there were hushed prayers. All seemed to know of his gift to them. Their eyes followed us until we rode over the next rise or around the farthest bend in the road.

Sileas and Harailt were among the first I saw on the path that lead up to the top of our hill. Behind them stood the young man whose broken leg we had fixed. Torrian, now grown into a fine, strong warrior, was promised to Kenric's guard. He would be one of those fighting in the front line with Kenric and the king's men. His father, Aonghus, stood beside him with several younger boys nearby. All faces had the look of awe and praise that had become common on this road of honor. My stomach ached when I saw their eyes. I had to close mine and take my mind far away to stop the flood of tears that constantly threatened to fall. I had promised. I had sworn not to cry.

Our group slowly rode through our small village center, surrounded by friends walking with us as we rode. Crisi waited ahead, her hand held by Kenric's wife, Caitrin. Kenric stood tall in the doorway to his lodge. Dressed as our chieftain, a leader of warriors, he carried his shield, the same one carried by Beathan so long ago, and had two long swords across his back and a short blade in his belt. He stood with his spear, eagle feathers and bear's teeth hanging from it, in his left hand. His hair was braided and hung down to his neck. He wore a plaid cape closed by the oak pin fashioned by Finlay. It brought back to my mind the mistletoe pin worn by the king and his brother. A stray thought ran through my head. *I must remember to tell Finlay about it.* As if it were important to me now.

The king's warriors slid off their ponies. "We bring the druids as the king ordered us. The Beltane sacrifice will be here, in your village. Firtha, the king's druidess, is here to conduct the ceremony. Do you take the oath to protect her and her followers?"

Kenric looked over the rest of us still mounted on the ponies. "I will have the honor of having the Beltane ceremony here. I will protect all who come to take part in this ceremony." At this, his head turned to Lovern. He nodded. "I am honored to know this sacred man."

Yes, Kenric, you knew him. He ate at your table repeatedly, sang your songs, laughed at your jokes, and healed your sick children. He mourned Beathan's death with you. I knew him too. When he was but a man. He made love to me in the cave. He cried when he killed the white stag for me. Now we will watch him die, give his life for ours. Yes, we knew him, this sacred chosen one.

The king's warriors stayed with Kenric and his warriors at the top of the hill. Lovern and the druids rode back down the hill toward the sacred spring where they would burn purifying fires until Beltane eve.

Sileas and Harailt took the reins of my pony and led me back to the hospice. They knew I could not go home. I sat on a cot, the world around me dreamlike, until Crisi came, carried in Eiric's arms, followed by Finlay.

I tried to stand, but my legs would not hold me, and I sat back down hard on the cot. "Forgive me for not standing. I have not eaten or slept well on this journey. What day is today?"

Eiric sat next to me and guided Crisi to my lap where I hugged her, my nose buried in her hair, inhaling the scent of honey. She carried Lovern's smell. My heart jumped, and tears seeped to the corners of my eyes, but did not fall.

"Tomorrow is Beltane," Finlay said. "We have begun preparing. The fire is being laid in the field. Eiric told me you would want to see Crisi so we brought her to you. I must go soon. Kenric is chaffed by this decision, though we know it must be done. I must convince him Lovern will be acting on our behalf. He told me he would rather Lovern act on our behalf as our healer, not as a sacrifice. I know he understands the importance of this event, but I must stand between him and the druids if by chance he says something that angers them. He is like our father, not careful with his words, speaking his mind with no regard to consequence."

"It is still hard for us all to understand that the goddess Scotia wants Lovern," said Eiric. She wrapped her arms around me and gently kissed my cheek.

"It all happens too soon," I said. "I have made a decision. I will not be here long after Lovern goes. You know that." Both Finlay and Eiric looked at me with understanding and nodded. "I charge you to take Crisi and keep her from harm. She has grown to be a part of your family and will do well with you. I love you both and trust my only child to be with you. I know the decisions you make for your children and her would be the same as my decisions. Watch over her. Watch over your children. Our children are our blood, our future."

Crisi sat on my knees and I looked into her face as I spoke to her. Her weight was almost too much for my weakened legs. My gut pain had grown difficult to bear, only kept in check by Rhona's drink. I drew in my breath and prayed for the strength I would need for this conversation. Crisi's wide eyes peered into mine and she said, "Mother, I went into the forest yesterday and I saw the biggest fox I have ever seen. Does Father know it is here?"

Ah, the fox. I understood, as soon as Lovern became the chosen one, that the sign I saw in front of the king's fort was a parting of my life with Lovern. The fox was saying goodbye. My ravens flew away from him, and he gave me his departing bow before he left. The fox followed us, followed Lovern, on this last journey. There were no ravens following us on our trip here.

"Yes," I said. "That is the king's fox and it followed us from his fort. It is here to watch over you. Your father and I will be going away. You will live with Broc now. I remember how you like to go hunting and exploring with him."

"But Mother, when are you coming back? When you go away, you always come back. Where is Father? I want to tell him about the fox."

"Crisi. You shall have to listen now. Listen well. Do you remember the story your father told you about the fox who gave his life to save his family?"

"Yes. I remember that fox. He was not as big as the one I saw yesterday."

"No. The one you saw yesterday is the fox that will be with you for the rest of your life. Watching over you. When you see it or think about it, you will remember your father. The fox will remind you your father watches over you, too. Remember how we looked for owls at night? Who watches through those owl eyes?"

"Grandmother," she said with a giggle. "I saw an owl catch a mouse. Does that mean Grandmother ate the mouse?"

"No," I hugged her closer to me with a smile. "No, the mouse will keep the owl alive so that Grandmother can look through its eyes. Grandmother is eating at the table of the gods on the other side of the river of death. I have told you this. Remember?"

"Yes, Mother. We are all going to be with her someday. She lives in a special place now, not here with us but not far."

"I am glad you remember," I said. "Soon your father and I will be living in that place. We will be watching you through the eyes of the animals near you, like Grandmother. Your father will be the fox, and I will be the raven who nests near your doorway."

Her face showed her confusion. I knew she did not understand. All I could give her was the memory of this day. One that she could call back eventually, when she was old enough to understand. I continued.

"I have a gift for you, Crisi. This is the bag your father carried from his home. And here, this is the bag your father made for me." I slipped both labyrinth bags from under my dress.

They were warm from my body. I opened them and shook the contents to the cot.

Out of Lovern's bag fell our hair, braided together and held by the red thread from our marriage. And the fur from the first fox he killed, small pieces of fur from every one since, and dried berries from the mistletoe we harvested just before the rain drove us into the cave. The cave where we found we loved each other. The crystals the bag once held lay buried under the posts of our home. His precious tokens from his past.

Out of mine fell Crisi's birth cord, bronze, red-gold and black hair tied together with a red thread, my mother's hair clasp, given to her by my father, and mistletoe berries. Yes, I had gathered some from the floor of that cave, too. I kept my armlets in the bag as well, since my arm grew too thin to wear them. They clanked as they fell out. Crisi laughed. "That is your sound, Mother."

"Crisi, these are things that will bring you comfort when you need it. Keep these bags close to your heart. You have a history here that you will not understand until you are older. Do not misplace them. Look, on the outside is painted a labyrinth. Learn to follow this path. First, use your finger and then your memory. It will lead you to where you are supposed to be in your life." I took hold of her little finger and led it around the path on my bag. I had often done this before, as a way to help her grow calm before sleeping. I sang to her at these times. She sang my song and followed the labyrinth, for the last time in my lap.

"It is good to hear you sing, Crisi. Your voice is clear and beautiful. Someday you will sing songs of your father."

We picked up the tokens on the cot, and put them back into the bags. I returned only one armlet to my bag. I was to be buried with the armlet Lovern gave me at her birth.

"Crisi, I am giving you the armlet my mother gave me. It has the spirals of our family. Someday you will look on it and understand the events that are to come. The spirals are our bloodline. See how they are unbroken."

"Yes, Mother. Can I go and play now?"

"Crisi. You are a child of my womb. Of all the spirits who have touched me, yours is the one I would truly give my life for. When you are grown and have a child of your own, hold him up to show me. Hold him high so your father and I can bless him." She turned her green eyes to me and I placed my hand on the crown of her hair. "Gods. If you listen to me on this earth, if you value the life sacrificed to you, bless this child and guide her on her life's journey, in my name, Jahna, and her father's name, Lovern."

Forbidden tears slipped from my eyes. She sat still as I slipped the strings over her head and placed the bags under her dress. She patted them into place. *They will become part of her body soon. She will stop thinking of them until she needs them.*

She moved quickly when I let her go, like a rabbit let out of a trap. I asked for a kiss and she grudgingly leaned and touched our lips together. Then she ran out the door with the energy of a child, my eyes following her as long as I could.

I sipped Sileas' broth and swallowed honey-sweetened mead laced with drops of the oil of the poppy. I rested to garner my feeble energy for tomorrow. Beltane. My stomach clutched as my mind refused to accept the passage of time. The day.... No, I could not think on it.

It was the day of his sacrifice.

CHAPTER 24

For we have met in this life
To dance in the light in the
time we have.
And I will call out your name
And through my pain
You will understand
The lover's song, though love
will live on
Long, long after life is gone.

And I will die in your arms
And all my sorrow will be
gone.
And all the things in my life
I held so dear must leave me
now.
But I will live on
Long after the silence ends
the song

Steve McDonald

82 AD May 1

Our heavy cloaks kept out the cold. Mine was lined and trimmed with the fur of the white stag. We passed the night holding each other tightly under the cloaks, skin to skin, and watched the journey of the moon and stars across the sky. I wanted to hear and feel every beat of his heart, to breathe in every breath he exhaled. We spoke little. I tried to forget, just for the moment, what was ahead. To calm my breathing, I traced my labyrinth, the pattern burned into my mind. I silently repeated the words I used in my work.

The gods give us the sun that sets but rises for a new day. We die, but will meet again in the home of the gods.

We sat on a small hill, just above the tree-line of the forest, alone for the few hours it took the night to pass. A late frost crept in and laid a crystal blanket of white sparkles reflecting moonlight over the farmer's fields.

Lovern shivered as I washed his body. Our jar of water was bitter cold. As I reached his feet, I caressed his toes. "Crisi has these toes."

"Ah, and she has your smile. She carries both of us to the future."

Now, the sun was about to crawl over the top of the mountain and promise a new day, a fresh new world. Just a few moon cycles ago, I rejoiced in the start of every new day, every sunrise, saying prayers of thankfulness to our goddess for my daughter, my husband, and my life in her work. This was a dawn that I did not want to see come.

The druids started to assemble around the fire, coming from the dark corners of the forest after a night of prayers. They had not been far, just out of sight. We heard their murmuring voices behind us all night long. I wanted to finish Lovern's ablutions myself.

I knelt in front of him and felt small stones dig into my knees. The sharp points of pain reminded me that this was not a dream. His eyes glinted with moonlight as he looked deep into mine. I took his sharp dirk in hand and shaved him as I had done many times before. This was the last time I would hold his face. Twice, I had to pull my hand away from his cheeks, trembling, trying not to cry. I did not want to cut him, to cause him pain on our last morning together.

The many times I helped ease the path of those dying and counseled their life mates, I had never felt the intense pain they were going through. I recalled the grief of losing Beathan and my mother, but that was like a bee sting to this anguish. I foolishly told the others to be strong. "You will see them in the Otherworld," I had naively said. Well meaning, but so unknowing. Now I understood. How does a person losing the mate of their life on earth stop the torturous pain of a dying heart? It was impossible. I knew I was ill and would not live long beyond his death. I would see him again, but those thoughts were hollow. They lived in the future. My life was now. My heart and stomach wrung itself into a ball and took up my whole chest. *Oh Goddess, help me. How can I not wail and tear out my hair?*

I prayed to believe that our bloodline would continue. A remembrance of Aine flooded my mind and heart. Was this the proof I so desperately sought? I forced myself to believe that she was of our blood – that she was our future. To reinforce my belief, I added a line to my prayer.

The gods give us the sun that sets, but rises for a new day. We die, but will meet again in the home of the gods. And through our children and their children we will live throughout all time.

Firtha and Rhona came to us. They bade us to follow them to a large bronze cauldron that contained smoldering, fragrant grasses. The smoke rose slowly in the heavy, cold air. The heat from the cauldron warmed us as we held hands. Rhona came to me, touched my shoulder, and gently tugged at me to tell me it was time to stand aside. I grasped Lovern's hand with both mine, and he turned to face me. His arms wrapped around me, as if to protect me from the upcoming event. *How can it be time already? We have not had long enough together.* I needed to talk to him.

"Do you remember the day we met ten years ago? I thought I hated you," I whispered. "I thought you had destroyed my life. You told Beathan I was not supposed to marry Harailt, and I did not think I would ever be able to live within the clan again." He nodded, his bronze hair free around his face, looking through to my soul with his dark eyes.

"Yes," he said, "the goddess had plans for us. It took time to find out what those plans were. Now we are here. We now know what is required of us, and I pray our efforts are rewarded."

"Yes." I shook my head in agreement. As I put my hand on his face, I remembered the feel of his red beard, rough on my fingertips. I remembered him inside of me. I remembered his tears at Crisi's birth. He leaned his now smooth face into my hand and my fingers traced his high cheekbones.

The gods give us the sun that sets, but rises for a new day. We die, but will meet again in the home of the gods. And through our children and their children we will live throughout all time.

His thin, sinewy body bent over me, and I looked deep into his calm, black-blue eyes. I wanted to live forever in those eyes. His eyes could find me anywhere and tell me he loved me without words. I loved his eyes.

The clan members smothered their peat fires. They would gather purifying flames to relight theirs from the Beltane fire. The heavy, acrid smoke still reached us and my eyes began to water. I bit my lip until I tasted my own blood. I could stand it no longer; I had to know his reason.

"Why? Why all the pain and dying?" I asked. "Your dying will not stop the war. We will still fight. Why not give in to the coming conquerors? Why do you have to die? Why do our clansmen have to die?"

"Oh, Jahna, my love. Your question has been asked by so many in the past. Is there an easy answer? I think not. Today we are able to hunt where we wish. We trade with those we call family or friends and kill those we call enemies. We ask for no permission except that of our own chieftains. They are our lords and rule-makers. We do not live at anyone else's call. We sleep and make love with those whom we alone choose. I have seen the Roman slaves. You were taken by one. They drove him mad. He never would have done that on his own. He was a guard for the queen! I have seen children with no names.

Crisi cannot live like that, I would rather she die. In her place, I die.

"For freedom, Jahna. It is a fight for life and for freedom. We must win, for all the coming clans and children. We fight for our daughters and sons to have the right to live free - run free. I die for my Queen, Bouddicea. I die for my mother and sisters. I die so we may win against our foe, now and forever. I give my life to our gods in trade for our freedom. I would do it again and again and again. For you. I do it for you."

The druids stepped closer and began to chant. Rosston, Nathraicean, all of them, even Rhona, had learned the song of the sacrifice.

"Lovern, I am trying to understand. I believe and trust in the gods and their demands. It is so hard because it is you I want now, not the gods' approval. But I will struggle to understand.

"I must tell you, I have spoken these words before in many ways: I would not know my life's path if you had not come to our clan. I would be a farmer's wife. In you, I found my teacher. You are my soul's mate. You are my only love. I love you here and I will love you in the Otherworld. I will cut your hair and shave your beard every day. I will weave gold cloth for us to wear. We will hunt the white stag when I come, and make love in our cave again. We will watch over Crisi and keep her safe. We will keep her free." My will was returning. I had to be strong for him.

"You are my heart," he said. "My strength comes from you. Alone, this would not be possible for me. The gods threw us together and we did our best. Now they demand this of us. Together, we will prevail in death as we did in life."

He gathered me into his strong arms and ran his soft hands through my loose hair. I crushed myself as close as I could up against his chest, curled into the circle he made around me. I felt the tickle of the fox fur band he wore on his arm against my face. He did not want to fail at this task, his last duty as our druid priest. I could not betray him.

"You know I love you. I have loved you since you first touched my mind. That is why I journeyed here so long ago. I had to find you," he murmured into my hair. Then, pulling back, he said, "It is time. We must go. The gods and the people await."

He lowered his mouth to mine, and we kissed, the last kiss of a husband and wife, of a master and mistress, of lovers.

Rhona drew me away and the druids stepped in. Rosston took off Lovern's cloak. He was naked except for his fox fur armband when Firtha called for the three pots of color. He stood tall and erect. My body reacted and readied itself for his entry. It was not to be in this life, ever again.

Firtha dipped her hand into a pot of alder red dye and rubbed her hands over his face and chest. His arms and back became weld yellow, and woad blue was used on his groin and legs. The colors melted into one another. As I watched him be painted, I remembered the bull he sacrificed at our first Samhain. The viper in my gut turned to stone. It pushed, heavy against my heart. It was impossible to breathe. Firtha finished. She nodded, holding her arms up to the gods. Her hands dripped the colors now streaked on the body of my husband. "He is done," she said. *We are both done,* I thought.

Yesterday, the druids prepared a sacred last meal for Lovern of unleavened barley bread, cooked on a stone until blackened and sprinkled with ground mistletoe berries. They sang a chant over it that I had not heard before. They named gods. Esus, Taranis, the thunder god, Teutates, the god of the clans. Firtha called these gods in their triumvirate. They are the gods we called for war.

Sing loud, druids, tell them my husband is coming to discuss war. Tell them to open their ears and take him to Lug and Bel and Morrigna and Scotia. Tell them he is leaving me and coming to them! Tell them he is coming. Tell them I love him.

Rhona brought the blackened bread to Lovern. He took a bite and his mouth twisted with its bitterness. A mug of mead was handed to her and she retrieved her tiny green jar of oil from her belt. She slightly tipped it to pour a small amount into the mead. She offered it to Lovern. He took a sip and then leaned forward to whisper into her ear. She turned and gave the rest of the drink to me. I was grateful to have it. Together, with the help of Rhona's elixir, we would gather the strength to walk to the fires and beyond. I tasted the honey of his lips as I drank, looking into his eyes while I swallowed.

Too soon, Finlay and Kenric appeared. "The fires are lit," said Kenric. "It is time to go."

"Where is Crisi?" I asked Finlay.

"She is with Eiric and the other children. She will be at the fires and the sacrifice, but at a distance so as not to see the whole event."

"Good. That is good," said Lovern. "She will be stronger for this." He sounded as if he were trying to talk himself into this thought. I knew she must be there and knew I would not be with her to talk her through what she would see.

"Eiric will need a soft hand for her today," I said. "Please tell Crisi we love her."

"She is well watched and is loved," he said.

The band of druids opened enough for Kenric to step in. "I wish there were another way to do this," he said. "I will miss you as a friend and healer. I know you will do your best for us, and if we have any chance with the gods, you will find it. It is time to go." We started to walk to the meadow of the giving fires.

A sudden thought scurried through my mind. *He will be cold. He needs my cloak.* I stumbled on a root, slippery from the frost, as I hurriedly shook off my cloak and held it up for him. He stopped walking and gazed toward the moon that hung still over the three hills. The fires were starting to blaze in the distance. I looked in the other direction, to the lake that reflected the late moon and beginning pink of a sunrise. The gray sky was clear of clouds. The memory of our first Samhain together, our first giving fires and its sacrifice, haunted me.

"Hear me now and believe!" He turned, and his eyes burned into mine. "With you near, I do not feel the cold. I do not feel anything." He reached out and grasped my shoulders with his strong hands. "When it is time, I will be with you, Crisi, and the gods. No pain can cross that barrier."

A moan leaked from my heart and escaped my mouth. I nodded and pulling my cloak back on, fell into step behind him. *I will not cry.* I tried to make my mind blank, but memories of the last ten years rolled through it. I was not sure I would be able carry out my task. How could I continue after today? *I will not cry.*

The gods give us the sun that sets but rises for a new day. We die, but will meet again in the home of the gods. And through our children and their children we will live throughout all time.

The stacked oak logs of the Beltane fires blazed and crackled with intense heat. We stood to the side, waiting for Firtha to speak.

"We are going back to our old ways," she told the crowd. As she started, their milling and talking subsided. I saw that the entire clan, and some from outside clans as well, were present, the children at the back. Sileas and Harailt were near them, and I knew they would also watch over Crisi.

"Today," she continued, "Beltane, is the day of sacrifice. The Romans are coming and we must stop them. The gods, through the king, ordered this sacrifice for the clans. We call on Bel and the Morrigna to hear us today. Lovern is here to give his life for you. He gives his life to the gods to bring victory to our cause. He will sit at the table of the gods and share a cup of mead. He will hunt with them and argue for our freedom. He does this of his own free will. I order songs to be sung about him for all time to come. He sacrifices his life so our blood will be free." At this, the crowd roared its approval. I swallowed several times to keep from retching.

"Follow us. Walk through the purifying fires. Go to the sacred waters of the lake. Follow us, be purified, and witness our gift to the gods." The crowd broke into yells of thankfulness. They also started calling Lovern's name. He was a god among us now.

Firtha led us between the towers of flames, and heat seared our faces. It was if the sun had come down to bear witness to this death. After we got through the path of flames, the night closed in around us again. Then we turned and headed toward the lake. To the point that Lovern and I had walked around so many seasons ago.

The druids walked before us on the narrow, worn path. I could see the small rise that was our destination. Then those who ran ahead to see the ceremony hid it. No matter. I would never forget what it looked like. The grass that grew on the rise always seemed greener than that beside it. Was it fed by the blood that had been spilled there so long ago?

Waves ate under the shoreline and caused an undercut of the land just at the edge of the lake, the frigid water that held our past human sacrifices and many bronze blades thrown to the gods. Even when the sky was clear of clouds and the sun blazed it seemed dark to me, at that spot on the lake. I hated it. I would never be able to look upon it again. Lovern's blood would now feed the grass.

The druids walked on. Fifteen white robes, fifteen druids to perform this deed. All were ready but me. I repeated my prayer over and over. I had to believe it or I would not live through this.

The gods give us the sun that sets but rises for a new day. We die, but will meet again in the home of the gods. And through our children and their children we will live throughout all time.

The crowd parted to allow us through. Behind them, the smooth black lake reflected the receding moon. My head pounded to the rhythm of the ceremonial drums. The druids' chant grew louder, drowning out my heartbeat, and then stopped as Firtha halted. She placed her hands on Lovern's shoulders and pulled him into place. Into the place of his death.

Lovern turned to face the three hills as the moon dipped behind them, his face devoid of expression. I fought with myself to hold back the flood of tears. Suddenly, the king's fox ran across the field next to us and a muffled sound of amazement went up from the crowd. I turned to Lovern, knowing this omen gave him power. I knew nothing would stop him from carrying through with his sacrifice.

Rhona, her white hair indistinguishable from her robe, carried an oak ember to the small stack of oak and rowan logs near us. She tossed in two sprigs of mistletoe. The fire burned bright and fast, and Lovern's face reflected its colors. No warmth emanated from it for me.

"I do this today to stop our valley from being overrun by the warriors who call themselves Romans." Lovern's clear, determined voice brought the crowd's eyes back to him. "They took the mines from my people and killed my mother, sisters and queen. I do not want them to come to this valley, to your clan, to my family. I do this so the gods will be here for you after today."

He paused and looked over their heads. I saw hope, his inner strength, in his eyes. "Look." He turned to a small nearby hill. On it grew one of our sacred oak trees. He smiled and seemed to become even taller in the light of the fire. Under the tree was the fox that had followed us from the king's fort, and the tree was filled with my ravens. They were back together again. A small bud of hope appeared in my heart.

I turned back, and he faced me. "Jahna, come tie back my hair."

I shuffled forward and pulled a piece of yarn from the fringe of my cloak. He leaned in so I could reach his head. My hands were numb as I combed his hair back with my fingers. I could barely tie the knot around its fullness. Every breath I was able to take leaked a silent "I will not cry." Finlay stepped forward and drew his bronze dirk. He reached over to Lovern's radiant, red hair, cut a lock, and handed it to me. I grasped it in my hand and then stumbled back to my place, his hair clasped in my tight fist, next to my heart.

Nathraichean and another white robed druid as tall as he stood on either side of Lovern. Each had a bronze axe gripped in one hand behind Lovern, their free hands grasping one of his arms. Firtha stepped up to Lovern and placed a braided fox-gut garrote attached to an alder branch around his neck, lifting his hair out of the way. Another in a white robe took hold of the stick, ready to turn it at Firtha's command. Firtha reached inside her cloak, withdrew a bronze dirk from her belt, and held it in her left hand. She stepped forward and placed her right hand over the center of Lovern's chest, over his heart.

Numb, I repeated again to myself, *the gods give us the sun that sets but rises for a new day. We die, but will meet again in the home of the gods. And through our children and their children we will live throughout all time.*

"I call on Lug and Scotia to listen to this man's words!" Firtha shouted to the sky. Then, looking back at Lovern's face, she continued. "Lovern, the gods require that you freely give your life to them. Tell them now if that is so."

His eyes stared into hers. "I give my life on earth freely in exchange for a life with the gods and freedom for my people."

Firtha glanced at Nathraichean and nodded.

Oh, gods be merciful to him and me. Let this death be not in vain. I will see him again. I will see him again. I will....

At the same time, both axes were raised over Lovern's head. Then the strong arms holding them arced down. I heard his skull break. His eyes closed and he sagged forward, held up by the strength of Nathraichean and the second druid. A third druid raised an axe I had not seen, and hit him again at the back of his head. His blood sprayed over my face. I tasted metal. His body was completely limp, head lolling, when the garrote tightened quickly and deeply around his neck. Firtha stepped closer and Nathraichean, his fingers entwined in Lovern's bloody hair, pulled his head back to expose his throat for her dirk. Lovern's blood seeped from the slice in his neck to join the dark, shimmering pool on the ground beneath him. Firtha's once white robe was now gory, covered with Lovern's life-blood.

The air around me wavered and Beathan appeared between Lovern and me, as tall and strong as he had been while alive. He reached his hands to Lovern and commanded him to come. My heart leapt in my chest. Beathan had come to receive Lovern! It was so. It was true. My prayer was answered.

The gods give us the sun that sets but rises for a new day. We die, but will meet again in the home of the gods. And through our children and their children we will live throughout all time. Oh, gods, thank you!

It must be so. I had to believe it so. For Lovern was dead on this earth.

Beathan turned and smiled. "We will come for you soon, my little mouse."

The roar of the river to the Otherworld filled my head and the vibrating air around me grew still and black. Acrid peat smoke still hung in the air. I closed my eyes and then opened them to see the druids loading Lovern's plaid cloak-wrapped body onto a small boat to carry him out to the deeper water. To lay him with the bronze blades.

I felt myself travel. My mind touched Aine's for an instant and I filled her with my anguish and the picture of Lovern's death.

CHAPTER 25

We were born to live again,   My only love,
And we will live again.   Nay,
One fond kiss   Forever,
And then we sever   Goodbye.
One Farewell,
Alas, forever

Steve McDonald

82 AD APRIL

The air slipped by like a meandering stream. Trees below were dressed in their summer greens, and white sheep grazed on the grassy hilltops. Golden warmth wrapped itself around me, made me lazy, and tasted like mead on a hot day. All my responsibilities and problems were magically gone. I laid suspended in purposeless floating. Why move? Why go back? Forever was too short a stay here. A deep breath brought no pain. A memory, no tears.

"Jahna," a voice from the sun whispered. "Jahna, dear. You must take the tea. If you do not, your pain will return."

Liquid entered my mouth without my knowing and made its way into my mind. It sheltered me in its woolen comfort. The taste of freedom was bitter. Time disappeared.

"Jahna, wake up!"

A familiar voice. One from my depths. One I could not disobey. I struggled to come home. My breathing changed, became shallow and fast. My heartbeat pounded in my ears as I pushed to the surface. I struggled to come up, climb out of the woolen cape in which I was wrapped. As I awoke, I realized I had dreamt of flying again. Gods, I did not want to leave. What has called me? Who dares to bring me back to the world of sorrow?

I saw only a thin slice of the room. I could open my eyes no wider. A breath larger than a spoonful caused the pain to roar its way through my body. To swallow or to even think of swallowing was beyond my imagination. When given, Rhona's magic drink sat in my mouth until it was gone and plowed its own course through my body. Every muscle fought against movement here. The pain was constant and unbearable.

It is not my soul that is ill; it is my body. My soul is pure. I will cross soon and be with him.

Lying on my side brought brief relief. My painted stone labyrinth lay on the floor next to me. I had only to turn my eyes downward to follow its peaceful path, my prayer repeated over and over.

It is not my soul that is ill; it is my body. My soul is pure. I will cross soon and be with him.

"Jahna." It spoke again. "Um," was all I could reply.

Peat smoke floated through the room, but now I caught the scent of coal, the fires of the gods and the smith's hearth. "Jahna," Finlay said. "I have gone through your home as you asked and brought these." My friend, my cousin, the adopted father of my child, Finlay, laid the folded white pelt on the floor near my stone and balanced my bronze bowl on top.

He sat cross-legged on the floor in front of me, to see into my eyes. Such a rugged face he had. Scarred from the sparks of metal he worked, his beard grew uneven. His eyes were creased with life tracks, some brought on by sadness but many with laughter. He was my link to the clan now, my only connection to my daughter.

I licked my lips to soften them so I could speak. "I will be forever grateful to you for watching over me now, Finlay. My hand will touch your shoulder often when I am gone from here. When I die, I wish to be buried with these. Do you think my bowl is large enough to hold my ashes? I want you to burn my body. Burn it in the hottest fire you can build. After, I want some of my body thrown over the lake where Lovern...." An arrow of icy pain shot threw my gut. I curled up, and tears squeezed out of my eyes. Was it caused by my viper or the memory of the icy lake where Lovern's body lay?

"Breathe, dear." Rhona stroked my back and used her soothing voice. "Breathe, and think of the field where Crisi took her first steps. Watch the child laugh and shine with pride as she stumbles to you." When we came home from the king's fort, I told her that story as we rode through the field where Crisi played.

Now, she used it to pull me away from the pain. I had done the same for so many of my clan. *Thank you, Morrigna, for allowing me to do such powerful work.*

I watched, in my mind, Crisi laughing and tripping, getting up and trying again. The pain receded just enough to allow me to take a shallow breath of relief. My eyes opened to see Finlay on his knees, his mouth twisted, eyes searching my face.

"You see, I need a hot fire to kill this snake in my belly. I have grown weary of it and do not want to take it with me when I cross the river." His face grew less concerned and more understanding. He nodded. "Is my bowl big enough? Did I make it big enough?"

"Yes, Jahna." He picked up my bowl as he settled back to the floor. Turning it reverently in his hands, I saw the fox. He stood on his two hind legs, his front legs placed on the trunk of a sacred oak tree, and his tail fanned out behind him. In the tree rested a raven and, just below it, a finch with a crossed bill. My family. My life. My resting place.

"Good. And my stone. My labyrinth. I want it placed on top of the bowl. Place them in the cave. The cave on the path over looking the fort. You know where. I told you. Lovern and I loved that spot to look over the valley. It is a shallow cave, but it will keep me safe. Crisi knows the cave. It will be good for her to know where I am. Oh, and these." I reached under the blanket that my head rested on and pulled out my acorn cloak pin and the bronze armlet Lovern had given me when Crisi was born. Finlay had made both. "I want these with me.'

"I will do as you ask," Finlay said.

"Now I must have some of the oil, Rhona. I do not want to be awake any longer," I groaned. My eyes closed, I heard the shuffling of Finlay rising and leaving and felt Rhona's hand on my head to steady it as she placed a drop of her oil on my lips.

It is not my soul that is ill; it is my body. My soul is pure. I will cross soon and be with him.

I flew again.

The lake was calm. Small, black wavelets rippled and glittered in the sunlight. Fragrant meadowsweet floated freely in the air. My head leaned to hear the twittering finches; I smiled in recognition. The dark, earthy smell of our lake penetrated me as I sat on its bank. A caress of my hair, a whisper of a song, and I was in his presence.

The light around him wavered with colors. His crystals in the sun. He was seated, but seemed to float just above the ground.

"Lovern," I sighed.

"Yes, my love. I am here." He wore the cape Beathan gave him. The one I wove with our clan plaid.

"My life, my heart, this world is sad without you. Have you come for me? I am ready to go. I am tired of fighting and want to rest now."

"You will cross soon, love. I will see you here very soon. I have seen your pain. Know that it will ease here. There are but a few things left to do, and then you may cross."

"I do not think I have the energy to do anything else, Lovern. What do you ask of me? My will to live left when I saw you die. I did not cry. I did as you asked and did not cry. Oh, but did it hurt, Lovern? I prayed it did not hurt."

Lovern's face turned to the place in the lake where they placed his body. "No." He faced me again with his mouth almost in a smile. "I felt nothing after the first blow. Your face was in my closed eyes, and I carried it with me until Beathan guided me to Scotia. It has been in my heart since."

I stretched my hand out to touch his cheek. He leaned back just out of reach.

"No, Jahna. You cannot touch me. You can hear me. You can smell me." His hand glided over my head, and the smell of leather, honey, and ground acorns fell around me.

"Are you a dream, a vision? Why are you here, if you cannot hold my face in your hands? If I cannot kiss your lips? Why do the gods tease me so?"

"I am here with the permission of Scotia and Morrigna. I have come to tell you of the future. I have come to have you ask Kenric to order the women and children of the clan to go. They must leave here. They must travel away. If our blood and the blood of the clan is to survive, they must go now. Their journey is not without peril, but they must go to the island where I gathered seagrasses."

"Why? The mothers are wives, too. They will not leave here without their husbands. And you know the men are training to fight the Romans. Why must the children leave?"

"The Romans still come and our children will die if they do not go."

"No, no, no! I cannot believe this! We gave your life to stop this! Why did you die? Why did the gods demand your life? We were to beat the Romans. You were to ask the gods to help us win!"

"Jahna." I felt his hand on my hair, the gentle weight of a feather. "Jahna, I gave my life for your freedom. For Crisi's freedom. The gods have allowed me to see the future and then come back to you. To show you and tell you. Look."

He waved his hand over the field behind me, and as I turned to look, it became a battlefield. The king flew down the hill in his chariot, his hair stiff with lime, and all the other manned chariots came rushing behind. The warriors, men and women, naked bodies painted the same blue I saw at his fort, hair stiffened with limewater, on horseback, followed. The runners came last, screaming and screeching, a battle-cry for the gods' protection on their lips. Shields and swords glinted in the sun, blinding me for a breath's time. Some even carried their farm tools as weapons. The king had called in all as his warriors. A huge army peopled from the Highlands.

The Romans were below, looking into the sun. We outnumbered them. The advantage should be ours. We should win easily. But they showed no fear.

Oh gods, the sounds, the screams of men and vibrations of horses' hooves on the ground. It hurt my ears, shook my heart, and took my breath away.

A mighty clash of chariots and horses; swords waved in the air and returned covered with blood. A memory of Lovern's blood taste came to my mouth. I tried not to gag. Spears thrown, and arrows flying that shields did not stop. Time was moving faster and faster. I felt so helpless watching the rout.

Then the Romans stood over our brave but dead warriors, slippery in their own blood and gore, and swore to their gods to capture all.

I heard King Calgacus yell to anyone listening, "Go! Allow no prisoners. Let no one be captured by the Romans. Our people would rather live with the gods! Go!"

I watched a few of our naked men run. Oh, gods, those still alive fled to the trees and hills and their clans. They ran to winter's starvation in the mountains and glens. They ran to gather families around them, not to live with but to sacrifice so they would not become slaves. They killed wives, husbands, children, and themselves. So few left to cry tears mixed with our blood. So few left to carry our memories. We would be gone.

I sobbed with grief, my head in my hands. Among the dead, I saw so many I knew. Kenric mac Beathan and his sons were there. Finlay mac Beathan and his son, Logan. Rhona's family, Chieftain Haye, his wife, Nairne, and son, Eanruig. Nathraicean's body was lying with Mouraug and Coira. They died together. No. They *will* die together. In this horrible battle of the future.

Rhona and Firtha stood on a far hill. The feathers of a sea osprey hung limp in Firtha's hair. Rhona's eyes were closed. I remembered what she told me so long ago, an echo in my ear. "Sometimes, all the preparations we make cannot help."

My stomach soured; I tasted it in my throat. I now understood why our children had to leave. We did not win the battle. We would not win the war.

"Why does this happen, Lovern?" I turned back to his wavering figure, outlined by the golden light of the setting sun. "Did you not speak with the gods?"

"Yes. I spoke with the gods. They gave me the sight to see this battle. They are giving us the choice, the chance to save our children. If enough go, the blood of our clans will survive. It is what I asked, to save our blood, our children. I have also seen Crisi. If she goes, she has babes. If she stays, she dies. We have been given this gift. You, who still live, must choose to take it or not. Choose to live as others want you to, or as you want to. Scotia, Morrigna and Bel have spoken. Do you listen?" He rose to one knee, his hair blazing around his face. His deep blue eyes that carried the wisdom of the gods looked to the skies. His voice carried over the valleys around us.

"Our children's children will carry on the fight of freedom, but only if they flee now and survive."

A whisper fell on my ears. "Now, the sun sets and I must leave. Go now, Jahna, and take the choice to Kenric. Take the choice to the people."

He rose to his feet, leaned over, and his fingertips came close to my cheek. I felt the fine hair move with his brush. "Jahna, prepare yourself. You will cross the river soon. I wait for you." A cold breeze flickered and moved my hair. He walked past me, and disappeared in the setting sun. When I shielded my eyes to try to see more of him, I saw the fox. He sat, looking at me, just under the trees. As I watched, he bowed his head, rose, turned, and disappeared into the forest without looking back. He was gone.

The air around me grew dark. I awoke on my cot in the hospice, the peat burning a bright spot in the middle of the room. With a start, and inhale of stale air, I realized where I was and that I had received a vision from the gods.

"Sileas, Rhona," I called out with as much strength as I could. "I need to speak with Kenric. Bring Kenric. I have a message."

Sileas ran to our chieftain's lodge with my request while Rhona tried to give me water that I could not swallow. "Rhona. I cannot go on in this pain any longer. After I deliver my message, I want to go to Lovern. I want to die. Do you understand?" I grabbed her hand with mine, the claw on the end of my arm, and would not let her go until she agreed that she would help me.

"I also see you are at the end, my dear friend. Your life on this earth is almost over. You have lived as the gods have asked and will be well received on your crossing. If it is now, or later, no matter. I will help ease your pain."

She moved to the end of the cot, never leaving my sight, as Kenric came into the dark room. He stumbled over a small stool on his way to my cot.

"Gods! Why is it so close and dank in here? I cannot see the end of my short sword. You should light torches or give more peat to the fire."

"Kenric," I said. "I am pleased you come. I am sorry to take you away from your evening meal with your guests. I have asked for the darkness. It pains my eyes to have the brightness of a larger fire. I am sorry if it causes you to seem unusually clumsy. But then your father, Beathan, always did call you clumsy as a boy." I smiled.

"Humph. That was many years ago, cousin. I remember he called you a *meanbh-chuileag*. A midge that was into everything and always a bother. It seems that we have grown out of those names. Or have we?" He wore a glint of humor on the corner of his eyes.

Sileas guided him to my bedside. She walked over to stand by Rhona, both hovering like protective quail mothers.

He sat on the floor beside my cot, picked up my bronze bowl, and looked at the patterns I had engraved in it. Then his eyes lifted and opened wide. He had not seen me for several days.

"My gods," he said. "Jahna. You are too thin - starving. My dogs look better than you."

"Oh, *ceann-cinnidh*. Soon, I will be dead. I hope your dogs live longer."

He became serious and leaned closer to me. "Jahna, I see you are in need. What is it you want from me?"

"I carry a message from the gods, through Lovern, to you. I had a vision. It is up to you to decide what to do from here. I deliver it only." I told him of Lovern's visit and some of the scene that was shown me. I did not tell of seeing his body or the body of his son, but I could see he understood. His head bowed.

"Lovern told me that this might not be the outcome of this battle. Things change with time and time may change the circumstances of the meeting with the Romans. But we must be ready. If it is the true outcome, our children must be given the chance to live. Kenric, I know you have the wisdom of all the chieftains who have come before you in your blood. The decision is yours. The battle comes."

"Your Lovern did not bring the news we wanted to hear. I am disappointed. But as you say, if we train harder and raise more warriors, we may still win. But I will think on his request. I will give it the reverence due and pray for help to find the answer."

"Kenric. Carry my love, my hopes for a good future to our clan. Now, good bye."

Rhona guided him out.

"Sileas, Sileas."

She took hold of my hands. "Yes, I am right here, Jahna."

"You must swear to me that you will take Crisi away to the island where Lovern gathered seagrasses."

"But should I not wait until Kenric makes his decision? We may have the clan's children to guide."

"Give him a few days, only two or three days, and then you and Harailt must go. No matter what Kenric decides, and especially if he has not decided by then. Tell Finlay I told you to take her. Tell him the fox and raven have spoken, and he will understand. Just go and do not stop until you get there. If all goes well and we do win the battle, you may come back someday. But do not take the chance. The gods seldom change their minds. You and Crisi will be protected there. Help her and you will be protected. Now go, start preparing. I must rest."

I groaned and doubled up in pain. Rhona came over and placed a drop on my lips.

"It is almost time, Rhona. I am cold. Place the pelt over me, please. Now I have one more thing I must do. Let me rest and I will call you when it is time."

It is not my soul that is ill; it is my body. My soul is pure. I will cross soon and be with him.

Lovern has told me he had seen Crisi in the future. I wanted that sight. I wanted to see her grown. Tears slipped from under my eyelids as I concentrated on creating my passage dream. I prayed I could make it come.

The peat smoke grew heavy in my lungs, and I coughed.

There was light. The sun streamed down around me. I looked up and on a small hill stood a beautiful young woman, her long black hair free and blowing around her. She stood next to a strong young man. His hair was also black, but bound and worn to the back. They looked at each other with love and tenderness.

Oh, gods. In her arms, there was a babe. Black hair and green eyes. It was all I could feel in my heart, the quest to tell Aine. I deepened my concentration and called her. There. There she was. She could now see what was in my eyes and heart. She seemed to be pleased.

We both looked upon Crisi and her family. Now the future will know of us, will remember us. We will not have died alone.

Crisi lifted the baby into the air, and his feet swung free. Yes, there was the sign. The sign of our family, Lovern's toes. We will be remembered. Lovern's sacrifice was not in vain.

Gods hear me! I will die when I choose to die.

And as I die, my thoughts will be of Fox who taught me to live, to talk to the gods, and to love. We failed to change the future, and now I beg the goddess Morrigna to allow my daughter a safe journey. I have only time for one more passage to tell our story.

Then, and only then, will I die.

And now my story is told. I have laid it on the winds of time, to be remembered and retold. It is like the sacred oak tree, its life evidenced in its splendorous existence in the spring and summer, and yet it looks like death through the fall and winter's storms, though it but in patience sleeps. My story, my life with Lovern, will lie waiting to be retold, reborn.

I have pain and am tired. My last passage dream is done. I am ready. Lovern and I walked a path designed by the gods. We honored them as we lived and died, and now I go to live among them.

Rhona pours the bitter liquid into my mouth. I cough but try to swallow as much as possible.

The pain is heavy. I choke. I cannot breathe.

"Be at peace, Jahna." Rhona's voice is far away. "Go and be without pain. They are waiting to help you cross, Jahna. Go and be free."

It does not matter any more. I hear a voice from my depths. A voice I cannot disobey. A voice I recognize.

"Jahna, little mouse. It is time to come with me."

"Beathan, I have missed you so! Where is my mother? I know Lovern will be here."

She answered behind me. "Yes, little one. Your father is here, too. We are all waiting for you. Come. Come be with us, now."

Those left behind are sad.

I am happy and well.

The river's water is fast and deep, but I cross.

CHAPTER 26

JUNE, 2005

As soon as Marc got to my apartment, we were inseparable. He held me through several teary nights. After the well-attended memorial, Meg told me she planned to take George's ashes to the Orkney Islands. He loved working at the Skara Brae site and wanted his ashes spread on the island.

He believed the henge builders and labyrinth designers came from the civilization that rose on those islands.

"Right now his ashes are in a mahogany box on the mantle of his home, next to Sophie," she said, her voice catching. "They wanted to be together so I'll take them both."

Even with him gone from my sight and touch, I knew he was watching over me, right there with my mom, dad, and Donny.

The night before Marc left for Wales, we sat wrapped in each other's arms on my small bed. A heavy, blue mood hung over me.

"Next time, I'm getting a hotel room," Marc mumbled into my hair.

Neither of us made it through the night in this tiny, cramped bed. We started the night making love, but after, one of us – usually me – ended up trying to sleep in my chair.

"I've loved seeing you again," said Marc. "It seems like months. I've done a lot of thinking while we were apart. I love you. I want us to start a family. What do you want?"

He held me close, and his chin rested on the top of my head. My cheek lay against his chest, listening to his heart beat, my heart racing. I couldn't see his face. I took a deep breath and was filled with his scent of wood smoke and loam, and then my breathing matched his. I felt safe enveloped in his arms, cushioned from the world.

But, a niggling feeling deep in my mind warned me to be careful. My psyche was still trying to work my way out from under Brad's thumb. It didn't matter that he was dead, or that I loved Marc. I thought about starting a family with Marc. Little boys with Marc's eyes, running around. I loved that idea. But....

"Marc." Reluctantly, I started pulling away from his warm, safe embrace. I still hadn't told him about the possible sale of the farm, or that I hadn't started the process to list the fort. I was afraid he would start giving me advice. "Please understand. I love you, too. I want you back. But if you come, you have to let me do my own work. This is my last chance. I'm afraid if I don't do well here, I won't be able to have my own projects anywhere. I won't be able to get any grants."

"I'm going to be busy for about a week, I have a report to finish. That'll give you some time to work with me not there and I promise, when I do come, you can tell me what to do and that is all I will do. Okay?"

We made love again and then he called a taxi.

My small room was deathly quiet while I packed to return to Scotland. The shrill ring of my phone startled me out of my reverie. It was Meg. She asked me to come over to the house before I left.

"There are a few things George asked me to do. We could get some of them done before you leave."

"Sure. I have tickets for tonight's train. I'll be there about two hours before I go, if that's a good time for you."

"That's perfect. I'm still here tidying up before the realtors come through. Take a taxi and I'll pay for the trip here and the trip to the station, later. See you about fourish."

Later, in George's study, Meg brought in a pot of fragrant tea and a plate of biscuits. The house was in disarray. Taped boxes were stacked in the hall and open ones scattered around this room. She'd been busy.

"Meg, you look tired. Aren't you sleeping well?"

"Oh, I've plenty of time for that. I've just a few things left to do. All the clothes are going to charity, and a few specific things to university. He took care of most of his personal things before he went up to see you. His labyrinths are going tomorrow. All but this one."

She walked to the now empty bookcase and picked up the bronze Chartre labyrinth. It was one I had taken to him. I'd left it there when he died and thought I'd lost it.

"St. John's sent this back and it's to be yours. George left a few written instructions and one was to make sure this got to you. He said you would be the one who would use it well and keep its spirit alive." She held it out to me and I gently took it from her. It was warm, as if George had been holding it in his hands.

"I didn't expect anything from him, Meg. I'll always treasure it." Tears started down my cheeks.

"One more thing, Aine. You know he loved you like a daughter. The one he and Sophie could never have." I wondered what heartache she was feeling right now. She loved him, too. I nodded and dug into my backpack for some tissues.

"Here, dear." She handed me a tissue box from the floor next to her chair. "I carry this with me all over the house. I've gone through two of them today."

I took a few and dabbed at my eyes.

"He had some money. Not a great deal, but enough to share with others. His solicitor will contact you, but I wanted to tell you first. He left some to university, and to me. But he also left some to you, dear. I can't tell you exactly how much, you'll be getting a letter, but it is a nice amount."

"Oh, no. I don't need anything else. This labyrinth is enough."

"Well, I heard you were looking for money for that site of yours – that hill fort? He would be very happy if you used it for that. He mentioned how important it was to you when he came back."

I gulped. Money for my site. George helping me even after his death. Angels watched over me.

"I'll use it well. He'd be proud of me, Meg."

"Aine, dear, he was already proud of you."

Tim picked me up at the station. "All is well and secure at the site. That chap, Stephen Treadwell, asked for you yesterday. I told him you'd be in tomorrow."

"Oh bloody hell. I wonder what he wants. Mr. Treadwell told me he'd call me if he got an offer on his land. I hope this isn't that news. Well, I suppose we'll find out."

I really wanted to go see the hill. It felt as if I wanted to go home.

"Who is on site tonight?"

"Matt and the new chap, Larry."

"Well, I have extra clothes and my toothbrush in my bag. I wonder if they'd mind if I bunked with them. If I remember correctly, we have an extra sleeping bag up there, right?"

"Yeah, and a pad, too. For whoever sleeps on the ground."

Two cots, three people. Yes, one of us will be on the ground. I hoped one of them was a gentleman and would give in without me having to ask.

A soft glow from the full moon reflected off the mountain and covered the fort in milky light. I was home. I said hi to Matt and Larry and dropped off my bag. I grabbed a torch and a cup of coffee and walked to Jahna's lodge. I closed my eyes and saw her smile as she stirred a rich rabbit stew, cooking over the peat fire. My thoughts confirmed what my heart felt. This was right. I was supposed to be here. I walked back to the tent, picked up the sleeping bag and pad, grabbed a hat and my labyrinth from my bag, and said goodnight. I wanted to sleep with Jahna tonight.

I settled near the perimeter of her home closest to the remains of the gate. My view encompassed the fields where Mr. Treadwell's sheep grazed and the bog where his Highland cattle wandered. Oak trees in the distance were silhouetted by the moonlight, throwing shadows across the fields. My finger traced the worn path on the labyrinth and I let my imagination wander. The clan was all around me, talking and laughing. Dogs barked and Jahna called to her goats. I loved it there. I stayed in that thought as long as I could, but the sounds and sight wavered and then were gone. I loved archaeology. It allowed me to live in times past.

It was about 4 AM when I woke up and stretched. The ground was hard, and I was chilled. Everything around me was dark and quiet. My eyes wandered over the outlying fields and bog and stopped on a ball of light.

"What the…?"

The light bobbed just above the ground near the trench where Mr. Treadwell had found the bronze horse harness fittings. I looked carefully. It seemed almost like a torch that was in need of batteries. The moon should cast a shadow of the person carrying it, but there was no shadow. I watched it for several minutes. It seemed to move in a small circle, never going far from the first area where I'd noticed it.

I had to go see what this thing was. I debated with myself as to whether I needed Mr. Treadwell's permission. If yes, I'd have to go to his home, wake him up and tromp through his fields in the middle of the night. Or.... There was a short cut down the path, around the foot of the hill and over a couple of fences. I could be there in about twenty minutes. I chose the short way, put the labyrinth in my pocket, and prayed there were no cattle roaming the bog.

Fences and small hills sometimes hid the dim circle of light as I walked, but when back in sight, it still bobbed, as if waiting for me.

I came to the last barrier, a rock wall surrounding the bog, climbed it, and stood watching, afraid and nervous about what I might see. There was no reason for this light to be bouncing in Mr. Treadwell's bog. Was I going completely bonkers? I squatted in place and decided to wait. A sneeze exploded to my left and I jumped, almost falling off the wall. The fox sat there, just out of my reach. It was the same fox I'd seen in the trees the other day, I was sure. There was no mistaking him; he was big. He sat watching the light bounce. He was glorious, even in the moonlight. His bronze fur glistened and his white-tipped, bushy tail wagged, slowly. Suddenly, he stiffened, ears forward and his eyes trained on the spot mine had left a moment ago. I turned back and gasped as I sat down hard, breathless, shocked at the vision in front of me.

Oh my God, he'd appeared out of the ground! He couldn't have walked here, I'd have heard him or seen him. My eyes hadn't left that spot except for a minute to look at the fox. He couldn't be there. But there he stood.

A man of about Marc's height stood straight and proud in front of me, at the edge of a cut trench. A faint aura of golden light shimmered around his body. He wore long pants, a tunic top tied with a cord, and a plaid cape, fastened at his neck. His loose red hair hung below his shoulders. One arm hung to his side, behind the cape. The fox stepped across the trench and sat next to that hand as if waiting to be petted. The other hand rested on his upper chest. His eyes looked into mine. I knew they were blue; the same blue Marc's eyes were.

He stared at me for a minute and then dropped the hand that rested on his chest. I saw the medicine bag. Healers and druids wore them to ward off evil spirits. He turned slightly to the left and moonlight highlighted its design. It was a labyrinth!

"Oh, gods above," I whispered. I suddenly thought I should show him my labyrinth and slipped it out of my pocket.

He smiled, and his hand dropped, palm up. He slowly waved it over the bog around him. Our eyes connected and he nodded as if he knew me. My heart stopped beating.

A cloud slid over the moon. I blinked, and the man and the fox had disappeared. They were both gone.

I sat on the damp ground, trying to figure out what I'd seen. As hard as I tried not to admit it, I finally concluded that either I was dreaming and sleepwalking, or Mr. Treadwell's ghost was roaming the fields in the moonlight. I pinched myself. "Ouch!" I was awake and left with one strong thought. There was something here I needed to find. To do that, I needed to speak to Mr. Treadwell.

"Good morning! Mr. Treadwell!" I was sure he rose with the sun hours ago. I didn't hesitate to knock hard on his door and call out. "Mr. Treadwell, it's me, Aine MacRae."

"I'm in the barn. Stop the yelling or ye'll wake the dead! Or my son, whichever first. I don't know where he learned to sleep so much."

I stepped into the frame of the barn door and peered inside. The sun shined brightly outside but didn't penetrate the dark interior. Bits of dust floated around the doorframe, reflecting sunlight like miniature flying fairies. "Hello, Mr. Treadwell. Can I speak with you for a moment?"

A striped yellow cat walked out of the darkness, rubbed against my legs, and purred. She looked well fed. Lots of mice in there, I guessed.

"Come on in, lassie."

I stepped inside, and my eyes grew accustomed to the shafts of light slipping in through the spaces in the barn walls. He stood over a workbench, so I headed his way. The cat followed me in, meowing.

"She's about to have kittens and begs all the time. Just pay her no mind. She'll go on a hunt in a bit. You're up early on this fine day. What can I do for ye?"

"Good morning, Mr. Treadwell. I hope you and your son are well. Stephen called and wanted to talk to me earlier in the week, but I need to talk to you first. I just returned from London last night."

His back was to me but I could see a motor in pieces on the table in front of him. He intently twisted a screwdriver, the strain showing in his stance.

"Ach! This blasted thing! I would've a new one if I were sure I would be on the land for a few more years."

My heart jumped into my throat. I hoped he'd not made a deal to sell yet. I hadn't told him yet about wanting to get the hilltop registered and protected. Registering it as a landmark might not restrict the sale of the rest of the land so I didn't want to upset him or his son needlessly. "Mr. Treadwell. I am here about your bog."

"My bog. What the bloody hell.... What do ye want with my bog? Oh hell. I give up. I'll have to take this into town." He turned to me. "Aye? What does my bog have that brings ye here?"

"Well, Mr. Treadwell. Remember the horse fittings you found? I think there may be more to find there, and I'd like the chance to bring a crew down and do some digging."

"Lassie. You want to dig holes in my bog? My cattle have a hard enough time as it is. Why would I want to be letting you dig more holes?"

"Mr. Treadwell. The bronze fittings are beautiful. And as I told you, it was not uncommon for the druids to throw other sacrifices into the water. I think there may be more in the bog. That it was once a lake that was sacred to the local ancient clans. I would like to be the one to find whatever else is there. Before it's gone or covered over." I heard a commotion in the corner. The yellow cat came out with a mouse in her mouth and laid it at my feet.

"Ah, she's laying a sacrifice at your feet, lassie. She only does that for those she likes. She will na even come near my son."

"Oh. Well. I'm honored." I reached down, petted the cat, and gently shifted my foot out from under the warm mouse body. She picked up the mouse and slowly walked to a dark corner. I expected to hear crunches soon. My stomach rebelled. Only coffee for breakfast seemed like a smart move right now.

"I'll tell ye what." His face brightened with an idea. "I'm going to cut peat there tomorrow. Ye can come and help. I can do with a few more spades working."

I wanted to start now and had to convince him to let my team into the bog today. I decided to tell him what I saw.

"Mr. Treadwell. I was outside, on the hill last night. I saw something. Remember the ghost you told me you saw?"

He stepped closer. I smelled his breakfast bacon on his breath.

"I do not talk about that to everyone, lassie."

"I haven't told anyone your story, Mr. Treadwell. I saw something down there. A bouncing light and a fox."

He stepped sideways so the sunlight silhouetted him. I couldn't see his face.

"Aye. A fox. He's a big one he is. The fox that doesna' eat the farm chickens." He paused. "What does the fox mean to ye, lassie?"

"I've always loved foxes. One followed me around when I was a kid. I think of them as my good luck charms. When I saw the big one last night, Mr. Treadwell, he was standing next to a man."

"What? What man was in my bog last night? What did ye see?"

"Well, Mr. Treadwell, to tell you the truth, I don't know what I saw. I think I saw a man, petting the fox. He was tall and wore brown with a cape slung over his shoulders."

"He showed himself to you."

"Was that what you saw? Was that your ghost? When you saw him, did he look at you?"

"No, he was pacing, walking over and over the same ground. He didn't look up at me. He seemed to be looking for something."

"When I saw him he was standing still. I think he was trying to tell me something. Mr. Treadwell, I have to go see why he came last night. Why he showed himself to me." I paused to think for a minute. "I have an idea. I have a whole group of young people with strong backs who would be a boon to you. We could dig rows of peat, look through them for relics and then transport the peat wherever you like."

His hands came up and rested on my shoulders. "I'll be lifting the peat alongside them. If there is something to find, I want to be there. The ghost." He slowly shook his head; his eyes never left mine. "He honored ye, too." He turned and walked back into the dark of the barn. When he returned he had four peat cutting shovels in hand. "We shouldn't let any more time pass, lassie. I'll go tell my son where I'll be, and you call your team here. We start today."

My team, Mr. Treadwell, and I dug trenches and poked through each piece of muggy, sticky peat and bog mud we dug up. I thought the dirt would never come out from under my nails again. We dug for hours, finding nothing except mud and goop. My biggest fear was Mr. Treadwell losing faith. I knew that I would stay and dig up the whole bog alone if needed. But I couldn't do it without his permission. Later, toward evening, his son Stephen tripped into the field where we were, carrying papers in his hands. I prayed it was bills to pay or some such.

"Da," he called. "Da. You need to see this."

My heart sunk. I knew what it was.

Mr. Treadwell carefully slogged his way to him and they spent their time together talking and leafing through the folder. Stephen quickly shook his head, and Mr. Treadwell seemed to agree by nodding. I knew we were in trouble.

"Aine," Mr. Treadwell called. He motioned me to come to him. "Lassie," he said when I stood next to him, knee deep in a furrow. "Stephen brought news of an offer from the hotel. It seems they want me to sign this week. I'm required to go to

London to meet with the purchasing company. I'll spend time with my solicitor and bank tomorrow. Stephen says I shouldn't allow ye on the property while I'm gone."

"But I know the land, I could have my team dig without your being here." I wanted to throttle Stephen and was ready to get on my knees to beg Mr. Treadwell to let us stay.

"He says we're too close to the deal to have anything happen to any of you. I told him, I'm still making the decisions here as long as the land is in my name. And I give ye permission for one more day. But girl, ye have only one more day. Now, the sun is setting and we will quit for today."

"Please! If we're to have only one more day, I want to dig in the moonlight!" I silently cursed the ghost for not being more specific with his sign. Why couldn't he have planted a flag where I was supposed to dig? I also cursed myself for not starting the process of getting the property listed. Now there was no way I could stop Mr. Treadwell from going. Maybe in time, time I didn't have, the hilltop would be protected, but I could lose this bog.

"Don't be daft. Let's wash our hands and eat a good supper." He raised his voice and called to my crew, "'Tis time to break for the night."

They all looked at me. "Okay. We can come back tomorrow." I turned back to him. "We haven't found what I'm looking for yet."

"Do we know what that item is?" he asked.

"No. Not yet. I'll know when I see it."

"Well, lassie, ye have another day."

Back at camp, I told everyone what Mr. Treadwell told me. "I'm calling the Regional Archaeologist tonight. If the hilltop is listed, the hotel still could buy the rest of the land. Unless we find something in the bog. We're going to have to work extra hard tomorrow, but tonight, why don't all of you go into town and have a good supper on me? Kendy, you know which place accepts my charge card, would you please take care of it? I'm going to spend the night here."

Laurie hugged me. "Aine, we'll stay as long as you need us. This is a fab site and we like working for you. No worries, it'll all work out. As my Mom says, 'Just think positive!'"

"Thank you, Laurie. I'll remember that." They descended to the vehicles.

"Don't forget we're working tomorrow. Don't you kids get lost in town!" Laughter and cheerios echoed after the departing cars. They were all kids. Boy, I really missed Marc.

"Just think positive. Just think...Oh, bloody hell. I'm talking to myself now. Well, if I'm going to talk to someone, I may as well talk to a ghost." With that, I picked up a torch and started down the back way to the bog.

Sitting on the wall of a cut row of peat, labyrinth in hand, I spoke again. "I know you're here. I need to know exactly where I'm supposed to dig. Is that a stupid thing to ask a ghost?" I looked around to see if anyone appeared, half worried it would be Stephen. No, still just an empty bog.

"What am I looking for?" I asked the air. No answer.

It was late, the moon was setting and I was chilled. I stood to start back to camp. "Hey! Out there. Yoohoo! I just remembered I brought my labyrinth. You liked it last time. If I say a prayer over it, will you come?" I decided to try. I closed my eyes, rubbed the path of the labyrinth and words floated easily into my mind.

Blood of our blood.
Do not forget us.
In the darkest of the nights, buried we lie.
We dream to have our voices heard again.
We beg you to find us, to bring us back.
Blood of our blood.
Do not forget us.
Our souls continue with the gods.
We died for you, we live through you.
Tell our story so we may live again.
Blood of our blood.

When the prayer was completed, I opened my eyes. "There you are!" The light bobbed again just in front of me. It bounced up about two feet above the ground and back down to touch it. "There? Is that where it is? Do we dig there tomorrow?" The light blinked out and I rushed over and laid my labyrinth on the spot. It was all I carried besides the torch, batteries almost gone, and my mobile. I spent the rest of the night fitfully sleeping and waking, cold and stiff, with the feeling of someone watching me and wondering just what I meant by "blood of my blood."

The sun's pink rays peaked over the mountain and I dialed Tim's mobile. Dew-covered and shivering I said, "Tim, I'm in the bog. Send the team, will you? And have them bring a big thermos of coffee and something to eat. I know I've woken you up and it'll take a while, but please get everyone on the move. Thanks. See you soon." Tim barely had time to utter a sound. I calculated ten minutes to brew a pot of coffee while dressing, and twenty minutes on the road. Another five minutes to hike in from the car and I'll have coffee in about thirty-five minutes if I didn't die from exposure before then. Ah, the sun was getting higher and warmer.

My crew, Larry, Darcy, Jane, and Tom arrived with coffee and baskets of food.

"Larry, please bring the yellow tape. I want to mark a grid." I walked a square around the spot where my labyrinth lay. As excited as I was about digging in that exact spot, I knew we had to go about this correctly or we might disturb something and devalue its importance. We started digging.

2:25. I looked at my watch for the umpteenth time. In the warm sun, the midges gathered around us. Until today, we were mercifully free from them, but it seemed they arrived in force. Maybe they knew we were leaving and wanted to be sure to get a taste of us before we were gone. Little buggers.

My job was slogging through the piles of mud that were shoveled my way. Larry and Tom were digging, and the girls pulled the peat apart, all looking for anything unusual. I stood to stretch my aching back, and felt nauseated. Had I eaten too many croissants? I stood up and walked to where we had a blanket out with water and snacks. I didn't want to lose my lunch in front of the kids.

Suddenly, an intense feeling washed over me. I had felt this when we buried Donny. I recognized it as grief and the agony of not understanding why he had to die. My body was bent over with silent sobs. Then, it passed. I tried to understand what had just happened. Did I miss George that much? I hoped I was quiet enough so no one noticed me.

Tom yelled out, "I've found something! Here!"

"Oh, wow!" Jane said. "It looks like a.... Oh my God. Come here everyone!" We were already crowding around her, me wiping tears from my face. "It looks like a leg!" she said.

I jumped into the trench and stooped down to look at its wall. Folds of a leathery material lay imbedded in the peat. "Let me see what you have there, Jane." She handed it to me. It was a human leg. A mummified, peat-dyed human leg that had lain in the bog for who knows how many years. Weak kneed, I leaned against a pile of peat. We'd found it. I'd found him.

Tom had shoveled through the leg of a bog body. In my heart, I knew it was the body of the ghost.

"Okay, okay." My mind raced to think of the procedure we should follow. "We can stop digging now." I laid the leg in the trench just below the rest of the uncovered body. "We need to have the authorities out here to assure them that this isn't a recent crime. Tom and Jane, please take pictures of this site and its surroundings. And make sure we have the GPS locators marked and recorded properly. Larry, could you go to Mr. Treadwell's and see if someone is home? We need to let them know about this. Darcy, get on your mobile and call in the local coroner and police. Call Tim to secure the hilltop. No one is to come up there until we have this figured out. I want to work with the police and make sure this recovery is recorded in every way possible as we dig the body out."

I climbed out of the trench. My hands trembled as I dialed Jimmy's number in Glasgow. "Hi, Jimmy?"

"Hello, Aine? What's up? More ashes?"

"No. Not more ashes, Jimmy. I need you to find the right person to come and help me protect this site. And if I'm right, I've something here that'll make your day. Heck, it'll make your year!"

Chapter 27

June, 2005

"I have a contact at the British Museum," Jimmy had said. "Dr. Andy Cardwell. He'll know how to get the ball rolling. I'll fax him my prelim report, and he'll jump on it like a fox on a mouse. Can I give him your mobile number?"

I called Marc, told him what I'd found and made arrangements to pick him up tomorrow evening at the train station.

Andy Cardwell called. I'd worked with him in London and respected him. He said he'd be flying in tomorrow evening as well, and had requested that the local coroner wait to inspect the scene until he was there.

"I know him," said Andy. "Dr. Jancle. He is a bit of an amateur archaeologist and is as excited about the possibilities of this as we are. I think he hopes as much as we do that this is not a modern crime scene. He said he'd wait."

The next morning, yellow police tape surrounded the bog and a uniformed policeman stood guard. We didn't have access, but I didn't have to worry about looters, just Stephen Treadwell, who was talking to the guard as I walked up.

"Constable?" said Stephen. "Do you think the sale of the property can still go through? I don't want anything to stand in the way of my father being able to retire." He had such an innocent and serious look on his face. I almost wanted to slap him. *Worried about his father retiring my foot, he just wanted the money.*

I definitely wasn't going to throw a spanner in the mix here, but I knew if it were what I suspected, the sale could be on hold for a while. And I didn't think the older Mr. Treadwell would mind a bit.

"I don't know about any sale of any land, sir," said the constable, "but you and the lady will have to leave now. My orders are to keep everyone away until we determine what this is."

Stephen took off in his truck, dust spinning from its back tires, and I walked up the hill.

All the evidence pointed to it being an ancient person. It must have been a sacred lake. Other sacrificial items had been found there. This body was probably an important person. I could hardly think straight, imagining all the possibilities. And I was dizzy and constantly having to pee. I spent the day on the hilltop, my crew working while I sat in a chair, watching the bog and making trips to our portable facility. Gods, I didn't need the flu on top of everything else.

I met Marc at the train station and after I made a stop in the WC, he said, "Aine, you're pale. Are you feeling well?"

"Not really. I think it's a touch of the flu. I've been so excited that I haven't slept well. That may be exacerbating it. I'll be better in the morning. Now come on, our bed is waiting."

I fell asleep after our lovemaking. The bed that had seemed so empty and cold was warm and comforting.

My mobile rang five times before I could find it under the pile of clothes that we had dumped in our rush last night. I laid back down and answered.

"Hello?" I sounded muffled to my ears, and my mouth tasted like pickled herring. Not a good way to start a day or a conversation. I told myself not to move too fast, and I might just be able to last through this call.

"Is this Aine MacRae?"

The voice was not familiar, and I winced. I had to pee, and my stomach was just beginning to wake up.

"Yes, it is."

"This is Mr. George Weymouth's solicitor, John Critchfield. I wanted to double-check the address we have for you. I am sending a messenger to you with papers for you to sign."

"What? What do I need to sign?" My bladder was beginning to scream.

"Mr. George Weymouth left you a good sized sum of money and you need to be able to prove your identity to the messenger and then sign the papers he is carrying. After he returns, we can transfer the funds to any financial institution you request." I walked to the bathroom as he spoke.

"Can't he just bring the check here and let me sign it so I can get the cash? I am short of funds and could use it now without going through a bank account."

"I don't think that would be a good idea, Ms. MacRae. We are talking about a very substantial amount here."

I didn't think George had much money, and as I sat down on the toilet, I remembered Sarah telling me he had divided it up between her, the university and me. I was sure not much was coming to me. "Just how much is a substantial amount?"

He told me. Later, I hoped my scream drowned out the sound of my peeing. One thought ran through my mind. I would have enough to buy Mr. Treadwell's farm and several surrounding farms if I wanted. Oh my God, I was going to be able to work on my site and not worry about making a living elsewhere for a very long time. Marc would be able to retire and work with me, to the chagrin of his peers.

Marc and I arrived at the bog to see Andy talking to a man I assumed was Dr. Jancle, and a woman with a camera, all crouched in the trench. Andy smiled at us through the muck on his face and gave us the thumbs up. A weight lifted off my chest. In a few minutes, he climbed out and walked to us.

"Hi, Aine. This looks really good. Dr. Jancle and I agree that a sample should go to Glasgow to have it carbon dated as soon as possible. I'm going to carry it myself. It should only take a day or two. We aren't going to move anything until the results come through. If it is what I think it is, then I will get a team here to remove the body."

"That's good news. I'm glad you're going to be a part of this, Andy."

"A part of it, yes, Aine. But if it is an ancient find, your name will be the one on everyone's tongue. Good job."

The rest of the day I was giddy and bounced around like a child. I blamed my now constant dizziness on not being able to eat. I blamed that on what Andy had said and the fact I had signed the solicitor's papers and designated a bank for the inheritance later that same day.

When I woke up the next morning and spent thirty minutes hanging over the toilet, Marc drove me into the doctor's office in Fort William.

"This is ridiculous. No flu lasts this long," he said.

He was right. I was seven weeks pregnant.

"Of course! That explains all the moodiness and throwing up! I'm pregnant! We're going to have a baby! Oh no, do you think I'm too old to be a mom? Marc, I am so sorry! I don't want to cry, but I don't know what to think."

"Aine. I love that we're going to have a baby. I'm happy! I've wanted a family, and now you're pregnant. With our baby."

He took my hand and led me to a bench surrounded by a small garden in a park across the street from the doctor's office. I sat down, and he sat next to me, both of my hands in his.

"Aine, we've had a lot of life experience since the last time I almost asked this question. You weren't ready then; hell, neither was I. I think we are ready now and can make a go of it if you want to."

He stopped, looking at me as if he were waiting for an answer.

"Make a go of what?" I would not let him off that easily.

"All right, all right. Aine, will you marry me?"

I looked at his beaming face, his sparkling blue eyes and smiled through my tears. "Do you know that when we get married I'll be as fat as a cow?"

"No, not fat. You'll be showing the world the proof of our love. You'll be showing them the next generation of Hunts."

"I love you. Yes! I'll marry you." We leaned in to kiss and my stomach chose that moment to remind us that I was pregnant. Fortunately, I turned my head just in time and hung on to the back of the bench as my hormones caused me to rid myself of my morning tea. Definitely not the romantic proposal I was sure Marc was expecting. We went back to the hilltop after stopping to get some soda crackers at the corner shop.

That night, after Marc finally fell asleep, I was restless. So much had happened in such a short time. I was still processing much of it, and as tired as I was, I still couldn't go to sleep. I was on the couch, a light throw over my legs, looking at the full moon. There it was, the rabbit holding the egg. I would point it out to my baby someday, just like my mother did for me.

Then I smelled smoke. Peat smoke. Jahna was coming. I hadn't had a visit from her for a long time, and I welcomed this one. I hoped she could tell how happy I was. The room faded from my sight, and I saw through her eyes.

Warm sunlight flooded the scene and a strong young man and woman stood tall in front of me. If I reached my hand out, I could touch them. Their raven black hair ruffled in a breeze and both looked at me with intense hazel eyes. The young woman held a baby. The man turned his head to look down on the woman with love, and his arms surrounded her in protection. This was an ancient picture. The woman held the baby girl up for me to see and then I saw the baby's bare feet. The babe had my toes, the first one after the big toe longer than the rest.

Then the woman looked at me and spoke. "My mother told me about you. I was too young to understand. She told me you would be the one to tell our story. I feel you now. See the babe my father died for. The infant my mother sent me away to protect. My clan is gone. We have heard stories of the deaths of many. But here, now, we are safe. We are on an island. I have married and love the man standing here with me. There are others here who also found this island. We have a new clan; my husband is the chieftain. This is now and our future. Understand that we will live on. You will see us in all the children and children's children that come. We will make it so. My father was sacrificed to make it so. It is time for you to sing our song, storyteller."

The prayer I prayed the night before I found the man in the bog ran through my head.

Blood of our blood, do not forget us.
Blood of our blood.

I understood.

Suddenly, the same intense grief that hit me when I first saw the body in the bog flooded over me again. My heart beat so fast I thought it would jump out of my body. A band constricted my chest and I could only take shallow breaths. Then, as fast as they had come, everyone was gone. The memory of it faded like a dream in the morning. Only a wisp of it was left in my heart.

I fell asleep wishing Jahna would come back one more time. Marc found me and gently carried me to bed where I snuggled next to him, the man who looked at me with love in his eyes. The man who would stand next to me in my search for my family. With him, I would continue the bloodline of the MacRaes with this baby. A girl with my raven black hair, my toes, and his blue eyes.

The phone woke me up for the second morning in a row.

"It's Jim, Aine."

I was beginning to like these early morning phone calls.

"Andy is talking to London right now, and let me call to tell you your good news. Holy cow, Aine, you have the discovery of the year for Great Britain. I'm going to venture a guess and say it is the find for the world this year. I dated the body of this man to about 80 AD. Give it plus or minus 15 years, still puts you in the category of this not being a recent crime." He chuckled. "I think the coppers will let you go now. Hey, this is close to the age of the woman in the bowl, right?"

"Yes, Jimmy. It all fits together. You've made me a very happy person!" Two things were now shaping my future, my new family and my discovery.

Andy called me to arrange the excavation and transportation of the body. Marc and I headed up the excavation team. We respectfully and carefully removed the body. Stephen and Mr. Treadwell helped and supplied almost all the equipment, with news crews from all over Great Britain watching.

I wanted to be married in Scotland, so before we left, we stopped into the Registrar's office and started the process of producing our previous spouses' death records and completing all the other paperwork. It would take several months to process. We flew to London with the body. Within the next week, Marc and I had moved back into my small apartment and purchased a new bed and a crib.

I continued getting fat while doing the most fascinating research I could ever think of doing, with Marc there to share in all the discoveries. Tim had decided to take a year off from his graduate program so he still managed the hill top site for me. I asked him to start plans to build a more permanent structure so we could thoroughly excavate the hilltop and the bog. His family was in construction so he knew the steps he needed to take and I had the money I needed to make it happen. We conferred with the Scotland Secretary of State's office to make sure we complied with the Planning Process and Scheduled Monuments Procedures policies.

Stephen Treadwell helped arrange an agreement with the hotel, even with the hilltop and bog on the List of Protected Monuments. The hotel decided they could build the parking lot on the other side of the building. Stephen actually led us through some tricky paperwork so it all ended well, especially with a bit of extra money from me. I'm sure it helped that I had asked the museum to name our bog man the Treadwell Man. I did it to honor Mr. Treadwell, but Stephen enjoyed the popularity as well. The museum agreed because we'd uncovered him on Treadwell land.

The research kept us so busy, I'd barely noticed time passing. One thing reminded me, however. I was getting bigger and bigger.

I had trouble finding a dress that I liked that would fit me for my wedding. Finally, my friend Rhonnie Craig took me shopping a few days before the wedding.

"Aine, you seem to be in a very good place. You have come to terms with your time with Brad and are ready to step onto a new path. You and Marc are supposed to be together and now the stars will line up to light your future. Your baby is healthy and you're going to find answers for questions you have had in your heart for a long time."

I hugged her to me when she told me my unborn baby girl was healthy. I didn't need to hear anything more.

We found a beautiful, long, forest-green dress that I felt comfortable in. Marc said the color was perfect with my eyes.

Marc and I were married in September at the Fort William registrar's office.

After, we invited a small gathering of friends to the hilltop. Rhonnie, of course, Kendy and Matt, now married themselves, and Tim came. Mr. Treadwell and Stephen were there. Jim Cowley from Glasgow and even Andy Cardwell and Susan, his wife, took the weekend off to come up. Everyone raised a champagne toast to us, though mine was apple juice. When I could break away, I took a walk to Jahna's home and lifted my glass to her.

"Thank you for leading me here and trusting me to tell your story. I will do the best I can." A brush of warm air lifted the ends of my hair as it lay on my shoulders like a mother's touch. I swallowed my juice and returned to the party.

JULY, 2007

Our beautiful baby girl, Janel, was born in February 2006. At the first chance, I unwrapped her and counted all her fingers and toes. Her first toes were longer than her big toes, just like mine. Just like the baby I saw in my last awake dream with Jahna. She also had a full head of black hair.

"She'll probably lose all this hair, it's normal," the nurse had said. "It would be a shame though, it's so long and pretty."

Janel hadn't lost her hair; it just kept getting longer. Now it shines as it curls and ripples down her back. And she kept Marc's blue eyes. She was of our blood.

I stayed home for three long weeks after her birth. I used my web cam, phone, and email to work with the lab. When I went back, we set up a corner nursery for Janel near us. She was fed and learned to laugh among the relics of an ancient people.

Day by day, we unraveled more of Lovern's secrets. I carried a respect for him that I will have until my death. His face was peaceful and his hands unbound. He'd volunteered for death. I couldn't fathom that. It was a question that followed me everywhere. We found and made copies of his many tattoos. We saw paint in crevices that told us he had been painted three colors before his death. We even looked into his stomach and listed the ingredients of his last meager meal, but none of these discoveries answered my question.

Finally, all the work we could do on him with the knowledge we had was done. The British Museum carefully preserved his body so that as our skills and knowledge increased, or new inventions came along, we would learn more about him. All the bog bodies that were found in Great Britain, and the world, brought life back into archaeology. Everyone who looked at these bodies wondered what kind of life they had lived. Looking at a human body, not just a piece of pottery, was so much more tangible for our minds to grasp. And a stained body trapped in a bog for centuries let our imaginations fly.

Tricia Jones, an artist and a member of our research team, created his face in wax, or what it might have looked like before the pressures of the bog deformed it. They displayed his body and wax face together. We published our report in February, on Janel's first birthday.

We were back in Scotland. Janel was eighteen months old. It seemed strange to count her age in months. I usually counted in hundreds or tens of hundreds of years. She was so young. And she moved so fast. When I took her to the hilltop site, I had to keep a constant watch out for her. Familiar with the people there, she was comfortable and thought the piles of dirt were hers to play in. I loved watching her play in the center of the fort, by the well where I imagined other babies learned to walk so many years ago. Marc would swing her up into his arms, place her on his shoulders and, both laughing, they would go pick the yellow flowers in the field below the fort.

I had the rights to use the Treadwell Man report as background and write a book. That is one reason we were back in Scotland. I wanted to be near the place where he had lived. I wanted to breathe the same air and see the same mountains. I also wanted to watch over the work on my hill.

My instincts told me the ashes I found and the man in the bog should be together. I gave the bronze bowl and its contents to Andy, to be displayed with the bog man. According to the carbon dating of the cremated remains, this man and woman could have lived simultaneously and I like to believe they knew each other. On certain days, especially when I had time to visit both displays, the romantic in me believed they had more of a relationship than we will ever be able to prove.

My scientific background would sometimes let in a picture of two people in love, walking and talking through the groves of trees or fields filled with sheep that surrounded the fort. Jahna, in my mind, had a face that looked somewhat like mine, the man, the face Tricia had given him.

I wondered what they would have thought of today's Scotland. Autos, planes, computers. As druids, they probably would have mourned the loss of nature. The freedom the Picts fought for was not realized. Their future held wars with the Romans and themselves, the Norse and the Irish. Even in modern times, Culloden and the loss of traditions and our kings. Now, we are at least able to have our own Parliament; a small freedom.

Jahna had not visited since the time we saw the baby. I hoped she was finally at peace.

I was editing the draft of my book.

"Marc," I said as I walked into the kitchen. He was fixing dinner and Janel was already in bed for the night. "I want to give him a name."

"Who?"

"The Treadwell Man. He needs a name. I can't go on calling him TTM. Let's give him a name."

"Alright, a name. Hmmm. Well, you know how important animal names were to the Celts."

"Most of his body was tattooed. He was a Pict," I said.

"He wore a fur band around his arm. What was it?"

"Fox."

"Right. Fox. A fox tail. I remember," Marc said as he stirred our pasta to keep it from boiling over. "Toss the salad."

I grabbed the oil and vinegar and began to lift lettuce and tomatoes around in a bowl. "He wouldn't have been wearing it unless it meant something to him. He also had reddish hair, like a fox."

"And the fox was important to the Celts or the Picts. It's found inscribed in the earliest writings and some folk sword dancers still wear fox hats. Pasta's ready."

"Then it's Lovernios or Lovern. The Fox. I'll be right there. I have to wash my hands." Actually, I had to wipe my eyes because tears started flowing as soon as I said the name Lovern. This was his story.

I walked into my study to write the name down and my stereo was on. I was listening to Scottish folk songs while I wrote, for inspiration. One, titled "Painted Men" by Steve McDonald, was playing and its words cut right through me.

> *With Spear and sword in their hand*
> *People from far away land*
> *Made their home here.*
>
> *The Scotties did battle them so*
> *They were a terrible foe*
> *Knowing no fear.*
>
> *I close my eyes, look deep inside,*
> *I see them again*
> *Pictures disguise, the fire in their eyes*
> *Like stars in the sky, the painted men.*

The last two lines rang so true.

> *Gone is the race, with the tattooed embrace*
> *The storybook face of the painted men.*

Lovern was a Painted Man, one who once had fire in his eyes.

Two days later, I asked Marc, "Why do you think he died?"

"I thought you had that figured out already. As you lifted the garrote from his neck you said you thought it was a sacrifice, not an execution."

"Yes. I still believe that, but I want to talk it through so I can make sure my facts are straight in my book."

"Well," Marc said, "he was a sacrifice or ritual killing. Not a slave or prisoner forced to death. They didn't tie his hands, and he had evidence of the ritual burned bread in his stomach, along with pieces of heather and mistletoe pollen," Marc said. "He was recently shaved and was painted three colors."

"We all agreed he was sacrificed to three gods. Esus, who required a stab or knife slash. His throat was cut. The burned bannock he ate just before death, which represented fire, and the three blows to his head honored Taranis, the god of family and clans. And because of the god Teutates, he was given a watery grave," I said. "We found him in a bog that was once a sacred lake, the Black Lake according to local legend."

"Remember his hands? Soft hands, not callused by physical work. He must have been a druid. Oh, and his toes? I compared them to yours when we took the x-ray of his foot." Marc had a silly grin on his face.

"Okay, I remember. It's not rare, just uncommon. But let's stay focused. I wonder if the sacrifice had anything to do with the Roman invasion? They were marauding in the Highlands about that time."

"Could have, but it's all conjecture, theory. Unless he starts talking, that's all we have."

"Yes. But it makes sense. I mean for the sacrifice. But I still can't understand how someone can give up his life, voluntarily, for something like that."

"Sorry, I don't have any more answers than you have."

"Oh well, thanks. I'll go work on my theory." I went back to my computer.

Several months later, still mulling over the question that was always in the back of my mind, I looked out the window of the small room I called my office over a garden filled with various colors of ranunculus bulbs in full bloom. With the blue sky as a backdrop, the vista was vivid, yet calming. My book was about ready to go to the editors, but my mind was still trying to come to terms with Lovern's sacrifice.

I knew his religious beliefs were strong. They were his reason for being a druid. He believed he would be going to live with the gods. It was hard for me to justify this as being enough to allow him to give his life so calmly as not to be tied up. Life was sacred. We fight for it subconsciously when in danger.

Marc and I, both lapsed Catholics, didn't practice our religion, but I remembered as a child that I firmly believed the saints watched over me. Many a time when I played tricks on my brother, Donny, I asked forgiveness from them, knowing I would be forgiven and be able to go to heaven. Terrorists in today's world claim religion as their reason for killing themselves and taking others with them. But can that be enough? Some of the so-called terrorists have to be tied into their cars made into bombs. How did Lovern give his life so calmly? And the thought still niggled the very dark recesses of my mind: how did Donny do what he did?

Our front door opened, and I heard Marc and Janel come in from their trip to the grocers. She was laughing, and he was talking about the big dog they had seen down the street.

"Woof. Woof. Doggy says woof."

I smiled as I marveled how our language skills have grown to include baby talk. She had a good-sized vocabulary now, but we had a hard time getting out of the habit of the hobbit language.

"Down. Down." I heard this and imagined her squirming in his arms, making it difficult to hold on to her.

"Okay, down," said Marc.

Her fast steps came in my direction and I squatted so she could run into my waiting arms.

She came barreling around the corner, her face filled with her smile. She was looking for me, wanting to be sure her family was whole and she was safe. I waited to reassure her safety and kiss her dark hair as she fell into my arms. Marc stepped into the doorframe, smiling. "It's a glorious day out there and we saw every cat and dog in the neighborhood, but she couldn't wait to get home to you."

The idea hit me so hard I sat down on the floor. He'd had a child! He'd had a family! Donny always said he joined the military to keep the fight away from his family, his kids, even before he had kids. I saw Lovern's family in my mind. In my dream, they were standing on the path above the hill fort looking down over his home. He was the man standing with Jahna, a child's hand in his.

It all fell into place. He'd died for his family. We'd give our lives for our loved ones, our blood. Now I understood the phrase in my prayer. "We died for you; we live through you. Blood of our blood." He gave up his life to Teutates, god of the family, the tribe. He was trying to keep his child from the Romans. I would die for Janel if I needed to. Of course! He died for his child.

"Marc. He had a child! Maybe the little girl I saw in my vision. He traded his life to the gods so she could live. I know she lived. I saw her with her husband and a baby. His blood continued."

"What? I thought druids were chaste. Like priests."

"So we think. But, what if…. And how many Popes have we had who had families before, and who knows how many children after becoming Popes? Maybe he was an exception."

"Exception or not, I don't think any of this will fit into your book. You can't prove it, it's all based on your dreams and ghost visits."

"Oh, I know. But now I understand how he could stand still and give his life without a fight. He must have done it to protect his child," I said.

"Well, I have to admit, I'd step in front of a speeding car to stop Janel from being hurt. I'd easily trade my life for hers. So, if that's what happened, I can understand that. I'll start dinner. Coming soon?"

"Yes. Please take Janel and give her some milk. I'll come give her some bananas in a few minutes."

A blank document came up on my screen, and I started typing.

Lovern's Sacrifice – Approx. AD 80

Mons Graupius – AD 84

Many early Picts or Celts were defeated and died during this battle between the naked painted men and the Romans. Those still alive after the battle ran to the hills or back to their villages. They killed, sacrificed loved ones, families, and themselves so the Romans couldn't enslave them.

I am sure some escaped. I believed Lovern's child escaped, and I saw her on a hill, maybe one on Skye, through Jahna's eyes, grown and holding a baby. I remembered the child's toes. I recalled the note from my ancestor describing the toes of his dead son after the battle of Glen Coe. I slipped off my shoe and looked at my toes, the same as Janel's toes. He had succeeded! His blood still flowed through our veins.

My heart skipped a beat as I realized how hard it must have been for Jahna to tell me her story. She led me to the hill to find her, and to the bog to find Lovern. I will never be able to share how I felt when Jahna entered my mind and gave me the pictures I needed to find her. I hope she knows how hard I will try to get her story told. In my deepest belief, I know Jahna and the man in the bog, the one I named Lovern, were partners, maybe husband and wife.

I promise, Jahna and Lovern, Janel will know your story, our family story, and I will never forget you.

> *Blood of our blood.*
> *Do not forget us.*
> *In the darkest of the nights, buried we lie.*
> *We dream to have our voices heard again.*
> *We beg you to find us, to bring us back.*
> *Blood of our blood.*
> *Do not forget us.*
> *Our souls continue with the gods.*
> *We died for you, we live through you.*
> *Tell our story so we may live again.*
> *Blood of our blood.*

I haven't told Marc, but every once in a while, especially just before falling asleep, I feel her again. She's a young soul, a strong soul and I know she wants me to find her. I've decided I will go back to Skye. I'm being pulled there. I've told Marc I want to find more about the young man in the note that had been handed down in my family, but most of all I have to try to find Crisi. I think she's the first MacRae on Skye. My blood. Donny's blood. Janel's blood. She's waiting for me to find her there, somewhere.

> *"One life, one love,*
> *but I shall remember thee*
> *from one life to the next,*
> *for the memory of the living*
> *is the dwelling place*
> *of the dead."*

Steve McDonald